Praise for Jackie Ivie's Lady of the Knight

"Compelling . . . dynamic . . . difficult to put down . . . with strong characters, sizzling sexual tension, plenty of passion, action, history, and great repartee, Ivie makes a strong debut and is destined to become a reader favorite."
—*Romantic Times BOOKclub*

"Thrilling . . . excellent . . . gives us hours of pure pleasure."
—*Rendezvous*

"Beautifully written and full of passion . . . a very exciting, excellent novel you will want to read again and again."
—*Romance Reader at Heart*

"Prepare to be amused, entertained, and moved almost to tears . . . delivers all that a discriminating reader demands—lush passions, soaring tempers, revenge, royalty, and a lass with an uncommon talent for finding trouble."
—*Fallen Angels Reviews*

"Completely captivating! Ivie does a wonderful job of entwining sensuality, treachery, and romance."
—*Romance Junkies*

"Very hot! A page-turner [and] a wonderful debut novel."
—*Round Table Reviews*

"The sex scenes are some of the best this reviewer has ever read . . . highly recommended!"
—*Loves Romance*

Also by Jackie Ivie:

Tender Is the Knight

Lady of the Knight

Published by Kensington Publishing Corporation

THE KNIGHT
BEFORE
CHRISTMAS

Jackie Ivie

ZEBRA BOOKS
Kensington Publishing Corp.
www.kensingtonbooks.com

ZEBRA BOOKS are published by

Kensington Publishing Corp.
850 Third Avenue
New York, NY 10022

All Kensington titles, imprints and distributed lines are available at special quantity discounts for bulk purchases for sales promotion, premiums, fund-raising, educational, or institutional use.

Special book excerpts or customized printings can also be created to fit specific needs. For details, write or phone the office of the Kensington Special Sales Manager: Attn. Special Sales Department. Kensington Publishing Corp., 850 Third Avenue, New York, NY 10022. Phone: 1-800-221-2647.

Zebra and the Z logo Reg. U.S. Pat. & TM Off.

First Printing: October 2006
10 9 8 7 6 5 4 3 2 1

Printed in the United States of America

To Audrey, for making reality from a dream.

CHAPTER 1

ad 1455

The man's directions were as bad as his food.

Myles hunched down into his fur, pulled the woolens farther over his nose, swallowed the bile, and forced his belly to keep the reaction to the tavern master's fare at bay. He was rarely ill and now wasn't the time to test whether the reason was the good Scot fare that was always available at his own table, or not. Worse conditions than he was facing were hard to come by. The wind-whipped pelting of sleet he'd endured had changed into a thick-falling world of white, blanketing everything and making the path even harder to find than before. He couldn't be ill. Falling from his stallion would be carving out his own grave.

He shivered. Buried deep in layers of linen, woolens, trews that looked rather silly when worn with the kilt, and wrapped with two fur robes; he still shivered. That brought a frown to Myles's brow, which sent a corresponding tremor through him as snowmelt dripped from there onto his upper lip.

He shouldn't have taken the time last eve to hone a skean to razor sharpness in order to scrape at his beard. He shouldn't have left as he had, smiling to himself at the eight groaning lumps of plaide-covered misery that were what was left of his own honor guard. There wasn't one of them who wasn't moaning and injured. It had been Myles's pleasure to leave them this morn to more of the tavern master's hospitality. It had been fated.

Now it just felt stupid. Worse than stupid. The entire venture was beginning to feel that way. What betrothed wanted a man who showed up unwanted, unheralded, unaccompanied, and fainting of weakness?

Certainly not the one his father had ordered him to report to. He didn't want her either. No one wanted the mistress of Eschoncan Keep, the land surrounding the rocky Fells of Eschon in Dumfries, or even the length of seacoast the family possessed. The woman was still untouched at a ripe age of a score and four because the man her family had betrothed to her wasn't interested in marriage. He wasn't interested in anything about her. Word throughout the glens was of the clansmen left cut and bleeding by just a touch of the sharpness of her tongue, and then blinded by her bulk and the plainness of her face.

Myles shivered again. He told himself it was reaction. He'd already wasted energy and blood on the fight over it. He'd taken to the field, fighting all comers to get out of this demon-inspired betrothal. It hadn't worked. He was still battered, bruised, and slightly disoriented from his fight. And his father had added insult. He'd sent the same men Myles had handpicked at puberty as the men he'd surround himself with for life. The laird of Donal had ordered his son's own Honor Guard into the fray. And he had even more

men to send should his son still balk even after he'd
fallen for the last time.

There was nothing for it. He could reach Eschoncan,
wed the harpy, and then flee . . . or he could waste
more time meandering out in a winter storm while his
horse plodded through ice-crusted drifts and he got
weaker. He couldn't decide which was worse. As he
huddled deeper in the mass of material and fur about
himself, listening to the steady breathing of his horse,
he realized the truth: either one was just as bad.

A glimmer of light touched the frost hovering in
front of his face, turning the crystals red and then
yellow, before going out. Myles blinked, shuddered at
that slight movement and how it sent icy drops about
his face, and tried to focus.

There hadn't been a sign of humanity since he'd left
Aberdeen at first light. Laird Eschon hadn't left a croft
untouched, or a body breathing, when he'd gone sys-
tematically about the glens, banishing and forcing off
any crofter in the area known as a demesne. Such was
the banc of having sided against yet another boy-king, a
Stewart who demanded such a thing. Myles's own clan
had only barely survived the same; and that was through
marriage. High marriage at that . . . with a traitorous
Douglass.

Myles had laughed and jested and called the teasing
words at his cousin when she'd been sacrificed on the
marriage altar. What he wouldn't give to take all of that
back, as he'd had to listen to it himself, just two short
years later.

The glimmer of light came again, tormenting and teasing and making him catch his breath with the giddiness
of actually finding shelter. Then, he had to deal with the
icy shock of the air he'd inhaled and the heaving of his

body as every part rebelled. That made the bruised ribs more painful and his grip on the rein precarious as he fought to stop the coughing spasm before it unseated him.

It was impossible. His mind was seeing things that his eyes were putting into existence in front of him. There wasn't a croft with anyone living in it between him and Eschoncan Keep. The alesman had warned him, but since he'd also been laughing as he had said it, Myles hadn't taken him seriously. It wasn't joint amusement. It was because he'd wheedled the reason behind who his guest was and already knew the acid-tongued skelpie who was waiting for him at the end of his quest.

The light came again, beckoning him, reaching out to him with the promised embrace of a mother's arms. Myles turned Rafe toward it. The animal didn't want to go. There was a hump of snow-covered deadfall between them and succor and Myles couldn't find the strength to compel Rafe. He had all he could do with holding his seat, keeping the sickness at bay, and forcing his bruised ribs to take one breath after the other, while his trembling increased.

Some bridegroom he was going to look at the altar. *If* he lived long enough to make the keep.

Rafe had decided the light really did mean warmth, shelter, and possible food, because he'd plodded to the end of the snow-covered fencing and rounded it. Myles forced himself to remain conscious. It really was a fence. At least, that's what it appeared to be. And fences meant people. And people meant life and warmth; mayhap even friendship. As much as he'd cursed God and claimed to want death rather than the hell his father was committing him to, it was a lie. Myles watched the round hump that became the front of a croft right in front of his eyes with something akin to shock.

It truly was a home. Further, there was light showing through the cracks of the shutters. Light meant warmth, and humanity, and by faith, he was tired of trying to pretend that he was strong and impervious. He wanted warmth, he wanted companionship, and he wanted time to recover—body and mind.

Rafe stopped, huffed a few times, and then turned his head to see what further his master was waiting for. Myles would have grinned at the steed but knew it would take too much effort. His face felt frozen into position. He let go of the reins and shifted his weight, preparatory to dismounting. All that happened was his entire snow-covered weight hovered for a moment in indecisive glory, before toppling into a heap at the horse's hooves.

At least the ground was soft. Myles found the stinging cold of all the snow coating his freshly shaven cheeks and chin and seeping down across his throat and into the opening of his shirt welcoming, and strangely reviving. He surprised himself by getting to his feet almost the moment the snow started melting, and then he was stumbling with a curse into the solid wood of a door jamb.

That hurt. Just about everything hurt, or had trembling attached to it, or was fevered, or was just too damn tender to touch. That's what came of taking on his father's entire clan before he'd accept the inevitable. He was being sacrificed to the witch of Eschoncan, because his father had promised it a decade earlier. And that because no one else would have her, and the Donals needed an ally with land, and that meant they wanted the dowry she came with.

The door had to have a handle, even though it was rough-hewn. All doors had handles. Myles shook his head in wonderment at the vagaries of fate that had brought him to a croft where light and warmth hovered just inside the portal and then kept him from claiming any of it because the door didn't have a blasted handle. Fate was fickle. It was also a hag of uncertain temperament and horrid shrieks of laughter that probably sounded like the ice storm had.

He backed two steps off, sucked in as much icy air as he could handle without having it burn a hole right through his chest, and rammed at the door.

The reason it hadn't had a handle was that it wasn't a door. It looked to be the remains of a wall; it had been propped into place, and it was now landing with a lot of noise, dust, and ceremony in the center of the one room. Myles shook his head slightly at the result of his act, watched the room reel at that, and gulped back the tavern master's fare yet again.

A gasp came from the loft and Myles forced himself to look up there, putting his hands on his waist in order to make the motion. It wasn't easy. His entire body was finding it difficult to maintain balance, and the only nonmoving spot looked to be right atop the planking at his feet. His head was hammering in time to his pulse, rivulets of snowmelt were just reaching his belt line and soaking into his drawers and undertunic, and his jaw dropped.

It was an angel. It had to be.

The lass looking down at him had the face of heaven, her reddish blond hair was of a length that would cascade well below her waist, if it wasn't falling forward over the edge of the wooden beam she was peering over, and she had the most luscious lips he'd ever seen. Myles knew then. He hadn't lived. He wasn't in a croft with heat at his front and a plank of wood at his feet. He was still outside, probably frozen stiff in position on his saddle, and regretting that he'd made Rafe suffer the same fate.

He just couldn't think of one thing he'd done to deserve such a heaven.

Then she opened her mouth and started such a screeching of noise, he stumbled back at the onslaught of it. She was calling out words of disdain, filling the small enclosure with a description of him that would have insulted the lowest village resident.

Myles's mouth shut. His angel wasn't an angel after all. She was more along the line of a banshee. *This* afterlife he probably did deserve.

"Well?"

She was asking him something. At least she'd stopped her tirade long enough to ask it. Myles shook in place, gulped down a too-dry throat as his head tried to lift from his shoulders, and glared back up at her.

"Are you going to come in out of the storm, or are you going to stand about like a dunce? Well?"

Her voice was rising again. Myles felt his shoulders hunching up as if to ward off her attack. He couldn't think. Steam was starting to rise from the melt of him as the heat she'd created in her home with the fire reached him. He moved his gaze to the hearth, ignoring the heaping of words she was still berating him with, and then he fell full out on what had been her door, right on his face. He only wished he'd reached unconsciousness before the pain hammered at him from bloodying his nose. Again.

CHAPTER 2

At least it wasn't a wild beast. Kendran's heart took
its own sweet time to calm and she used the time to
size up her opponent. She already had him figured as
such because that's exactly what he was doing—
opposing her. The mass of fur-covered bulk could just
move off the only available thing she had for a door,
too. And then he could go about setting it back up.
That's what he could do.

What he wasn't going to do was lie there, slumbering . . . while icy snowflakes filled the entryway and
sifted down to cover him. She sucked in air to screech
that at him as well but had to let it go. It was futile to
waste further breath on an unconscious man and her
voice had cracked more than once at the strain. She was
in danger of catching further sickness and he wasn't capable of understanding. He was either deaf, dense, or
a foreigner. That was easy to ascertain because of the
odd, amazed, and confused look in the eyes peering
over the edge of his fur as he'd listened to her.

She was just going to have to do it by herself, just
like always. Which shouldn't surprise her anymore, but

ward, and shoved harder. He didn't move. Not even a little bit. She frowned at that. Men didn't come in quite this bulk. He might as well be a horse.

As if she'd said it aloud, a horse head appeared in the door, huffing his presence at her, which sounded annoyingly like he was lecturing her.

"Let me guess. You're a male, too," she said, as semi-intelligent eyes regarded her from a long distance up. The man's horse was a Clydesdale; very sturdy, very large, very strong. He was also moving to a broadside position, as if to block the elements. Kendran told herself she was being witless. It didn't help. She told herself that no horse had that much in smarts. That didn't work, either. She tried telling herself he was obviously getting what warmth he could since he wasn't capable of fitting through the door. But that wasn't true. The fire was going to go out if she dawdled much longer, and the horse really was blocking some of the elements with his size. She looked across at the back of her visitor's head. He'd actually had the sense to have a mount this intelligent? Maybe he wasn't a dimwit after all.

She leveraged her fingers beneath the plank until she had a good hold, tried to stand, and finished that off by falling onto her buttocks while a foot slid beneath the wood. Then, Sir Good-for-Nothing decided to roll, and since he was following his gender's creed and doing nothing helpful, it was toward her. That sealed her left foot right where it was . . . beneath him, pinching her ankle, and starting such a torrent of pain, all she could do was rant at him, pummel the fur she could reach, and finish it off by a screech to the ceiling. All of which got her little more than a sharp pain in her throat, wet tears on her cheeks, and she could have sworn his horse was laughing at her with each head toss, too.

"I have never tasted horseflesh, nor have I e're considered it. But, I swear to you, horse, I'll very much enjoy slicing the meat from your bones and roasting it. That's what I'm going to do!"

The last of her words didn't make sound and Kendran grabbed her throat in the beginning of what might actually be panic. She was going to finish her days locked beneath a plank of wood while a stranger slumbered atop it and his horse mocked her? Lady Sybil would certainly enjoy that! As one of the only blood relatives to Laird Eschon, Sybil would reap rewards, while a half sister and legitimate heir froze to death as a result of her own stupidity.

Her ankle was starting to throb, making it difficult to ignore how his weight was cutting off the circulation to it, and then the pain reached her knee. Kendran wedged her free right foot beneath the structure edge, lay fully on her back, and shoved. Absolutely nothing moved, although there was a long, drawn-out groan coming from either the wood or the man. She couldn't decide, nor did she care.

The horse whickered softly, shook its head back and forth, and she speared it with a glance. Male. Obviously. Men only rode stallions. She knew that already without the proof just coming into view through the door.

"You are na' coming in here," she whispered, since that was the only sound that came out of her throat, and even that hurt.

He ignored her.

"Dinna' think you can do whatever you wish! I'll have you know—"

What voice she had trailed off as the horse bent its

head, placing reins atop her hand, and then she held her breath as he appeared to wait for her. Kendran caught her breath in surprise. The man had a horse *this* chivalrous?

She sat up; wrapped the rein about a plank edge, securing it in a split in the wood; and gave a tug. It wasn't necessary. The animal already knew what to do. She gaped as the door lifted, releasing her foot to a flood of pain as the blood returned, and sliding the man off and into a heap right beside her hearth.

Then her rescuer backed out the same doorway, taking the wood with him, until it was almost in the perfect position to lift it back into place.

Kendran would have sprung to her feet, but her ankle was tender and that made it take a bit longer and it was awkward. She took a long, considering look at this beast, which appeared to be almost the exact same look he was giving her. Considering. Sizing up the other. She wondered if any woman had looked favorably upon a man just for his horse, and she knew if such a thing was possible, she was in danger of being the woman to do it.

She grinned.

"Mayhap he'll do us both a favor and perish. Then, I'll gain you by right of possession." She gave up whispering the words. It hurt too much. She mouthed them, instead. It didn't matter. She was talking to a beast of burden. A smart beast of burden, but a beast.

He blinked.

Kendran hobbled over to him and unfastened the rein. He surprised her again by backing out of the way so she could put the door back into place. She promised him silently that if there were oats to be found, she'd find them and get them to him, and then he fully amazed her by turning about and showing the sled attached at the back of him.

Kendran looked down at the fur-covered lump with something akin to astonishment. He'd brought his own supplies? What was he—some kind of guardian angel?

No, she answered to herself. Inaccurate comparison and complete fantasy. He was a slumbering wretch that was soaked to the bone, unconscious to the elements, and worse, he was a man. It was a good thing he had the sense to own such a wondrous beast. She reached for a skean in her belt.

Kendran hobbled out the opening and onto the snow-covered stoop, earning herself a chill clear to her knees, and then she was sawing away at the ropes with which this man had bound his supplies. She didn't have time for knots. Her hands were in danger of losing feeling before she got the ropes undone and lugged the bundles back into the croft. She didn't bother unwrapping anything. She simply dumped the bundles onto the ground and shoved them in front of her, down the stoop and into the now chilled room, snow and all.

The door wedged well into the space, and she shoved handfuls of snow along the sides of it, making the seal even better. Her fingers were giving her trouble now, with small pings of sensation traveling from each digit to her elbow, but she had other things to worry over. The snow would melt, it might even form the ice barrier she needed along the outside of the door, but she had to get the fire strong again before it went out. It had taken her over half the day to get it started the first time, and that had been with hands covered with gloves.

She grimaced. Her gloves were hanging before the fireplace. Still. Attached there by a dirk she'd used to pin them with. They were probably dry and warm. She should have taken the time to don them before following the horse outside. That way she wouldn't be flirting with pain and sore-rot. All of which went through her mind as she looked at three cracked nails—one all the way to the nib—and the darkening bloodline of a long scratch on her forefinger.

She sighed, snarled as even that pained her throat, and went to the remains of her fire. She could heat snow later. There was enough of it lying about. She selected another chunk of rafter wood, stirred the coals, and added it to the top, before bending to blow gently. There wasn't much dry wood available to her, although she'd gathered it all day. Everything she'd found was sodden with exposure to elements and needed time to dry before it would be of any use. Anything else she'd had to locate in this croft and take apart in order to burn.

Kendran looked up at where she'd made her bed. There was enough planking in the loft to get them through until the deadfall dried, although she'd have to re-form a pallet elsewhere. There was also plenty of snow to make a good kettle of something edible. *If* he had a kettle and something with him worth cooking.

Her hands were still numbed feeling. She was forced to use her shawl. She wrapped her hands with the material in order to hold her knife and cut the ties apart on a bundle, spilling not only an iron kettle and the iron stand needed to place it atop an open flame, but wrapped parcels of what appeared to be dried meats and—Lord help her!—her man had fresh vegetables. She speared a glance at the slumbering lump. Fresh vegetables in the midst of November? What force of wizardry was this? Only a castellan was capable of growing such a thing. And castellans owned castles. They owned the land to do it; they had the heat, lighting, and warm soil to do so;

and they had the sense to devote a section of their keep to such a thing.

Only Lady Sybil at Eschoncan Keep kept an indoor garden, and that was because she was growing her herbs of succor. Kendran actually thought she was more capable of cultivating poisons than cures, but she wisely kept the thought to herself. Sybil wasn't a woman to be thwarted, and she did make some of the fare tastier with her additions than when it had started out.

She was one to be feared, however. Kendran looked again at the lump of man and shivered. Then she shook it off. She was being imaginative and stupid again. No man had the ability to do what Lady Sybil did. Then Kendran opened a particularly heavy bundle, spilling gold coins into her lap and making her gasp, and that just made her throat start cursing her for such a thing as trying to use it.

My man carries gold? she asked it of herself, even with the proof in front of her eyes. He carried a lot of gold. He carried a treasury of gold, he had a very smart mount, and he was stupid enough to collapse in front of a woman? He must not know that a woman covets gold more than she loves the flesh. At least that was what Father shouted more than once at her mother. What an enigma this man was beginning to be. Her hands were starting to feel like they belonged to her again, and that meant she didn't need the shawl. Kendran wrapped it about the gold pieces, ignoring the clink of it and the glimmer of it as firelight caught each piece. She shrugged. So he was rich. He was still a man. She dumped the entire bundle of it on the floor.

She dragged up the kettle and limped over to the fire, settling it atop the rack like all of it belonged. Then she was adding a bit of the boar fat her nose found for her, and slicing strips of his dried venison into it to fry. At least it looked to be venison, and as it warmed and sizzled, it started smelling exactly like it.

Kendran had already decided the best way to get snow was through the shuttered window and she went there next. She could have used the snow she'd shoved in with the supplies, except it had already begun melting into rivulets on the packed sod floor, running in streams toward the slumbering bulk at her fire. That caught her attention for a moment. She couldn't just leave him there, could she? She pursed her lips and answered herself. Nay. He'd brought her bounty. She was going to have to see to him. Once she got sup going, anyway. That would be soon enough.

She had her nose pinched when she returned to the fire. It wasn't at the thought of unfastening and assisting a member of the enemy gender; it was because the wrappings he had about himself were starting to steam, and that was putting a musty odor into being. She shoveled handfuls of snow into the kettle, where it popped and sizzled before turning into a liquid that would eventually make a stew.

She wondered if he came with the rudimentary equipment of a spoon and then decided it didn't matter. She had more than one skean with her. Her long-handled one was still in the loft, but that couldn't be helped. She could fetch it. She could finish preparing the stew. And then she'd see to the man. She wasn't going to see to him until she had everything else in place. He was the least of her worries.

She jumped, catching an inner beam, and swung herself back up to the loft, found her blade, and returned. The man hadn't moved . . . much. He was definitely breathing, too, although it came with grunts and whistling attached to it.

Kendran snickered at him as she heard it. He was a snorer, too? Her luck was as bad as always. The water was starting to bubble, and it was giving off the most heavenly smell. It almost covered over the smell of wet hair. Almost.

She went to fetch a packet of his vegetables, looked at her options, and shrugged. He was close enough, he was unmoveable by normal force, and he was oblivious. He'd never know. Kendran hobbled back over to him, put a piece of broken planking atop him so he could keep his wetness to himself, sat ungently on the bulk of man, and settled herself, using him as a bench in order to slice very thin pieces of first carrots and then potatoes, and God bless the man, he had cabbages, too! She ran her hands along each piece, almost sensuously caressing the bounty that had been gifted to her. She'd been as foul tempered as always, full of conceit, and her reward for these faults had been to find an empty, bereft croft, in order to wait out the blizzom Lady Sybil had warned her was coming. Never once had she guessed a man would actually arrive, bearing gifts such as these for her. Kendran glanced over at him and fought to keep her color and her ability to breathe as everything on her entire body absolutely stalled in place.

He was lying on his side, the fur had parted, letting her see a good portion of what it had been hiding, and the poor fellow had bruising and lumps all over the immensity of throat and chest that she could see. He was also sporting a split lip that hadn't healed from when he'd first earned it, and he was coated with his own dried blood. Even with such damage, he had the most handsome male face she'd ever seen, or believed existed. And that was completely and totally unfair! And unexpected. And breath stealing. And a hundred other horrible things.

Kendran turned, gulped, finished slicing the last of the cabbage into the stew, and stirred it thoughtfully, using the time to temper her reaction before she turned back to this man. Sybil had told her she would regret this impulsive ride. Kendran was putting into play things she couldn't change. She was going to regret it. That's what she'd been told.

Lady Sybil truly was a witch. That was the only explanation. Because men that looked like the mass she was still sitting on didn't exist. They couldn't. And if they did, they certainly weren't unconscious, at the fingertips, and available to the one woman who had sworn off them for good.

She slid onto the floor, took a deep breath, and pivoted toward him. The impression didn't fade. Even with the dried blood, and his nose a slightly redder shade than the rest of his sculptured jaw, he was still breath stealing.

She scooted closer. It was a good thing he'd landed on his face. That way the blood from his nose wouldn't have choked him, as it coated him from lying in it. Then again, if he'd fallen on his back, he probably wouldn't have bloodied his nose and needed to worry over drowning in his own fluid.

She looked over him to the smaller pot he'd had with him. It was perfect for heating more water in order to wash him off. She debated it a moment and then shrugged. He was still breathing. It was probably more important to get his wet clothing off.

The man had his fur robe fastened to him with

rawhide strips. And they were very difficult to force. Rawhide just got tighter and more resistant, and it was nearly impossible to unfasten when wet. Kendran sucked in her cheeks, considered it, and then put the point of her long blade beneath one and sliced. She didn't have to do much else. The fur was saturated to the point it opened itself. And it was making the sodden shirt beneath it pull apart as well.

Kendran cut the next tie, and the next, and the next until she reached the one at his knees. That the only point where she had to assist the removal. He had the fur looped between his legs for some reason, and that was just more male stupidity as far as she was concerned. Kendran pulled. She cut every available tie that could possibly be holding the garment to him, grabbed handfuls of wet fur, and pulled again. She put her uninjured foot against him and pushed while her arms pulled, and all that happened was her shoulders ached, her hurt leg joined in, and she dripped great quantities of his snowmelt just about everywhere. About the only good thing seemed to be the lukewarm temperature of the water as it melted.

She set her lips and gritted her teeth. She still let out the sound of a curse. He was strapped into the fur like it was permanent! She knew he'd strapped it about himself to block out the elements. Well, maybe he should have made certain to fall into a strong man's croft, then, if he wished it removed!

Kendran rocked him off of her, looked down at the dousing of water she'd suffered, and nearly gave vent to the scream of frustration. Except that he was still oblivious to the world and her throat hurt. Her heart had decided to join the fray, sending every beat to where the raw, burning feeling was, too. Swallowing didn't help. She knew nothing shy of Lady Sybil's warm honey-hop brew would.

Kendran went to her knees and tried again. If she could just get the mass of soaked layers off his chest . . . that might be enough. She could at least get that part of him warm and dry. She concentrated, pulled, and wrenched until her fingers ached with it.

He had several layers of woolens about him, swathing so much of him it was no wonder he'd looked like a great beast. It had also muted much of his form, which as she kept pulling and unwrapping, she could see was still going to be considerable. And formed well. And muscled. And it all felt strange beneath her fingers . . . and he was a lot warmer than he was supposed to be, too. He was also starting to mutter loudly and indistinctly and with disjointed words.

Well! He should talk.

Kendran spared his face a glance. He had the fever. The man had the sickness worse than she did. He was probably going to spread it back to her, and they would both perish, and then that wonderful horse of his would perish, too. Unless he had more smarts than the two of them and wandered away to the stronghold of Eschoncan by himself. For some reason she knew the horse would manage it.

Beneath it all, her fellow had on a tightly woven linen undertunic. It was plastered to his frame, rising and falling from the humps of muscle it was clinging to, and her fingers were having even more trouble as she slid the button fastenings apart. If what she was observing was true, the man's physique matched the beauty of his face. And that was most unfair of all. Most.

Kendran peeled the tunic placket apart and caught her breath at all the bruising and barely healed, scuffed-looking patches that seemed to be all over him. The man had taken a severe beating recently. Severe. That was odd. Such a beating should have parted him from his gold, if not his life.

She was frowning now. The man had ropelike muscles in his belly, and they were moving and flexing beneath her hands as she worked at him, prompting her more than once to check his features again. His heavy, snored breaths hadn't abated, nor had they changed much, and now there were droplets of sweat glazing that brow and peppering his upper lip . . . where whiskers should have been doing their job at hiding what truly kissable lips he looked to have.

At that thought, Kendran's hands completely halted while her eyes went their widest.

She was up on her knees to reach him better, and that had her hovering above him, running her hands over and over the exposed portions of him, the fingers spreading about his neck, shoulders . . . then his chest and then his belly, and she could swear her every pore was jumping at the sensation of his flesh. Kendran's mouth opened and she gaped at him. This wasn't happening. *It couldn't be.* She hated men. All men.

She shook her head and forced her own mouth shut. Her man was fevered. He was putting out a fire pit full of heat. That was it. It had to be. But what the devil was wrong with her? She hadn't been this hot before touching him. There shouldn't be tremors going all the way from her fingertips to her toes, and from thence to the top of her head, before they were moving to a most horrid point of all, her breast tips. . . .

She jerked her hands from him as if scorched. And maybe she was. Kendran looked at her own palms in dismay and something else. Something worse. She'd almost looked like she wanted to touch him. That she'd been enjoying it! She wasn't caressing him. She wasn't! This was a man. And men were horrid creatures. They were vermin. They took from a woman, and then they kept taking and taking and taking. She hated them. Hadn't everything her mother had ranted sunk in? There was no excuse for what she'd just been doing. None. And she thanked God the man was still unconscious to all of it. She only wished she had been.

And she still had the bottom half of him to uncover and expose!

At that thought, Kendran covered her face with her own palms, muting some of the heat there with cool flesh she could've sworn had been burned, just from touching him.

CHAPTER 3

He had a very smart horse. His name was Rafe. His saddle had been engraved with that name, anyway. It could be her man's name just as easily, but the horse answered to it immediately, so that's what she called him.

There was a lean-to behind the croft, built into the same hill, and her spare leather skirt made an acceptable manger of sorts, and the man had oats, so Rafe was secured, curried and seemed happy enough, once she had the man's cast-off, dried and stiffened fur tossed across Rafe's back and secured in place. He looked well fed and happy to be weathered in so completely.

They should be so lucky.

Kendran slid into the window, using the thick ice shelf as a ladder. It didn't resemble the same croft. It didn't even resemble the same country. If it wasn't for the thin ribbon of smoke that threaded its way through even more looming, thickly threatening cloud cover, none would think it more than a larger hump of snow in a world of the same.

Kendran dropped to her feet, swiveled to latch the shutters behind her, and checked the stew . . . going on four days. She'd been feeding it water and the bare minimum of vegetables for all those days, too. It was almost time to add more meat to it. It was actually fairly plain tasting, but it was healthy. There wasn't one reason why the barely aware, almost naked hulk of man she was tending kept gagging and spitting every time she wasted effort to spoon-feed it to him.

She looked over at the cause of her anxiety; watched the bared chest rise and fall with uninterrupted, un-fevered sleep; and almost felt satisfied. Then she shook her own head at her foolishness. She'd nursed him through his sickness for days now, swishing cold snowballs that melted upon contact all over that chest and throat, and even over the width and down the length of his arms and legs. She'd tended to another person. No one at the keep would believe it.

She grinned over at him. She was rather satisfied at herself, actually.

She was also tired of her own smell, a shift stiffened with sweat, and underdrawers and chemise that seemed glued to her with filth. He slept. He hadn't awakened in hours . . . the fire was dim, the eve far off. She'd hung an entire row of his clothing along the second-to-last rafter to dry them, depleting his supply of skeans and then his dirks to pin them up. Not only had her ingenu-ity dried his entire wardrobe, including the changes of clothing he'd packed, but it had made a piecemeal di-viding wall, as well.

All in all, she was very satisfied with herself. If only she had her voice back, everything would probably be close to perfect.

She went to fetch the smaller pot, the one she'd used to feed him and get him water, and hold the snow she'd used to make balls out of to swish along him, and dropped a hasty hand to his chest in passing. Then she stopped, snagged into breathless immobility by the feel of him under her fingers. Again.

It wasn't his fever. There wasn't any sign of it. He'd been sweat soaked and raving like a madman the first two nights. She hadn't had the strength to keep him abed. So, she hadn't tried. She'd waited until he ceased thrashing, got himself well off the padding she'd fashioned as a bed, and then had tossed a cold pan of melted snow water on him. That had stopped him almost instantly and he'd pierced her with hate-filled, bleary eyes of an indeterminate color before crawling back onto the padding—which was where he belonged. With the coverlet securely in place, so it could cover over his long, thick, muscled limbs. The cold water splash had had other benefits as well. It had had a calming effect on all the bruising and swelling on him and it had immediately put a halt to the fever's ascent. From that time on, she'd taken to making snowballs and running them all over him, letting his heat melt them. He'd cursed at her, making her think he was lucid and aware to form such sentences. He wasn't a dimwit, either. He had an excellent vocabulary, although most of it seemed useful strictly for ranting and cursing.

She twisted her lips and bent to touch them to his. That was another guess of hers. Useful for testing his temperature, and other things. Things like . . . finding out for herself what a kiss from such a mouth would feel like. The answer had been nothing. It had felt like kissing her own hand. But something was different this time. Kendran realized it as the lips beneath her pursed slightly, molding to her own, and her eyes flew open. She jerked back; glared at the calm, still sleeping form, and considered him. It was difficult to know if he was asleep or awake. He wasn't giving her any sign.

She shivered involuntarily. She didn't want him awake and knowing of the liberties she'd taken . . . deep in the dark, with the fire banked and no one else knowing. She didn't want him able to recall how she'd run her hands all over just about every part of him . . . except one. She'd kept his short trews in place and let it dry as it would. She didn't want to see what he possessed. It would ruin her budding fantasies. Men only wanted one thing from a woman: a brood mare. *That* part of him he could just keep to himself!

She twitched the woven coverlet that was one of her cloaks into place to his chin. Watching and waiting for him to wake enough to feed him was her evening pastime. She still had chores to do before then. She had a damp bath to take, garments to rinse and hang, and then she was going to decide which of his wealthy wardrobe she was going to wear this time.

Kendran went to refill her pot with snow from outside the window. It didn't take much effort. The snow was almost knee depth and it was crusty with a layering of ice, making it easy to scoop. Her efforts had another benefit as well. Leaning across the sleet-covered sill had a jolting effect right beneath her bosom.

She stirred the fire coals, added another chunk of dried peat along with some deadfall to it, and put her pot on to boil. Then she glanced over her shoulder, checking her patient. She had the strangest feeling of being watched, but that wasn't possible. There was only one other person in the room, and he was still sleeping, if the rhythmic cadence of his chest was any indication.

She stood and looked at him, consideringly. He still had the same even breathing, the same deep, rumbling kinds of noises accompanying it. There was only one thing that seemed to halt his snores . . . and she blushed to recall it.

The light was too bright for such recollections. Mayhap she'd experiment with it again tonight. Once the fire was banked, and she slid in behind him, to share warmth with him . . . and to do other things. Things like exploration. Things that couldn't possibly stand the light. Like . . . how well put together her man was. How the muscles bunched and coiled as they were stroked and skimmed across.

Kendran's fingers trembled on the little hooks of her shift, and then she lifted it over her head. The under-drawers followed, leaving her just the fine satin che-mise that reached barely to her upper thigh. She always had them crafted this short. Made it easier to do just about everything in. Climbing stairs; mounting horses; and, most especially, outrunning her mother's voice and her sisters' tirades. It was scandalous, but most of what she did was such a thing. She shrugged and pulled the light blue ribbon tie at the juncture of her breasts. The garment was crafted with gathers beneath each breast, and the ribbon was the tension point for creating the type of support she needed. It hadn't been adjusted in days—since she'd donned it. Kendran bent her head and pulled it off.

There was no swishing sound such as fine satin was supposed to make. It was much too crusted and filthy. She must have gotten used to it, and such a thing would have horrified just about everyone in the kirk, let alone Eschoncan Keep. There was a rustle of noise behind her and Kendran jerked her head. The man had turned onto his side, the movement making the cover slide. He was still asleep though, or he was very adept at pretending to it. Her shoulders sagged minutely.

She closed her eyes and sucked a sob back. She didn't even know why. Kendran Eschon never cried! She was adept at hiding emotion. No one ever saw her cry. Such a thing had gotten her father's attention—and his fists—more than once. She'd learned a long time ago. Rapidly.

She was tired of being lonely. She was tired of listening to her own thoughts, since her voice didn't work. She was tired of taking care of an ungrateful, unconscious invalid and his horse. She was just plain tired.

She reached for the warmed water and pulled the pot from the fire. Then, she crept behind the wall of clothing and started sponging. She used a two-handed method, filling both hands with soaked, warmed cloths and running them from her throat, crossing them over her torso, between her legs, over her thighs . . . down to her feet. Then, she heard the groans.

Sweetest Lord! Myles rolled to his back, lifted both thighs, slammed his hands onto the blanket-covered humps of his knees, and tried to send the desire back to purgatory, where it belonged. He truly *was* in heaven. Or hell. The angel he'd just seen couldn't be real. And if she was, she couldn't possibly be the creature who'd hissed and spit and tormented him, putting his body through such icy hell she should have been roasted alive by now with the strength of his cursing. Could it? Why was such a thing happening to him? He was on his way to contract a wedding with the harridan of all harridans! He wasn't supposed to be dallying with crofters from the self-same clan! And if he did, it wasn't supposed to be the woman who had probably saved his life!

An oath nearly exploded through his clenched teeth. It had been bad enough tamping his desire when she'd run her hands all along his back and sides, before enwrapping her arms about him just last night. It had only worked because he'd rolled onto his front, burying the part of him that wouldn't stay deadened well out of her reach. And now she was bathing naked in front of him!

He groaned again, venting the sound through tight teeth. She'd moved behind the curtain of cloth. That hadn't helped much. Her nakedness in silhouette was almost worse to watch. Vicious. Vixen. Tempting. Luscious. Womanly. Was she ever womanly! She had rounded thighs attached to the most glorious buttocks he could have conjured into being, a very small waist, very long legs, and a bosom that made him gape. If she'd looked then, she'd have seen every bit of passion he was trying to hide . . . every bit of it.

Oh, Lord!

It wasn't working. He was driving himself mad with it. Myles did the only thing he could think of. He turned toward the wall and slammed his head into it.

The next thing Myles was aware of was warmth. Body warmth. She hadn't put her clothing back on, if the contact at his back was any indication, and his problem raged again . . . full force. Unbidden hunger pumped through him, making his forehead pound and reminding him of the blow he'd taken there, while that was accompanied by a spasm of his entire lower body with the strength of it. And all that did was pilot him directly into the scooped-out section of her body it felt like she'd made for him.

Blast and damn the woman!

"Stop. I beg you. Cease. Please?" Myles was shuddering with the plea, and the effort at restraining his own body. And all that happened was she moved, going onto her haunches so she could study him some more. At least, that's what he suspected she was doing. He didn't open his eyes to verify it. He was doing his best to keep from lunging for her.

Then she was tapping her fingertips against his cheek, increasing the tempo until he had no choice. Myles cocked open an eye.

Up close she was even more ravishingly beautiful . . . all soft curves and loveliness, set off by that halo cloud of red-gold hair. It was possible to tell that her eyes were blue, too. She possessed a pert nose, long lashes, a large mouth. . . .

He groaned again and lunged up for it.

This time, he was kissing her like a man was supposed to, plying her lips with his own and caressing soft tissues, sweet heat, and showing her what a kiss from a man was truly like.

She was fighting then. As frail as she was? Myles chuckled at her efforts, and that gave her a bit of space between their mouths. What she did with it stunned and angered him. She nipped at his already split lip.

He had her on her back, both arms at the sides of her while his hands held her head in place so he could glare down at her. And he was breathing hard, the motion pushing his abdomen into hers. She wasn't far behind him. Her own hard breathing showed that she wasn't cowed at all. Far from it. She had her teeth bared and was hissing, and she was raising welts with the claws she had attached like leeches to his waist.

"Perhaps we should start anew?" he asked, cocking his head.

She spit. He was in luck that she hadn't much spittle at her disposal, and all that happened was a slight raining of moisture on his features, while she sucked for more. He knew how to counteract that. Proximity.

Myles bent his head, lowering it to her collarbone, and started nuzzling with his nose along the soft flesh there. He felt the instant reaction as she went sword stiff in his arms. Then he was doing to her what she'd done to him . . . just last eve, when she'd thought him oblivious. He opened his mouth and ran his tongue along her neck to her shoulder, tasting freshly washed flesh, and then he felt the tremors her entire body was suffering to such an extent it moved his own body with it.

He lifted his head. She was crying. Silently.

"Damnation!"

Myles ground out the curse. He'd never taken a woman by force, regardless of the instigation. He wasn't about to start now. He looked down at the scrunched-up features and wondered why she sobbed soundlessly. Then he realized the truth. She was a deaf-mute.

He'd been about to ravish a deaf-mute. A woman who couldn't tell him nay. The desire was dying now. He didn't question why. This was as cowardly and despicable as he wanted to feel.

"You canna' speak?" he asked, when all she did was continue the silent course of her tears.

She shook her head, making her hair move with the motion and drawing him to watch it. She wasn't naked, either. His mind had put that fact into being, as well as her desire for him. Both were patently false. Especially the latter. She looked like she'd rather be touching a snake.

"Myles."

He offered the name when it looked like she was about spent with her emotion and was down to little jerks of breath. She didn't look like the type used to crying. Myles wondered why he thought himself an expert on such a thing. And then he was shaking his head at that observation. She was a woman. Women cried their woman tears at the most opportune time . . . for them. He cocked his head to the side again and waited for her.

She'd finished. At least there weren't any tears sliding from beneath her lashes anymore. She was wearing one of his fancy shirts. It actually looked like she was wearing the one they'd sewn specially for his presentation to his bride.

His bride?

Jesu'!

His head started pounding again, in rhythm with his pulse. He was on his way to the ceremony. He had the loveliest wench in his arms, and with the weight of him he was pushing her into the pallet she'd made. He was afraid to roll over, however. He knew she'd flee him. That, he didn't want.

"My name is Myles," he tried again.

She whispered something that started with a "k" sound. He bent his head closer.

"What?"

"Ken . . ." Her name had two syllables, if the effort she was making was any indication, and the first of them was Ken. He decided not to guess at the rest. He was also grinning, releasing his own mantle of guilt. She wasn't mute. Nor was she deaf. She was toying with him.

"Your name is Ken . . . what?" he asked.

"Dran," she replied.

"Ken . . . dran?"

She nodded. Then she opened her eyes.

Myles had to look away. She had riveting eyes . . . meant for gazing into and getting lost. That would be another mistake in an evening full of them. The pounding in his head got worse. He looked at the fire.

"I have you to thank for my continued health, Kendran?" he asked.

She nodded.

At least that's what he thought she did. He sucked in a breath to withstand the assault of her entire body on his and looked back down at her. She had her eyes open wider, for some strange reason, and he wondered at it until he realized the obvious. His indrawn breath had pushed more of him solidly against more of her, and she had too much bosom for such a thing to happen and not get noticed. He glanced down at cleavage that begged to be adored and then he swallowed.

"You're a very desirable woman, Mistress Kendran. You ken?" he asked.

Her eyes reflected the shock at his words, and he wondered what was wrong with the entire male population in Eschon Kirk. The woman was an angel with the body of a siren and the heat of Hades, all wrapped nice and neatly and packaged with such a man-pleasing form, she had to know of it.

"And I'm a man. At best, a lowly creature. And at worst . . . a beast."

She blinked. She didn't say a word, but she didn't have to. Her eyes were reflecting the truth back at him. She agreed with every word. He kept the satisfaction deep, where it wouldn't show.

"And that would mean that I'm a bit useless at controlling basic things."

She narrowed her eyes a bit.

"Things like lust . . . desire . . . passion . . . heat. Things like these."

Now he had her. He knew it as he lowered his voice to say the words, ending on a whisper of sound. He watched as a spasm ran her body and transferred directly into his. She licked her lips. He had to force himself not to react, but it was taking everything he had not to. He had to tense every muscle he owned and hope she didn't guess at the why. A bead of sweat was leaving his hairline and following a crazed path to the top of his nose as he fought it.

"And if I lift from you, I'm afeared you'll escape me."

She huffed the disgust at what had to be his stupidity.

"You'd na' escape?" he asked, his voice catching on the phrase.

"We're . . . weathered in."

She had a bit of voice and it would have been cutting if she had use of all of it. Her whisper of sound was bad enough. Myles lowered his head a bit, sent his gaze to her cleavage, where it was shoving against him, and then he moved to look at her through lowered brows.

"Ah. Prayers do get answered," he replied.

She gasped. The movement nearly undid him, and the vicious pounding at his temple was his reward. He looked heavenward and waited for the droplet to slide down his nose, so it wouldn't stray toward her. Then, he was licking at the saltiness as it touched his lip.

"You're . . . still unwell?"

He almost wished her voiceless again as she asked it, confused sounding and unsure. She'd unhinged her claws from his side, if the slackening of pain was any indication, which meant she was in serious danger of being attacked again. Myles wondered if any woman was this naive, this provocative, and this insensitive to a man's needs. He lowered his head. "I would na' push much more of yourself into me," he said.

Her eyes went their widest, showing him the depth of their color, and also that they were a strange shade of dark gold at the center, before they turned to blue. Myles was instantly hooked. Completely and desperately, and with a viciousness with which only his little brothers could have cursed him. He didn't know all that much about this love emotion, losing his mother at such an early age, and living with men all the rest of his years, but he knew he had it. He just didn't know what he was going to do about it, now that it hit.

He cleared his throat. "You do ken of what I speak? Nod your head for aye."

She nodded.

"Good. I'm going to roll from you now. It's na' going to be easy."

"You're still hurt?"

And she used that breathless whisper again that was sending warm air all over his chest and into the hollow where her breasts still nestled. He shook at the instant sensation and what thoughts came with it.

"You *are* hurt," she said.

"Have a care, maid," he growled.

Her brows lifted at that. Myles swore again and kept swearing until he ran out of curse words, and the adjectives were blending together. The only good thing looked to be that she wasn't familiar with a lot of them. At least that's what he inferred from her wide-eyed stare when he finished and gathered more air.

"I've been tempted to the extent of my reason, and yet you do it more."

"T-tempted?" she stammered on the question, making him smile slightly.

"Aye," he answered, sending the word through clenched teeth.

"By . . . me?"

"Of course by you! You see any other fetching females about?"

"Fetch . . . ing?"

"Christ! Has nae one ever said these things to you? Are all the men in the glens blind?"

Her mouth was open to the same extent as her eyes. Myles glared down at all of it, cursed his always rotten luck, did a push-up of motion so he could heave himself off of her, and then huddled into a ball of misery to ward the sensations off. And vicious wench that she was, she hovered about him, stroking his back as he shook with wanting her, and forcing himself not to do a thing about it.

It was definitely hell.

CHAPTER 4

Pounding woke her. Steady, heavy, pounding . . . dragging her pulse into rhythm with it as it carried across the packed earthen floor and sought out where she was bedded down on piles of his dried clothing.

A solid thud sounded next; another . . . and then she knew what it was.

Kendran's eyes flew open. He was breaking their door seal! He was exhibiting every bit of male insensitivity and lack of ingenuity. If he broke the seal, he was going to flood the enclosure with ice and snow . . . and worse! They couldn't keep the enclosure warm with the amount of firewood they had. She opened her mouth and started yelling. All that happened was a pinched-off siren wail followed by a bit of choking as she grabbed her own throat to halt the pain. And she'd just started getting her voice back!

Imbecile! Dunce! Fool!

None of her mouthed words made sound, but he had stopped his assault on their door. He'd swiveled toward her, too, and was glaring at her with dark eyes and a snarl on his face, which was a very ruddy shade of rose. He was also wearing several items she'd had hanging, which was only lower-body clothing; then he'd draped her cloak about the whole of it, and he'd taken off pounding with his fists against the wood, so that he could ram a shoulder into it.

"Nay!"

The whisper of sound didn't make a dent in the stillness, but she was on her feet and in front of him, and using her body to block his efforts next. They still shuddered two steps before his rush was halted. Then he was turning a devil-dark gaze on her.

"I canna' get the door open," he told her, "and I'm as weak as a new-birthed pup. Come, assist me."

Kendran blinked to give herself time and attempt to find her wits. It didn't work. He was still immense, stirring, and half naked. He didn't look remotely weak. Anywhere. She swallowed.

"'Tis sealed," she whispered and tried to show him. His efforts had produced cracks in the ice, but it hadn't gone beyond that. She was probably in luck that he hadn't picked up the hand ax.

"You sealed it with ice? How do you do such a thing?" Astonishment colored his features now. That was almost as devastating as his gaze.

"Packed snow . . . melts," she replied, although it was whispered.

He whistled. Kendran pinkened at what sounded like praise. Then he put both hands on her shoulders and actually lifted her fully from the ground in order to put her on one side, proving he wasn't near as weak as he claimed.

"Then it can remelt," he said, as if that explained such actions.

"It is too large!" Saying the words with the volume

she attempted it hurt her throat. She narrowed her eyes at him over that.

"Too large?" At least he'd stopped his rush and was examining the door instead of trying to rupture his way through it. "Where?"

"Top." Kendran pointed. It was easier. The slab of wood that was their door had started out as a piece of the loft floor. She'd had to hack it down with a hand ax. She hadn't been perfect with the size. She'd been close, though. She watched as he looked it over.

"You did this?"

She nodded.

"You ken your way about a cleaver. Good. You can cleave it into the proper shape whilst I'm out. That would give you something to do rather than waste breath and your voice to argue with me."

Kendran's mouth dropped. He was right. It was a waste of her breath, and she'd done nothing to stop his assault on the door. She watched in horror as he gave it another blow that should have split the center of it.

Men! He'd been right about another thing, as well. She knew her way about a cleaver. She was designing which portion of him might deserve the largest blow as he sucked in another breath. Kendran reached out and wrapped both hands about an arm, clinging to it before he rushed the door again.

"You'll break . . . seal," she whispered, the words sounding every bit of how they were scratching at her throat and making her wince.

"That's my intent," he replied.

She shook her head. Vigorously.

"Why? You dinna' wish me to relieve myself? You dinna' wish me to see to my horse? You dinna' wish me to leave? That bears thinking on, lass."

He was standing and looking down at her, as if he had nothing better to do than consider the reasons behind not allowing him to break through their door.

"Rafe . . . is fine," she managed.

He cocked one eyebrow up. Now that she was being given the full assault of his handsomeness, she could tell he really did have devil-dark eyes, of a deep brown. Almost black. No . . . black-brown. Bottomless, black-brown. Everything she was arguing went right out of her head.

"I would like to get some meat to flavor this swill you make. I also have need of relieving myself. 'Tis a normal condition. I assure you."

She reddened with a blush. She could actually feel it happening, and how heated it made the skin attaching her hair to her forehead feel. She forced her gaze away and stepped back, uncurling her fingers from where they'd been wrapped about his upper arm. Then she turned and pointed to the window.

"You access through the window?"

She nodded.

"That's very bright of you. I'll na' fit. I'm a large size."

That was an understatement. He was more than large. She reached to his lower jaw. He was incredibly large. "You . . . will." She winced at the useless waste of voice. It hurt, it wasn't more than a scratch of sound, and she was using it to argue with a man. Doubly wasteful.

"I will na'."

"Will." Blast him for making her say the quibbling word!

"Will . . . na'." He stretched out the words as if daring her to respond.

Kendran glared at his nose. She didn't feel quite

ready to meet his gaze again just yet. She needed a bit more preparation.

He let out a sigh. The coverlet he wore, which was her cloak, rose and fell with the force of it, and then he pivoted toward the window. "Very well, lass. We'll have a try at it."

He crossed the room with floor-eating strides and pulled the shutters open with a force that broke her bolt stick and should have unseated all of it from its fastenings. She almost expected that very thing. *That* was exactly what she expected of a man, after all. Brute force; creating havoc and solving little. If this was what he called as weak as a pup, he was going to have to put another description on it. Or she was going to have to gain some stouter weapons.

He turned and launched himself onto his buttocks, bending forward into an arch in order to fit. Kendran couldn't help the intake of breath. His frame was taking up the entire width and height of the space as he looked across at her.

"Dinna' think this a win. I do it to spare your voice. I happen to like the sound of it. When it is na' screeching at me, that is."

He was pushing himself up and out of range and there wasn't anything she could answer anyway. She had to resort to picking up the smaller pot and launching it at the wall, where it thudded, taking out a good section of what was left of the insulation of packed, dried peat. His laughter answered for her, and then it turned into cursing. Kendran smiled to herself as she heard the litany of words, said over and over, and then she noted something strange. He went through almost the same listing of them in the same order each time. She guessed what had happened. He'd broken through the drift she'd turned into a long slide, with the massive quantity of his weight.

Myles didn't waste time returning to the croft. The air was brisk, full of the frost crystals that coated first, and chilled next, while the lone path leading to where Rafe was stabled in his own snow hut and from thence to the tree line was narrow and drifted and treacherously iced at the center. He glanced back at the croft. The wench was beauteous, but she was also selfish and argumentative. She'd done well by his horse, however. Too well. Rafe was not only content and warm, covered over as he was with his master's fur, but he was engrossed in partaking of what was probably a good portion of the dried oats. The wench should have saved some for a nice gruel. It would have been more beneficial to him than the steamed water she kept trying to make him swallow.

She was obviously not a poor crofter.

Not only was she ready and willing and—when healed—probably extremely able to use her voice to berate a man, but she had no skills about a cook fire. Admittedly not signs of a poor crofter. Her culinary talent was weak at best, and what broth she made was no better labeled than swill. He went to the saddlebags that were dumped unceremoniously over a felled log at the back of Rafe's enclosure and heaved them atop a shoulder. The wench wasn't much of a horsewoman, either. If she had been, she wouldn't have left good leather bags to freeze, nor would she have allowed herself to be stranded, horseless, in an empty croft with a stranger.

So . . . she wasn't a poor crofter, she couldn't cook,

and she wasn't a very good horsewoman, if she was one at all. He said another curse at the wench just for good measure. She was damning them with every moment prolonged by this storm. He was in hell, all right. Both of them were. She just didn't know to what extent.

Had she been a poor crofter woman, he'd be doing his best to convince her that dallying with him was a much better way to pass time than arguing. That would enable him to give in to the massive urge that nothing seemed to temper and every moment seemed to enhance. He ached to make her his own. Hours spent whiling away time worshipping that woman's frame had such a vast appeal Myles caught himself choking on the excess spittle in his mouth at the thought. But . . . as she couldn't cook, had no skills about a horse, and had a refined way of speaking, she was obviously a noblewoman. And that meant he couldn't do what his body was demanding. That kind he had to leave untouched.

Myles moved the cover off his head, bent forward, and shoved his face into the first available heap of snow, to revive him, sting his flesh, and clear his thoughts. It didn't work. Even when she was raging at him, she was arousing him. How was such a thing possible? He only hoped what he was suspicioning might have truth to it, and that the virago he was sharing a croft with might actually be the horrid heiress of Eschoncan.

But if that were true, they were really damned. He didn't have much that would keep him from claiming his bride to be well before he gave his vows. And it wasn't going to be much trouble to keep her from screeching at him in the future. He had much better things to think of to keep those lips occupied.

His heart was hammering fully before he reached

the croft and started edging his way along the sides to the window again. It wasn't from the exertion of carrying full saddlebags and balancing atop slippery drifts. It was thoughts of the exertions he couldn't allow to happen and couldn't seem to banish, either.

He found the access window, positioned himself in the relative solidity of the crusted drift, and pushed. That's when he found she'd barred the shutters against him. Myles had to suck in the laugh. What bolt it had, or that she'd put into place, would be easily burst should he try it. That would also mean he'd have to repair it, or listen to her whispered raging at him. Of course, when she did that, her emotion would make two spots of color touch the tops of her cheeks, her eyes would flash blue fire at him, and her bosom would heave against his shirt that she was wearing—and little else—with every breath. Myles tilted his head to one side as he considered it. All of that was tempting. Very. Almost more than he could fight.

He tilted his head the other way. He could also take the civilized approach and actually knock for entry. He knew that would surprise her. She wouldn't expect that.

He decided on the latter. He settled the pack more securely on his shoulder, reached forward, knocked lightly . . . and waited. The wench knew there was not another soul in the immediate area and she knew he'd be needing entrance back in. Yet she barred him, made him wait, and then ignored his knock when he gave it?

He made a fist and knocked loudly enough it rattled the shutters in their frame. It also started a slight hum of noise above him. Myles looked up at that, which put him in the perfect position to receive the entire head and body covering of snow that he got as it was dumped on him from the roof.

"Blasted wench! Ah!" Myles had to spit snow out in order to make the words, he had to ignore the burn of instant freeze as the snowmelt slid beneath the coverlet and soaked him again, and then he had to wrap both hands about the roof joist, in order to bust his feet through the obstruction of a shuttered window.

The force sent him right into the room, scraping his side and bumping his head, since the wicked lass had decided at that moment to answer his knocking. Myles was on his feet the moment he landed, however, and if she were a man, she wouldn't be standing, weaponless, staring at his entrance like she was. He heaved the entire mass of saddlebags and cloaking to the floor, sucked in a breath, and hollered his anger at the ceiling.

Kendran gaped. She couldn't close her mouth if she'd wanted to. He'd swung through the window opening with the agility of an acrobat, tossed the same saddlebags she'd been unable to lift higher than her waist to the floor like they weighed nothing, and he didn't even seem to be aware that he was now shirtless and wet, and scattering droplets all about their floor, while cold from the window sucked the heat right out of their room.

"Blasted wench! Selfish, vicious, hate-filled—!" And then he stopped his own words with another loud yell at the ceiling. All of which was gaining him not a thing toward getting them sealed in and warm again.

He'd finished. Kendran was at the window, trying to shove the shutters shut again, so she could seal them. She hadn't known how long he'd be gone, but if she hadn't bolted the shutters, they wouldn't have stayed together, and it would have been stupidity to leave them agape while he took his sweet time returning to the croft. It was almost too cold already, although it was still daylight, and it had only been a moment or two since she'd opened them!

"You shouldn't roam about in so little, lass. You make the punishment too easy to devise . . . and enjoy." The heavy breath at her ear was all the warning she got. Then Kendran was swiveled and held against snow-chilled flesh, and if he thought that was going to get him anywhere, he was very much mistaken.

She started struggling. All she gained for that was arms the texture of iron bars about her, her body crushed against water-soaked chest and belly, and the long shirt she was wearing soaked through. She was gaining something else, as well. She was gaining warmth. A lot of warmth. And she was gaining size and strength and rigidity against where he was shoving his pelvis into hers, and she was getting a gut load of turmoil and fright over that.

"You barred me from the lone shelter." He growled the words at her cheek.

"Nay!" She was screeching it. It sounded like a scratching of vermin.

"For leagues. Barred me. Without reason. Without thought. Without a care. That act requires consequences. *Severe* . . . consequences."

And then she got the mother of all shocks. She got his kiss again . . . hard, heated lips, right against hers, molding and lightly sucking, and making all manner of wonders burst through her entire frame until there wasn't a thing cold about an open window in the midst of a snow-locked day in late November in the Highlands. There was only this emotion, this feeling, this amazement . . . this jolt.

Breath deepened at her nose; he turned his head farther, taking hers with it; and then he started toying with her lips, pulling them awry the slightest bit, so he could taste her. He caught her gasp in his mouth and Kendran's entire world felt like it rolled as he held her, sucked on her, and made everything spin. She couldn't think. She couldn't breathe. She couldn't move.

His left arm wasn't about her waist anymore. She felt branded as he slid his fingers upward beneath the shirt, grazing her ribs, before grasping a breast fully in his palm, as if testing the weight, the size, the fullness. Kendran moaned, gained herself more of his mouth with the motion, and that had him moving until her back was against the wall, and lifted into place, so he could angle his loins more fully against hers. His hand squeezed her gently, he flicked a thumb against her peak, once . . . again. . . . Then he was rotating it with his fingers, and sending fire everywhere. Liquid heat went down her entire frame, coating her, possessing her, blessing her.

Kendran shuddered; she melted, she crooned with what sound she had . . . and then she exploded. Ecstasy such as she'd never known flooded her, owning and claiming her and upending everything she knew about the entire world. She didn't even realize she'd moved her legs, wantonly straddling his hips so she could shove herself against the solid maleness that was him, rocking in place until the shudders ebbed. None of that sunk through until the emotion crested, and then it slowly faded . . . leaving nothing in its wake but bliss. And that was followed almost immediately by a horrid mixture of shame and confusion and abject fear.

Kendran's eyes were wide, she felt dazed, and she began shaking, violently. He felt it, for the lips he'd been plying hers apart with softened, and then he was lifting his head, spearing her with that black gaze of his, and he had an eyebrow raised, as well.

"Gently, love," he whispered. "We have time. We have lots of it."

The most horrible thing was happening and she couldn't stop it. Tears were coming. There wasn't anything she could do, and what was worse, a man was going to be the witness to it . . . again. She already knew it was a man causing it. They always did, but to have him see? She already knew if she showed a man the breaking point, he would always be ready and willing to get to it.

She turned her head to the side, slammed her eyes shut, and shook with restraining it.

"But we must pause this long enough to secure yon window."

He was moving his chest, and he was releasing the breast he'd held, so he could move the arm behind him to unlatch her still-locked ankles. Kendran felt his motion, as much with where her bosom was now clutched against him, as with his fingers when they reached her feet.

He didn't have to unfasten her. Her legs gave up the post and slid back down, taking a bit of her dress shirt with them. It wasn't much. She could still feel where it had bunched to the waist, laying her open and naked where she was still wedged on him. She could also feel a solid throbbing problem where he seemed to be nestled, right between her legs, parting them with his size.

"You should have told me you knew your way about a man," he commented at her ear. "We could have saved some wood with creating our own fire. No worry, though. We can always start."

She forgot all about crying and turned back to him . . .

to his mouth. He was smiling. He wasn't just smiling. He was openly grinning. Kendran had never seen him smile. It was devastating. He was devastating. She didn't dare look anywhere else on him. She wondered if he knew.

"We've got a powerful start to it," he continued. The grin spread farther, revealing perfectly spaced, white teeth. "I only hope I can withstand the temptation of your frame long enough to satisfy you, lass. That's what I hope." And he finished the words with a twinge of the part of him with which she still had intimate contact.

Kendran gasped the shock at his crudeness. Then she was shaking her head, vigorously.

"What do you mean nay? Your body does na' say nay."

Only because she hadn't known! Who was she supposed to ask? Her mother—the woman who hated all men? Mother must not know feelings such as this existed. She couldn't. She'd never rail against Laird Eschon if he made her feel like this! Which must also mean that Father didn't know how to create such emotions. Kendran didn't need to ask it, either. She instinctively knew, and the surety frightened her more than what had just happened. It changed everything she thought she knew and surmised about this sexual thing between men and women.

What was she dealing with? And why had no one told her?

He was moving sideways, taking her with him, and rolling that part of him against her as he did so. She wondered if he knew how mystifying and enticing and sensual it felt, and instinctively she knew he did. That was why he was taking such small steps and swiveling his hips a bit as he did so. He knew. He just didn't know how far he'd rocked her world with the feelings he'd aroused.

"Please?" she asked.

He grunted, turned his head, and speared her into breathlessness again. "Take care what you ask for, woman. There are only so many things I'm capable of granting, at present. The ability to satisfy you may na' even be one of them, although given how easily you reach it . . . gives me reason to hope."

She choked. Then she was coughing the reaction to that. And then she was getting to feel how amazing it felt to slam her chest against his with every coughing spasm she made. Through it all he didn't release her. If anything the right arm still holding her latched to him tightened on her waist, sealing her further to him. Kendran's coughs calmed. She tried again. "Please?" she repeated. They were almost at the window, if the blast of cold air against her back was any indication.

"No plea needed, lass. I'm all yours. Just give me a moment. We'll have another start to it."

She caught the gasp against his chest. He didn't seem to feel it. "Release me. Now. Right now."

"Release you? Good Lord, why? I'll have this latched in a moment. . . ."

He was fussing with the shutters. He had probably given the open window time to drift, making it impossible to latch unless he swished the snow and ice out of the way. And it would be impossible to stay shut unless he put the stick back in the bolt irons. He was also softening a bit in the part he still had entrenched between her legs.

"Blasted window! 'Tis filled with snow."

He was moving his chest from side to side, shoving snow out of his way, and sending bits of it to sprinkle onto where she felt bared from the back of her waist down. That made her cling closer to him, which was true stupidity from hearing his reaction to her movement.

"You're a lusty wench, are na' you? You really should na' have kept it so well hid for so long. I was over my illness last eve. We wasted the time. We wasted all morn as well."

"The snow is *cold.*" Her whisper didn't make much sound, but the intent of it wasn't lost on him.

"Mayhap you should have waited to accost me, then."

"Accost you? Me?" Each word hurt. They didn't make sound, either.

He grinned again. Her heart caught and then decided that it really was going to resume beating, albeit raggedly.

"You should save your arguments for when you have voice. I prefer your mouth occupied with other things. Things . . . I'll see to . . . the moment I get this . . . shut!"

He had to release her then in order to shove at both shutters at the same time. Kendran dropped from her tiptoes to their earthen floor and shimmied to one side, although her legs were giving her such trouble she had to brace herself against the wall just to remain standing. Her knees were even quivering, and everything was very cold. She told herself it was the amount of air he'd let in but knew she lied. It was reaction . . . and loss of contact with him.

"We'll both catch our death if we dinna' get this window latched! Why does it na' . . . stay shuttered?"

Kendran pushed away from the wall; went immediately to her haunches, with legs that were still badly trembling; and grabbed at the stick right behind him. Then she was standing upright.

She held the stick out to him but he was ignoring her as he puzzled the problem. That was stupid of him. The window wasn't going to stay latched unless he secured it with the stick. There wasn't any other way. Of course, it was rather interesting to watch him hold both sides together, shoving at the burden of snow that must be there. His stance was making every part of his upper chest, arms, and shoulders bunched and taut, and showing her very distinctly why she'd been unable to break the power of his grasp once she had it. It was also making it difficult for him to do such a thing again, since he was apparently going to stay and hold the shutters closed.

She grunted at that, and surprisingly it had a little bit of sound. He wrenched his head over to glare at her.

"You have something to say?"

She raised her eyebrows.

"What?"

She turned toward the wall beside him, pantomiming his position and the uselessness of it, before raising her hands. He didn't understand. *Men.* Then, she leaned close to point at the bolt latch in front of him.

"It needs a bolt?"

She nodded.

"And you have one?"

She lifted the stick, waved it in front of his nose, and waited.

"You had the method and you dinna' use it?" He was hissing it through his teeth.

Kendran reached out, keeping well away from any contact with all that half-naked male, and dropped the odd-shaped branch into the bolt holders. Myles released the wood, but he did it slowly, and they both watched the wood bow slightly, but it held.

"You have to bar the window to keep it shut," he commented, with a voice that sounded just a bit shaken and unsure.

She nodded. Since he was still looking at their handiwork, he couldn't have seen it.

"You didn't bar me out. You were keeping the space warm. You had to keep it shuttered."

She nodded her head again. He didn't see that, either. He just kept musing. He was also taking great huffs of breaths, if the heaving of his shoulders was any indication.

"There was no punishment deserved by you . . . for you did naught."

She didn't move.

He sighed hugely. "I behaved a fool and a lout."

She nodded vigorously over that one.

"What else am I so mistaken about, I wonder?"

And then he turned fully, folded his arms, and looked her over. Insolently, and with a dark gaze that felt like it was slipping beneath the one garment she had and was laying her bare.

Again.

CHAPTER 5

"I've won. Hmm. Again. Fancy that. Pay up."

Kendran looked at him with the same tight, unconcerned look and yet he knew it bothered her immensely. She was giving off enough sparks from her blue eyes, they shouldn't need to keep the fire kindled.

"You ken the rules. You were the one designing and then demanding that we follow them." He pointed to where she'd etched the rules of the contest into the dirt farthest from the door. It was her idea to make him pay for attempting to ravish her for punishment. And it was her idea to use tosses of his game cube to gain it. He should have warned her of his luck.

Warn her? he wondered anew and smiled to himself. *Never.*

She wasn't meeting his eye as she opened her pouch and spilled out three dried broad beans. She carefully plucked one up, rolled it between her thumb and forefinger while Myles made a great show of patting the overfull pouch in front of his crossed legs before opening it.

"You realize once you're depleted of beans, you'll have no choice."

She hissed something at him. He sucked the smile back into his cheeks.

"'Twas your own contest rules. Na' mine."

She pitched the bean at him. It stung momentarily at where she'd speared his cheek. One thing he had to give her—she was accurate . . . with a bean, anyway. He grinned, broadly and widely. He couldn't help it. Then he plucked the bean from the drape of his plaide, opened his drawstring to add it to his pouch, and made great ceremony out of how difficult it was to refasten, since it was so full. Then he was looking over at her again.

He rolled the die between his hands, blew on it as if to warm it, grinned over at her before tossing it to the earth between them, and watched without saying a word as it came up a ram all three times. It had also been her making the decision of what each symbol was worth. He looked at the beautifully carved ram, which equaled a four. Low for him, but he wasn't worried. She hadn't had a decent toss all eve. He sighed in an exaggerated fashion and pushed the die over to her.

"Your toss."

The rules were simple. Three tosses. Largest score won. Pay a bean or a truth. They'd each started with a share of thirty-two beans. That was all he was willing to spare from the soup that was simmering over the fire. It smelled delicious. He'd noticed more than once that she'd looked toward it. His own belly was rumbling with the hunger, but victory was too close, and he was tired of the guilty feeling in his lower belly. Besides, the beans weren't soft yet. They had time to finish this.

She rolled and got a rabbit. Three. She was being cursed with low scores, and he watched how white her knuckles got when she retrieved the piece for another toss. *So angry?* She got so angry over a little game of chance?

Ram. Myles started up a tuneless whistle as she gathered the cube again. He'd noticed how much that particular noise bothered her, and it was his pleasure to see the two spots of color appear on her cheeks. She was going to lose again. Actually, she wasn't ever going to win against him. Not with games.

Six. His eyes widened on the perfectly etched Celtic cross. It had been his own design, worked last winter when weather made it impossible to do much else. He'd spent the entire season making a collection of dice, one for each member of his family. He'd even glazed it with resin and char, shining it until the only reddish tint was in the deeply etched lines.

It didn't help staring. It was still a six. The highest she could get. She was clapping the delight before the cube settled. She hadn't rolled a cross all eve. She now had a higher score than him. And she was holding her hand out to get a broad bean back.

"I believe I'd rather give a truth," he said.

She narrowed her eyes at him. She glanced to the plump bag on his lap-spread kilt. She moved her gaze back to him.

"'Twas your rules," he reminded her.

She turned her head away, as if dismissing him from her thoughts. She'd already tried that ploy twice. It was amusing to watch. Myles sucked in both cheeks in consideration. It was her idea to place point values on the carvings and then decide the penalty. Pay with a bean . . . or a truth.

"So . . . what do you want to know?" he asked and licked his lips.

She shrugged. She'd only offered this payment up

once to him, when she'd first realized how badly she was going to lose. He'd asked what she normally wore closest to her body. He didn't think it was the blush she'd given him, especially when he'd pointed it out to her. Then she'd gone to the bundle of material she still slept on and yanked out a flimsy-looking piece and unfurled it to reveal a gauzy piece of garment that got his palms instantly wet. She hadn't offered that payment since.

She was pointing at him.

"What?" he asked.

Then she was pointing to the ground where he sat, the door, and then shrugging her shoulders before pointing back at him.

"What?" he asked again.

If grinding one's teeth made sound, that's what he was hearing. Myles couldn't hold the reaction in but kept his laughter to a snort of noise. He knew what she wanted, but it was so much fun to tease and torment her. It was the least he could do . . . to repay her.

She was digging her carved stick into the dirt, making slashes of letters.

"Oh. You wish to know who, why, and what," he offered.

She folded her arms and waited.

"Myles. Eldest son. I'm on a quest. I dinna' possess much of a knack for directions and I got lost."

She was etching more.

"You wish to know of my injuries? My bruising? Oh. Well . . . I dinna' wish to go on this quest. I had my mind changed for me."

By whom? she wrote.

"My father."

His eyes widened as her face drained of color. Myles

was reaching for her when she recovered, jerking her own body taut. Then she was looking at him with such disgust he recoiled.

"What now?" he asked.

You lie, she wrote.

"If you dinna' believe me, how will you ken I've paid up or na'?" he asked.

She stamped the dirt with her stick and then she was writing again. *How then?* she wrote.

"How then—? Oh! You mean how did he do so much damage, since he's an auld man, and I am na'? Nor am I a weak sort."

She gave him a level look that didn't reveal anything. Then she nodded.

"He dinna' do it alone. He called on as many able-bodied men as he needed. Dinna' fash yourself. I held out well . . . at first. He just had more of them to use and I went down eventually."

She had tears in her eyes. Myles watched them gather and he started frowning. "Dinna' cry. I'm a stubborn man. My da had little choice. I was na' going on this quest willingly, and he had given his word that I would."

She turned away.

"Satisfied?" he asked and received her nod.

"Good. Then roll. We have na' got all day. I've a fine pot of beans readying on my fire and a wench to humiliate. I've yet to decide what questions I'll ask. Once you've run out of beans, that is."

And two hands later, he had all the beans. He watched as she lifted her shoulders slightly in what was a defensive position, if he'd ever seen one.

"Why do you hate men so?" he asked softly.

Her eyes were wide, they were definitely blue, and

they were looking at him with a shocked expression
like she must have thought him too stupid to decipher
such a thing by himself. Then she was tearing up
again. Myles watched it happen. She got to her feet
and she was shaking. He felt like a bear.

She was wrapping her hair into a large, unwieldy
knot and securing it atop her head with her writing
stick. Then she was going to her pile of clothing and
putting a piece of cloth about her shoulder to make a
shawl and then she was scrunching her face into an
ugly frown and then she was pointing her finger at
him, shaking it, and mouthing words that looked a lot
like her screeching had.

Myles was mystified. He shook his head. She went
to her knees beside him and poked her finger into his
chest. It looked for all the world like she was berating
him, and he couldn't think of one thing he'd done to
deserve it, other than win her at die tossing and take all
her beans. That was her own fault, since she'd selected
the payment and the contest—with a little chiding
from him. And he had such luck at dice that no one
who knew him ever challenged him. It was still no
reason for acting like this.

"I dinna' understand. What have I done now?" he
asked.

She tossed her hands in the air, looked across at him
like he'd lost his wits, and then she was pummeling a
fist into her other palm, beating her hand until he
reached out to stop her.

She evaded him and got to her feet so she could continue pointing, and mouthing, but she wasn't aiming
the words at him this time. She was aiming at the air
beside her. Then she skipped over, moving a couple
of paces to the side so she could pummel her hand

again. Then she was back at the original stance to berate the air again.

Pointing. Pummeling. Pointing. Pummeling. She started sobbing dryly during the fourth repetition and she didn't even seem to be aware of it. Myles got to his feet slowly. He watched as the pointing side of her parody started losing, hunching farther and farther down into a crouch, and then she was putting her hands over her head. He knew what Kendran was doing now. He reached for her, plucked her up, and caught her against his chest. That way, she could hit at him for a change, rather than her hand.

"A man has hit you," he whispered.

She shrugged sadly and slowly, teasing his nostrils with the smell of her hair beneath his nose while her hands continued flaying at him.

"A woman has hit you." He tried again.

She snorted the response and her hands continued jerking.

"Well, somebody has hit somebody," he replied.

She nodded. That sent whiffs of her particular scent wafting toward his nose again. He inhaled deeply.

"Who? A man?"

She nodded again. She was stiff. Unmoving. Except for her hands.

"A man hits . . . a woman?"

She nodded again.

"And you see this?"

She shook her head. Then, she nodded.

"I dinna' ken. Who would beat a woman in front of you?"

"My . . . da," she whispered.

Myles choked on the spittle in his mouth in reaction.

It explained everything. "Your da . . . hits a woman? Is it your mother, then?"

She didn't act like she was listening, but her hands weren't hitting at anything any longer. They were tapping at his chest in a disjointed beat that had nothing rhythmic about it. She nodded slightly.

Myles didn't know anything about it. There hadn't been a feminine touch at the Donal Keep for years. None. Unless he counted the servant woman. And his father would never have hit at them. And if he did, he'd never do it viciously or to cause harm. Such a thing wouldn't make a woman warm and willing in your bed. It couldn't. Myles narrowed his eyes in thought. Such a thing would probably make a shrew. What man wished a shrew to his bed?

"Men and women . . . they do fight," he said it to her ear. "We fight."

She caught her breath. Her hands went completely still on his chest.

"'Tis a natural state of life, I think. You saw it wrong."

She was shoving against him then, and she was struggling. He tightened his arms until she ceased it. Her heart was moving like a hummingbird's again, and he put his lips to her temple. He couldn't help it. His heart hurt.

"I would never hit you," he finished.

"Let . . . go!" she hissed.

At least that's what he thought she said. It was impossible to make it out with as little sound as she gave anything. He shook his head.

"Nay!"

She was probably talking through clenched teeth as she said it. She was also moving her face, grazing his lips across her brow as she did so. Then she was tilting her head upward, making the connection of his lips slide along her nose, to the end of it. Myles moved his caress to her lips and stopped himself. He was comforting her—not making love to her. That's what had gotten him into this predicament in the first place! Trying to seduce where he wasn't wanted.

"I'm sorry." He lifted his head to look toward the roof beams.

She repaid his gallantry by moving, pulling away so she could knee him directly in the groin. Hard. Wickedly hard. He dropped. Bone-cracking hard. But he took her with him.

Kendran couldn't breathe. She was in shock. She was in fear. She was in a torment of worry, and she was being crushed by the body weight of the man, Myles, since he'd wrapped himself about her. And she'd done it to him. She didn't know what he'd do now. He was trembling and he was ashen, and he was sweating, but it was a cold sweat. He also had his face scrunched into such a tight grimace it bared his teeth.

"What . . . did you do . . . that for?" he whispered, catching his breath partway through it and groaning at the end.

"You held me," she answered, spacing each word through the ache of her throat.

"You hurt me for that?" He slit an eye open as he asked it.

She nodded.

"Good Lord, why?" He shuddered slightly as he asked it. She felt it all the way along her back and into her knees, and from thence into the dirt floor.

"You held me," she whispered again.

"I ken that already. I held you. 'Tis punishable?"

"You held me," she repeated again, since he wasn't listening.

He sighed heavily. Everything he was doing seemed to have heaviness and weight attached to it. Even his words. Especially his words.

"I was holding you to comfort you. Jesu'! Has nae one ever done so?"

She hesitated breathing after his question. His voice got softer.

"I would na' have hurt you. I just said as much."

Kendran shook her head.

"Dinna' anyone ever hold you afore?"

Kendran frowned at that. Then she nodded. She'd been held. That's why she was so adept at running and moving. It was harder to catch her in order to hold her, imprison her, punish her. "I've been . . . held. 'Tis awful."

"Some holds are na' holds. You ken the difference?"

She shook her head. There was no difference. She wanted free. He hadn't granted it. She whispered some of it. His weight got worse, if that was possible.

"Holds for comfort are different. Much."

"Holds are for punishment. Keeping. Na' letting loose." She tried to say all of it, but most was just a whisper of sound, nearly indecipherable to her own ears. She was surprised to receive his answer.

"Na' true." His breath tickled past her shoulder. She scrunched it. "Na' all holds are used as punishment. You ken?"

"You wouldn't let me go."

"For that you unman me?"

"I dinna' ken," she continued, as if she had a wealth of voice and not the squeak it hurt to use, ribs that felt scrunched together, and his weight pushing her knees into the floor.

"What dinna' . . . you ken? Why you did such a thing? Comfort? What?"

"*Nae*. This. Unmanning."

He was still shuddering, but his breath wasn't as short and huffed as it had been. Kendran hunched further, to avoid where it was slithering over her flesh and making her very aware of the fact that the man, Myles, was perched atop her, he hadn't been wearing but a length of tartan when he fell, and she hadn't enough material to squelch how any of it felt.

"And . . . now that you ken?"

"'Tis this way? Every time?" She rolled halfway, onto one hip, moving the weight from grinding her knees into the beaten floor and probably making grooves in it. She also did it so she could get a better look at him as he answered.

"What?"

He wasn't as ashen, but there was a definite line of sweat droplets dusting his upper lip, drawing her glance for a moment. That was dangerous. He had kissable lips and he knew how to use them with devastating results. She already knew that. Everything on her body was experiencing it . . . and that just from his breath? *Not good, Kendran,* she told herself. *Definitely not good.* She forced a swallow and answered him. It was still a scratch of sound, but it was sound.

"You fell. Oft?"

He was frowning at her now, and if looks could wound, he was attempting it. She couldn't help the triumph that had been in her voice, nor could she halt her own amazement. She'd heard that a man could be harmed in such a fashion; even the largest man. She just didn't know it was this devastating. A woman could save herself this way . . . if she wasn't stupid enough to be seized and smashed in place when the man fell.

"Oft?" he asked, and it was from between clenched teeth again, from the sound of it.

She nodded.

"You mean should you try this again, does it work the same?"

She nodded again.

"Perhaps. Most men have themselves protected. They would na' leave themselves open to attack by a hellcat. I certainly will na' in future."

Her eyes went wide. It matched her mouth. She watched him glance there and back.

"I will just have to learn how to spot them quicker."

"Whom?" she asked, pursing her lips with making the word. He was looking there when he answered.

"Hellcats."

Kendran's eyes narrowed. That gesture was followed by her mouth again. She licked her lower lip and drew it into her mouth and sucked on it. A tremor scored all along him. He couldn't have hidden it. She experienced it, too.

"You seek to increase the pain?" he asked and moved his gaze to hers.

She considered that, wrinkled her brow, and tried again. "So does it?" she asked.

"Does it . . . what?" He was having trouble with his breathing, if the little grunts of noise accompanying them were any indication. That was as mystifying as anything he was making her experience.

"Always? Every time?"

She watched as he blinked, slowly and steadily, and

then he sucked in on both cheeks, pursing his lips. Everything on her body pulsed as she reacted. She couldn't help it and there was no hiding it. She didn't even know where the response came from.

"I'm na' so certain I should answer that," he said when the world returned to normal. Or as normal as it could be with the man weight atop her, warming her . . . damning her.

She kept her gaze on his nose, where it seemed safest. There was also a slight shadow of whisker he was sprouting on his upper lip. She hadn't noted that before. "Why?" she asked finally, when all he did was watch her.

"When you whisper, it does na' hurt?"

She shook her head.

"Good. Then whisper and we can cease the playing at it."

"Playing . . . at it?" Her heart really was going to cease with what those words must mean.

"Speaking. Understanding. You whisper and I'll get close enough to hear it. I've tired of guessing your meaning. I've tired of a lot."

"You're heavy," she answered when all he did was wait.

He chuckled. Breath touched her neck, her skin . . . her bosom, causing a riot of sensation and strangeness at each peak of both breasts. She only hoped he wouldn't look there!

"I was ever large. What of it?"

"I canna' . . . get breath."

He grunted at that, pushing more of her into the floor. His weight was easily his gravest weapon, and a pulse was starting to thump in her temple, gaining her annoyance, and not much else. Kendran squirmed her way onto her back. Then she reached up, put both hands on his chest, and pushed. And absolutely nothing happened.

"You think to move me now?"

She nodded.

His lips twisted. "Perhaps they should have warned you."

"Who?" She did the movement again and watched his glance flicker there, and this time it was he who licked his lips. The tremor went through her entire body this time. And he felt it.

"Those who told you of this little trick of yours. Takes a man's legs out from under him and renders him weak. Powerfully weak."

"Weak?"

"Aye. He canna' move. Na' even a little. He has to settle his belly from the pain. He has to absorb it and move on. 'Tisn't nice."

Kendran considered him. Then she pushed again. "You lie," she hissed.

"I am very tired of hearing that from your lips. I am na' in the habit of lying. The next time, you're forfeiting a kiss to me. A long kiss. A heavy kiss. Be warned."

She pushed up at his chest again. Nothing. Again. She held her breath and pushed. Still nothing.

"Are you amusing yourself, or is this for me?"

Kendran snarled and pushed again.

"You believe me, yet?"

"What?"

"I've nae strength to my limbs, and na' much desire to find it."

"Why na'?" she whispered.

"Because there's a definite advantage to this position. I'd think it easily seen and noted. And I rather like it."

"What?"

"You. Beneath me. Exactly as it was meant to be. If you hadn't unmanned me first, that is."

Kendran's eyes went wide, her arms lost their strength, and that just put all his weight on her as he dropped.

"See?"

"Heave . . . off!" If she had a voice, it would have screeched it. The force of it over her throat hurt enough just to pretend to it. And that was before her ribs joined in, feeling like they were crushed between the sod and him, neither of which was unbending.

"Oh . . . I dinna' think so."

"Why . . . na'?" He wasn't giving her enough room to breathe, and those breaths she managed to gain were tortuous and slight.

"Because you'll be able to exercise more of your power."

That was laughable. If she had voice enough to make it audible, and if she had room to pull enough breath. He called her powerful? The man was mad.

"I have *nae* power," she panted each word with what space she had.

"A woman of beauty has too much power. A woman with softness and passion about her frame has even more of it. You reek of both."

He was getting some strength back, or whatever it was he'd lost, because he put both hands out, splayed them on the dirt at her sides, and lifted his chest up. And then he was tensing up his stomach, making ridges of muscle pulse against her hip, where he was still holding her down.

Kendran gasped the air in, lost it, and gasped in another. What he was shoving against her felt large, hard, and powerful. And not at all weak. He couldn't possibly be expanding and hard for her again! He couldn't! If he was, everything else he'd said was a lie. "But—you've been unmanned," she told him. "You said so."

"And powerfully painful it was—is—too," he answered.

"It is?"

"Aye."

"Liar!" She hissed, and her mouth was still making the motion when he seized it.

CHAPTER 6

The bean soup was bland, but filling. The kilt he was wearing was warm and comfortable. Everything was warm . . . almost hot. Even if the sett had been made of a lighter weave it wouldn't have been troublesome or cold since the room seemed filled with enough heat it wasn't an issue. He rather liked going about with his upper torso uncovered. Even bruised and battered, his nakedness put a tether on her tongue. That was satisfying and enjoyable . . . and something more. It was flirting with the forbidden. That was proving intoxicating. In fact, the entire evening was starting to arrive at that state, he decided, as he pushed through the pieces of kindling he'd purloined earlier. He settled on a piece, with a good thick knot in it, perfect for the die he was going to carve. Knowing he'd bested her, and better yet, that she knew of it was making the forbidden that much more seductive, alluring, intoxicating . . . and tangible.

She hissed something at him from her position at the far wall. Myles ignored her and shook his head. He'd warned her what would happen if she called him a liar one more time. He'd warned her, and he stilled at the recollection. It was just a kiss. Just one in a series that had become more than one. And he was damn lucky the beans had sputtered when they had and stopped him. What was surprising was she'd been assisting him, regardless of the words she'd mouthed at him once he had let her up. He knew the truth. That woman responded. Passionately.

And that was ambrosia to the senses.

It was her fault. She had no excuse for straining her voice with invectives hurled at his head, making what squeak of a voice she owned high and sharp. She'd called him on when she'd called him a liar. What was damn surprising was she'd actually thought the thick tangle of material at his hip was a sign that he wanted her in the flesh, and not what it was: his kilt knot. As accurately as she'd kneed him? He'd be lucky to want any woman immediately following that.

That much really was a lie. He reflected on it as he twirled the bit of wood in his fingers. She would never know of it, but he was rapidly approaching exactly that stage of want again. Nothing was dampening it. Nothing. Perhaps if she wore more on that frame of hers. Perhaps if she were thin, spindly, or weak . . . or mayhap if she were overlarge with huge clumps of fat-filled flesh to each handhold of her. Either of those options might work at cooling him and keeping his thoughts from straying to exactly what they were.

The fire wasn't blazing, although it was keeping the beans simmering and warm enough to make a fine sop for the hard bread he'd packed for when he needed it. But it was hot—bloody hot—and that was making slight moisture glimmer on his skin whenever he moved. That was another advantage of having her in possession and control of what wardrobe he'd had with him. He needed the air about him for the cooling effect. He probably needed more than that. Myles squirmed on his pallet made from the folded-over tartan of the sled cover. She probably thought she was being generous by gifting him with that. She did allow him a kilt to wear, while the other one was hanging from one of his dirks as a divider, and failing miserably at it. She should have given the divider curtain sett to him to wear. It was one of his coarser, woolen ones. That way mayhap the prickling would help mute some of this want that he couldn't.

Myles groaned softly. The chafe and itch of roughly carded wool against any part of him would be worse. He knew it. He didn't have to guess. He shifted on his bed, drew his legs beneath him in a cross-legged pose, and settled what material he could in his lap. Then he turned away from her. He could always face the wall, but that would be too obvious. Then, she'd know. Or guess.

There was one thing left to try, but it was too bitterly cold to attempt it. He already knew that, too. When last he'd checked, the air hurt to breathe, and Rafe wasn't even interested in eating, preferring instead to sleep, covered over in his master's fur. Myles would have to be powerfully aroused to try a full-body plunge into a drift of snow mixed with ice, and then there was his other problem: getting to the window access without alerting the vixen who was tempting him to his troubles.

She was a vixen, too. Tempting. Luscious. Womanly. Vindictive.

He knew the last for certain, as she traipsed across his vision once again, highlighting herself in the firelight as she plundered his saddlebags. Myles couldn't help it. His eyes followed her, even though he had to crane his neck to continue. She should just take the bags over to her pallet. That would be the generous thing to do. And it was her turn to be generous!

He rubbed the whisker growth on his jaw in thought. Then he turned sideways and settled the skean onto his face, sliding it down to his jaw and over his chin, using years of practice as his mirror. It was a good thing this blade could use a good sharpening stone. Myles couldn't control the slight tremble of his fingers. The scrape sound didn't soothe it, either. Nothing did. And it was her fault.

She went back across the room, scattering firelight in her wake. Vicious. Vixen. He already allowed her everything she wanted. Anything else meant a fight, and to fight with her meant proximity so he could hear. That was the one thing he wasn't allowing! So he let her plunder at will. He only had one thing left that she hadn't claimed and he had it with him. His clan *feile breacan*. The one woven specially to be worn when presenting himself for his betrothal.

To what could only be her.

He turned his head fully away and swallowed, but it was more of a gulp. There wasn't any estate in several leagues' distance, save the obvious: Eschoncan Keep. And there was only one family inhabiting that hall, and it had a daughter of marriageable age who was known as a shrew and a harridan and a skelpie . . . and she was known to be large. They should have specified the large, he mused. This one was large, all right. In womanly, tall, willowy ways. Her head reached his cheekbone and if he raised her a bit, absolutely everything on her fit well with the size of him. Everything.

The Eschoncan heiress was his roommate in this croft filled with unmitigated desire. This Kendran . . .

was his intended bride. The woman he'd nearly killed himself to avoid. She could be no other. His. Myles's eyes widened on the sight of his own hand shaking too much to continue for a moment. He couldn't believe his luck. This was the woman he'd fought his entire clan to keep from wedding?

He groaned again, but it was louder this time, prompting him to glance over his shoulder and check for a reaction from her side of their space. She was ensconced back on her pallet. She'd already decreed the spot nearest the fire to be hers. She had right of first possession. He didn't fight that, either. It was already too hot, even here at the far wall, and he'd let her have any part of the room she wanted as long as it was on the other side of her curtain of clothing and well away from him!

Myles watched her through a slit in her veiling at where she was engrossed with picking at a thread in one of his workday plaides. She should definitely wear more. That might help. She shouldn't mock him with every breath he took by wearing so little in front of him! Women showing what skin this Kendran was were available and used for one thing: the one thing he was fighting his entire body over. He finished his shave and slid the blade along the side of his pallet to dust it. He passed his free hand over his face, massaging at the jaw knot his clenched teeth was making. It didn't work. Nothing did. He was suffering. Suffering! With the effects of desire and heat and frustration and pain. It was growing toward pain. Real, gut-twisting pain, almost the extent of her kneeing him earlier had been. Myles shook his head. That was stupid. This pain was worse. More personal. Burning, making him hard . . . pulsatingly hard.

Damn her! He knew it wasn't her fault she'd been stranded in only the clothing she wore. It was probably not her fault that a winter blizzard had cropped up, chasing and then sealing her into this inhospitable croft, either. It was probably not her fault that Myles had been wandering about, lost and ill. It was definitely her fault that she'd bathed before him just last eve, though! And no amount of telling his mind to ignore it worked, either. He knew what she had beneath the broadcloth shirt she was wearing. Even if it was one of his longest and grazed her knees, he knew what it hid. Knew it as if he'd already touched it, teased his fingers along it . . . tasted it.

Myles groaned, shook his head, and turned his focus back to the stick, although it was sweaty in his hands. He began to wonder if he was going to be able to wield the skean properly. But he had to have something to do with his hands or he was going to be finding out exactly what she felt like beneath that shirt! The space in front of him on the pallet wavered, he twisted the hilt in his hand, rotating it as the blade caught the firelight, and he wondered what next he could try.

There was the whisper of cloth, and then she dropped into place right where he was staring, unconcernedly crossing her legs to sit in exactly the same position he was in, and sending his imagination right into the shadowy recess between her thighs. Myles gulped, squeezed, and the stick shot right out of his hand, before coming to a clattering stop against the wall. Luckily, the hilt of the skean was made for such a movement, for all that happened was his knuckles went almost white with the pressure he had exerted on it. She glanced to where the stick lay and then back at him, meeting his eyes like there was nothing more to it than that. And then she smiled.

* * *

"Watch this," she whispered and held out her hands. It was probably an unnecessary request, but he was acting very strangely. Myles hadn't moved his eyes. He hadn't even blinked as far as she could tell.

Kendran waved her fingers within the strands of dyed wool that she'd tied into a large circlet and then made it into a weave that needed all her fingers just to hold. She watched him inhale. There was no way not to watch it. He wasn't wearing any material on his chest, he was shiny with moisture beads, and it looked like he was trembling as well. Kendran's brow drew down, as well as her hands. He couldn't be ill again! It had taken all the nursing skills she knew, and that wasn't much, to make him well the first time.

"You . . . ill?" she whispered.

He didn't answer. His eyes were dark, revealing nothing. That didn't give her anything to go by. It was probably his fault. He was turned so the fire was at his back, shadowing him. If he was as fevered as it looked, he didn't need the fire, though. He probably needed to be wiped off with snow again.

"Well?"

Nothing. He didn't even blink, although his eyes narrowed. His lips were in a thin line, too. He was angry? That was ridiculous. Every contest he'd set up he'd won. That's what had decided her. He couldn't know the basket-weave game. No man did. This one she could win. She lifted her hands again, reaching outward and upward with her fingers to pull the strands tighter.

"My turn. My game. Do you ken how it's played?" She had to tip forward until her face nearly touched his to make certain he heard the whisper. Other than a sharp intake of breath, he acted like he hadn't even heard it. She scooted a bit closer, rocking on her thighs to make the motion, since her hands were woven into the wool strand. Her knees touched his. First the left one, then the right. She stopped and looked up toward him again. If anything he was sitting even straighter than before, and angling away from her. That was intensely stupid. He couldn't hear anything she said if he did that.

Mysterious. But he was ever that. Since she'd first seen him, he was mysterious, and dark, and enticing and provoking, and a thousand other emotions and descriptions that she didn't know enough about to name. Kendran felt the blush just looking up at him was causing her. Then she watched his nostrils flare as he sucked in a huge breath.

Good. He wasn't ill. He was just acting strangely. That was another word she could use to describe him. Strange. Strange . . . and large and muscled, and heated. Very heated. A smile toyed at her mouth as she watched him shudder with exhaling that breath and then take in another of the same depth and size.

"You ready? Watch." She dropped her fingers, releasing the weave into the one long, knotted strand it was.

"You want me to play a . . . game?"

Kendran hadn't known she'd been fretting until she heard his voice. She felt the tangible relief. He wasn't ill. He was just tired. Perhaps that was it.

She nodded.

"Now?" he continued.

She nodded again.

"With you?"

She giggled, scanned the entire room for effect, and then returned her gaze to him to nod. Whom else could she mean?

"Right now? Here?"

Kendran gave him her best big-sister look and bent close so he'd hear the whisper. "Here. Now. You and me. My game." He wasn't breathing the entire time she spoke. He didn't appear to be moving at all. He might as well be a statue and about as animated. Except for the sheen of moisture coating every inch of him, making the skin-wrapped muscle of his entire upper torso shine as she waited. . . .

"This is my bed," he said finally. He didn't inhale breath for it, and that meant he'd been holding it.

Kendran gasped. Then watched as he turned the skean he was still holding outward, and stabbed it into the wall at his left side, where, impaled, it was quivering with the force of it. Kendran jumped but didn't move otherwise. Force didn't mean much to her. Show of force meant even less.

"Na' a bed," she answered, hoping the waver in her whispered voice wasn't as noticeable as it felt like it was. " 'Tis a cover. And I had to come. You were ignoring me."

His answer was ground between his teeth, but it could have been anything. She rather fancied it was one of his curse words. He was also running his free palms along his kilt-covered knees over and over, pulling at the material with the force he was using. Strange. Dark. Fascinating.

"Watch now." Kendran stuck her hands, palms inward and fingers straight and together, into the loop. Then she pulled it tight, stretching her arms wider than the span of his shoulders, which she had the gauge of since they were right in front of her eyes. He'd given off pulling at his kilt-wrapped thighs to put his fingers through his hair now, combing it back and holding it there. It was probably a shade close to the black-brown of his eyes. At least that's what she suspected it would be once it was washed and then groomed with a comb, rather than his fingers. It was also longer than shoulder length, since the ends of it were lying limply to that span of flesh before grazing the large humps of his chest. Her fingers started tingling. That was odd. That was wondrously, horribly odd.

"Uh . . ." She swiveled her hands, wrapping a loop about each palm as she did so. Then she lifted herself the space between them to get close enough he'd hear her whispered words. "This is the basket game."

"The basket game," he echoed. "'Tis . . . a game?"

She blinked slowly, to stay the first response to roll her eyes toward the ceiling, and then she nodded yet again. "Watch closely." That was probably a stupid request, since he hadn't taken his eyes from any part of her since she first sat down. A tingle stirred within her at the thought and she sent it away. She was whiling away the time. That's what she was doing. That's all she was doing. The other part of her was doing something completely different. That part, the one she hadn't even known existed, and that he'd brought into being with his kisses . . .

She narrowed her eyes. *That* part of Kendran Eschon wasn't playing games. That one was set on vengeance. Swift and sure vengeance. And both were excellent courses of action when stranded by a winter storm in a deserted croft with a member of the detested gender.

Detested . . .

How was such a word supposed to survive when applied to the male sitting facing her? There wasn't any room for such an emotion. Kendran gulped. She didn't know why there wasn't room, and she didn't want to know. She wasn't ever going to find out. But she was going to make him pay. That's what she was doing.

That's all she was doing. If he wished to call it a game, so be it.

This Kendran was gaining full measure for her humiliation, first at losing the bean game, and then for turning into a siren of desire from the lesson in kissing he'd given her. That lesson had turned her into a writhing, panting, overly heated, sensual slip of flesh, created and willed into being by such mind-numbing hunger, she still shook with it if she didn't control it. Fiercely. That creature wasn't playing. It was getting vengeance.

Kendran laced her middle finger through the loop at each palm and pulled the string taut again. There was now a rudimentary basketweave showing, just like before. "You do this," she whispered, the sound coming out just a bit hoarser than before.

"Why?"

"You drop the weave, you remake it."

"Why?"

"'Tis how you play! First to drop a thread, loses."

"Why?"

She did roll her eyes then. It didn't make a dent in the mass of man in front of her. She leaned closer. "A dropped thread . . . ruins the weave," she told him.

"So?"

The one word sent breath caressing her throat and shoulders. She had to force herself to ignore it. "If the weave is ruined, you canna' keep the basket shape."

"So?"

She sighed and watched as he appeared to flinch when her breath touched him. That was interesting. The craven Kendran smiled—inwardly. The outward one who was game playing smiled flirtatiously. "You ruin the weave, you lose."

He groaned. The solid mass made the sound with just a slight opening of his lips. She could see he was clenching his teeth, too. That was interesting. And enjoyable. And thrilling. And stirring. And hot. Kendran stopped the litany of wonderment playing through her mind. She wasn't here for that Kendran. That one might actually want his kiss again!

"We play . . . to thirty-two." She stumbled through the whisper but got it all out. Then she pulled her head away and regarded him with the same blank look he was giving her. Saying nothing. Showing less.

"Why thirty-two?" he asked.

Kendran snarled. "Because I want my beans back." It wasn't said with a whisper. It was more a hiss.

He smiled then, a long, slow smile, revealing white teeth amidst all that dark, swarthy skin, and then he licked his lips. Kendran gasped, felt the reaction clear to her toes, and then it got worse! The response traveled across her shoulders and centered in her breasts, making the nipples taut against the broadcloth. There wasn't any way to hide it, either. Her hands were in use. She scooted even closer to him, to force the shirt to slacken, and watched as his eyes completely closed. Then his entire frame pulsed in a strong movement that went right from him then into her.

Kendran opened her mouth, but nothing came out at first. There wasn't much for it. She'd started this. She'd finish it. She'd win. She tried again. This time there was a bit of sound to the whisper. "Pinch your fingers," she whispered.

"What?" he asked, in a much lower tone than before.

"Thumb and finger. Pinch them together. Like this." She lifted the thread and pointed with her nose where he was supposed to grasp at it. "Then lift . . . over the sides . . . and take it."

"I am na' . . . touching you," he replied, and there was something so unsteady about the words, or the phrasing of them, that she frowned slightly.

"'Tis simple. Children play it."

"I dinna' play it."

Kendran pulled back farther and considered that. Then she pulled one hand out and shook the string loose. "Learn. Hold out your hands."

"Nae."

She wanted to launch a tirade at him but settled with whispering a few words while she filled in the blanks. "Blackguard!" *You'd give me* "no chance!" *to gain back what I've lost? 'Tis most* "unchivalrous!" *of you. Most* "ungallant!" *Most* "unmanly!" *Most* "unfair!" *Most—*

"Enough!"

He grabbed for the string and pulled it out of her grasp. Kendran watched his motions as he viciously strapped his hands into the string to form the basket as if he were born to it. That was odd. Either he was lying about knowing the game or he was a very quick study. That bore thinking on. He'd finished and was glaring at her with that unblinking, dark stare of his. Kendran gasped and dropped her eyes to the mesh of basket, where it was safer.

"Watch."

She reached for the crosses on display between them and pinched them as she'd just described to him before maneuvering her hands beneath the outer strings. When she brought her upturned hands through the center, she touched skin.

A strange spark, almost painful in its intensity, was

immediately followed by what could only be their combined groan. Kendran's eyes went wide, her legs turned into so much bog-filled stability, and where she'd inadvertently touched him was actually itching. She didn't know what to say. She didn't know if she was supposed to say anything. She didn't even know what had happened.

He didn't act like he did, either. There was nothing for it but to finish the play and move the thread onto her hands. He wasn't loosening it, though. She couldn't grasp it unless he did, and his entire body seemed to be shuddering and not much else.

"Let . . . go," she snapped, but since it was in a whisper, it didn't have much authority to it.

"You touched me," he replied.

She shrugged. "So?"

"You are na' to touch me!"

Kendran uncrossed her legs and went to her knees, placing her a bit above where he was still sitting. It would also make it easier to get the string off him. She couldn't get much farther, however. She hovered over him for several moments, sucking in and then releasing breath, while his seemed to increase in depth, strength, and volume right beneath her. She gulped the reaction away. That Kendran wasn't playing this game. The vengeful one was. "Loosen your hold!" she hissed down at him.

He moved his arms inward, relaxing the tension of thread. Kendran lifted it away from him and sat back on her haunches although she rolled a bit before regaining her balance. Such a thing happens when one has no use of her own hands. He had no right to start howling curse words at her. None.

But that's exactly what he was doing, and adding in

names for her behavior such as jezebel and wanton. Kendran sucked in a breath full of shock and hurt and then disgust. And then it was anger. He was not only a poor player; he was a bad loser. Totally unmanly. She almost wasted what voice she had with saying it but settled for returning the glare he was giving her with exactly the same amount of venom.

"Finished?" she asked, baring her teeth.

"I'll na' play this game with you. 'Tis silly and childish."

"Nae. You're silly and childish," she replied. "And you lose poorly."

His jaw set, if the knot bulging out the side was any indication, and he was having difficulty breathing. He shouldn't toss out insults if he couldn't handle having them paid back.

"I have na' lost . . . yet." His voice went so low as he finished that Kendran could barely make it out.

"You have. You are."

"I am na' losing."

Kendran nodded the answer. She was finished wasting her voice on him. She was finished playing with him. It was senseless. He didn't know the rules.

"You can only lose if you choose to play. I'm na' playing. Therefore, I canna' lose."

"Loser," she mouthed.

"I'm na' losing!" It was totally unfair now. He had command of his voice and he was using it to shout across less than an arm's span of distance. He should have guessed by now that loud speech wasn't going to get him anything other than a fight.

He swore and then started filling the void with words that shocked and angered and stunned. "Hell sounds better than this! Jesu'! I'm locked in with a wench who craves attention regardless of the cost! And when she does na' get it, she plays! I am na' losing! She is."

Kendran's mouth opened with surprise. Oh, if only she had use of her voice he'd not be looking at her with such an expression on his face! She had no voice, so she did the next best thing. She made a fist and slugged him, and all that happened was her blow bounced from the plateau of muscle she'd aimed for.

He lowered his head and growled at her through his eyebrows. He *growled* at her?

Kendran wrapped the looped string about both fists and shoved them against each other over and over, making friction and heat run from her palms to her elbows, and that wasn't enough to mute what she was feeling. Nothing was. She should have aimed for his jaw! Better yet, she should have smacked at the almost healed split in his lip.

And then he started laughing. At her. At her actions. Kendran launched herself at him, swinging with the joined fists, but he caught both of them easily, fell completely off his pallet onto the hard dirt floor, and then he wasn't laughing at all. He was nuzzling, and sucking, and sending his breath all along where the shirt placket hadn't buttons enough, and murmuring sweet words that hadn't one thing devoted to losing, or cursing, or anger, or anything other than absolute need, want, and desire.

Kendran was in shock, yet she wasn't. Her entire being should have been angered and stiff, and unyielding. Instead, the other Kendran took over. This one was moaning and moving, sliding sinuously in the space he gave her, since he'd captured her legs within his own. And that was no kilt knot she felt this time as he rolled her over and went atop her, the movement separating her legs as she made the space for him. There wasn't any material hiding it this time. She didn't have to look to make certain. The heat and texture of it against her upper thighs was enough.

"Wondrous fair. Womanly. Sweet. Passionate. Love. Heat . . . hot." He was using a slow cadence of words each time he rubbed his lips against her, tracing the line of her jaw, along her neck, and then to the base of her throat. Then he was huffing little heated swirls of air onto the skin he'd just tongued to wetness with his words.

"I want you, lass. Nae games. Nae lies. You. Your womanhood. Now. Right now."

She was left in no confusion over what that meant, as he moved his mouth lower, separating the neckline of her shirt like there were no buttons there at all. And then he was scraping the growth of whisker from his upper lip against flesh that had never felt the like. Rubbing. Scraping. Moving his face from side to side as he strove for first one nipple and then the next, going closer and closer each time. Closer . . . And the wanton Kendran was helping him.

It was her hands in his hair, holding fistfuls of the brownish black strands to keep him right where he was, while everything about her lower body was in an agony of want, need, and exquisite torment. He was guaranteeing it, too, with each swipe of his body against her, each movement placing the man part of him between her knees, then carving open her thighs, arching his back at the same time, and she wanted it so badly she was screaming with it, even if she had no voice to do so.

He'd reached a peak, licked it, scraped his mouth across it, and then he pulled the entire piece into his mouth and started suckling, and Kendran went absolutely wild with how it felt. She was bucking and heaving, and shivering and screaming, and existing in such a realm of excitement and fantasy that everything on her exploded. Heat such as she'd never known filled her, owned her, claimed her, making an inferno unlike anything she'd ever experienced, and she wanted more of it. So much more. More . . .

He was chuckling as she shimmied, her movement shoving him to the neglected breast, and that just made it more tortuous and more sensuous and more rapturous and more . . . more . . . more.

Kendran was moaning in rhythm with the continuum of pushes he was making against her very core. She felt his hands sliding beneath the shirt, blazing fire across her thighs, then onto her buttocks as he lifted her, exposing her . . . to him. Then he was touching, pressing . . . entering and fusing and making such pain race through her back that she arched with it and sucked in on the shock.

And then the most thunderous boom hit the door, making dust rain down from the rafters, coating the entire scene and dancing on fire flecks until it looked like a fantasy scene from his hell.

Another boom came, making more old dust.

"Bloody hell! Christ! Jesu'!" Myles began the usual litany of his cursing, starting through the words as if by rote, but he was on his feet instantly, pushing that male part of himself beneath the kilt, while he moved sideways to pluck his skean from the wall. Kendran couldn't move. She felt riveted in place, her shirt hanging open at each side, showing it had more than one button torn from its hole, while legs were akimbo, and everything was shivering with the reaction. Everything.

Myles didn't have the same problem. She didn't know how he managed it.

Kendran watched as he moved, walking in a slight crouch. He didn't even stop to reach up with his free arm and yank down one of his kilts before tossing it toward her. His aim was accurate, too, for the material landed perfectly, covering over everything she slammed her eyes to keep from seeing.

Kendran had her hands over her face then, holding in the emotion. She didn't know what it was, and she didn't want to find out. It was enough that it was lurid and evil and she was almost naked and lying atop nothing more than an old beaten earth floor, trembling with the shivers going up and down her spine.

And it was cold.

She knew when he reached the window, heard the shutter moving, the sound of his body going over the sill. And then she waited, hearing nothing but the beating of her own pulse in her ears.

CHAPTER 7

It was Rafe.

Myles tipped a head around the corner of the croft, keeping to a crouch, not only for the stealth, but also because the air hadn't warmed any. It was so bitter cold it even hurt to breathe. It was also frosting everything on his upper body every time he moved. He would have groaned, but that would have been a waste of body warmth when he expelled. He couldn't afford it.

He also would have berated his horse if Rafe wasn't getting ready to take another swipe at the doorjamb with what looked to be the back post of what had been his lean-to. Myles launched across the space, reaching the stallion before he could back into the door again. The animal quieted the moment he was there. Then, he was soothing the nose and looking into what could only be terror-stricken eyes. *Terror?* he wondered, stroking the animal while he checked for damage.

There was a light grazing of torn flesh at one shoulder. It looked the type brought on by knocking against the pillar that had supported the lean-to roof. There was also a bit of blood drip on one of his flanks. Myles examined it briefly in what light was available. Then he was at a semicrouch again, cursing the ill timing of his luck again. He was silent about it this time. He didn't know the extent of the threat. He was preparing to gird an unknown quantity with nothing more dangerous than a skean? He possessed a sword, a broad bow with a quiver of arrows, a hand ax, a beltfull of dirks, a shield . . . and all he'd managed to grab was one skean?

This was not encouraging. Especially when faced with the ice-formed gargoyles that the trees just outside the clearing looked to be. There was also a frost-filled fog hanging just below the treetops, making it difficult for what sun there was to penetrate. *Sun? 'Tis still day?* Myles wondered, looking up for a moment at the proof of it. It didn't seem possible. He'd suspected an entire day of woman-induced torment had passed, not just an afternoon of it. He patted Rafe's side, gathered the reins, and tried to make the animal take one step he didn't want to.

Whatever was at the lean-to, the horse wasn't having anything more to do with it. Myles had to give up. He couldn't force Rafe to go where he didn't wish to, not without jabbing at him, and the animal was still trembling from whatever had accosted him. It was better to lead him to the opposite side of their croft and it garnered the same thing, his horse tied again and out of harm's way, while Myles had the mobility and stealth he'd need.

He looped around behind the croft, skimming along the roof where it had been formed out of the hillside, all the while wishing he'd shown more sense. Not only to have a graver weapon, but more than a kilt on his frame, and he'd have put on socks, too. Myles stifled the curse at wearing sockless boots that filled with snow every time he took a misstep into a drift. Then, he reached what was left of the lean-to.

There were wolf tracks all about the ground, some scuffed through by hoofprints, some covered over by snow that had fallen when the roof collapsed. They were still big prints, and they were definitely made by a wolf; a large, mature wolf. Myles put a hand out as a measure and considered it. The prints were the same size as his spread hand. He was facing a very large wolf. He rolled the skean in his hand. The only good thing looked to be it was a lone animal, and not a pack of them. One skean would have to be enough.

Myles bent forward and started following the trail.

The animal was crazed. Illness, hunger, or disease had been rumored to do such a thing, but Miles had never seen it. This wolf wasn't following a scent; it wasn't honing in on prey; it wasn't doing anything more than zigzagging amongst deadfall and heaps of snow-covered obstacles, and causing Myles more than once to fall full out on his backside with chasing it. That just got him bare loins covered in snow and melt and an acid temper to match. The ungodly creature wasn't just causing him the burn of ice-cold snow against his nakedness and making every intake of breath painful; he was making a fool of him as well. Myles was about to give up chase, and follow the same path back to the warmth of Kendran's fire, when the tracks turned that way, themselves.

That had him loping faster as he followed them, sliding more often, falling even more, but there wasn't anything cold or frozen or anything other than heated and worried as the tracks got closer and closer to their croft. Myles was inhaling ice burn and exhaling heated worry, and everything on him was taut and prepared when he reached the window, where shutters weren't latched against him anymore. They weren't anything other than gaped open and showing a black hole where the tracks showed the size of the body that had burst them open.

Myles's heart stopped when he saw it and then decided it really would continue beating. But it was painful. Almost as painful as the ache in his side, now that he'd reached the croft, and then he heard the sound of scuffling.

He sprang through the aperture like he was born to it, rolled instantly to a crouch, and had the skean poised for flight at his fingertips. He didn't know what stopped his throwing arm. He never did puzzle it out, either.

Kendran was standing in front of the animal, her entire body protecting what proved to be exactly what he'd thought: a very large gray wolf. And what was worse, she was frantic, but not at him. For the animal. She didn't voice it, but everything about her was in that position. Myles dropped the skean and came out of his crouch to face them. He could feel the flush overtaking his entire body. He couldn't do anything to prevent it. He wasn't remotely cold.

"You . . . ken this creature?" he asked.

She nodded.

"Well?"

In answer she stepped to the side of him and started stroking his fur. The animal arched its back in appreciation. Myles could relate to that. His own back clenched, reminding him. She probably should have put more clothing on than the shirt she was barely wearing since he'd ripped the buttons loose.

He looked away. He had to. He didn't know why his

mind wouldn't rid him of the images or why desire for her dogged him like a plague. And yet he did, at the same time. Because it was unfinished. All of it.

He swallowed and looked back at her. She was still standing with the wolf kept protectively at her side, and she was scratching the animal's ears now.

"A pet. He's a pet."

She nodded again.

"Yours?"

She nodded.

"I hope you dinna' think to use him."

Her eyebrows rose.

"As anything other than comfort while I'm off."

Her brows drew down again.

"You puzzle the why of another trip into the snow?"

She nodded.

"Rafe."

"Rafe?" At least that's what he thought she said. He had to assume that's what she mouthed since he wasn't in hearing distance of any whisper she might have made with the sound.

"My mount doesn't find your pet . . . pleasant."

She frowned.

"He tore down his shelter to get away. That's what made the noise . . . interrupting us."

Her eyes went wide and then she looked down. It didn't cover her blush. Myles watched it and smiled—inwardly. He was doing his best to halt what his body was experiencing at the temptation she presented, and look stern at the same time. He didn't know if it was working, but it was the best he could manage.

"And now I have to rebuild one for him. Perhaps you could make yourself useful by fanning the fire up some more. It's powerful cold out there. I'm going to need it when I return."

Then she amazed him by waving her fingers in a gesture of farewell. Myles was grateful he didn't react and kept the flash of anger from showing as well. The wolf was responding. He was giving a low, menacing, deep-belly growling sound.

Kendran watched him don one of his serviceable, thick shirts, pulling it brutally over his head and shoving his arms in, although he left the placket untied clear to his midchest. He didn't tuck it in. He grunted while pulling off his boots, and then he grunted worse after donning two pairs of socks before putting the boots back on. Then he was taking his pallet apart to tie the covering over his shoulders. He wasn't paying any attention to her or Waif, either.

That was probably a good thing. Kendran barely had control of the animal herself. The upraised hair beneath her hands was telling of it. The low growl that was barely making sound was continuously pumping from his throat, too.

She'd lied. Waif wasn't hers and he certainly wasn't a pet. And if he was, it was the Lady Sybil who claimed him and taught him. And it was the lady who had sent him out in a winter storm hunting out her sister, too. Lady Sybil was like that. Always knowing what to do.

Kendran hadn't given much thought to what her nonattendance at family functions might mean. She supposed her absence in a deathly blizzom was bound to have been discovered by now. The entire keep would have been tossed looking for her before they would accept the inevitable. Especially if her mare had returned riderless.

Kendran had gone riding, and now she was missing. In weather such as this, being missing meant exposure, and exposure meant death.

They would probably already be preparing and changing the dowries.

Only Lady Sybil wouldn't join in the general confusion. She'd know what to do. The wolf beneath Kendran's fingers was the proof of that. Sybil always sent the animal out if her half sister was missing. It was their secret.

Waif would find her. He always did. And he'd have herbs with him that would be exactly what Kendran needed. Not a season hence, she'd stumbled upon a hornet's nest, earning herself several vicious stings and a face so swelled she couldn't see through what eye slits she had left.

Kendran had fought off the fever and found herself a cave to shelter in before succumbing to shaking that wouldn't cease. And then Waif had appeared in that cave, a packet tied beneath his neck chain. That time the packet had contained ground barley tops mixed with some sort of smelly unguent, and she'd also been sent a tiny silvered flask of spirits. The powder had made a heady soup. The unguent had taken the pain and swelling down, and the whiskey had been heavensent, too.

Waif hadn't waited around to make certain she survived, but he never did. He was going to return to his mistress, and then she'd be making vague words to assure everyone of how groundless their worries were. It was no wonder she was considered fey. She'd probably even know exactly how far and where her sister was by the length of time the animal was missing.

Lady Sybil knew exactly what to send and she knew

exactly how to make certain it arrived. She sent it with her wolf, Waif. Kendran just hadn't had time to untie the bundle and get the animal on its way before Myles had reappeared through the window, looking more menacing than a clan assassin.

She didn't think Waif was dangerous, but he was certainly exhibiting every sign of it for the entire time it took Myles to clothe himself properly. He probably needed to wear everything in the croft—the open window was telling of the evening's bitter cold—but he wasn't.

"Dinna' think your animal will protect you forever."

"What?" Her word didn't make sound, but he had to know what it was. He'd finished with his preparations and was standing in the midst of the room favoring both Waif and her with that devil-dark stare. That was the only portion of his body left uncovered, since he'd also folded a plaide about his head and face and tucked it beneath the shoulders of his cloak.

"From me!" He was yelling it. He had to be since the sound should have been muffled but was still loud.

"I—" She stopped. Her voice wasn't working, and she didn't have an answer, anyway.

"We've unfinished business, you and I." He was pointing at her and then at himself.

Kendran's eyes went wide. She didn't have to respond to that, either.

"And if you think a trained wolf is barrier enough, let me assure you, animals dinna' work that way."

"How would you ken?" she replied, goaded into answering. Only the first word had sound, but that seemed enough.

"My clan keeps dogs, too. Sometimes a wolf or two joins up with the pack. I dinna' know from whence they come, nor do I care. Wolves are kin to dogs. Dogs are pack animals, my lady. Pack. And pack animals follow a leader. A male leader. A strong male leader."

Now she was annoyed. It probably showed in the way she straightened, lifting enough on Waif's hair that his growl deepened.

"Besides which, you're covered in my scent."

"What?" She didn't have to ask. He was waiting for it, though.

"A dog will na' attack a scent he knows and loves. You're covered in mine, and I, nae doubt, reek of you. Your pet will na' attack me. He'll probably welcome me. Think on that whilst I'm gone."

He was still talking as he walked over to the window, keeping an eye on Waif the entire time. Kendran didn't know enough about Sybil's pet to argue it, but Myles couldn't be right. The animal was silently menacing, his hair was grazing her wrist from where it was still raised, and she could feel how taut and ready to spring he was simply by the close proximity to him. He didn't seem cowed, or disinclined to attack. Myles must think the same, for he didn't do his typical maneuver and lift himself to his seat in order to back out the window space. He simply swiveled toward it and dove right through it.

And then there was only silence broken by her uneven breathing.

Waif relaxed the moment Myles disappeared and that made it easier to pull on his collar, spinning it around so she could reach the wrapped bundle that had been tied beneath his jaw. There was the honey-hop herbal tea mixture she'd been looking for, and there was something more. A strange purple-toned vial that came packaged in a small square of soft leather.

Kendran unwrapped it reverently and scraped off the wax tip, smelling the savory the moment she had. *Savory?* she wondered. Why would Sybil pack such a thing? Savory wasn't useful on a sore throat. It actually wasn't of much use, one way or another. Kendran had only known Sybil to use it once before. As an aphrodisiac. It was called the ambrosia of the gods. A stimulant. For mating.

Kendran went cold. Then hot. And then she was shaking. If there was ever an example of Lady Sybil's sorcery, this was it. She settled the wax back onto the top, but it wouldn't fit properly, and she spilled some of the potion on her fingertips, and from there it dribbled onto the shirt in small droplets scented of lust and excitement and longing. And then it dribbled onto the floor at her feet.

This wouldn't do at all! If Myles caught a whiff of this scent, he'd think she wanted what he'd stirred into being within her. He'd think her desirous of it, rather than so horrid that she'd held him at bay with a wolf to avoid it.

Kendran put the bottle behind an open slat in the wall and then she started sorting through the other clothing for something to wear. Clothing that wasn't saturated with a potion designed to bring to fruition exactly what she had to evade. She didn't want the man Myles! She didn't want what he did to her! She didn't want to feel the other-worldly possession of her body, the exquisite tension deep within her, nor the wellspring of want that was still cursing her hands with tremors. She didn't!

And she didn't want Lady Sybil devining that she did!

It wasn't fair! No one had warned her. She had no weapons to fight such an unknown quantity as this stranger was. She hadn't known feelings such as he aroused within her existed. No one had ever mentioned them. The entire Eschon Keep was filled with hate-spawned taunts and violence and anger. There hadn't been any lessons in love given.

Love?

Kendran's thought stalled and her eyes went wide in horror as she backed from the wall holding the vial. Why had she put that word into existence? She didn't even know this man, Myles. All she knew was he possessed a temper. And a visage so handsome it was a heady experience just looking at him. And he had intensity and strength and brawn and the emotion of lust following him like a cloud. And her fingers were bothering her again for want of touching him. That's all she knew. She certainly hadn't known he could create an emotion akin to heaven with that body of his. No one had told her!

It seemed the cruelest thing they could have done. If she'd known such feelings existed, she could have readied a defense. Kendran put cool hands to her hot cheeks. She didn't love him! She couldn't! No Eschon female loved a male! They were hated creatures. Taking, vicious, vile, horrid, sweat-soaked and smelly creatures! That's what they were!

She watched Waif as he watched her. The wolf had always made her anxious. Myles hadn't known what bravery it took to hold to Waif like it was an everyday occurrence while his shackles had risen in aggression. No man would know how her entire body had shook just from clinging to the animal's neck like she had been. Myles wasn't going to find out, either.

She had to rid herself of this smell, however. And before the day got much older. The little purplish savory flower had always had an unmistakable aroma. Now, it felt like it was enveloping her, creating a cloud about her, wafting up from the fine linen shirt of his that she still wore, enwrapping her with such a craving she had to swallow to still it.

Which reminded her. She still had a sore throat and Waif had delivered the perfect brew for it. All she had to do was put kindling on the fire, blow it back to life, boil herself a pot of herb-filled tea, and sip it. And that had to wait for the rebolting of the window.

Kendran looked over at the yawning aperture with a feeling akin to shock. The window was wide, the fire was down to gray-shaded coals, the animal beside her was quiet and still, and his fur had a chill to it she should have associated with the slow freeze entering the room, and yet she felt none of it? Kendran's eyes widened. It was the savory. It had to be. Why else would she be standing in such surroundings thinking and experiencing such thoughts of the man she shared the space with, to the point that she felt enwrapped in a heat-filled haze?

Kendran shook her head and heard the ringing sensation of that, and then she could even sense the sound behind every blink of her eyes. She rubbed both hands together and felt such heat from her motion that her hands felt scorched by it. Each and every sensation was being heightened to such a degree she was frightening herself. She was also accomplishing nothing toward getting the space warm again and her tea brewed.

Lady Sybil had cursed her! Kendran started searching for the bolt stick, so aware of the sinuous glide of her own body beneath the shirt she wore that even that material felt too confining, too stiff, unyielding, strange. She caught her own hands working at the bottom three buttons—the ones Myles had left fastened—and then sent the snarl soundlessly into space that should have chilled her teeth, but didn't. It was Waif putting a howl into existence in her stead. Kendran glanced over at where he'd moved and watched him pace, pawing slightly at the dusting of droplets she'd put on the packed earthen floor before prowling again, circuiting the room. Then he surprised her completely by selecting the remnants of Myles's messed and scattered pallet upon which to sit, panting slightly, as if even he felt too hot in the room.

It was ridiculous to consider. It was horrid. It was magic and sorcery, and witchcraft at work. That's what it was. The savory oil Lady Sybil had sent was working . . . already! Kendran watched her own hands shaking as she found the sliver of wood that was left of their bolt and latched the shutters together. She was going to see that sorceress banished for this! That's what she was going to do! As soon as she found something less stiff and scratchy against her skin.

And that was more important than seeing to her fire?

Kendran watched her own hands finding one of his silken-feeling shirts, watched each button slide into its hole while she massaged them, feeling the nuances of each sanded and shaped bit of shell they'd used for his buttons. And through it all her body grew more heated, more tense, more strange. The sensation didn't cease. Even when she knelt and blew on their coals, earning herself a nose full of wood smoke and a chest wracked with coughing, she smelled the savory. And it was blending with other smells, making them stronger . . . more intense . . . more stirring. More distinctive.

She recognized his.

Kendran was on her knees, leaning back onto upraised heels, breathing deeply of the combination of man scent—strong, hard male scent—and she was still in that position, breathing lungs full of air as the fire stirred and caught, sending more wood smoke into the hole that had been cut for their chimney.

She couldn't quite place it although it wasn't an odd smell. Just unique. Because it was a blend. And she'd been mistaken earlier. Myles wasn't vile, sweat soaked, and smelly. Not at all. Myles had the most intoxicating smell. It seemed to follow her about almost worse than the savory did. His scent was akin to the wood smoke and it was the smell of heather. Added to that was the aroma of rain wash . . . and that was mixed with fire heat. Intense fire heat. Then it was all combined to form the most arousing, stirring, and exciting aroma. . . . That's what he smelled like. It was intoxicating. It was stimulating. It was—

Kendran forced the musings away and looked directly at what was now a roaring fire. The flames crackled and spit, sending bits of colored soot into being, to float atop the draft and from thence waft upward toward the chimney. She watched them with eyes half slit, knowing she hadn't finished with the chores she'd set for herself, and wondering what they were . . . and worse! Why it wasn't bothering her. She should be livid. She should be ranting every curse she knew onto Lady Sybil's head, rather than sitting watching a fire swell and grow.

She'd been spelled with savory . . . and it was by her own hand!

Kendran looked down at her own fingers, watched as they shook, rubbed the pads of her fingers against her thumbs, and then brought them to her temples. It didn't help. If anything, it made her head drop back as even the weight of her own hair worked against her. She felt the ends of it brushing against her bare toes . . . the bottoms of her feet . . . tickling her.

There was a stir in the room behind her. It was the wolf, Waif, and he was rubbing his face into the remains of Myles's pallet, pushing the padding he'd made into a heap. Myles wasn't going to like that, unless he chose to point out how right he'd been. The wolf didn't look menacing. He looked almost sedated by the touch, feel, and sensation of Myles's bed . . . and his smell.

He took his sweet time returning to the croft. Kendran's nerves were stretched to a screaming pitch, her entire body was tormenting her over and over again with sweat soak followed by bone chill, and that was chased away by trembling. She'd remembered her herbal tea. And when the honey-hop brew was simmering, it seemed to add even more aroma into the distressing combination already filling the room.

Kendran was annoyed; she was tense; she was frightened. Frightened? Of a little thing like a love potion?

She tried working at a finger-knitted belt. The sett she'd been picking at earlier in order to make the string for the basket game yielded more strings easily. She braided three of them together to make herself a length of rope. Then she was making a loop at one end, securing the other beneath a thigh, and pulling a new loop through each preceding one, entwining them into a rope of strength, flexibility, and tensile strength. That way she could find something useful to do with herself. She could make something of use. Maybe a strap to hold his belongings together so he could pack. That was helpful.

If the wolf could get through the storm, there was every chance a man on horseback could also. There was also the chance the Eschoncan Honor Guard would follow. The last thing Kendran wanted at the moment was the twelve select men whose duty it was to guard and protect the laird and his family. That would be disastrous.

It would also be fortuitous.

It was useless. Her hands wouldn't cease fumbling, and her body wouldn't cease annoying her with its troubles. And the silken weave of this shirt she'd chosen was clinging to sweat-soaked skin, outlining her easily in the firelight, and if that weren't enough, even that felt too heavy, erotic, and sensuous against her skin!

And then into this volatile mix came the sound she most dreaded and yet most yearned for at the same time. Her heart stumbled as a knock came on the shutters.

CHAPTER 8

It took him six tries to get that one in. Myles waited for the reaction from her side of the room. It wasn't long in coming, although the wolf she had at her side was where the scratching sounds were emanating. The animal was comfortable, sprawled as it was atop the remnants of Myles's pallet. She wasn't as comfortable. Nor was she as warm. All of which was her own fault.

She wouldn't call off her pet. And if she was going to be stubborn, then Myles had a new game for her. He could be more stubborn than anyone. Any of his brothers could tell her so. And she deserved every bit of what he could pay.

It was cold outside, bitterly cold. It was probably seeping through the wall where she was encamped. He hoped so. It was her turn to suffer.

He'd been sweating with his exertions, soaking all his layers of clothing. And then she'd made him stand, panting to breathe in air that burned with each gulp, while she'd taken her own sweet time with answering his knock. The wait had frozen the outer layering of his woolens, so that by the time she'd opened the shutters for him, it was all he could manage to lean forward and fall through the opening. He was tired, he was frozen, he was hungry, and he was annoyed.

He got more so the longer she threatened him with her pet. That animal had spent the time it took to fashion another shelter in the snow for Rafe in comparative luxury and warmth, as it claimed the remnants of Myles's bed. *Very well,* Myles thought. If she wouldn't remove her pet, she could lose the use of her own pallet, which was the one he now had possession of. He wasn't moving.

He'd limped over on numbed feet to where the fire was blazing, filling the croft with more heat than it needed, more light than he wanted, and a stench worse than the swill she'd been making while he'd been ill. He'd held his gloved hands out toward the flames, thawing them enough he could peel the frosted wool off. The smell of that combined with what she'd been cooking, making him very aware that she hadn't gained any culinary skills in his absence. It also made him aware that wet wool was a better aroma than what she was cooking.

His belly had lurched queerly as he'd lifted his head and sniffed, and that got him a cry of sound from where she was still hovering, her hand on the animal's collar.

Exactly as she was still doing now.

Myles flipped another dried broad bean toward the little pan he'd emptied into the dirt after taking another whiff of the contents. She'd screeched at him over emptying it, but she hadn't stopped him. She was too busy with making certain the wolf she held kept menacing Myles. That was what she'd been doing and was still doing— making certain he knew just how little she thought of what he'd said to her about finishing it. That must also show what she thought of the conflagration of desire they'd created earlier, and that she didn't want it. Or him.

The bean made a clanking sound as it glanced off the rim and landed somewhere beyond it. Myles heard the rustle of reaction coming from her side again. He almost smiled. He knew how much it bothered her. Knew it because she'd let him know of it. Maybe she shouldn't have pointed her finger at him and then shaken it at him like he had all the wits of a snowbank.

He picked another bean out of his pouch, held it between his thumb and forefinger, sighted the range, and flipped it with his other forefinger. That bean missed, too. Myles sighed softly, covering over any sound she or her pet might have made. He was losing his touch. The first ones had thumped and clanged as they hit, unerringly filling the pot until he'd run out of them, and then he'd had to empty it onto his lap, refill the pouch, and start anew.

All of which bothered her excessively.

She wasn't giving him much sign of it, although she hadn't moved her eyes from him most of the evening. She'd been gazing at him when he'd put fat strips from the dried venison into melting boar fat and waited for it to sizzle. She'd been watching him when he'd gone to the window and filled the little pot with snow—all three times. He hadn't checked. He'd felt her gaze. That was odd, but there had been a lot odd about the evening.

She'd been watching silently as he'd scooped the snow into the big pot, where it had instantly melted, making a sputtering and spitting noise that had almost covered up the ones she had been making, and she hadn't said much when he'd carved the last bit of cabbage into it, either. He'd known she was bothered, all the same. The low-throat growl of her pet had told him of it.

And when he'd had enough of being menaced by such a creature and asked what it would take to get her to stand the animal down, she'd gone and done the unforgivable. She'd turned her back on him and given him the stiff, silent sight of her back, showing how little she thought of him. And since she'd clothed herself in one of his fancy dress shirts—one spun from cream-soaked flax until it draped and slid over flesh—the sight started an ache. Physically. Continually. Reminding him. Myles had been more annoyed than she could be at what the sight of that shirt caressing her back and loins had done to him.

He was even more annoyed that the wolf had been watching all of it.

Myles flipped another bean toward the pot, arcing it with a move that looked like he'd practiced until it was perfect, and the bean sailed into the little pot without touching any of the sides. It made a satisfying thunk when it landed, too.

He tipped his head to see her reaction, or even if she had one. Other than a tighter look to her lips and both arms wrapped about the wolf's neck, she didn't look like it affected her at all. He knew it was a lie. He reached for the pouch and pulled another bean without taking his eyes from either of them. Then, he turned back to his little game.

Perhaps she should have told him sooner that her new swill was a brew for her throat. He wouldn't have emptied her little pot into the dirt if he'd known it was medicinal. Perhaps she should have been finding and brewing it a lot sooner, if she had something like that with her. That would have been more beneficial than shrieking at him until what little voice she had turned into her usual croak of sound before silencing.

Myles shrugged, sighted the rim of the pot, and flipped. The bean glanced off the edge.

Perhaps she should put rules on her pet. Perhaps she should have made the animal heave off what was left of Myles's pathetic pallet. Perhaps she should be packing and readying herself to follow the animal back to her keep. That would give her something to do, other than watch him with a wounded look to her that he couldn't erase no matter how many beans he flipped. She should also put more clothing on the pleasures she was denying him. *Denying?* he wondered. Nay, she was threatening him away from.

The shirt she'd decided to wear required ties to keep the neckline closed. She hadn't fastened them, or she hadn't found them and laced them into their holes, where they should be pulled tight, rather than left loose, giving him glimpses of flesh when he least needed it. Especially with the restraint she'd put on him and his desire for her.

"Call off your pet," he said, breaking the oddly companionable silence with words that had her sitting straighter. And that had the animal going to its feet and baring teeth while she did little to control it. That was her answer?

Myles had no choice. He shrugged and turned back to the beans. He could flip beans all night into the pot. She'd just have to sit back and watch it. Perhaps she shouldn't have let him know how much her earlier loss had meant and how much she wanted her beans back. Perhaps she shouldn't have put a price on making her pet stand down. Perhaps she shouldn't have gestured wildly at the bean pouch and held three digits of one hand up before changing them to two at least five times, since he'd been too amazed, too surprised, and too annoyed that she actually was threatening him in order to get her beans back. As if a wolf would actually help her cheat.

Myles hadn't any need of the fire, then. He'd been so angered, he'd broken into a sweat all over his entire body. It was all he could do to choke it down. *Her beans back?* That's what she wanted?

He got another bean out almost viciously, making a slight tear in the bag, spilling several of the beans into the stretched kilt between his knees. He looked at them for a moment, then shrugged. Perhaps it was time to try two at a time. Things couldn't get much worse.

Both missed.

She was about ready to allow Waif to do what he wished. If that hulking man didn't cease acting like he was the age of a young, spoiled bairn, she was ready to release Waif and watch the wolf make short work of all the skin Myles wouldn't keep covered! That's what was going to happen!

Kendran shook with it. She ached with it, burned with it, and kept swallowing to still it, and nothing was muting what the potion had put into effect. She wanted him. Her entire body wanted him . . . desperately. Completely. With all the fervor of the bubbles he'd had bursting from the top of his stew before he'd moved it farther from the flame. And all Myles could do about any of that was flip beans into the small pot? The man made no sense. The wolf made no sense. Nothing made any. It was maddening. Why, always before when Waif had found her, delivered what he had for her, he'd desert her. Except now.

Kendran didn't know why, although she had a very good guess. The animal belonged to Lady Sybil. That was enough recommendation. Then again, keeping him at bay was giving her hands something to do other than what they wanted to do. Despite what a silly, childish, arrogant male this specific one was proving himself to be . . . despite everything, Kendran wanted

him and what he'd given her a glimpse of. Wanted with
a fervor, passion, and intensity she didn't have any
ability to grasp. Every time she watched any part of
him flex or move, everything in her body pulsed, or
lunged, or vibrated, reacting with such strength it was
a wonder Waif hadn't already attacked what could be
the only source for her discomfiture.

He thought she wanted her beans back? She was actually surprised that he'd thought it true, and that it had
worked, because she didn't know what else to reply
when he'd asked her to call off the wolf. Stupid, silly,
blind male. Didn't he realize by now that the animal
was reacting to his every action and gesture? She had
no more power to call Waif off than she had to halt this
storm that had made close unfriendly companions out
of two strangers.

She was only surprised Waif hadn't already attacked.
She watched Myles flip another bean, and then he put both
hands over his head, arched his back, and stretched—with
a long, lithe movement. It had every bit of skin sliding over
every corresponding bit of iron it wrapped and made her
mouth open so she could pant for breath. The man had to
have every idea what he was doing! He just had to! She
was spelled with a potion and having to fight the effects
of it while doing everything in her power to keep a dangerous animal from attacking. And then the bane of her existence, this Myles, was putting on such an arousing display
for her it was making everything a hundred times more
potent than any bit of savory petal–enhanced oil could
possibly be. Stupid man! Stupid, foolish, childish man!

Kendran groaned and watched as Myles finished his
stretch. Then she had to watch as he leaned onto his back
and rolled over, sinuously sliding fully onto his belly,
while the kilt barely did its job at grazing his upper
thighs. The least he could do was take the coverlet that

had been hers and blanket himself. That way she'd not have the added stimulant of fighting her own longings, while the thing she craved and already knew was hard and hot and very tingly feeling beneath her fingers was directly in her sights and available . . . so . . . available.

"Call off your pet." He'd turned his head toward her and pursed his lips.

Kendran felt every bit of the reaction as her entire body pulsed again, and then she had to grasp Waif around the neck tighter, as he moved slightly, lowering his front shoulders preparatory to a lunge.

Myles's lips twisted in what was probably a smile, although he didn't look amused.

"The bed's softer over here. And warmer," he finally said. "Nay. Make that . . . hot."

The last word was deeper said and with a breathless tone that had every hair on her head reacting. Waif wasn't much better, and his back showed every bit of how it felt to be taunted, teased, and tormented, and unable to do anything about it. Kendran swallowed with a dry throat and blinked on eyes that felt just as dry. She sent a command to her neck to turn away, for her body to move, disdaining what he was offering. Nothing was working. Except her eyelids. She blinked again. It felt just as dry and unrelenting as before.

He sighed heavily, the motion expanding his chest so that his back rose with it. Kendran swallowed again. She blinked. Her throat and eyes seemed to be the only parts of her entire body that were cooperating with the order to cease staring. She hadn't known the potion made with savory had such power.

"Verra well. Suit yourself."

He turned his head from her and started a steady, deep rhythm of breathing that was too steady and in too perfect of a cadence to be real. Then, it deepened and she knew it was. She was being tormented within a speck of her sanity, and the object of her torture was sleeping? Her fingers tightened on the wolf's fur until she had strands of it between her white knuckles. She sensed the animal relaxing, and then he was also going to his belly. Kendran unwrapped her own fingers and lifted them away. Then she had to watch as even the wolf managed to find the deep, even breathing of slumber, leaving her to deal with the effects of this powerful aphrodisiac all by herself.

And she detested males even more.

"I . . . want to touch you."

Myles stirred, unsure if the whisper was in his mind, his dreams, or this reality of his that was this hell.

"What?" He rolled his head and lifted it.

The wolf wasn't glaring at him like it had been, nor was there any sign of it. He looked around. There wasn't any clue to the voice behind the words, either. He sighed and put his head back down. Dreams. Cursed dreams.

"Only . . . you."

If he hadn't fallen asleep on his front, shoving his cheek into the pallet covering, he wouldn't have to do a semi push-up in order to turn his head completely. The words were still being whispered, and they were still coming, and it was Kendran making them. He shook his head to clear it. It didn't work.

"No?" she asked.

"Nay, lass. Na' that. What . . . did you just say?" He was waking and it was a rapid thing. He shifted onto his side to see her better. The plaide on him shifted with the motion, unwrapping about his nakedness.

She pinkened. He rather thought this blush worse

than any previous ones, for it met the collar of his shirt, and probably went beneath it as well.

"I . . ."

It surprised him that she was on the pallet at his side. It was also strange that she was on this side of the croft. As she'd also dismissed the threat of her wolf, it was very surprising that she'd approach him. And waken him. And say what she just had. All of it was dreamlike. He cleared his throat and wondered where his spittle had gone to.

"Did you just say . . . you wished to . . ." He gulped with another dry motion. He watched her go even redder. "Touch me?" he finished.

She looked up at him then. The roar in his ears crested and his heart lurched into the depths of his belly before rising right into his throat, where it became a pounding block of more dryness. He could melt in the depths of her gold-starred blue eyes. He longed to, wanted to, nearly begged to. . . .

She nodded.

His own heartbeat went to a deafening level in his ears, and his eyes widened. He was afraid his mouth wasn't far behind. He was afraid to breathe.

"Now?" he asked.

She looked away, focused somewhere on the length of plaide that had unwound from him and lay at his side. Then she nodded again. To the coverlet. Not to him.

Myles reached out a hand and lifted her jaw, making her face him.

"Why?" he asked.

That made her blush worse. He watched her eyes film over with a sheen of moisture. He truly didn't think she'd answer him.

"Because you're beautiful," she whispered, so softly he

had to crane forward to hear it. "And . . . I've never been around a man of such . . . beauty and such . . . brawn."

Myles's lips pursed to stop the feeling. He knew what it was although he'd never experienced quite that combination with this strength and fervor before. It was unmitigated satisfaction. And it was followed almost immediately with hunger. The reaction was worse in his groin. He was grateful she didn't glance there as everything jumped and grew and started tormenting him with its own pulse. He moved his fingers away and gazed at her. Gazed deep.

"And?"

Her forehead crinkled as she watched him.

"You also said you wanted it to be only me. Only me? What does that mean?"

She looked to the right of him and then the left. The firelight was fickle and was lighting only a portion of her face. He watched as she chewed on her lip. Then she met his eyes again.

"I dinna' wish you . . . touching me."

"What?" Surprise colored the word, making her jump. It was also the emotion flooding him, making him rosy up nearly as much as she had. Only his wasn't embarrassment. It was baser than that. It was anger. And intrigue. And savage interest.

"Why?" he asked, finally.

She shrugged. Then she answered, "What . . . happened . . . this morn. I dinna' ken."

"What dinna' you ken?" he asked.

"This . . . thing." She waved a finger toward him and then pointed it back to herself, and then she sent it back to him, only this time she hovered a hair's breadth away from his shoulder. It didn't help. She might as well have already been touching him and caressing and doing a thousand other things. It felt like every part of him was trying to leap toward it.

He swallowed around the obstruction still blocking his throat, although it wasn't pounding as severely as before. "What thing?" he asked.

She tipped her head a bit to the side and regarded him. He knew the look. He felt belittled and chided just from receiving it.

"Verra well. This . . . thing, as you call it, what dinna' you understand?"

"What . . . and why."

"'Tis want and desire and lust and craving and hunger. Base hunger. That is what it is to me. I fought it. I lost. Now you want me to sit still . . . while you practice at all of that? On me?"

Her lips were probably going through the same emotions he had earlier when he'd stifled his humor. Then, she lost out to it and simply smiled. It wasn't a gentle smile, either. It was bright and it was dazzling, and it was followed almost immediately with sober awareness. And she was breathing harder as well, if the swell of her bosom from beneath his shirt was any indication.

"That's it. Exactly." She whispered the words. They still sounded like music. Sweet, oiled, and perfumed music. Myles lifted his eyebrows and eased himself into a sit, puddling the material into his lap to hide what she wasn't ready to handle.

"How much of this touching do you wish to do, lass?" Myles was amazed his voice came out as smooth and unaffected as it sounded. If it matched every piece of his body, he'd have been yelling it.

She lifted a shoulder in a shrug. He watched her do it and tempered every other reaction on his entire body. He did it for a reason. He wanted to play this new game of hers. And he wanted to win at it.

"And what am I to get from this . . . game?" he asked, finally.

She gave another half shrug.

"What if I refuse?"

She lifted those blue-gold eyes to his and there wasn't a hint of guile within them that he could see. She just wanted to explore. She hadn't been around men. Well, damn it, he wanted the same thing! But not for the same reason. Myles had been with women before. He just hadn't been with this one, and he was still aching over their aborted session earlier.

"If I allow this thing, if I dinna' move . . . am I to get a turn?"

Her eyes were wide, and her new blush made them more blue than before with the contrast. He didn't care. She'd started it. And deep into the night, there wasn't much reining him in. He wondered if she knew.

She shouldn't have dismissed her wolf.

"What . . . of my maidenhood?"

Myles's ears were cresting with the roar of sound. He knew it came from his own blood rushing through his ears. It wasn't easier to bear for the knowledge. He was jubilant and almost whooped it aloud. He forced himself to calm. To swallow around the obstruction pounding in his throat. He was going to have her. Open, wanting, wanton, willing, warm . . . ready.

He rubbed his hands along where the plaide was still trying to coat his thighs all the way to his knees before returning back the same path.

"What of it?" he asked.

"'Tis—"

"Gone," he supplied when she just sat there looking at him with luminous eyes that held the secrets of the world within them.

"Gone?" she asked.

"You dinna' possess a maidenhood 'ere longer, lass. You gave it to me. This day. Earlier. Afore your wolf interrupted."

"Nae."

The word contained her horror. Myles knew why. She thought she'd lost her value. She didn't realize how little all of that meant to him. Of course, they'd have to say the vows even before the New Year ceremony his father had demanded of him. *Cristes maesse*. Christ's mass. That was it. She'd be his Yule bride.

"'Tis nae worry, lass. You've nae need of another to husband. You gave your maidenhead to the man you'll wed. Me. From this night onward. I vow it."

"You . . . wish me . . . to wife?"

He did. Even without the beating he'd sustained. Myles nodded.

"Why?"

Why? He sat straighter, sucked in a breath, and started talking. "Because you've a body that tempts my dreams, a face I wish my bairns to see with their first look, and I'm all afire for you, and only you. That's why."

"Oh."

Oh? Myles was surprised he hadn't stumbled over every bit of his declaration, and that's all she had for an answer. He watched as she tilted her head to one side, consideringly. As if she still had a choice.

"You have . . . gold?" She swallowed before the last word.

"I have lots of gold, lass. More than I can carry. Strong rooms full."

"Enough?"

He grinned. "Your sire will na' be disappointed."

"It has to be enough to break a betrothal."

Myles's eyebrows raised and he couldn't resist teasing. "You've been promised to another man? And now, in the deep of night, with verra little between us, and going through the rules of this great game of yours—now is when you're deciding to tell me? Heartless. You're truly heartless, lass."

A smile toyed at her mouth. He had to prevent the motion to kiss at it. He couldn't. Not yet. Not until they had the rules of her game established and agreed upon.

"He's powerful."

"Who?" he asked.

He got the look that told him what she thought of his witlessness. He almost responded. "My betrothed," she supplied, finally.

"So?" He shrugged, watched her vision drop to where the motion had moved his chest, and then she returned to looking at him.

"My clan . . . needs his power."

"I'm powerful, too, lass. And rich. Verra rich."

"You'll need to be both."

"Anything else?" Myles couldn't resist teasing.

"He's auld."

He bristled with indignation. He didn't even know he had the capacity in him to feel insulted. He was two months shy of his twenty-ninth birthday. He wasn't old.

She was twisting her fingers together and then she was moving her glance up to him, almost pleading with him. For what? She already had him wrapped about each of her digits.

"How auld?" he asked, since she was waiting for something.

"And ugly."

Myles straightened. *Ugly?* He was considered one of the most handsome of the entire Donal clan and any other clan that cared to voice an opinion on such a thing. It was his right since he'd grown to manhood and discovered such a visage had merit in a woman's eyes. He knew he was handsome. Anyone with eyes knew it, too. Now, he was insulted.

"And none other will have him to husband."

"What? How do you know all this?" he asked, and he spoke with such force she had no choice but to know now how angered her words were making him. Which was stupid, if he wanted her to remain in ignorance.

"I've . . . heard tales."

"Tales? You condemn a man on words? That is na' very generous . . . of you, lass." He almost got all the words out before the import hit him and he stumbled through the last three of them. It was exactly what he'd done with regard to her! Exactly! Why, he'd had such a dread of what was only known through rumor that he'd managed to be beaten in combat for the first time in his life. The fact that it had taken more than seven of his father's best men didn't mute it, either. And he'd been fighting to keep from the one thing he was nearly begging for now.

Perhaps he really was the fool she continually thought him.

He fought down the reaction. They hadn't established the ground rules of her little game.

"So. Which is it to be? Either you hie yourself over to your own side of this croft, or you accept the offer of my hand so we can start this game . . . or . . ."

Her eyebrows went up. There was the slightest teasing smile on her lips at the same time. "Or?" she repeated.

"Or I'm going to do what I'm barely preventing myself from doing. I'm going to take that shirt completely off your body, feast my eyes and my mouth on you, and take you completely this time. And you're going to enjoy every moment of it. That's what's to happen. You haven't much time for a decision. I wouldn't waste it."

"Oh."

He was very tired of her tiny answers to what was

tantamount to bearing his soul. He hoped when she had use of her voice, she'd speak more. Especially since he was beginning to believe tales of her acid tongue were just that—tales. He huffed out the breath before sucking in more so he could put every bit of it in words, and then she forestalled him with her next words, making him hold to the air he'd gained until it pained.

"You have . . . to close your eyes."

Even if the rule was whispered, it wasn't happening. He refused.

"I will na'!"

She was blushing again. Myles nearly swore. His palms were leaving wet trails on the material and he could feel his legs trembling. He hadn't been coy. She really didn't have much time.

"I canna' touch you . . . otherwise."

"You close your eyes, then."

She considered that for three full measures of his own heartbeat. And then she did it.

CHAPTER 9

Kendran started with her middle finger against Myles's. It wasn't planned, but that's where she connected first. Kendran licked her lips at the flash of heat that seemed to light through her, leaving trembling in its wake. Underneath her, Myles seemed to have had the same reaction, resulting in the same sort of tremor. She slid the one finger up the length of his, running it along ridges of bone and sinew that made up his hand, and then she was gliding up his arm.

She knew one finger wasn't going to get her enough sensory value, but she was keeping herself from the full impact for a reason. She realized it as her lower body lurched forward slightly before settling back onto the reality that was her pallet bed that he'd usurped. Kendran parted her lips to let the little gasps of breath out. There was no reaction from him. Right in front of her.

She reached his inner elbow and went about the circumference of a lower arm rippled with tendons and striations of muscle that might as well be iron. Kendran allowed herself another finger with which to feel him, adding her index finger to the one already touching him. There was still no sound coming from the man she was exploring, although he was trembling a bit more than before. And there was a slight touch of moisture starting to coat him. Both of which were encouraging and exciting and intoxicating, and a thousand other things as well.

Kendran had been seated atop her bent legs. From that position, it was easy to lift her feet, raising herself just a bit higher as she pushed her fingers into flesh that hadn't much give to it. She reached a knot of muscle in his upper arm that had her gasping. She forgot all about self-denial, and slowness, as she tipped her wrist, putting as much of her palm flesh against him as possible. He was hard, and thick, and impossibly rigid. She couldn't span half of his arm with the one hand, and so she brought the other one, too.

She was also giving up on staying seated. Her thighs took the brunt of her new position as she lifted farther, placing her above him, although she didn't open her eyes to check. She didn't have to. His breath was sending little rivulets of sensation from where it kept caressing her throat and from there to the tops of her bosom. Kendran had never felt the like. She'd never had such a feeling of power. It was euphoric. She wasted a thought as to why no one had ever told her sensations such as these existed, and then let it go. Either they didn't know, because they'd never felt them, or they didn't want anyone else to know, because they were too enjoyable, and there was no way to keep men and women who knew such things apart.

Kendran tried very hard not to smile at the thought. She wasn't successful. The response was a growl of sound from the male at her fingertips. She lifted her hands as if scalded.

"What is it, lass?"

"You . . . growled."

"There was naught said about sound. I would never have agreed to this had you placed such a condition. Never. I've the patience of a well-experienced man, but you're testing it. To put a leash on my own tongue! Nae. I'll na' do it. I'll na'. Why, in a moment—"

His words ended with the pressure of her left index finger against his lips. Kendran was in shock at the sensation as he immediately pursed them and sucked on the tip, sliding his tongue around the nail and making everything on her jump. She was swaying, like a liquid ethereal being, and he was her rock, her foundation, her core . . . her man. She reached out and steadied herself against him with her other hand, coming into contact with the ridge of muscle encasing his shoulder.

She pulled her finger from him the moment she was steadied. There was a distinctive kissing noise as he released it. Kendran pulsed at it. So did the man in front of her. Then, he was making more than a growling noise, and it was said in a deep-throated fashion. Kendran's fingers were drawn there, to caress the thickness, and the knot in the midst of his throat that vibrated under her touch.

"You're powerfully close to being scized, wench. I hope you ken this." The deep whisper was threatening and serious, and making the riot of gooseflesh that was lifting her hair from her forehead even worse. Kendran went fully to her knees, moved both hands up the sides of that handsome face, sliding her thumbs along the lines of his jaw, over to his ears, as she pulled his hair back and out of her way. And then she leaned forward the tiniest bit and hovered above lips that seemed wrought from heaven just for the art of kissing.

"You're a verra handsome specimen, Myles," she whispered against the flesh of his lips. "So perfect of face and form that it's nearly painful to look at such bounty."

"So . . . you approve?" he replied.

She snorted the amusement.

"Damn you, lass," he said to that, and then he moved.

The croft rocked, turning into a storm-tossed ship, and Kendran held to him for balance as he took her mouth with his, sucking and licking and then touching delicate little kisses all over her lips until they felt overripe and large and ached for even more. He wasn't getting all of it, however. He'd taught her a thing or two about this kissing, and she had more leverage.

Then, hard hands gripped her waist and pulled her into his lap and smashed her so close to all the flesh she hadn't even explored yet that she pulled her mouth away in protest.

"You . . . cheat."

"You can have your thirty-two beans back. You can have sixty-four. You can have all of them."

"What?" Kendran opened her eyes. She did it more to regain some balance. And that didn't work. Myles hadn't a speck of anything other than black glinting from those devil-dark eyes and they weren't but a fraction of space from her own.

"The game. 'Tis finished."

"Nay."

Kendran's whispered reply didn't make much sound, and not simply because it was whispered. It was because he'd spread his hands even farther open and was sliding them up the span of her waist and back over and over, moving fabric against her skin and making the material stick worse to her from moisture that seemed to spring from his hands to her.

It was too hot. It was too steamy. It was too erotic and sensual and sensory, and Kendran hadn't enough experience with any of that. She pulled farther away from him, bringing his face back into focus and narrowing her eyes at the beauty of it. She hadn't lied earlier. She'd never seen such beauty. She didn't think anyone else had. Her old sister, Merriam, was going to be in raptures of jealousy over the man Kendran had managed to snag.

Especially given the reality that was her signed betrothed, the aging earl of Kilchurning. She'd lied earlier. Her betrothed wasn't just a rumor. He was fact. And that was another reason to hate these creatures called men and avoid going to the place her station in life decreed she must eventually go. Kilchurn Keep was real hell. Everyone said so, even the ones who survived the visit.

"I'm right here, lass," Myles whispered. He'd pursed his lips a bit and tilted his head as he brought her attention back to him.

Kendran blinked. There wasn't anything scratchy about the motion and she wondered at her own sanity. Men with the form and face of the man she was perched atop weren't lying about for any woman to find. And she was thinking of Kilchurning? She was going mad.

"You . . . cheat," she replied.

His jaw locked. That had to be what sent a nerve bulging out one side of it, and the hands holding to

her waist softened their grasp. Then they were
removed completely.

A heavy sigh came out of him next, and the force
of it moved her with it, since she was still clinging and
seemingly stuck to him. Then there was the problem of
where his breath slithered all over her upper torso,
cooling flesh that had been wrapped in heat and sweat
a moment earlier. Kendran trembled as she released
where her fingers were still grasped, holding his hair
back and making every bit of that defined face easily
seen and watched.

She hadn't been lying earlier. He really was too perfect of face and form. It almost hurt to look and keep
looking. She watched her own hands moving until she
had them centered atop each of the two mounds he had
on his upper chest. Then she closed her eyes and
pushed herself away.

The shirt didn't make the move with her. She knew
it was clinging to him, enjoying what she didn't dare
to. It was also giving him a very good view of breast
and belly. She knew it from the groan emanating from
the chest she held, making even her fingers vibrate.

"You tease and test sorely, lass."

"Close your eyes, then," she replied.

"Nae."

"Then watch."

Kendran had her own thighs beneath her again, although she couldn't tell if she was still on the pallet, a
portion of plaide, or the beaten earth floor. That's how
little the surface beneath her mattered. The chest her
hands were spread apart on . . . now that was a different undertaking, entirely. The size and scope of it was
hard to grasp in the flesh. Kendran had never seen a
man this large, this brawny, or this amazing. Her eyes

already knew it. Now her hands did, too. She glided her fingers along him, making certain the pads of her fingers and the entire span of her palm flesh was always in contact with him, and nearly frightened herself with the wellspring of want and moisture and lust she was creating in her own core. He wasn't helping, either. He was breathing quickly and deeply, and that was bringing into being glens and valleys and strips of muscle that had the consistency of rock. No . . . that wasn't accurate, she realized, as her fingers grazed and bumped and slid along him. Rocks weren't this hot, nor were they this slick with moisture, nor did they move with each touch, tensing and bunching and making it difficult to hold on to. Kendran's hands wouldn't stay connected like she wanted, but it wasn't entirely his fault. It was also hers. She was shaking too badly.

She slit her eyes open and caught the gasp inside. She'd reached what should have been his belt line, if he wore a belt rather than a wayward plaide that wasn't covering much. It was hovering near her belly, though, with a strength and rigidity beneath it she was too afraid to touch. It was also swaying, touching minutely to her every so often before he'd groan, shake, and move away.

Kendran was fascinated despite her misgivings. Fascinated and amazed. She leaned forward, the intensely tender surface of her nipples reached and touched flesh, and that sent such a surge through her that the groan wasn't coming from his throat, and it was not whispered, either. It was from hers.

"Christ." Myles breathed the curse. Then, he was going through the usual litany of curse words before adding several she hadn't heard yet, and when he finished, he was breathing even harder, making where she was still attached to him sway with a rocking motion with each of them. Kendran didn't move. She didn't want the contact ended. She had never felt such heat and erotic magnetism as what existed at the tips of each of her breasts, and it was making her crazed with whatever emotion the stupid potion had first created when she'd spilled it.

"Lie back," she whispered.

"Why? So you can finish killing me?"

Kendran giggled. That had him clenching muscle she thought he'd already tightened to an impossible state, and her fingers curved along with each one.

"You go too far, lass. I'm warning you."

"Lie back," she repeated, this time using the low octave of tone that her voice was gifting her with, for some strange reason.

His answer wasn't intelligible as anything, but she fancied it was more cursing. He was doing what she asked, however. Kendran hadn't known that a man's belly tensed into strips of sinew and muscle when he forced himself to lie back, but her hands knew it now. There wasn't any way her fingers were coming un- latched from him, and that meant she went with him. Stretching out all the way to the pallet, although he seemed suspended for more time than necessary in a sweat-sustained arch that kept them hovering just above the pallet.

"Now, Myles," she said. "Now. Lie down. Now."

He dropped.

Kendran was right behind him, stretching fully from her kneeling position earlier, although her feet were well off the end of the pallet past his. She raised her- self, locking her elbows in order to make her own arms hold her away. The shirt of his wasn't assisting, either.

It was still clinging to him, opening wide a view clear to her belly, where the great mass of his manhood was straining beyond. She watched as he lifted his head and looked there. And she watched the purplish flush that started near his neck and spread until he seemed a creature of fire and glow and was shaking so badly she rocked in motion with it.

"Jesu'! I have never been held to such a limit! Release me, lass! Finish the game! Dinna' make me beg! Ah!"

"Nae," she whispered in reply.

"Wench."

The word was hissed between his teeth. He was using it in place of yet another curse. Kendran smiled slightly and eased herself down . . . all the way down, although the brunt of him right beneath her breasts was hot and heavy and massive and trying to cleave its way between them. She reached just below his chin from this position, and then she was opening her mouth, tipping out her tongue and touching it to one of his nipples.

She thought he was going to fly right off the pallet with the lunge he made. Kendran drew back in haste and watched with wide eyes as he glared at her. He wasn't as beautiful with his nostrils flared wide, sweat plastering hair to his head, and a gaze that wasn't just devil dark—it was black with intent and anger. And he was the most stirringly handsome sight she'd ever seen.

She tipped her head again and did it again, lapping at the nub and giggling slightly at the entire effect as tremors shook the man she lay atop and everything on him tightened and lunged.

"Very well, lass. I'm begging! Cease this! Allow me a turn. Now!"

In reply, Kendran nipped at him. The reaction was immediate and intense. Myles grabbed her, squeezed her waist between both hands, and moved her physically, hauling her up his entire frame, scraping and moving cloth with the mass of him, and then he had her mouth with his and was sucking the very breath from her the moment she exhaled it.

The entire world spun. Then it reversed and went the other way. Kendran reeled with the motion and fought for breath. There wasn't anything else she could do, since he was stealing it, and replacing it with his own. He was also moving her, over and over with his hands at her hips, clenching solid handfuls of flesh, where she hadn't given him permission to touch, in order to rub himself against her over and over. He was creating a friction of desire and intimacy that had her entire spirit soaring, and her heart stalling, and then the lightning filled her, sending shoots of electricity through her entire being. Kendran yanked her mouth from his in order to give it voice, sending the moan to the highest reaches of the sky, since there was no way the little croft could contain it.

Myles rolled, holding her so tightly to him that she never even touched ground before he had her beneath him, back against the pallet, the shirt sticking everywhere to both of them, and his plaide bunched into a mass at where their bellies should have been touching.

"I did warn you, lass. I did."

Then he was splitting her legs, dividing them with the strength and power and hardness of himself, and she was actually helping. It wasn't until he had the mass of it against her that she stiffened, preparing herself for the pain. And there wasn't any. Bulk. There was that. And heat. Firelike and intense, licking at her core and making her shudder, and then she was filled—totally, completely, and intimately.

"Oh, God." Myles was crooning it, and then he was moving, pulling out so he could lunge back in.

Kendran arched her back, purred and accepted him, learning, sharing, positioning . . . before spilling over a waterfall of such height and wildness she didn't know if she'd survive the eventual drenching when she landed. Her scream didn't make much sound, although it should have with the strength she gave it. Myles must have known for he had his lips pressed against the section of her throat that ached worst from the use. And then he was sucking, gently, furtively, and then he was lapping at the skin as if he gained succor for his tongue there.

"Lass. Oh, dear God . . . lass." Myles crooned words, filling the space with the slight depth of his voice, the harshness of his breathing, the torture of his motions.

Kendran keened with it, filling her chest over and over with breath that burned, before she was releasing it with a motion that cooled and relieved. Still he moved, rocking against her, pulling . . . pushing, leaning into her and manipulating her until there was nothing else that mattered in the entire world save this.

The sensation grew, molding and mutating into a feeling of strength and vitality and pain and panic and lust and everything the damn potion had put into play in her body and mind, and then it surpassed even that. Kendran felt it again, was pulled into the ecstasy again, with a fervency that defied time and space, and then he paused, seemingly held in place by invisible cords, as his body pulsated and trembled, and if she wasn't mistaken the sounds coming from him were akin to sobbing. Kendran held to him for dear life, encased him, embraced him and accepted him, and just when it seemed he couldn't possibly stay in that position another moment, he moved his head and looked down at her with the most amazed expression. She looked deep and could see the moisture-coated eyes hadn't a thing devoted to evil. They were too beautiful.

Then he collapsed, sending such weight and sweat-soaked heat onto her that it expelled every hint of breath she might have within her. Kendran lay for several heart-stopping moments while she absorbed the size and bulk of him, and then she was squirming, pushing, and straining at his entire weight until she had enough of her upper body free she could take in great gulps of air. He wasn't moving the entire time, although he was still trembling and twitching with a disjointed rhythm. That was oddly comforting, and satisfying, and the most intense sensation struck straight at her heart, making Kendran's eyes open fully on the span that was the thatch roof of the croft, where several loft beams had already been filched in order to make a fire. It should have been tormenting and evil feeling, much like the earlier feeling. It wasn't. It was beautiful. Kendran eased a breath out and pulled in another, absorbing the glow and euphoria of it. She realized there wasn't anything ugly about anything.

She was losing feeling in her legs, however, and even tensing her thighs didn't seem to make any difference in the male still enwrapped in her flesh. It didn't seem to affect him one way or another. Kendran slid a fingernail along his side, earning herself a twitch of the flesh beneath her motion, and not much else.

"Myles?" she whispered.

He didn't exactly answer, but she fancied the harsh sound beneath his breath was a try at one.

"I canna' move."

He chuckled slightly at that and Kendran gasped at

how that felt. She wasn't prepared for any of this. And there wasn't anything she hated about this particular man. Nothing.

"Myles?" she tried again, only this time she put a croak of sound to the name.

A groan was her answer this time. And she watched and felt the tremor that accompanied it. That was strange. He was acting very strange. Almost like he was ill . . . or hurt.

"Are you hurt?" she whispered.

He chuckled again, which got him the exact same reaction.

"If you dinna' cease that—"

"What, lass? This?"

And then he twinged himself in the deepest part of her. Kendran's eyes were huge. And worse. She was caught with that expression on her face when he rolled his head to the side to look over at her. He wasn't the least bit injured, if the grin on his face was any indication. She nearly put both hands on him and attempted to push him off. Two things stopped her. One was she already knew she hadn't the strength to move him, even without a covering of snow-drenched fur. The second was because his closest arm came out and he placed a hand squarely between her breasts, stalling everything, even time.

"That was . . . wondrous," he finally said, when all she did was stare.

Kendran blinked. There was moisture behind it. That was stupid. She had nothing to cry over. She kept blinking until it cleared away.

"And we will verra much enjoy our wedding night. If not our entire wedded existence. Trust me."

Her eyebrows rose.

"You think me fey? Nay, lass. I only know from experience. You've a ripe shape and a winsome face. And there's the added depth to you that none tapped afore me. Which is a verra good thing, I might add at this moment." Parts of him were tensing at his own words, and that was interesting to note. Kendran watched as even his shoulder seemed to clench with it.

"There is?"

"Oh, aye. You're loaded with passion. Womanly passion. Such a thing is powerful. Extremely so."

"It is?" she asked.

"*Cristes maesse*. Nae longer. I'll na' wait a day longer."

The words made no sense. Kendran's brows drew down as she puzzled it. Christmas. The day was five weeks off. *Surely he doesn't mean to wait—* Her thoughts stalled.

"You wish to wed . . . on Christ's mass?" She mouthed most of the words since her throat was annoying her with the use of it again.

He grinned broader if such a thing was possible. "I'll na' wait a moment longer. You'll be my wife. Mine. Before the eyes of all men. Come Christmas."

"I canna' . . . get prepared so quickly!"

Now she knew his grin wasn't the widest, since this one dazzled with the amount of teeth he was showing. "If I thought you unwomanly afore, it was an oversight. Only a woman would worry over preparation at such a time." And then he flexed the encased portion of himself against her again.

Kendran's gasp answered him.

"I'll na' delay it. I'll have you to wife before the Yule, or I'll have none. Our firstborn's legitimacy hangs in the balance."

"But—"

"And I'll na' have it said my first son is a bastard. Five weeks. You've five weeks to prepare for your vows. Five. Rather than fret over the amount of time available to you, you'd do better to worry over the length of this storm, and the time lost due to it. That's what I'd be for worrying. As sated as I feel, I'd wed you in nothing more than this here sett." He lifted one end of the plaide he'd been sleeping with. Kendran knew she was coloring. She didn't know how to stop it.

"And I'd wed you in this shirt you are wearing and naught much else. I may make it a condition of the wedding. That's how much I like how you wear it."

"Nay!"

She should have known he was teasing before the grin came again. Kendran had to look away. With such an expression, he was even more beautiful than before. She hadn't lied. No man should be so perfect of form and face. It was unworldly. It was perfect. The man was perfect.

A man. All these years, she'd been wrong.

CHAPTER 10

Warmth woke Kendran . . . liquid warmth, toying along her ribs and dancing across her buttocks, since they were bare and uncovered.

Kendran gasped herself awake. *Bare and uncovered?* she wondered. But when she tried to roll over, changing the situation, the warmth became a hand, and then it became a bond, stopping her.

"Ah nae you dinna', lass."

"Myles?"

There was a sound of a chuckle, a feel of air across not only uncovered thighs, but there was naught on her back, either. "In the flesh, love."

"The . . . flesh?" Her whisper wasn't making much sound, but it contained every bit of her dismay with the last word.

His answer was a growl of noise, followed by what could only be a kiss on her shoulder. Kendran gasped and hunched it from further assault.

"You attempt a cheat? Again?"

Her eyes went wide on that insult, and then her back stiffened. "I dinna' cheat!"

"I thought the wolf ploy was bad enough. Yet now, you surpass even that."

"I dinna' cheat!" she repeated, with the rasp of voice she had.

"Verra well. I'll call it different. You forget the bargains you make once the time to pay up arrives. This is what you do."

"I dinna'!" Anger was the emotion strengthening her arms into lifting and rolling, even with his weight bearing on her. The result was she was on her back, half on, half off the pallet, and a full, broad span of bare, muscled chest was now hovering directly above her. Worse still was how it was tingling where her own belly skin was touching his, and then the feeling flared right to her breasts, where everything reacted as if yearning for it.

Kendran gasped and crossed both arms over herself, shielding where he'd been eyeing. Her movement had his gaze moving the heat he was imprinting her with to her eyes. And what she saw there made everything go perfectly still.

"Perhaps 'tis best if you close your eyes again," he whispered.

"What?" she replied.

"Your eyes. You may wish to close them again."

"Close . . . them?"

"Or leave them open. I've little care. I am na' the beginner here."

Kendran's eyes went wider. She'd not thought it possible. "You . . . jest."

"Jest? Me? Nae. Na' when I've such bounty before me. Mayhap later. After I've . . ." He lowered his head, and Kendran had it in her grasp before he reached skin. She had to release herself to do so and knew that's where he was looking, as a shudder ran his frame. Since it was plastered to hers, the tremble went all along hers, as well.

"Ah, lass. You've no knowledge of what you do."

"Myles . . . I—"

"You made a bargain. 'Tis time to pay up."

"P-pay?" She stammered the word, making it two syllables.

"'Twas your game, lass. And you may na' ken the ways of men and women yet, but you're a quick study. I give you that."

"I dinna' ken a word you say, Myles. Nary a one."

"You got to touch me. I dinna' move. Now . . . 'tis my turn." The slight lift of his eyebrows as he said it made it worse.

"You moved. You did. You did na' hold to the bargain. You even took the shirt from me while I slept."

He was fully grinning now, showing very white teeth that glinted in the dim light tossed out from their coals. "True. That does na' change the pact you made. I get to touch you. And I will na' take exception should you also . . . move. In fact, I would appreciate that you do so."

"Wait!" She pulled on his hair, stopping him again.

"Now what is it?"

The way she'd gripped at him had his hair pulled back tightly, exposing every bit of his handsomeness. There wasn't much light for her to see, but what there was fell fully on his dark eyebrows, moisture-tipped eyes, and features that probably sent any maid into a swoon if she had this man at her fingertips. Kendran was no exception. She realized it as her heart fully lurched within her, surprising her. Frightening her.

"'Tis . . . too soon."

The gentleness in his expression twisted her innards

even worse. Kendran had to part her lips to gain pants of breath.

"'Tis painful?"

She shook her head.

"Then what?"

"I—we—I—"

"If you canna' put two words together, you canna' argue, Kendran, love."

"We're . . . na' wed. This is wrong."

"The moment I arrange it, we will be. I vow it."

"But . . . we're na' wed . . . right now."

He blew a sigh across her breasts, cooling and warming at the same time. Kendran couldn't stop how it felt, any more than she could stop the intake of breath alerting him to it. All she could do was hold on to him and force him to continue watching her face, rather than anything else.

"You . . . are a viciously desirable woman, lass."

"I am?" she replied.

"And I'm nae saint. I'm verra far from it, actually. Now, release me."

Her answer was to grip her fingers, knotting his hair even tighter. She watched as he assimilated that. Then, he tipped his head, tilting his features, and proving how little control she actually had as her hands moved with it.

"You still seek to stay me?"

She nodded. Rapidly.

"Why now?"

"I . . . dinna' ken."

"Kendran, you may na' ken much about men and women, but surely you ken the workings of your own home."

"My . . . home?" She was mystified and it sounded it.

"And knowing such, you'll realize how precious these moments are. This night. Right here. You and me. Nae one else. Just us. Together. Alone."

Every word created shivers. They were transferring to a weakness that spread and encompassed everything.

"The moment I arrive and make my presence known, I'll be settlin' the bride price, and then I'll na' be allowed within the same room with you. Na' alone, anyway. Times like these will na' exist for us. Now, will you release me?"

She shook her head.

"Why na' now?"

"I already told you. 'Tis too soon."

"Kendran, I am na' one for woman fears. I dinna' even ken that women suffered them."

"I dinna' fear you!"

"Then why do you stop me?"

"I . . . dinna' ken feelings such as this . . . were. I dinna' ken—"

He laughed, and with his belly fully against her, it wasn't possible to ignore the reaction. Kendran's voice halted midsentence and her mouth went to the same width as her eyes. Her hands were not the barrier she'd suspected, either, as he moved easily and fully, lifting himself to his haunches and taking her with him.

That was an interesting perch. Myles was cross-legged, had her settled in the crook of his legs, with her back against his chest, and his arms wrapped about her from behind. It felt wondrously safe and secure. And strange.

"Close your eyes," he whispered against her neck. And then he licked the spot.

Kendran squealed, started, and was brought back

down to nestle against him again. She had no choice. She shut her eyes.

She didn't have enough experience for how it was going to feel. She was trembling with waiting. The smell of wood coals—still glowing—warmed her senses next. Kendran filled her chest with the smell, exhaled it, and then took in another deep breath.

Behind her Myles chuckled and then his arms moved, unleashing her, but not letting her go. She wouldn't have gone, anyway. He was right. She had made the bargain of sorts with him. Aside from which, she didn't want to move. And with her eyes closed, nothing looked evil or wicked or wrong. It didn't feel it, either.

His fingers trailed down her arms, sliding all the way to her hands, and then he spread her fingers so he could entwine his with them. Kendran trembled but didn't give him any other sign. Then he was lifting her arms, up and over her shoulders, and assisting her with latching her fingers together at the back of his neck. Kendran almost opened her eyes. Almost. She was too afraid. He'd put her in an arch, wantonly displaying everything to the fire's light . . . and to him.

That didn't feel evil or wicked, either. It felt reckless and wild, and everything he'd shown her earlier. But it was tempered by a slight edging of fear. She knew why. He hadn't moved. He was breathing heavily, sending shock waves of sensation all over her shoulders, and from there to her breasts, and still he didn't move. Then he started speaking, using low, soft words rather than touch. Everything on her shuddered at the first word.

"Such perfection. Such lush womanliness. Ah, Kendran. You are a lovely wench. A siren, a vixen, a goddess. You are so beauteous . . . 'tis difficult to believe you real."

Kendran fought the smile, then just let it curve on her mouth. He couldn't see it anyway. He was still behind her. Finger pads touched her lower belly, starting sparks and heat and sensation into existence, and then his fingers spread, following a path of his making. He went over her hips, around the indentation of her waist, up the sides of her torso, thrilling and exciting the entire way. Then there was the low growling noise, seeming to emanate from his chest, and from there it moved to his throat. He didn't open his mouth for the issuance of it. He didn't need to. It rumbled over the back of her neck and made a solid aching sensation out of both nipples. Kendran arched even more fully, leaning her head into his shoulder in order to make the movement, displaying more of herself, with more fullness, more craving, and just more, more, more.

And then he denied her!

The low growl came again, with a poignant note at the end of it, and Kendran tried to twist to make him give her the embrace she needed. Her breasts had never felt so needy, nor as grasping. She knew what she needed, she knew he'd brought her to this sensation, and she also knew he was going to deny her. The moment she made the movement, his hands slammed to her waist, holding her pinioned exactly where she was. And then he was clicking his tongue, letting her know of his displeasure.

The moan wasn't coming from him this time, but her.

"Myles . . ."

"Hush."

"'Tis . . . strange."

His answer was a movement of a hand . . . moving

finally to caress her abdomen, starting a swirling vortex of shooting hunger. Kendran melted into it, swayed with it, leaned whichever way he was moving her, and heard the throb of rhythm so clearly in her soul she could have hummed it aloud.

Myles moved her to the right, sliding her back against his chest, and making everything that was solid become imbued with an insubstantial, cloudlike quality. Kendran opened her mouth to pant for breath. It was all she was capable of.

"Love . . ." His whispered word whistled through her consciousness, filling gaps and valleys and creating a world of desire and hunger, and heat—massive heat. Almost like fire.

"Myles . . ." She breathed the name like a chant. And then added to it, "Myles . . . Myles . . ."

He swayed them to the left, moving with a sinuousness that had nothing to do with a Scot night in December, and everything to do with fire and light. Kendran let her head fall forward, putting tresses against her own torso, and then she was moving her head back and forth, making the locks of hair do what he wasn't—fit to her, slide against her . . . caress her.

The moan was from hunger this time. She even recognized it.

"Myles." Her mouth was open to gasp it this time.

His answer was a light touch of his tongue against the skin beside her throat, and then she felt the slide of moisture to the end of her shoulder and back. Again. Over and over. Kendran leaned with it, slid with it, moaned with it . . . flexed with it. Learned it . . . loved it . . . made him take it and own it.

He'd changed the tongue motion, making it one of suction as his mouth nibbled at her throat, pulling the skin and then releasing it, and making certain she felt each bit of it.

Kendran shuddered the second time he did it. On the third she was shoving against him, and on the fourth she was begging.

"Please . . . Myles . . . please?"

"You dinna' even ken what it is you ask for, lass," he answered, cooling the spot he'd just sucked into a canker of fire.

She yanked on him for an answer, using her body weight to move him nearer. At the same time, she was arching into an impossible bow, in order to maintain contact with the thick male hardness he was keeping from her.

Nearer . . . Again.

Kendran let the moans slip from her lips. She no longer cared if he heard them and correctly translated them. She only wanted him. Deep. As deep as she could get him.

"Na' so fast, lass."

Myles's hands were like talons on her flesh, pinioning her hips where they were and holding her in place as he pulsed toward what she wanted . . . what he wanted. What he was denying. Kendran turned her head and found his mouth with hers.

Then there wasn't anything cold or lonely or vicious in the entire world. There was only the sensation of his breathing with her, and the slow motion of his mouth as he sucked on first her upper lip and then the lower, imprinting ownership everywhere he touched. Kendran was careening without substance. She was as liquid as one of Lady Sybil's brews. And he knew it.

"Please . . . Myles. Please?"

Kendran kept up the cadence of her plea against his

lips, the words filling any gaps between skin, and each time he shuddered.

"What is it you need, lass?" he asked, the words filling her ears.

Her answer was a twist of her entire body, and then a lunge, pulling him to her with her entire weight, making certain he'd not need to ask such stupid questions ever again. Ever.

He was chuckling, though, and leaning back onto the pallet of covered straw, which could have been floor just as easily. Kendran molded everywhere along him, sliding with him, and then she used her feet on the tops of his as leverage once he'd unfolded enough she could do so. She wasn't leaving the caress of his lips; she wasn't moving from the contact with any part of him.

Myles had her hips still, but he wasn't denying. He was moving her, alternately pulling her upward and then downward, as everything that was male about him branded the tender flesh of her thighs . . . her lower abdomen . . . her thighs again. Kendran unlatched her own fingers and spread her hands out on the pallet beside his head and used the motion to lift from him, putting herself in a push-up of motion in order to see, when she opened her eyes, exactly what she expected to.

She slit her eyes open, and the resultant view caused a spasm through her entire form. He felt it, for the slight smile curving his full lips showed it easily. Kendran lowered her head, shaking it from side to side to part her hair enough, and took his mouth with exactly the same motion he'd used on her.

"Ah . . . lass."

The words were said as an endearment and showed her how clearly he was enjoying what she was doing. Kendran snorted the amusement and felt the corresponding reaction in the body she was straddling, dividing her legs so all that was Myles could fit between them. And then she was moving, sliding ever closer . . . moving away. Closer. Moving away. Now it was her turn. She realized it as she teased him. Teased herself.

"Wondrous. Perfect. Lass. Temptress." His words continued with more titles he was naming her. Softly, at first, and then increasing in volume as he strove for what she wasn't allowing him to have.

Kendran had never felt as powerful, as wild, as free. Her hands moved, finding a solid berth on the dual mounds of his chest, so she could raise herself even more, going to a slant of provocation. Her legs moved as well, going to a crouch, so she could tighten her thighs on the hips between them, holding him firm . . . holding him poised, in position. Ready.

"Now, lass! Now."

Myles was slick with a sheen of moisture, making everything on him gleam, and it was pooling in the shadowy recesses about his muscle. Kendran bent her head, lapped at the salty trail in the midst of his chest, and then she was chuckling as well, and blowing on the spot, and holding on with every bit of strength in her thighs to the writhing entity he became.

"Lass! Now!"

Kendran used every muscle at her disposal to pose herself above him, panting for breath, panting for reason, and wondering at her sanity. And then she smiled.

"Beg me," she said.

Beautiful devil-dark eyes opened, surprise and something else glimmering in them, and then he narrowed them, sending everything on her body into absolute shock with the dangerous intent everywhere on him.

He didn't beg her. He spread his hands wider, holding her hips with a grip that defied argument, and slammed her down onto him.

Kendran warped, enveloping and encasing and enjoining. She hadn't a hope of keeping the cry from sounding and knew it tore at every bit of her recently healed throat. She couldn't prevent it. Ecstasy was ripping through her veins, taking every thud of her heart and turning it into a powerful surge of light, heat, and joy. She hadn't a prayer of containing it. She didn't even mind the use of her voice.

And when the throbs of feeling ebbed, Myles was still her rock, her sanity, her base . . . still holding her to him and still making her move, the ripples of his chest following every motion of his arms as he made her mold to him, lift from him, and then return over and over again until Kendran thought she'd go mad with it. She scrunched her eyes shut . . . strove for it. Careened over the edge and owned every bit of the thrilling realm he sent her to again.

And again. And so many times she lost any recollection of them. The only notice of their passage was the ripping sensation deep in her throat, the crescendos of fulfillment that he sent her to, and then the tears as he made her go even further. Kendran didn't even know what brought on the tears. But she was weeping, and with an abandon she'd never before felt, her tears falling on the mass of man, mixing and blending with the sheen of sweat he already had coating him. And all of it was making a shine that was nearly blinding every time she opened her eyes.

Sounds grew about her, adding to the mass of

experience, filling her ears with grunts and anger and rage and joy and intensity, and then Myles added to it, with a long drawn-out groan, seemingly without end. When he ran out of breath, he held her in place, sucked in another, and moaned the quantity of it out as well. Kendran held to him with all her might as his bucking motion faded and then stilled altogether. And she watched. She couldn't tear her eyes away. Cords seemed stretched beneath the skin as he finished, their color dark against an even darker shade. She'd never seen, felt, or heard anything as amazing.

And he was all hers. Forever. Or as soon as the betrothal could be arranged. For some reason, she didn't think it would present much of a problem.

She skimmed atop the cushion of air that seemed to be surrounding him as she matched to him, sinking until her head was lying right against his throat, where a vein was still pulsing in disjointed rhythm.

"Ah, Kendran. 'Twas . . . wondrous. Nae?" He had to space the words with what breath he was gaining. He was also rubbing both hands along her back with a tempo she could learn to like, and very much at that.

"How would I ken such a thing? I'm just a beginner," she answered.

That got her a whiff of what was probably amusement. He didn't give it enough effort to even raise her. That was odd. Kendran lifted her head, propped her arms across his chest, and waited.

"What . . . is it, lass?"

"You," she answered.

One eye slit open. Then, the other. He groaned.

"What?" she asked.

"You've drained me, lass. I've nae strength."

"No!" she responded.

He nodded. "Aye. 'Twas wondrous, too."

"This unmans a man, as well?" she asked.

If he'd give it some effort, it was probably meant as a wide smile, but with the way he was acting, all it looked like was a smirk.

"This is God-given weakness, love."

"You're weak now? Is this what you'd have me believe?"

"My legs are atremble, and my arms are na' far behind. Does that answer your question?"

"Is it as bad as the other?"

"What other?"

"A knee."

He huffed out the chuckle. She rose with it. "'Tis world's apart, love. Worlds."

"Are you laughing at me?" she asked.

"Never."

"What are you doing, then?"

"Thanking my luck that I found you, although I may na' last the entire length of our wedded life, at this rate."

"What does that mean?" Kendran asked.

"That I feel a need of a sennight's worth of sleep of a sudden and am being thwarted by a lass with pestering questions. That's what it means."

"I dinna' understand a bit of this, Myles."

He really was laughing now. That had to be what was making her rise and fall, and then he rolled to one side, pinioning her on her back with a leg the weight of his horse across her thighs.

"Jesu'!" Kendran swore. And she never swore.

That got her an eye opened. "What is it now?" he asked.

"You're the size of your horse, and you'll numb my legs if you dinna' move."

"Well, at least you see the reason for my weakness."

"I see a man with a volume of heft to each limb, and a mouthful of words. None which make sense."

"If I move, will you hush?"

"You want me to hush? Why dinna' you just say so?"

He had his lips pursed, was already breathing fairly heavily, and it took a stiff jab to his ribs before he answered.

"'Tis a good thing I had already decided on your perfection, lass. You're sorely testing it. Sorely."

"You find me . . . perfect?" Her voice caught. As did her breathing. She was amazed her mind was still functioning. This matchless man . . . found her perfect?

"Afore I knew your love talk, I did. Can you na' hush now?"

"If you'll move the deadweight of your leg!"

Kendran shoved at him and rolled from it before it fell again. He didn't let her get far, as an arm snaked out and pulled her unerringly right back against the enclosure he seemed to have made for her.

"Ah yes, lass. Right there. 'Tis . . . perfect." His words slurred to an end, and then he was breathing too deeply to be anything other than asleep.

Kendran pulled the coverlet over them. He was right. It was perfect.

CHAPTER 11

Kendran had her mind changed when she woke. Perfect? No man was such a thing! And as for thinking Myles unworldly, well . . . he was that. He was also deceitful, a rogue, and a blackguard. All of which was proven the moment she opened her eyes and found him gone. Vanished. Every trace removed. As if he'd never been.

That much was a lie, since the shutters were being held together by two loops that looked a lot like the braided rope she'd been weaving the night before. And when she slid a skean tip beneath one of them and sawed until it burst, she found it to be exactly that. He'd taken all his belongings, every crumb of food, every bit of material, every piece of coin, and then he'd snuck away—like the lowest Highland reaver!

Kendran ignored the brilliance behind his method of latching the window shut, and it wasn't as much due to her mounting headache as it was the small pile of beans beside the fireplace, which when she counted them came to exactly sixty-four. That's when she started crying.

* * *

Myles broke through the snow again for the fiftieth time. Then he remembered he'd ceased counting hours earlier. As had he ceased complaining about it. It didn't change his luck, it didn't change his circumstances, and it didn't help. He was still lost, or the wolf knew it would be followed and wasn't returning to its home for that reason. He'd ceased tormenting himself with his lack of wits. There was nothing else he could do, and he'd spent hours last eve watching that wondrous woman slumbering so heavily and worrying over what would happen when it was discovered that she'd been sheltering with a man.

And had given herself to him.

Knowing what he did of her father, and his temper, and guessing the rest of it, Myles was determined she wouldn't be beaten. Not for something that was inevitable, and so heavenly, that if he concentrated enough, he wasn't wandering about in a haze of frost-filled air, approaching darkness, while he kept an eye on the wolf's trail to his right. He was safe, warm, and ensconced in that woman's body, and he was nearing his own personal heaven again.

He sighed, climbed out of the hole the snow had been hiding, and kept walking, Rafe at his heels. It wasn't because he wished to walk; it was because the ground was treacherous with hidden holes and bogs, and frozen bridges, and it was unsafe for the stallion. It was also making him wonder at his sire's sanity. What clan wished such a deserted landscape as the one he was walking through?

He'd realized the wolf was following a large, flat, frozen burn as it meandered through the boulder-strewn and treacherously snow-covered Fells of Eschon. That much hadn't been open to question. He also knew if her pet could reach her, any number of her clan also could. And he wanted no whisper attached to her. None. She was perfect. She really was an angel. And thoughts of her warmed him all over again, making it feel even colder when he fell through another drift again.

Myles started cursing. Loudly. Making the air rumble with the sound before he could help himself. He stopped when he ran out of breath and sucked in more, then listened to the echo of his own voice, eerily returning to him. And naught much else. It was stupid. The entire thing was, actually. He could have stayed warm and dry, and caressing that woman's body while the time passed, instead of wandering about, attempting stealth, when someone his size had never, and would never, accomplish it. Not only that, but the trees had thinned before disappearing altogether, making him very easy to spot against all the white blanketing the entire world.

Now it seemed even more witless. The wolf was taking the easier path, it was lighter on its feet, and it knew where it was going. Or it was following a scent of a crazed hare. There wasn't much to recommend what the animal was up to, one way or another. The trail it was making wasn't giving any clue as much as it wove and bobbed about.

Myles sighed and pulled himself out of the caved-in drift, settling his foot on iced-over snow before putting his full weight atop it. What he was doing was stupid, now that he had time to put thought to it without having the image of the sleeping Kendran in his sights, instead. He was going to reach her keep. He was going to present himself to his future in-laws—exactly as had been planned originally—and he was going to make their betrothal a certainty before she arrived back, her reputation intact and her honor sacrosanct. That, and he was going to make certain the laird of Eschoncan Keep had sent a guard of men out to search for her, by following the wolf's tracks. Or he was going to see that one was sent.

He rather hoped it was the former, which was why he was keeping so far wide of the animal's tracks. Myles wasn't good at subtlety. He didn't know how he was supposed to mention following the animal without giving up his knowledge of how he knew where the tracks led and what they'd find at the end of it. He sighed and took another tentative step. He was just going to have to try.

He was staying from the easiest path in the event they were already using it to reach her. What he'd managed to do instead was get lost, go around and through any number of ice-splashed small burns, and more than once question his own sanity.

He was betrothed to her. What did it matter if he'd consummated the union before the ceremony? At least he'd been warm, well fed, and alive. All of which had great merit at the moment, with night darkness looming ever closer, and not one light nor one hint of a large keep anywhere in sighting distance. And then he heard the calls.

Myles raised his head, saw the contingency of men immediately, and his hand raised before they gave another shout. He'd been right! His head felt like it might burst as a score and more men strode into sight, their presence showing clearly what they were doing— following tracks—and also that they were heavily armed. Myles could take a few of them, but he'd never be able to take all of them. The laird of Eschoncan was bright to send such a thing. He was fetching his wayward daughter, and he was probably already deciding the punishment for her. Myles had the grin under control before the air made his teeth ache. He already knew what punishment he was devising. His. Because that woman had a reservoir of passion as yet untapped and he wanted to be the one discovering and enjoying it.

They were upon him quicker than he realized. They had strange webbing attached to their boots, making walking atop the snow look effortless in comparison, and they were grouped together in a united front of threatening proportions. Myles drew himself to his full height, brought Rafe nearer, and waited.

"Your name and mission, friend?" One of the men called out loudly. They all wore full beards, probably making him look effeminate with the scraped condition of his own cheeks and jaw.

"Donal! Myles Magnus Donal, firstborn son and heir to Laird Donal."

"Donal?"

"Aye."

"You the intended husband, then?"

One of the men jostled another one and Myles watched as the motion was perpetuated until they all seemed to be rocking with the merriment. Myles forced the proper look of confusion to his features and fought down the rising anger. It was the same thing he'd once thought.

"Our sympathies, friend Donal. But why is it you wander about in such dread weather, and on such a foul plain?"

"The entire clan holding is a foul plain as far as I can tell," Myles replied.

"Aye." One of them replied. He stepped forward a bit and reached out a welcoming hand. "That it is. Name's Kenneth Kilchurn. Of Drumrig Castle."

The man had a firm, hard grip to his handshake. He was also stifling an emotion that looked and felt suspiciously like animosity. That was odd.

"Kenneth," Myles returned the greeting.

"And what is it you're about again, Donal? You lost?"

"I am na' lost," Myles said.

"Nay?" Kenneth asked.

"I was but pondering my fate."

"Pondering, you say?"

"Aye. And doing a bit of deciding on which one was worse."

There was loud laughter at that reply. Myles went grimmer at the insult being shown his beloved, but he kept it inside, where it wouldn't show. The outer Myles was bobbing his head and grinning like a fool.

"And what is it you've decided?" one of them asked.

"That a large grouping of men standing about and jawing in devil weather is about as useless as teats on a boar. That's what I've put a decision to."

They roared with laughter at that.

"Welcome, friend Donal!"

Myles met all of them, although names and faces eluded him, and since they all had like-shaped fur caps about their heads, unkempt beards and wore a variation of blue and black plaide, it was difficult to tell them apart anyway.

"Grinnell! Take friend Donal to the keep. Make it a

THE KNIGHT BEFORE CHRISTMAS   165

quick journey. Tell the laird we found a lost pigeon while on our journey."

Lost pigeon? Myles nearly snorted his anger. It was bad enough portraying that death was a preferable choice to this upcoming betrothal, but hearing what they thought of him made it worse, somehow.

"Is it far?" Myles asked.

"Aye. 'Tis a fair piece of walking to Eschoncan Keep, and the prize awaiting you there. You certain you wish a rescue? Death. She is a valuable option at time."

Myles set his jaw and nodded. It was better to keep it to himself. They didn't know her true nature. All they knew was the Kendran that she showed them. He uncoiled his fist about Rafe's rein, nodded to all, and followed this man named Grinnell.

It was a fair piece and more. He realized it as he dogged the lighter man's footsteps, keeping Rafe close at hand. It was also brutally cold, the night clear and with a moon cast that made a glow come from the snow they walked atop, and it was companionable since the younger man said little and kept a steady, ground-eating pace. Myles only fell through one drift, too.

This Grinnell didn't even halt his step and wait, leaving Myles to jog along until he reached him. It was impossible to tell how late it was when they crested a hill looking down on the blackness of a square keep seeming to rise from the rock it was hatching from, but it was late. Nearer morn, if Myles was any guess. He was sore, too. That's what came of lazing about in a croft for days with little to do but lust for a woman.

They gave him a drafty room in a drafty corner of what was rapidly being unveiled as an unkempt, badly maintained, poorly constructed, and ill-conceived castle. Myles kept his lips from curling and showing his disdain with such an effort of will, he surprised himself. He was exhausted, he was sore and tired and hungry, and all they offered him was a room with poorly fitted shutters, a bed that sagged in the middle, and a fireplace that had to be cleared out first before it could support a fire's smoke.

Myles stood to one side of the door, arms crossed about his belly, and watched the servants scurry about, trying to make the unused room look and feel warm and welcoming. His father hadn't been distinctive enough. He'd said the Eschons possessed land but no coin. What he should have said was they possessed little worth saving even with coin. Myles scanned to the ceiling, roughly two stories above his head. He thought there might even be a bird's nest high among the rafters, but he could be mistaken. If it was a nest, it was last season's and thus uninhabited. It was still disgusting.

There was a fine film of snow dust on the sill, and he watched one of the serfs whisk at it with a broom, sending bits of snow fleck and dust to hassle everyone with a cough, Myles included.

"God's blood! I'll await this room in the hall!" He knew his voice thundered. He couldn't help it. He didn't much care, either. If he hadn't met Kendran already, he'd be for running. No wonder the lass ran from here. Anyone would.

There was a small, cowled figure in the depths of the hall, barely showing in the light cast from dawn, shedding down as it was from slits cut in the walls. That made the hall even more chill than his room, and that was competing with the frigid air outside. Every room they'd passed felt the same way, and there had only been one fire lit that he recalled—the one in the great room—where he'd first been greeted.

Myles frowned. They had so little funds that they couldn't build a fire to warm themselves? No wonder they were desperate to wed their daughter off, even offering the keep, half the lands about it, and the Rocky Fells with her hand. It was a pity the man hadn't managed to produce a son. Perhaps a dowered bride would have saved the castle. Myles checked the chinks of light showing through cracked mortar in the rock opposite him. *No*, he mused, *there isn't any amount of gold that will save Eschoncan Keep*. It needed razing. A good fire. Perhaps a battering ram taken to all the walls.

"You . . . are the intended husband? This Myles . . . of Donal clan?"

The creature hovering in the shadows asked it, annoying him with the waifishness of her appearance and the slight whisper of her voice. He'd heard the Eschon females possessed voices rivaling the banshees for volume, yet all he'd run across was whispering, cowed figures. He couldn't prevent it this time. His lip curled.

"You're correct. We're poor. Verra poor," she remarked.

Myles crossed a foot in front of the other and swiveled, leaning against the inner wall to observe her.

"Nay!" she hissed. "None must know I'm here! Turn back!"

Myles pivoted back. He was leaning against the wall for a reason. A day and night of walking in deep snow was it. The wall was slimy with frost, cold and lumpy with the poor construction and haste with which it was built. He still leaned against it, earning himself the dampness of his cloak as the frost melted with his own body heat. He waited.

"You are he. Dinna' bother denial."

"I've denied naught. Nor shall I," he replied.

"Good."

The door opened beside him and a serf stumbled out, his arms full of old and dried rushes. He watched the man's progress down the hall, away from them. And he waited.

"You've strength as well as honor. The laird has done well."

"Have you a reason to stand about, wasting away as well as wasting time?" he asked the wall in front of him.

She snickered beside him. "Wasting away. You've a great depth of humor. You'll need it."

"I need a good meal and sleep. That is what I need. From the looks of it, I'll na' be receiving either."

"We're poor. Dinna' you just hear me?"

"Your castle speaks for itself. You needn't put words to what I can see with my own eyes. 'Tis lucky for the Eschons that I have gold—lots of it—and that they betrothed their daughter to me with this heap."

"Food is scarce at times."

"None look starved . . . much," Myles commented.

She snickered again. He supposed that went for humor. Then she surprised him.

"Waif did mention your size. He said naught of your handsomeness," the little wench continued.

"I've na' met a person named Waif, and had I, he would have forsworn being called by such a fanciful name. Any man would."

"Waif is na' a person. He is my pet. You met. Trust me."

"The wolf?"

She snickered again.

"You tell me a wolf speaks with you?"

"He dinna' tell me enough. I can see that for myself. Things are about to become verra interesting. And verra entertaining."

"Nae animal speaks to a human. You're daft. That's it. You shouldn't be out without your keeper. You'd best leave."

"Waif speaks. It's just humans that dinna' listen. He mentioned your stubbornness as well. I see that much was nae tale."

"Lady, I'm warning you—"

She giggled at that and stepped out from the shadows. Her voice was melodious and sweet, as was her visage once she got the cowl from her features. She reminded him of Kendran for some reason, and he watched as she nodded, devining his thoughts.

"Younger sister, my laird," she whispered.

"She has a sister?"

"She has more than one. More's the pity. You'd do best to remember that. It will come in handy in your near future. It will."

"What?"

"Go softly, knight. That is what your name means. You ken? Myles. Knight. That is what you are, and will be. And remember—whatever happens in your future, you must agree. You must."

Myles shook his head. The little woman facing him didn't move. She might be Kendran's sister but she hadn't been gifted with the blue eyes, nor the wealth of reddish gold hair, nor any of the other's height and womanly frame. All told, she was probably the height of his sword.

"I must, must I?" he asked.

"I'll na' beg."

Myles snorted. "Seems to me all I must do is find myself some warm gruel in this sty, an uncomfortable ancient bed needing replacement, and an audience with the laird. Then . . . we shall see, won't we?"

"You must agree! Whatever happens. I flirt with punishment simply meeting with you! You must agree."

"Tell me one reason why."

"He'll beat us. All of us. Especially . . . Kendran. He enjoys that the most."

Myles's gut coiled, tightening into an empty knot of worry. He sucked in a breath and held it. "Why?"

"Because she doesn't respond. He canna' break her. That's why she runs. She knows. That's why she was there. She was running. It will na' go well with her once she's brought back. Dinna' you see?"

"I see a touched woman, with a bit of madness to her, a hall filled with frost and decay, and a day ahead of me that's going to make my head ache. That's what I see. Do you wish to hear how I feel next?"

"Ah! Men!" She put both hands in the air, lifting the folds of her cloak at the same time. Her wimple shifted, and he could see she wasn't remotely like Kendran, for her hair was dark brown, nearly the match to his. "I dinna' ken why I bother with speech!"

And then she tossed a bit of dust up into the air, where it mingled with the dust motes and sparkles of frost-laded air, and then settled . . . all over him.

CHAPTER 12

Kendran knew the amount of trouble she was in for by the amount of men sent for her. She always had. This didn't bode well.

She walked between the ranks of her father's Honor Guard, who still weren't speaking to her, and knew she was in dire trouble. Never had Father sent so many. Kendran had counted more than thirty when they'd first reached the croft and made short work of the door. At least Kenneth was leading them. He'd always shown a bit of chivalry in his dealings with her. Of course it was tied more to her betrothal to his great-uncle, but still. She liked to think he had some honorable instincts.

He was leading them and they set a brutal pace. She knew it was because he wanted to reach the keep before dark came again. He was already annoyed that they'd had to spend a night in the croft, resting and eating their dried cakes while they awaited daylight. The croft hadn't seemed large before, but with all those men sitting about, it had shrunk to such a proportion the last bit of loft had looked heavensent as a place to hide. That way no one would know of her tears, either.

Kendran had been running all her life, and she knew the time for that was over. As was her youthful exuberance, her faith . . . her innocence. There was nothing for it. They knew she'd run from what had been decided. They all knew. She was going to wed with the earl of Kilchurning. She had no choice. She couldn't outrun it. And just when she'd decided freezing or starving to death was a much better fate, the man she'd always hoped was out there had come.

She hadn't had enough time to enjoy the miracle that was being gifted to her. She hadn't known men like him existed outside of dreams. She also hadn't known he'd turn out to be so foul and base. Nor had she known what it felt like to be heartsore. It was an ache that went clear to the bone. That much she knew now, however. There wasn't anything worse.

Myles had offered her heaven, and then he'd shown that it was in his grasp to give it . . . and then he'd taken it away. If it wasn't for the blood specks on her thighs when she'd awakened, and the throb of awakened flesh in her most inner place, she'd think him a vision she'd conjured into being. But he wasn't that. He was a stranger, a blackguard, a man. Men. She should have remembered. She should never have let her guard down. She should never have trusted him.

That's what hurt the worst. She'd given herself to a man who'd discarded her once he'd had her. Used. Kendran felt used, and then abandoned. And she hadn't a clue to the why. Had he found her wanting? Was he, even now, off to his next conquest? A man that gifted by nature could have any woman he wanted—and probably had. She'd been easy for him. She tried to tell herself she couldn't possibly be alone in that. Any woman looking upon him would find it amazing and awe inspiring that he wished contact with them . . . especially intimate contact. He could have any woman; all he had to do was crook a finger. And yet he'd wanted her. He'd spoken words of honor and betrothal and of a future. It had made her feel so . . . special.

And now she felt used. Worn, tired, alone, and old. Feeble old. She wondered if Lady Sybil had seen that in the future when she stared into the colored smoke she created with her dried herbs and potions. Kendran barely found the strength to pivot herself up into the loft once she'd been given her own hard cakes to munch on, and there wasn't much up there for comfort. There was only her own coverlet that reeked of him, and the hard-packed peat the crofters had used for their loft floor.

Good thing it was dry. It absorbed tears easily.

Kendran huddled and shivered and sobbed until her head ached worse than her throat possibly could. And worse than all of that combined was this heartsick feeling. She'd known she wasn't special. She'd known he was never for one such as her. She'd known. All along she'd known. And still she'd loved him. And still did. And that made her a bigger fool.

She really did hate men.

Eschoncan Keep was alive with light when they reached it. Kendran didn't wonder at the why. She couldn't. She was barely conscious enough to keep putting one foot in front of the other, since that's all they required of her. That, and she had to stay in the middle of the pack of them. What were they thinking? That she'd run away again? Stupid. Foolish. Men. Where was she to go, and how was she to do it? She hadn't known that being sick at heart drained one of strength like it did. She, who never had a moment of weakness and could usually outrun any, was having trouble making each thigh lift the leg it was attached to. The flesh was jiggling, the muscles within were trembling, and her belly was actually heaving with the sensation of simply walking.

She swallowed that away. She knew what the problem was. Knew it! She'd tasted freedom and rebellion. She'd experienced joy and ecstasy and euphoria. She hadn't even known her body was capable of such wonder. And now that she knew, it was harder to face what she knew. Never again.

And now she had to pay.

The stables were alive with serfs and horses, making it warm with steamed breath. Kendran was escorted right through the midst of the confusion and marched to the back of the keep. They weren't taking her through the front door. They were taking her to the back, where prisoners were brought. Where trash was hauled out.

The wood door had seen better days. Most of the keep had. Kendran kept her eyes on the water-stained oak while the knock was answered. This door didn't even have an outside handle. One had to wait. Offal wasn't giving the option of entering. Not unless they were invited to. Kendran swallowed another round of tears. Her body had never betrayed her as much as it was doing. She couldn't afford such weakness. Any show of weakness. Her father was going to be waiting. He was going to be ready.

She never let him see her cry. Kendran dabbed at her nose and eyes with her cloak, put every emotion as far down into her core as possible, and banished the man who'd shown her heaven from her very existence. He was too perfect of form and face to be real; therefore, he wasn't. That was it. He was a figment of her imagination, conjured into being by Lady Sybil's potions. That's what it had been. Nothing more. Ever.

The ranks of her guards had thinned to just eight of them before she knew her destination. The tower. She was going to his tower. The place where Merriam always had to attend to him. Kendran's heart decided it still existed and pumped the fright into her cheeks. Kendran couldn't believe it. *Fright?* She'd never shown him anything except hatred and disdain. He craved fear. That's why he did it.

The door was shut behind her and she heard the bolt falling. It was her father's steward, Minchon. The man was a wizened, old piece of leather. He obeyed everything the laird asked of him, no matter how horrid. Kendran didn't wish to know what the man was capable of hiding. She didn't think she could stomach it.

"You think a bit of time away makes your hand more desirable? Is this what you think?"

He was shouting it. Kendran lifted her head.

"Well?"

She shook her head. She didn't have enough voice to answer, anyway.

His face darkened. Kendran knew what that meant. Anger.

"The earl has offered for you again. I've accepted. You'll wed with him."

She shook her head again.

He had a board the length of his sword. A long, flat board. Kendran watched as he slapped it against his palm hard enough to leave blisters.

"The earl demands an obedient wife."

"I . . . refuse." Her vow wasn't as authoritative as she would have liked, especially since there was only a squeak of sound to the last word, but it was all that came out. It didn't help that he'd taken several steps closer, slapping his hand the entire time. He should have raised welts by now or at least looked like it was paining him.

"You'll wed!"

She glared at him in reply, thanked God soundlessly for giving her back a spine when she most needed it, and let the hate fill her. Hate for all of them. Men. All of them. Her father, the earl . . . Myles.

He was shouting. Kendran refused to reply. It wasn't going to stop him. Nothing was. She was still glaring at him when the first blow hit her on the back, sending her to her knees.

Myles had never slept harder. He couldn't even remember reaching the bed, let alone unclothing himself, covering himself over with a blanket, and finding sleep. And he was hungry, ravenously hungry. He reached out to flick off the blanket and realized there wasn't one. Nor was he unclothed. He was stretched full out on the sagging mattress, with one foot hanging over the end, the other over the side, since he'd not even taken the time to doff his boots.

That was odd. He never slept with his boots on. Such a thing was barbaric. And rude. And did little good to fine linens such as Donal Castle was known for. He turned his head, rubbed his cheek against linen that felt like sack cloth, and groaned.

"You've awakened? Right. What is it you want first?"

The voice rang in his head. Myles groaned worse.

"I'm to fetch whatever you require. At whatever hour you require it. As the intended husband to their eldest daughter, you can have whatever you wish. Although I'm na' so certain you are of the Donal clan, let alone *The* Donal."

"What?" Myles asked.

"The Donal. From the Donal clan. I've heard tell of them since I was a wee one. They're rich. Gold flows from their wells. A laird of such a clan wouldn't arrive with little more than a horse and a change of clothing and naught else."

"What?" Myles muttered, again.

"A horse and a change of clothing. That's all you have. All. And you were wandering about lost. In the dead of winter. Without an escort."

Myles groaned. The lad didn't stop.

"Which is rather strange. Nae clan leader from such a powerful clan is about without his guard. Why dinna' you have one? Are you an impostor?"

"An . . . impostor?" Myles repeated. The words made no sense. The lad speaking them wasn't making much of it, either.

"Impostor. By the saints! Have you nae wits, either? Why would they saddle me with such as you?"

"I left them," Myles replied finally.

"Who?"

"My Honor Guard."

"Honor Guards canna' be left. They stay at a laird's side through all. That's why they're called Honor Guards."

"They also . . . *betray*." Myles didn't say the last word aloud. He didn't want it out until he had his feet beneath him again and his wits at his disposal.

"You're The Donal? Truly?"

"Yea and nay, lad." Myles tried sucking moisture into his mouth. It might make his words less garbled sounding even to his own ears.

"How can you be either?"

"Eldest son. Heir. That's how."

There was a huff of annoyance, and then the fellow cleared his throat. "Verra well, then. All's correct. They've given me to you. I'm to squire for you. I'm to get you whatever you wish. You being The Donal, and all."

"Silence," Myles answered.

"I canna' get what you wish if I'm silent. I just remarked on it."

"Silence!" Myles tried to put enough emphasis on it, but all that came out was a growl of sound. He didn't understand why his head felt so filled with cloth wool, nor why his tongue felt the size of a muckle wheel of thread. He tried moving it in his mouth and found it glued to the side. That was odd.

"I'll na' say another word. I vow it."

"Christ." Myles put his hands on the rails to either side of him and pushed himself up and out of the depression he'd made in the sunken mattress. Then he had one foot on the ground, as he straddled the outer wooden edge of the bed to keep from sinking back in. The room rocked in front of him at that small act.

"I'm to see you have all that's required. All. Just ask."

"Why?" Myles asked.

"Why?"

Myles sighed heavily and brought both hands up to rake them through his hair. He could use a bath. And a sharp skean for a shave. He could use all of that, but first he needed sup. A large joint of well-roasted meat, a platter full of vegetables, a trencher of gravy. He opened his mouth to speak of it.

"I can see you wake poorly. We'll work on that."

"What?" Myles asked, turning his head.

"Beggin."

"For what?" Myles replied. His head was starting to pound in rhythm to his pulse, and it was heavy and painful.

"Nae. That's my name. Beggin."

"What fool names their offspring Beggin?"

"Well! I'll have you ken 'tis an ancient name. Given afore the Celts. Long afore we were on this sorry earth. And you were in this sorry condition and in this sorrier keep, and going to wed the sorriest nagging woman on the planet, making you the sorriest excuse for a master I've yet served. That's what it is."

"Jesu'!" Myles replied and put both hands to his ears. The man could put a sentence together with a rapidity that defied the listening. It increased the tempo of his pulse, and, therefore, it was transferring into his head.

"Go." He moved one hand and pointed to the door.

"I canna' go. Unless you wish me to fetch you something. Do you? Wish me to fetch something?"

"I just wish for some silence."

"As a tomb. I vow it."

Myles turned his head. This Beggin was a slip of a lad, perhaps the age of his youngest sibling, Ethan. That would make the lad sixteen. He was also bobbing his head and moving his arms and torso about in a pace that made the room's rocking seem mild.

"Canna' you keep still?" he said.

"There's nae reason to shout. I'll keep powerfully still. I'll na' move. I'll just stand and await your request. That's what I'll do. I vow it."

Myles would have rolled his eyes, but he sensed it

would hurt too much. And he wondered what that little sprite of a girl had done to him to have such an effect.

"How long have I been here?"

"That depends on what you mean by here."

Myles sighed—long and loud. It unglued his tongue from the side of his mouth and he moved it about slowly, sucking up spittle and wondering how to get his tongue back to its normal size. He also wondered what he'd done to be shackled with the lad bobbing and weaving before him.

"So. What is it to be?"

"How long?"

"Do you wish answers to questions, or would you rather have a repast? You look like the type who rarely goes hungry. I bet you can eat a half a stag. All by yourself. At one sitting. That would be a sight to see. That would."

"Mead," Myles replied.

"You probably drink barrels of that, too."

"Can you get some?"

"Of course I can get some. I'm a squire. All you have to do is ask and I get what's required."

"Then, why dinna' you?" Myles was losing patience. It sounded in his voice. He moved his hands and placed them on the railing and swiveled so both feet were on the floor. He watched the room move and rotate before settling into a slight hum of movement.

"Why dinna' I what?"

"Get what I require?"

"Because you've na' yet given me an order!"

"Silence!" Myles tried to yell it. His tongue still wasn't working properly, and all that came out was a garbled word, sounding like a curse. He grimaced. For some reason it made his head ache worse.

"Well! I've served many a master, but never one with such a sore temper. I'll have you ken—"

Myles lurched to his feet, glared down at the diminutive fellow who hadn't ceased moving and jiggling everywhere on his body. It was a better alternative to leaning forward and heaving out the nothing that was on this belly, but not by much.

"I want mead! Now!"

"Well! Why dinna' you just say so?"

Myles took a step. The lad moved rapidly away from him. He wasn't surprised. He suspected the pace of this Beggin's steps, just from the time he'd already known him.

"There's *nae* need to rage and rant at me. I've been a squire for years. I'm well trained. I've been given to you for your use. You've *nae* squire. Therefore, I'll be yours. You'll have *nae* complaints."

"Mead." Myles repeated. "And with it meat. And with that, vegetables, bread, and water." He started unfastening the ties of his tunic and spread the placket wide. The garment had been on him for some time, and he'd sweated in it during the long walk to the keep, and then during his long sleep.

"You want mead? And water? Both? Why?"

"I want water to bathe in. Heated water. A tub full. And a skean."

"What is that for?"

Myles toyed with telling him to slice his tongue off but held back. He only wanted the wretch out of the chamber so he could bolt him out. "Shaving," he answered finally.

"You shave? Why? A full, healthy beard is what makes a man."

"Brawn, and size, and strength and honor are what

make a man, lad. Dinna' mistake it for aught else."
And Myles pulled the tunic over his head. He watched
as the lad gaped openmouthed at the array of muscle,
healing scuff marks, and yellowish-tinted bruising that
his shirt had hidden. He watched and waited and then
he couldn't resist the taunt. "Would you be carin' to
test your theory on what makes a man? Out on the list,
Squire Beggin? Against me? I've na' met a challenge
for a good sennight. Mayhap longer. What say you?"

"You want mead? And sup? And a bath with a skean?
I'll be seeing to your needs, that's what I'm saying."

"All good. I'll await you."

Like hell he would. He just wanted the little lad out
of his sight and out of his head, and then he wanted the
sickness purged from his frame.

The door shut, rattling slightly with the poor fit. Or
perhaps it was rattling from the force with which the
little runt had shut it. Or perhaps it was because it was
aged and had taken more than one good dousing of
water during its lifetime. Or perhaps it was because the
hinges looked old and rusty even to his blurred vision.
Myles took a step, then another, making his legs move,
although it looked to be a lurching, haphazard fashion.
Then he went to his knees. It wasn't worth the effort,
either. The door didn't have a bolt.

CHAPTER 13

Myle's had been invited to attend to the laird of Eschoncan in the chieftain room before their banquet. He knew why. He was to present himself to his future father-by-law, commit to the wedding and documents giving him ownership of Rocky Fells and leadership of Clan Eschon. They'd also be making him owner and chief executor of this drafty, badly constructed, and even more poorly maintained keep. He hoped there wasn't anyone in the clan who would fight it when he sent for enough men to raze the castle to the ground. Myles's lips twisted at the thought. He'd keep that plan to himself. There would also be the gift he had of gold coin, the lengthy listing of his assets—prime among them being eldest son and heir to Donal—and there was every chance Kendran would be there, too.

There was no need of hurrying, although everything on his body seemed of a differing opinion. He couldn't wait to see her again. It felt like months had passed, rather than the course of days. And each moment that was prolonged made seeing her again that much more desirable, alluring, and craved.

His entire being craved her. He hadn't known it happened that way. None at Castle Donal spoke of a love like he must feel for her. None. In the whole of his lands, none had even whispered about the existence of an emotion akin to this. All they spoke of—and chided each other over—was carnality, lust, and a play love that felt cheap and tawdry in comparison. None told him of the hard knot that was forming where his heart was supposed to be, making it a thumping ache, sending more of the same into his limbs rather than blood, just from being apart from her. And from not knowing. That was the worst. Such a love clouded his senses, took over his form, and compelled his every motion. It was heady. Powerful. Draining. He couldn't concentrate. He couldn't move smoothly when he needed to, and he couldn't comprehend why. Myles forced himself to calm—to stop the tremble of his frame, the increase of his pulse, the shallowness of his breaths—yet each bit of time that passed made it harder to accomplish any of it.

He probably shouldn't have left her as he had, but he'd thought it the best move at the time. He hadn't known how much time they had before her clan would come for her . . . and he'd wanted to surprise her. He wanted to see her face when she found out the truth: that the man she detested wedding was her very own croft partner. He hoped she liked the bean gesture, too.

They had their banquet scheduled for late. Near midnight. Myles assumed it was so they could get the proper cooking time to the game they'd decided to roast, but all he had to go by was the undercooked fare Beggin had procured for him. It was a feast of poorly seasoned, undercooked venison, accompanied by a platter of washed-out looking carrots, a loaf of bread that had seen better days, and mead that had been so diluted with water it might as well be considered that.

He shoveled it all in as if it were the best sup he'd ever tasted. And then he sent the squire for more. That was the best way to keep Squire Beggin's mouth from spewing out more words than any one person should have to listen to: keep the lad busy. That's also how he found out that Squire Beggin was a thief, as well as a braggart, a nuisance, and a general twitcher. The one thing he wasn't being—after he'd purloined another tray full of sup—was annoyingly talkative, but that was more due to the length of leather Myles had strapped about his squire's mouth, muting the words he kept speaking, than anything else.

He smirked over at where the lad was busily arranging his chieftain *feile breacan* and almost felt sorry for the lad. Then, he got to listen to more of the squire's words. Poorly spoken, but spoken all the same. Myles shook his head. The bath looked more inviting than the sup had been, and if he made enough splashing noise, it might drown out his new squire's ceaseless tongue.

It didn't. The lad had managed to figure out how to talk with a square of leather blocking his mouth, and the garbled words he spoke were still understandable, and full of the abused state of Myles's clothing, the amount of gold he had to his person, the length and weight of his sword, along with the quality of the gems at the hilt, and then he went over the amount of time spent with scraping his chin and cheeks to smoothness. And what a waste of it all of these preparations were.

He said more than enough words over that. As if the lad had never had to dress for such an occasion before, or ever seen it done.

Myles listened halfheartedly, and then he tried ignoring

him completely. He had enough to do with calming the tremor of his hands in order to keep the skean scraping at his skin and not pricking beneath it. Myles already knew he had rich attire that hadn't been rinsed in rainwater and worked over with a brush in order to impart softness and drape. It would be stiff and scratchy, but it was his own fault. He'd left it to dry where Kendran had placed it— from the rafters of a deserted croft. He also knew the shirt he planned on wearing needed rinsing. He wasn't going to allow it. It carried her smell. That was enough for him.

Myles also already knew he was a handsome fellow. Everyone in sighting distance of him had been telling him of it since he was a lad. He well knew what he had to do and the impression he wanted to make. She hadn't seen him in his best light. She was going to, now. The entire clan of Eschon was going to see what the harridan of harridans had been betrothed to, and they'd also find out that he was willing and ready to marry her. In fact, he was going to demand the ceremony moved up, even before Christmas Eve, in order to have her.

That thought was transferring to his every movement until he looked clumsy enough he actually needed a squire in order to make certain his plaide was correctly crossed over one shoulder, caressing the silken shirt, and holding the medallion given the Donals from The Bruce's court, more than a century past. Then he was raking his hair back into a long, loosely braided queue and tying it with a length of black cord when something the squire mumbled caught his attention.

". . . prodigal is brought back, marching atween the guard like a prisoner. That surely upset her, but it was her turn, I would say. And that just went and upset their banquet plans even more than you did. That's the why—"

"What did you just say?" Myles spun on the one boot he'd managed to lace and glared across at the lad, who was engrossed with picking up the discarded drying cloths and the *feile breacan* Myles had arrived, collapsed, and then slept in.

"Oh. So you wish to listen to me now?" The lad dropped his armload, put both hands on his hips, and bobbed his head even more than his usual. Then, he added a shuffling step from side to side. "Mayhap you should na' have made it impossible for me to speak, then."

"Impossible?" Myles was across the floor and slicing the leather band before the lad took another breath. "Stay the argument. Tell of this delay." Then, he had to put his hand over the lad's mouth, since he already heard the sucked-in breath. "And naught else. You ken?"

Beggin nodded. Myles removed his hand. The words started, almost too quickly to hear.

"There's been banquets held afore this one. Larger than this one. With more folk attending, and more mead, and more game and more entertainments. Eschoncan Keep has the reputation for such a thing. We can drink any man beneath a table and eat our fill for days. It's a legacy we got from the Norsemen, which, if you hadn't noted, share some ancestry with us. It's due to our setting. The Vikings always land here first. They conquer everyone here first. We're the most Northern clan, unless you count those at the islands of Orkney and—"

"Can you simply tell me of the delay?" Myles asked, stopping the nearly ceaseless barrage of words for a moment.

"Like I said, this was a large fest, but not our largest, although you wouldn't have known that. You've importance, but it is midwinter, travel is difficult, and none truly thought you'd come. After all, she is . . . well—

Ugh, I'll na' say. I'll let your own eyes and ears learn of it. She's been difficult for the laird to wed off. That's why they made such an effort to greet you and show you what the clan is capable of. They've been preparing for your banquet for a sennight. Perhaps more. The logs were felled, the best mead was set aside to age more, bread was baked, the game cured, and then—"

"Tell me of the delay!" Myles interrupted him.

The lad sucked in more breath. "What's to say? You dinna' arrive. The preparations went back to the buttery, the game back to the curing shed, and the ladies retired back to the solar, which is the one spot they always keep warmed with what wood has been gathered—"

"The delay!" Myles tried again.

The lad glared at him. "I am telling of it! The laird was in a temper. All assumed it was due to your absence. A messenger was sent to your stronghold. I dinna' know if he arrived, or not. It's na' been enough time. And you traveled without your own guard. Why would you do such a thing?"

Myles forced himself to a calm he was far from feeling. He swallowed, uncoiled his fist from where it had been wrapped about his sword hilt, and looked over the lad's head. He listened to eight of his own heartbeats before he had the frustration covered enough that it didn't sound in his voice. He didn't control the guard, his father did. They'd already shown him that. He wouldn't be mourning if they'd perished from eating the tavern master's ill-cooked fare. It would be justice for their betrayal of him. His Honor Guard had been handpicked by him a decade earlier. *Handpicked!* And they'd still turned on him, beating him into submission when the laird's men hadn't proved to be enough. He filled his chest with air and let it out. Then he asked his question, putting in so little emotion it didn't even sound like him. "So finish. My absence was na' the reason?"

"*Nae.* 'Twas the Lady Kendran. She was lost out in the storm. She was just brought back this day." His voice lowered. "And she was taken to . . . the tower."

Myles swallowed. "This is bad?"

"'Tis where the laird . . . well . . . where he chastises . . . uh . . . those who need chastisement."

If he'd touched one finger to her, Myles was breaking his arm. He had it decided before the haze cleared in front of him, and the lad ceased wriggling in his hand. It took him a moment to realize he had the lad's shoulder within his fingers.

"I had naught to do with it! You can unhand me and seek out another enemy! I have never served a more base knight! Little in manners, nothing whatsoever in charm. I think you'd best find another squire."

"And I may own myself well satisfied with your service. I may speak of it with His Lordship when we meet. I may even request you along with the dowry."

Beggin looked heavenward and then started speaking again. Myles shut the sound out of his consciousness. He was moving again, shoving the other boot on, and lacing it with a precision birthed by years of warfare. He didn't know how many guards the laird of Eschoncan kept around him, but the auld coward was going to need all of them for protection if he'd touched her.

"Well, hasten me to the chieftain room, young Beggin. I've a betrothal banquet to attend! Haste!"

The lad was speechless at the speed with which Myles finished. It didn't last. He started his pestering words before the bolt was lifted and then he was guiding. Myles listened for any further remark of Kendran but in vain. Beggin was full of words that weren't worth a listen, and then he gave more.

Myles sighed and followed on the lad's heels.

The great hall had looked deserted when he'd arrived, early yester morn, but it was decidedly crowded now. Myles stood on the last step of the stair and looked about as those there absorbed his presence, and his size, and what he hoped was his grim expression. This was his future? If he hadn't such love for Kendran, he'd be turning about and leaving them to their own ends.

They were already drinking, as the volume of kegs on the trestle tables attested. That was rude of them as well as stupid on the host's part. A banquet wasn't to start until the guest of honor attended, and drunkenness was never a good way to control any large gathering.

They were already well into the latter. He could tell as sounds of revelry swelled about him. There was a huge fire roaring in the fireplace at the end opposite the front entryway, on Myles's left. It wasn't necessary. Any laird worth his power knew a room this full had no need of that much heat. Not Eschoncan. That laird had ordered a log the size of an entire tree placed and lit, making the enclosure reek of wood smoke, sweat, and aromatic perfume concoctions that all seemed to blend together, making what they'd serve even more unappetizing.

Myles looked it over while everyone appeared to be doing the same to him, while the entire time Beggin was yanking on his sleeve. Then, he was being led down into the room and through it, past a myriad of diminutive, well-dressed ladies and their escorts, men who stood a head shorter than him, if not more.

He passed straight across the room and into a hall flanking the large fireplace, above which a large length of plaide hung, and little else. Myles noted it was fraying and looked like it had lost the bottom half of its color to torch smoke and years of neglect. It wasn't hard to look grim.

It was more steps later, taking him another story higher, before he was facing a large, fairly impressive impediment of a double-sized door carved from what looked like one length of wood. It was set in place with wrought ironwork hinges that would have been equally as imposing and magnificent if they'd only been given a good cleaning. Myles looked it over as he waited for their knock to be answered. He had it decided that the door was one thing he'd be saving from the castle before he gutted it, when the door showed how poorly designed it was by swinging outward, sending Squire Beggin back a good four steps to avoid falling on his flanks at the surprise of it.

Myles barely kept the smile from his lips, as that was the first thing the lad glanced at as he caught himself. It was obvious, despite the other's continual bragging about how the festivities were being put on for Myles, and how he'd come about this knowledge from his attendance at so many of them, that it was a another fable. Not only hadn't Beggin been to these hallowed halls, but he hadn't been allowed in the chieftain's rooms and graced with the laird's presence much, if his openmouthed expression was any gauge.

Myles was the opposite. He'd been in chieftain's rooms since he was born. He'd been settled into the largest of the chairs and had taken to handling every sort of weapon on the walls since he could walk. He'd been the known heir to all of it since the day he first took breath, and Castle Donal not only had a room easily twice the width of this one, as well as being longer, but it had weaponry covering all the walls, the ceilings draped with the banners from clans they'd won in battle, and all of it was perfectly maintained and displayed and valued.

Not so the Eschoncan Keep. Myles stopped the disdain from settling on his lips with sheer act of will, but he had to hood his eyes to keep his emotion to himself. The claymores, swords, skeans, daggers, hand axes, and spears along the wall were in such disrepair and neglect the Eschon clan would have trouble slicing their own banquet meat with any blade there. They were all in need of a good cleaning, a good sharpening, and a good bit of use. The bows looked too warped to be accurate, and more than one spear shaft showed the results of bore worms at work. As did the leather of their shields. Myles looked over the array, sucking in on his cheeks and taking his time. He suspected they were thinking he was admiring and showing respect for the display.

He was actually deciding which among them was worth saving.

There was an enormous needlework tapestry hanging from one of the ceiling beams to fall behind the upraised platform that held the laird. Myles's eyes went to it next, and he took his time. He had it decided that, even if that bit of blue plaide was in disrepair and fading in rectangles of space that showed where the archer slits in the upper wall caught the full glare of day sun, he was still saving it. He moved his head down to look at Kendran's sire.

He was disappointed. Severely. Completely.

The man facing him didn't look capable of harming a worm, let alone keeping the females in his keep in fear of his temper. One of the large, white tufts of hair that went for an eyebrow lifted as they appraised each other.

Laird Eschoncan was large, but it was a girth brought about by years of gluttony atop a frame that might have held muscle at some point. He also sported a large shock of white hair, ringed about his head with the pattern of his balding, and a dark red- and gray-streaked beard. If he was in the chieftain plaide, it had seen better days; if not better years. He was also short. Probably the height of his daughter, or little taller. That much was evident, since even ensconced in an elevated chair that had gilded wood separating from the framework, he was forced to look up and across at Myles.

"Donal?" he finally spoke. At least the man's voice had nothing feeble or weak about it.

The chair he was in was definitely going to the refuse pile, Myles decided. He didn't even think the gilding was real gold, but he could be wrong. He waited before he replied. He was waiting for the dozen men standing about to absorb him. He was also deciding which of them would be the toughest to take and, therefore, would be the first one he'd be taking.

"Well? Are you The Donal, or na'?"

"Not," Myles replied finally. And then he took himself to his full height to cross his arms about his chest. He watched as the laird took in the stance, the richness of his attire, and the set look of his jaw.

"Emissary?"

"Nae," Myles returned.

"Well speak up, lad. You're either The Donal, or you're his emissary. I've na' got all eve! I've a fest to attend."

"You've a fest to control, I would say," Myles returned.

The man did have a temper. His cheeks reddened as he watched. "Your meaning?" Kendran's father asked.

"Control. And your lack of it. Your household. Your guests. Your fest. 'Tis a betrothal party, is it na'?"

"Aye," the man said the word louder than before. Myles smiled.

"And is na' a betrothal party in celebration of a wedding?"

"You're insolent."

"And you've na' shown me a bride . . . or a dowry."

"Show me a groom and an offer."

Myles nodded, opened one of the pouches hanging beside his sporran, and started spilling gold coins all over the floor at his feet. He heard the reaction from those about him. He didn't take his eyes from the laird. He waited until the gold ceased moving and just lay there, winking in the torchlight.

"That is a verra nice offer."

"'Tis but a fraction of what the Donals bring to the table. And it will be doubled as long as the new term is met."

"New terms? I said naught of new terms."

"By the Yule. The vows are to be taken by Christmas. *Nae* longer. That is the new term."

"The wedding is to take place in less than five sennights? You're mad."

In answer, Myles moved his hands to the other bag and started flipping more coins onto the puddle of them on the floor. He knew it was impressive. He didn't have long to wait for the answer. He could tell what it would be by the choked sounds coming from his host. "By Christmas. That eve. We agreed?"

"Aye," came the answer.

"Good. And now . . . your offer?"

"The Rocky Fells of Eschon, the coast of Dumfries, and the keep, itself."

"You say naught of the bride," Myles countered.

"And you haven't shown me The Donal. The offer is for him. The laird. I'll na' take another."

"My father is too auld to take a bride. He sent me in his place. Myles Magnus Donal. Firstborn. Heir."

The man smirked. At least that's what Myles assumed the expression was, since all that happened was the beard moved.

"So . . . you are The Donal."

"Not until my sire's demise. Dinna' mistake my words. He may live a lengthy spell yet. I am na' The Donal. But I will be."

"I rather fancy you, young Myles. You've spirit. That's sadly lacking in my home. I trust my daughter will fancy you, as well. Kenneth? Fetch the bride."

The man Myles had targeted for his first blow was the one answering the request. Myles's back tightened without his order to do so. He knew it was the look of malice this Kenneth had given him. Myles uncrossed his arms, placed his left hand on a skean handle at his belt, while the other caressed his sword hilt.

There was something wrong at Eschon Keep; lack of guidance and leadership was it. Perhaps the laird was too tired and old to manage it. Perhaps he was too caught up in punishing and abusing his womenfolk. Whatever it was, Myles was going to see it halted. And it was going to be halted before he took his vows. They had two fortnights. Two. Christ's Mass. That's the length of time he was giving the laird before he usurped power and did what one was supposed to with such a thing. Govern. Lead. Guide. Direct. Influence. Establish order and then maintain it. And if the old man facing him had put one finger on Kendran, he wasn't going to live to see any of it.

Myles had it decided when he heard her steps . . . or someone's steps.

He swiveled to watch her enter, following this man Kenneth. She was walking strangely, with her head bowed. And she was heavily veiled, her head and shoulders covered with a length of velvet the color and weight of her gown. It was a rich-looking fabric. It had also seen better days. Myles's lips thinned and he narrowed his eyes as he watched her walk. If he wasn't mistaken, she was hunched a bit, too. The laird was going to pay for that. Myles was going to be making certain of it.

"Daughter!"

The hunched figure was moving forward, on shuffling steps. Myles's heart completely stopped as he watched it. She looked cowed, beaten, hurt. He no longer cared for ceremony or effect. He was at her side and lifting the veil and feeling the shock soaking clear into his entire being at what he saw there before anyone stopped him. It wasn't Kendran. It was a relative, but it wasn't Kendran. She had the same red-gold hair, a nearly exact shade of blue eyes, but it wasn't Kendran. The heat that had filled him since he'd awakened evaporated, leaving ice in his veins, and a quiver of motion that was all it felt like his heart was giving him. And this woman really hated him. She wasn't just acting it. Her entire body was coated with it.

Agree. . . .

The word went right into his ear like it had been whispered there. Myles swallowed. Now he had the proof. He was dreaming. Or he was going mad. There wasn't a soul near him.

Whatever it is . . . agree!

It was the voice again, sounding just like the first

and only time he'd heard it. He knew then whose voice it was. That little wench who had dusted him with powder and sent him into oblivion. It was her words, and her command, but the sweat soaking his entire body was entirely his.

"This is na'—" he began. His legs wobbled slightly before he caught them.

"My daughter, Merriam. Your betrothed. And soon to be . . . your wife. Verra soon. By Christmas, Merriam."

"What?" Her eyes went wide as she glared at him. Then she had her nose wrinkled as if smelling something distasteful. He only hoped his own expression wasn't a mirror image of hers.

"He's demanding a Christmas ceremony. You heard me."

"I . . . refuse," she replied.

Myles heard the old wood creaking as the laird moved. His shoulder clenched as if a hand was on it . . . a small hand.

"As do I." The words were spoken by him, but they hadn't voice to them. The hand had moved to midback and felt like it was pushing right through him, into his chest, squeezing the bulbous mass that used to be his heart, but felt now like it was a stomped-on, abused shard of ice.

"And he refuses also. See!"

She had a vicious voice, sharp and penetrating. She was pointing at him. He knew why. Myles was in a shake, his head swinging back and forth as he absorbed it. He only hoped he didn't faint.

Agree! The voice in his head was shouting it.

"Are you refusing my daughter's hand, Donal?"

The auld laird had a sword, but he hadn't unsheathed it. He didn't have to. Myles noted more than seven of them coming out of their scabbards out of the corners of his eyes. It wasn't the fight he'd planned in his mind earlier. Back then, he'd had strength to his limbs, power in his body, and love in his heart. Now all he had was black.

Agree . . . Now. Right now.

"I agree," Myles repeated and wrenched himself back from the spite-filled woman who was angrily shoving her velvet back over her head, covering over any other expression. He feared he was going to be ill. His entire frame was covered with the shivers racing his skin to center at his scalp. He swallowed the bile away, sent the weakness back where it couldn't bother him, and turned his head to focus on the tapestry.

About the only good thing was the pressure that had seemed to come from a little hand wrapped about his heart had evaporated as if it had never been.

CHAPTER 14

"I'm dying." Kendran shuddered through another tearful breath.

"You're na' dying. Nor will you. You've little more than a bit of bruising to you, and that's only on your hip." A rag swished over her skin with the words. It carried as little sympathy as the words did.

"It is na' the bruising that's killing me," Kendran mumbled to the sheet.

There was silence for a bit, broken only by the sound of water dripping from fingertips prior to drying them off. Then, Sybil spoke again. "I had heard this of heart-sickness. I dinna' think it had merit. I dinna' ken such a thing existed. I was wrong. I will remember it in future, however."

"Heartsick?" The disdain would have had more weight if it wasn't whispered and if she hadn't lost it on a sob.

"Little else has feeling. Only the heart. And it burns, sending pain from thence to overtake even the soul. Death is preferable. This is what I was told."

Kendran swayed her head back and forth on the

sheet. No one spoke to Lady Sybil. They wouldn't dare. It was said she was touched by the faeries.

"I had also heard of the bitterness. The blackness. The despair. The desire to lash out." Sybil sighed. "All true. All of it."

Kendran clenched her lips. "Nae one speaks . . . such things," she whispered. There was a bit of voice behind the words but it came in spurts of use.

"The air is alive with voices. They always speak. You just dinna' listen. You could. You just dinna'."

Kendran lay on her belly, arms spread wide, so that her hands hung from both sides of the bed, and absorbed the ache of flesh moving over bruised ribs with each and every breath. She had no choice but to accept it. Sybil was very accurate. The burn coming from her heart hurt much more than any other part of her. She hadn't known what heartsickness felt like, either.

"You must have shocked him," Sybil continued as if she'd said nothing of moment. "Severely."

Myles? she wondered. "Whom?" Kendran asked.

"Our sire."

"Why?"

Sybil sighed again and went back to spreading some sort of unguent on Kendran's hip and across the welt on one shoulder. From the smell, the salve had rosehips in it and a bit of mint, but beyond that, Kendran hadn't a clue what it contained. She didn't much care, either. She hadn't been exaggerating. She really did feel like she was dying. Why else would her heart continue to beat so painfully? Why else would tears cloud her vision, shivers run her frame, and loss fill every part of her that it could? Strange, that. She'd never known such an emotion existed.

"Because he only hit you three times. Thrice."

"You . . . lie." She had to swallow between the words.

"Nae. I was there. I counted."

"Only the troll Minchon was there."

"You still doubt me?"

Lady Sybil clucked her tongue and then went onto her knees to reach the same level at which Kendran was lying. Sybil was beautiful, in a way that owed more to the mysteries behind her gray-green eyes than anything about her face or her form. She always had been. She was strange, though, and frightened most everyone away even before she spoke.

"Father. Me. Minchon. You speak false. Again. Always." The words were all whispered. Sybil heard them all, though.

She sighed. "You gave him what he wanted too easily. You cried."

"I never cry!" It was a foolish use of her voice. Kendran realized it as the hoarse tone died away.

In answer, Sybil lifted a finger and traced a tear path down the incline of Kendran's nose. Then she was rubbing the wetness away between her forefinger and thumb. "That's what stopped him, I think."

"He's an auld man, his gout pains, his arm tires, and his face was bright with blood color. He's ill. That's why he stopped." The words were all whispered. It didn't hurt her throat as much.

"Perhaps. I dinna' think so, though."

"You speak riddles, Sybil. As always. I would have another tend to me."

"There are no others. They make preparations for your sister's banquet. You'll attend as well. As soon as we finish here."

"Celebrate? Me?"

"The entire clan celebrates. Why should you be different?"

"Because I'm dying. That's why."

Lady Sybil clicked her tongue once. Then, she was smoothing a lock of hair from Kendran's brow. "That's why he does this . . . you ken?"

Myles? Kendran instantly wondered. She swallowed it away. "Who?"

"He needs to break us. It makes him feel more manly, since he's too weak and spineless to earn it the proper way."

"What are you speaking of now?"

"Men. Strange creatures. Even that dark, immense one. Especially him."

Kendran's heart stopped and then decided it would continue beating since she must not have enough ache filling her. Sybil didn't know him. She couldn't. None of them could.

"Verra strange. They need to feel alive. They need to feel valued. They need victory. This is what drives them."

"Whom?"

"Men."

"You ken naught of men, Sybil. Just as you ken so little about me."

"Poor Kendran."

"You dare pity me?"

The girl gave a little snort. "Nae. You dinna' need pity."

"What is it I do need, then? Since you're so wise?"

"Him."

Kendran shivered all the way to her toes, and then she felt the shivers as they climbed back up to the base of her neck and went right up over her head beneath her scalp. She didn't need him! Never. Ever. She opened her mouth to refute it, but Sybil started talking again, stealing the space.

"It is different with men."

"You know nothing, yet pester with upset and torment. Find another sickbed to attend. I've little use of you and your potions."

"True. All of it."

"Then why stay?"

"Because I want to."

Kendran frowned. "Why?" she asked.

"The new year is less then six sennights away."

"So?" This time Kendran had an aggressive note in her voice.

"And it's a boring time. It can be a boring . . . lonely time."

"If you canna' make sense, go. Leave. Now."

Sybil sighed. "I make sense. You just dinna' wish to listen. Just as you are na' listening about men."

"Them again?"

"Them. Always."

"If I listen, will you leave?"

"If you still wish me to."

"Verra well. Have your say and go. I canna' stop you. I dinna' ask for you, I dinna' wish company, nor did I want it, yet here you are. Pestering. Again."

"You asked. Just not aloud."

Kendran sighed heavily this time. "You always go forever around something afore you say what you mean. Would you please begin? You make everything ache worse just from the listening."

"Men are strange creatures. Different from us. Strong. 'Tis what sets them apart from each other. They ken this. They crave it."

Myles. The vision of him rammed into Kendran's consciousness, filling her vision. She closed her eyes to make it go away. It didn't work. It was worse.

"Some are more blessed than others. 'Tis gifted to them at birth. Others must work at it. Hard. They fight. They play. They meet on the list. You ken?"

Kendran moved her head on the sheet in a nod.

"Still others? They never receive the gift of strength. They have to find it in other ways. Smart ways. Devious ways. Underhanded ways."

"Like Father?" Kendran whispered.

"Such a thing makes them men. And then they have to test it."

"Test . . . it?" Her whisper stumbled. She didn't mean it to.

"He dinna' leave because he wished to, Kendran."

Kendran gulped away the knot from her throat. She was so tired of crying. She rarely cried. She knew why. It didn't do any good.

"He was saving you," Sybil continued, in the same soft, modulated tone.

"From what? Snow?"

"Disgrace."

Hope flared, making the hard clump that was her heart pulsate and quiver. She gulped again. "Dis . . . grace?"

"A man and a woman in a croft. Sharing space for days? Alone? With little more than a share of clothing atween them? Disgraceful."

"Naught happened," Kendran lied.

There wasn't an answer for a bit. Then Sybil spoke again. "I ken as much. But would others? He could na' risk it. He would na' risk it. Na' with you."

Why did Sybil have to light the spark of hope and

light again? Wasn't it better to paint men all the same color? Did her sister really have to change it? "Why are you doing this?" Kendran whispered.

"Because he did what I required. I'm repaying him."

"Repaying?"

"Remember what I've been saying? About men?"

Kendran licked her lips. "Aye."

"Then listen. Understand these creatures. The males. It's about honor. And duty. And what it costs. Even for our father."

"Father? You go too far, Sybil. I'll na' listen. Father does na' ken the meaning of the words."

"He kens them well. He just does na' have them. That is the problem."

"Little sisters with long-winded speech saying little and meaning less—that is the problem," Kendran replied.

By the feel of air on her arm, Sybil was probably chuckling, although it didn't make sound. "All men need it. So much so that it's a sickness. They crave it. They fight to gain it because they have to have it. And if there's nae other clan about with issues enough to warrant a war, then they'll fight amongst themselves. It happens—time and again. Our father is nae different. He's just too much a coward to fight on the list, as any other man would do. He'd lose. So . . . he ensures his balance and his place in this life by taking up his issues against those he can still conquer. Us. That way he keeps his honor and duty in his own head."

"Have you finished yet?" Kendran asked.

"And you. Look at you."

"Aye. Look at me. What of it?"

"It was easy to break you this time. You cried. Early on. He dinna' even have to sweat. You never give in. He's probably still crowing his victory."

"Nay, I did naught." Sometimes Sybil made too much sense.

"You did everything. He broke you. Finally. Merriam always takes a dozen blows, whilst your mother? She does na' ken when to stay silent. She suffers greatly, too."

"I dinna' break!" The thought was mortifying. Almost worse than Myles leaving her.

"You needn't cower in shame. It was bright of you. I already spoke on it."

"Are you finished yet?"

"He is verra handsome. Verra. Better than I could have conjured into being. Perfect in face, form . . . speech. Is he as perfect . . . elsewhere?"

Kendran went white hot with the embarrassment. Sweat broke out everywhere. Then she was cold. Icewater cold. "I dinna' ken of what you speak," she whispered finally.

Sybil giggled. It was a strange sound. The youngest Eschon female rarely, if ever, giggled. Kendran cracked open an eye and peered at her.

"I've met him," Sybil whispered.

Kendran rolled her eyes and shut them again. Lady Sybil was forever speaking of things that couldn't be. She couldn't have met Myles, just as she couldn't have been in the tower when Father wielded his board. She was right, however. There had only been three of his blows. That was an easy thing to guess, however. There were only three welts across her body.

"It was a lucky thing, too. Any more and he'd have changed his own history. Again. Just like when he made your mother lose the son she carried. He causes his own dissatisfaction. He just does na' see it. None of you do."

"What are you speaking of now?" Kendran's brows knit together. She didn't open her eyes.

"Our father. His punishment. His own stupidity. You were bright to cry when you did and stop him. Any more blows and he would have unseated the bairn."

Oh, Jesu'! Kendran's eyes flew wide as she recoiled from the thought instantly and completely and with such horror she shook with it. "Nay. Please nay," she whispered.

"It's to be a male bairn, too. The image of his sire. Tall. Dark. Handsome. Brawny. You'll name him Brently. He'll bring honor to the Eschon name."

"You lie."

"Are we back to that, again?"

"You have nae knowledge of such things. Nae one can."

Sybil's breath reached Kendran's cheek with a sigh. "You're right, of course. I but guess. I might be right, however. If I am, I'll be called a witch. If I'm wrong, I can shrug and be called mad. Either way, it will be some time afore it can be proved. You'll need all of it. You have much to do."

"I'll na' carry that man's bairn! I'll not. None can make me."

Sybil giggled. Again.

"And you can cease your laughter! I dinna' ask for this, and I'll na' accept it. Never. You're wrong. You are."

"I may be," Sybil returned.

"You are."

"Such faith. I warned you what would happen if you put into play events you could na' change."

"Help me change it, then!"

"I dinna' have that much power."

"Brew me a potion. Make it bitter and yet sweet. Much like the memory of it. Make it unseat this bairn."

"I canna' brew any such potion. You ken this? There is naught I can do."

"You brewed the savory. You made certain I had it. This is your fault, and you must help me undo it."

"The lone thing I must help you do is get your own betrothed to come and fetch you. The ancient earl of Kilchurning must arrive afore the snow melts. It will be difficult enough convincing him of the bairn's parentage. Especially if one gets a good look at your sister's bairns."

"My sister does na' have bairns! Ah!" Kendran slammed her fists onto the hard side of the bed in which she lay. It didn't relieve the frustration. All it did was make the sides of her hands thump with pain.

"She will."

"Will you cease taunting me! This is all your fault!"

"Mine?" Sybil asked, and then she clicked her tongue several times.

The hands might as well still be rubbing, still kneading the potion into her back, but something was different. The peaceful, calming sensation was gone, changed into one charged with anger, action, and intent. Kendran's skin started itching with it. Her heart started hammering with something besides ache and pain, as well.

"It was your potion," Kendran bit out.

"It was no potion; a bit of herbs suspended in oil. That's all."

"I would na' have done it without the potion!"

Sybil giggled again.

"And you can cease your laughter. You cause havoc and then laugh?"

"Me? You were the one who ran. I warned you of the

trouble that would ensue if you ran. Did you listen? Nay. You never listen."

"And so you sent the potion, guaranteeing my trouble so you could be right and toss it in my face?"

"The oil contained no savory, Kendran. It contained linden flower and a bit of comfrey. Nothing more."

"'Twas savory. I smelled it. I know. I was there."

"Ah . . . the mind. It puts into play that which does na' exist. That is another bit of knowledge I'd heard, but dinna' understand."

"And you put into play words and things that dinna' exist! I dinna' carry a bairn, there's nae need of hastening my bridegroom to the altar, and aside from a bit of discomfort, I can put it all behind me."

"That man takes your innocence and makes you a woman. You call it discomfort? Strange."

"Let me up. Now."

"Better," Sybil replied.

"What?"

"You've the sound of Kendran again. You'll na' run?"

"From what? To where? You speak riddles and taunts until I yearn to scream!"

"Most of which you owe to my honey-hop brew."

"What?"

"Your voice. You have it back. Na' quite as strong, but back."

Kendran's eyes widened fully. It was true. She hadn't even noticed it. "You're a witch, Sybil. You'll be burned as one, yet."

"I'm naught. A youngling. A bastard. A waif. Nothing special."

Kendran pushed herself into a sitting position. Nothing

on her body ached. That was strange as well. "And I am a Middlemass elf," she returned.

Sybil giggled again. "You'd best prepare. You've a banquet to attend."

"Oh, yes. My sister's banquet. Has her groom arrived, then?"

"Aye. The day afore you . . . were caught."

There was a distinct pause between the words. Kendran went to her feet, wobbled for a moment, and then strengthened. "So. He actually came?"

"Aye."

"And he agreed to this union?"

Sybil smiled softly. "Again, aye."

"Even after he met with her?"

"And even without the dozen swordsmen your father was readied to put into use should he balk. Aye, the groom came. The Donal heir. He came. He matches his reputation, too."

"What? Mad? Cowed? Ready to be abused by a woman's tongue?"

"Nay. Large. Handsome. Strong. Brave. Filled with a sense of duty. And honor. And self-sacrifice."

"Nonsense. Nae man can be such a thing."

"Your sister detests him."

"So? She detests all men. As do I," Kendran finished, almost as an afterthought.

"Do you now?"

She didn't give that an answer. Sybil was already holding all the answers she needed. Kendran simply shrugged.

"I dinna' believe he's desirous of the union. His sense of duty and honor are what forces him."

"He still agreed, dinna' he?" Kendran asked.

"Aye. And paid. With gold coin. Enough to bow a

man with the weight. Except na' this man. He's as strong as he looks."

"So?" Kendran said again.

"And his name . . . is Myles," Sybil replied, so softly, it might as well have been whispered.

That's when Kendran got her first thud of the pain her heart was capable of feeling. Nothing Father could do compared. Nothing.

So. Her sister was to marry him. And he'd agreed. He'd taken Kendran's innocence and her love, knowing all along it was never to be, and then he'd come to fetch his bride. Kendran readied herself for the banquet with a skill and steady hand she didn't know she possessed. It was easier the more time that passed. She just put all her emotions as far down into her soul as they'd go, and then she walled them in there. Nothing was getting out. Nothing was getting in.

And birth a child of his? She'd rather die. She would die.

Aside from which, Lady Sybil could be wrong. She'd been wrong before. Kendran wasn't carrying a bastard child. She wasn't fetching her groom to prevent the disgrace. She was going to do what she always had done— wait out the old man's death and hope his nephew and heir wouldn't take up the betrothal in his stead. Even if he did, she'd decided long ago that having the man Kenneth Kilchurn as her groom wouldn't be too onerous a chore.

What was she thinking?

Kendran's hands trembled on the final touches to her bliant. She pulled on the twisted lacing, tightening it just beneath her bosom; held her fingers to the spot where a heart used to be; and stopped the instantaneous ache with the pressure of her fingers. Kenneth was a handsome sort. He was fit. He was very strong. He was one of her father's greatest knights. He was an excellent choice for a husband.

But he wasn't Myles.

Damn him! Damn him! Damn him! She'd do anything to banish him from her consciousness, but he wouldn't go! All she had to do was close her eyes, and he was there—taunting, grinning, playing . . . loving.

Kendran pulled in a shaky breath, held it until it burned, and let it go. Mooning for her sister's groom wasn't going to get her through the evening, or the next few sennights. But she didn't know what would.

CHAPTER 15

The aleman was first to go.

If Myles still cared enough to correct the estate, their aleman was changing occupations—that, or leaving. No man serving such a spineless, underaged brew was staying employed. He gulped down the eighth tankard of it, slammed it to the table, watched as several of his soon-to-be clansmen stared, and grimaced back at them. He wasn't stewed. The only thing he was, was filled with liquid. They had to have bite to their drink if they wished to see Myles Magnus Donal deep in his cups. Which would be an improvement to the current state he was in.

"You're a drunkard . . . too?"

The deceptively sweet voice at his right side asked it. Now that voice had an acid bite to it that the ale lacked. They should decipher a way of bottling the venom contained in every softspoken word his betrothed spoke. They'd make a fortune, keep their barren lands, and save his future, as well.

Myles smirked at the trail of his thoughts. She hadn't spoken to him since the meal had been brought to them and he'd discovered that they really did know the proper way to roast meat. He'd ignored her then and she'd hushed. That couldn't last. He turned to her now and slit his eyes. It didn't work. Even looking at her in that fashion didn't make her look enough like Kendran to quirk interest. All it did was make the large knot in his belly twinge as it coiled tighter.

"Too?" he asked.

"Aside from being witless."

His back clenched. He felt it and consciously forced it to relax. Everything she said had a challenge attached to it, and was said in a snide fashion. He hadn't the reason, yet, but she was definitely living up to her reputation. His lips twisted as he fought the smile. Then, he just did it.

"See? Witless."

He shook his head.

"Wondrous. I'm saddled with a drunk and an idiot. Are you spineless as well? Or is that too much to wish for?"

"You wish a spine in your spouse?" he asked.

"Stupid question. All men are spineless, my lord."

"Hmmn." Myles signaled for more of their watered-down mead. He also tore off a chunk of his bread loaf. They'd managed to bake fresh bread, too, he noted, as he scooped out a section of the softness inside. The bakers were staying employed after all.

"A glutton, as well?"

Myles ignored her. She made it easy. It wasn't that she was ugly. She looked too much like Kendran to warrant such a description. She was worth a second look if one hadn't seen her sister first. She had reddish gold hair woven about her head in a braid before falling down the back. The tresses were being caressed by a length of opaque light blue silk, all the way to the small of her back, showing the length of it. That was impressive. As was the wealth of bosom her square-neck bodice was pushing toward the edge where dark blue ribbon was threaded, drawing his glance more than once.

Definitely worth another look. And the talk of her size was just that: talk. Either that, or it hinged on her height. She was a tall woman. She reached his chin. Very few women did. Except Kendran.

Myles groaned and bit savagely on the crust of his bread. It didn't work. Nothing was working. He'd still have to bed the woman at his side. Somehow. He wondered if she'd be insulted over having her face covered during the act itself. He snickered to himself. She'd probably find it more offensive when he tied a gag about her mouth first.

"Do you never speak?"

Myles took his time chewing, swallowing, and enjoying the baker's skill. He might even give that fellow a larger wage for such a thing as fresh bread.

"Why?" he asked, when he'd finished. He didn't turn to look at her as he asked it. He watched the entire room in front of him. They still had it too hot, although it was well past midnight, but the fire had lost some of its heat. It was also dimmer. The others hadn't the same idea of the quality of their mead. He could see revelers lolling about on benches, and some were even beneath tables. If he wasn't mistaken, Squire Beggin's boots were among them.

That wasn't fair. The lad couldn't hold his ale, and the others had started before him.

"Because I might wish to converse with you."

"Why?" Myles asked again. He could also see both entrances to the great room from the one all-encompassing glance. The castle boasted this room at the very center of it, but it was long and narrow, and since they'd seen fit to place him at the farthest end of it, opposite their fireplace, he had a perfect view of the entire room.

And Kendran. When she came. If she came. He almost groaned again.

"You'll be sharing my bed in less than a month, and you ask why? By the saints! You are a simpleton!"

Myles had to force his shoulders not to hunch up to ward off the image. If he had the little waif who'd forced his tongue in front of him, he'd squeeze her throat just for putting the words into his head and forcing them from his lips. Share this harridan's bed? Never.

"If I grace your bed, it will be only long enough to beget an heir. I'll na' share my bed with you."

"Why na'?"

"Because I require women in my bed."

Her quick intake of breath was his reward. Myles couldn't stop the expression as he turned to her and narrowed his eyes again. It didn't work. She still wasn't Kendran.

"And what am I?"

"You dinna' wish to know what I think of you, mistress. I would na' ask it if I were you."

"Why na'?"

"Because it is na' flattering."

She frowned. It didn't improve her. In fact, if she wasn't careful, she was going to have deep grooves carving her face exactly like her mother's in very few years. She hissed something about his base beginnings and turned back to her own goblet of mead.

That was fine with him. She'd been trying to anger him since they'd met. He couldn't fathom why, unless it was to solidify and protect her version of men. He felt a stir of movement on the left, where the staircase led to the chieftain's rooms, and those apartments in which the family lived. He could only hope they were better constructed and less drafty than his were. Kendran deserved it.

"Are you the violent sort?" she asked, surprising him.

Myles turned his head from scanning the room and looked her over. Everything she asked had an intent behind it. He wondered what this one was.

"If I've a use for it," he replied finally.

"There's never a use for violence."

"I never lose on the list, my lady. Never."

"Do you use your fists?"

"If need be," he answered.

"On . . . a woman?"

She cared about the answer. Very much so. Myles shook his head slightly. "I've never hit a woman. I never will."

"Never?"

"Nae woman would survive my blow, Lady Merriam. Dinna' you just hear me? I dinna' lose. Ever. To anyone."

"You just haven't had the proper challenger. Sir Kilchurn could win you. He's also never lost."

"I've little doubt of that if the examples of his challengers are the men in your clan."

"He'd win you, as well."

"As it will na' come to pass, 'tis a moot bit of words. You do that oft."

"What?"

"Overuse words. To incite and inflict. Too bad you do it so . . . *poorly*." He couldn't resist adding emphasis to the last word.

Her eyes widened, her mouth opened, and she

looked close to sputtering. Myles put his finger up to stay her response.

"Remember, my lady. I'm witless. Spineless. A glutton . . . and a drunkard. Your words. Your evaluation. Your mistake."

She was speechless. At least, until she'd regrouped and reevaluated her enemy. That gave him a little time. He used it, swiveling forward in the large oaken chair they'd given him and scanning the room. Again. Ceaselessly. For one woman. Just one. All he needed was a glimpse. Just one.

Then she was there, stepping down onto the landing between the stone archway and just standing there, looking. She had a light behind her, too, highlighting her, and making every eye go there. Myles was no exception.

"Oh, look. My sister has decided to grace us with her presence. I suppose she spent the time in preparation. She rarely leaves. . . ."

The woman at his side said more. He didn't even hear it. There was the sound of a rain-swollen burn rushing through his ears, and it felt like the top of his head wanted to fly off. And through all of it he felt the coil in his belly twinging, tightening, squeezing. . . .

Kendran moved her gaze to him, and then everything went still. Myles no longer saw or felt anything as time suspended; ache and worry and finality faded away, leaving only irrepressible joy in its wake. The room may have been dim, the light behind her may have been in his mind, and the steam of too many bodies packed into the space may have muted everything, but it was as naught. Nothing meant as much to him as the way her mouth parted, allowing breath; the way her eyes opened just slightly, showing the soft blue he loved so much, that was so unlike the harsh, frozen shade of his betrothed's; the quick way she took each breath. Then she blinked and turned her face away, shutting him out so completely it might as well have been a door shutting.

Reality intruded, sending the steam back into his nostrils, the din of the room back into his ears, and showing the lack of illumination the room actually possessed. It made it difficult to see where she disappeared to as she walked down the final two steps and into the crowd. He lost sight of her, and with it the ability to breathe. The pressure in his belly was coloring everything with a dull haze of red. It wasn't the angry shade he'd envisioned earlier. It was more like loss . . . blood loss.

"My sister. Always one for an entrance."

"What?" Myles cocked his head. He didn't move his eyes. He was still searching for her. She was wearing a wimple of pale tan, sheathing the hair he'd have known instantly. It shouldn't be difficult to spot, yet it was.

"She fancies herself a beauty. Spends hours whiling away time at her mirror watching herself. I can see you noticed."

"Whom?" Myles replied.

"Kendran. My little sister. That was the woman you just saw and stared openmouthed at."

"Oh." The word sounded like a groan. It wasn't meant that way. It was due to the dryness in his mouth. It had gone parched. Dust dry. As was his throat. Too dry to swallow, although he tried.

"Must you?" His betrothed asked.

"What?" Myles probably did sound like a simpleton, if not look it. He was straining to find her. How could she disappear so easily?

"Act love besotted the moment you see her?"

"Besotted?" Myles closed his eyes; pushed the ache into the depths of his bowels, where everything was rumbling and hating him; and forced himself to sit until he reached the back of his chair. He had to use his chest to assist. The heavy arms of his chair were well constructed from sturdy wood, and the chair only moved a fraction before holding the motion as he gripped with each fist and shoved. Then he was pushing until the thick knots of wood carved at the chair's back felt like they were imprinted into his spine before being satisfied. His betrothed didn't know the meaning of the word *besotted,* but she was very accurate. He was exactly that—exactly.

"With her. Everyone she meets falls over himself for a glimpse of her. Everyone. Why should my own husband to be behave any different? Look there? She's speaking with Sir Kilchurn. Apt."

The wood in each fist creaked and groaned, then warped as it came unfastened from the dowels that had seated the arms. Myles used it to temper the reaction and knew the harpy at his side was watching. He hadn't known jealousy felt this way! He hadn't known the ache and the anger and the frustration and the rage. And he had to hide all of it?

Sweat droplets broke out all along his forehead and still he fought it. Someone should have warned him about this! Or they should have brewed stronger mead! Or he should have done a thousand things differently, such as not being born the Donal heir, nor getting lost in a blizzom, and especially not falling so heavily for a woman he wasn't destined for.

His arms lifted, taking the carved, wooden ends with them, while the chair arms swayed uselessly downward to each side.

"It's a good thing you're not a violent type."

She had such a snide way of saying everything. Myles turned to her, blinked the stinging salt out of his eyes, and gave her the same expression she was giving him: a sneer.

"We've na' got enough chairs," she finished.

"What makes you say that?" he asked.

"That is my father's favorite chair."

"So?" He wiped a forearm across his brow and then looked at the object in his hands. They'd carved a lion's paw into the ends of their chair arms. It had weakened the wood, and it looked even more insubstantial in the palm of his hand. Myles stared down at it in surprise. He hadn't even felt it. None of it.

Kendran tripped over a man's boot, caught herself before the stumble showed, and wondered how she was supposed to keep command of her breathing, her motion, and her senses if Myles was anywhere in the room. It was impossible for a man to look so wondrous, and yet there he was—in the flesh! Presiding over the assemblage like he belonged there, and making everyone else look insignificant and plain.

Even Kenneth.

Sir Kenneth Kilchurn was a brawny man, striking, with a wealth of sandy-colored hair and blue eyes. He was a bit of a flirt, a wonder with animals, and he was a terror in battle. All of which made him an excellent candidate for husband, if his uncle would do them the favor of expiring. And if she'd never met Myles.

"Lady Kendran?"

It was Sir Kenneth. He was clad in a doublet of dark blue, atop a kilt of Eschoncan blue; his hair was neatly slicked back; and he'd even made an effort to scrape the whiskers from his face. All in all, he should be setting her pulses afire, not making everything go cold.

"Sir?"

He escorted her over to a stool and gestured for a trencher to be filled for her. Kendran wasn't hungry. She didn't think she'd be able to swallow. Her body felt tied in knots and everything was trembling. And why? Because there was the most handsome man she'd ever seen glowering down from his place atop the dais. That's why.

And Merriam was with him, putting her hand atop his knee for a moment, grazing her shoulder against his, smiling with him. Kendran ground her teeth, squelched the reaction, and felt her throat twinge again. She'd barely got some voice back. She wasn't going to waste it. Not on him. He deserved Merriam. He deserved her screeches, her snide words, her spite-filled looks.

Kendran watched the sup that was set before her turn into a wash of green and brown and putrid grayish tan. She didn't dare blink. It wasn't that she was crying—never! It was the smells in the room. They were making her eyes water. That was it. Mother should have seen the rushes swept out and new ones placed before she started the fest. They should have taken a few buckets of snowmelt, mixed it with boiled fat, and scrubbed at the floor before they started serving food. They shouldn't have used so much wood in the fireplace, creating an inferno of heat that wasn't necessary. They'd have been better served lighting all the torches scattered high on the walls, rather than making such a huge fire that it created a sweltering heat filled with such noxious fumes. They should have opened the large double doors earlier, to let in frost-filled air to put a damper on the moist heat all about her. They should have started the dancing already, rather than wait until everyone was falling down drunk, or too filled to enjoy it. Kendran watched with the blurred product of tear-filled eyes as tables were shoved to the walls, their passage pulling the majority of snoring and stewed revelers with them. They should have done a thousand things different.

Starting with keeping that man from betrothing Merriam.

Kendran looked down at her sup and blinked rapidly until her vision cleared. It didn't help. She wasn't hungry, and the sup he'd gathered for her was unappetizing. They'd filled a hollowed-out bread loaf cavity with a mixture of meat, vegetables, and gravy, creating a stew that if she were hungry, and it wasn't hours old, would probably be tempting her palate, instead of making her belly churn. She handed it to a passing serf when Kenneth went to check on the minstrels.

Father had hired them over a fortnight ago, and he'd been feeding them, and keeping a roof over their head—although it was a loft in the stables, it was still warm—and they hadn't much to do for such bounty, save strum on their lyres and lift their voices together. Both of which they did terribly.

She grimaced as the first strains started up. They'd be hard put to dance to anything this trio produced. She wondered what Myles thought and immediately cursed the fates that always brought him directly into her thoughts, into her sight, into her hearing . . . into her sphere. And then, he was right in front of her, stalling everything into insignificance.

"I've claimed a dance, fairest maid," he commented,

with the deep voice she hadn't managed to banish from her recollection, either.

"I—"

He didn't let her finish. He didn't let her say yea or nay. He didn't allow for more than keeping step at his side as he led her toward the front of the great hall, which, now that it was dimmed, and the tables had cleared, looked less like a wreck of a celebratory banquet, and more like a fitted-stone floor readied for dancing. Kendran wouldn't have been able to get her voice to finish, anyway. The first touch of his fingers on hers had silenced her with the trembling he had attached to them, and he wasn't disguising it very well.

They weren't the lone couple on the floor. And the dance steps wouldn't keep them near each other, save every eighth note, which was slow in coming, and when it did sound was sadly out of tune, but it was magical at the same time. Mystical. Heavenly. Soul stirring.

It had been since the first time she'd set eyes on him. And nothing was changing it. He was whispering something the third time their palms matched, her right to his left, finger to finger, flesh to flesh. The very first time, the spot had ignited, swelled, taken over her body. Kendran had moved her hand to her cheek the moment he had turned from her. And seven notes later, he was back. This time he lifted his right hand palm outward to her left, only now he was using his thumb, holding for an infinitesimal amount of time before releasing her again.

Kendran's breath caught. Her heart leaped. Everything pulsed. She was very afraid she was glowing.

The third time he whispered something, nearly inaudible. Kendran tried to decipher it from the movement of his lips but failed. She had to form the question the next time. That time the hand touching hers shook, making it difficult to press her palm to his even for the length of the note. Kendran blushed. Despite everything she and this man had shared, she blushed. She was only grateful it was very dim, the watchers at each side were bleary-eyed and decimated, and the other dancers about them wobbled more than they swayed.

"Balcony!" The hissed word was clearly whispered the next time. It was still senseless. Kendran had to mouth the question again when next he neared.

"Well?" This time he sounded frustrated and angry. Now he was angry? Kendran didn't have time to answer, and seven more notes later he was back.

"Have you a balcony or na'?"

He stayed with her long enough to ask the entire question, causing a lurch in the line of dancers, one of whom stumbled before ending up in a riot of laughter against another partner.

Kendran nodded. Then, she was chiding herself for idiocy, lunacy, and stupidity. She knew very well what he wanted to know that information for. He wanted to see if she had access. She longed to hit herself for allowing such a thing.

"I must see you!" The next sentence was said in a quick fashion, and he gave himself enough time since he'd stepped closer before the dance warranted it, and lingered a moment longer, as well.

Kendran shook her head. He wasn't looking. He was moving around an unsteady gent before being set upon by a pushy woman who looked like she couldn't put much more of her frame against Myles and have it still be considered dancing. Three more notes and he was back.

"Well?"

Doubt clogged her throat. She'd never seen anything

as stirring as the way he looked at her, boring right into her very soul. She gulped it away and turned before she could do what her whole body felt like it was longing for. *Say yes, Kendran. Yes. Yes.*

The next time he was in front of her, he had his jaw clenched, defining the line of it, and then he was sending a large amount of air through her wimple that had a slight shade of groan attached to it. She was never going to hold out for another meeting of their palms. She was afire with the sensation and each time it was getting worse. Her legs felt like twigs bowing in the wind, her thighs were worse than melting candle tallow, and everything on her was pounding with a rhythm the minstrels couldn't seem to find.

"The morrow!" He had the word whispered right into her ear, since he'd gripped her fingers with his and pulled her so closely it had to attract notice. And then he was moving away again, finding himself swiveling around another lady he was ignoring since his gaze was still locked with Kendran's as the song ended. She couldn't move her eyes. The music stopped, the last note dying into somewhere above her, and all she seemed capable of doing was standing, struck immobile by devil-dark eyes.

CHAPTER 16

"Come, Squire Beggin! Time's awasting. I need that drawing."

"In . . . a bit."

The lad was huffing and panting between the words. Myles grinned further.

"A bit? 'Tis what you said na' an hour hence! Now. I've a hankering to begin work on this heap of stones. I'll na' be able to do so without a drawing of each floor, door, and roof joist. You said you could do it."

"Can . . . you na' . . . give a body . . . rest . . . first?"

"Rest? Ha! 'Twas na' you taking challengers, and showing who has the strongest sword arm! Rest? Save it for when you've a bit of a battle beneath you! And for that, you'll need a mite more practice."

"Prac . . . tice?" The lad split it into two words since he was still huffing for breath. And all they'd done was run every set of steps a dozen times at least. The lad acted like it was he who was meeting five of the Eschon Honor Guards and annihilating them so they couldn't heft their weapons to carry them from the stable when he'd finished with them, as Myles had

done just this morn. Since Kenneth had been put onto
an errand and wasn't available, Myles had started with
one of their strongest, and then he'd taken on one after
the other until they'd shaken their heads and refused
another pounding he was ready, willing, and capable
of giving. It was exhilarating. It was exciting. It was
strengthening and rousing and enough to feel as if a
thousand needles were pricking at him, barely making
contact with the skin and yet enough to make everything on his body itch. And it was almost enough to
make him forget that he had a nighttime assignation to
attempt with the woman he obsessed so over that he
couldn't think. For that he was going to need a drawing of the castle's layout, and a good scope of the entire
perimeter, and a good knowledge of where each staircase led and where the weaknesses were in them.

And the lad thought him exercising?

There was no help for it. Since he'd awakened, he'd
been on the move; keeping his heartbeat paced to the
thump of anticipation that was soaring through his
soul, bringing her closer with each and every one.

He'd worked up such a sweat by midday that he'd had
to follow up his exhibition in the yard with a brief dip,
breaking through ice until he couldn't stand it any
longer. Then, he'd retreated. Grateful. Refreshed. Alive.
And as a bonus, he'd also been out of listening distance
of the lad's ceaseless words of complaint; primarily
over the temperature and over the weight of Myles's
sword, and how was a young lad to carry such a thing
when it weighed almost as much as he did? Myles
thought him very amusing. He still wasn't budging.
The lad wanted to be a decent squire for a knight? So
be it. He was behind on his training. There was nothing
for it, but to double it.

The rhythm of anticipation had started up again the moment he'd pushed himself out of the water, rubbing at the ice that was trying to form on his body with rough motions of his plaide. It was still there when they reached the castle. It was the driving force behind his steps as he ran the stairs, going over so many of them that he'd ceased counting, and it was the thumping rhythm of the blood singing through his ears.

He knew exactly what it was. He was in love. And it was wondrous!

"When you've finished resting, see me a tray fetched. And a tankard of the brine that these fools call ale! Go, Beggin! See to it."

The lad's shoulders slumped. Myles almost felt sorry for him. Almost. He had to rid himself of the lad long enough to get a good view of the outside of the castle. Where the family resided. He had to see Kendran. He had to get her to understand. He had to tell her. He'd thought it was Kendran he was betrothed to, not her sister. He hadn't even known she had an older sister! He had to see her. He had to hold her.

He didn't want anything more. Just to hold her.

The outer walls of Castle Eschoncan had a better look to them than the inside, although that wasn't devining much. The rocks they'd used for construction hadn't the wear and dilapidated appearance of the interior woods and tapestries. That was to be expected. As long as they'd fitted them closely and hadn't used mud-based mortar in the construction, it might be more feasible to gut the interior and start anew, rather than pound the walls to the ground.

That was a forlorn idea. They'd used mud mixed with straw. It was cracked and missing in places altogether, even in the balconies, which he knew counted to four on each side. He had eight chances, then. One was the right one. One also had a hole large enough to fall through it near the edge. All told, the state of the castle was going to be very beneficial to him. Especially if there wasn't any moon, and the frost coating would make every grip precarious. Every little chink and opening in the rock face made a toehold and fingerhold for a man bent on accessing a woman. Despite the lack of tree cover all about the castle's perimeter, there was a wealth of leverage spots for any maneuver. It was going to be child's play.

For him. Not for Beggin. That lad was collapsed on the stairs, right outside of Myles's rooms, and he was snoring. There also was no platter of food in sight. Myles did the same thing he'd done last night immediately after finishing the dance with Kendran. He picked the boy up, tossed him across his shoulder, and hauled him into the drafty rooms given to him. Then, he went looking for his own meal.

She wasn't going to allow him in. He had no right to request such a thing of her, and she had no right to even *think* about allowing it! None! Kendran finished combing through her hair; checked and then rechecked the buttons leading up the placket of her voluminous, and very concealing, and very warm woven flax and wool nightgown; and wondered what was keeping him.

She hadn't latched the large door leading to her balcony. Just in case he really did try to climb to her and actually made it. She didn't want him rousing any of the guards with the pounding he'd undoubtedly do. It was also bitterly cold outside. She knew. She'd checked.

More times than she could count on both hands. Still, he hadn't come.

It was also icy, with frost crystals coating every surface. And there was a dense fog shrouding everything outside her balcony. It wasn't even a real balcony. There weren't any stairs leading to it. She was too high. And on the top floor, the ledges outside were called oriels. Only a fool would try to access her by climbing to one. And Myles didn't know which one. He couldn't know . . . and he couldn't possibly be foolish enough to attempt a winter night climb! It was too dangerous. It was insanity. It was brave. It was chivalrous.

Kendran caught her breath again at a sound outside the balcony door, went to check it, and then even went so far as to look out over the sides before slinking back to her chamber. Even that small contact made her stocking-clad feet cringe from the cold, and then she slid, banging a thigh against the door handle, showing how slippery it was, and everywhere she touched came away with frost coating it.

He couldn't do anything so foolish! He couldn't! And if he did, he wouldn't have told anyone, so if he slid and fell, there would be no one to hear him. None would even know. None would attempt a rescue, because they wouldn't know. Kendran's mirror reflected the worry in her eyes right back at her.

She had no choice but to give it up, and she eyed the bed next. They'd built a fire in her grate earlier, just enough to dent the chill. It was down to coals now, flickering and giving out very little light. That's why she still had the candles lit, deep into the night, when she should already be asleep, and thinking of no more than the upcoming Yule season. That's what she should be doing!

He had no right to disrupt her sleep this way, either! Why, he'd made her wait until any soothing heat of her warming pan had long dissipated, meaning her sheets were going to be so cold she'd have to wait out the warmth that would come from her own shivering. Eventually. Maybe. She might have to get another quilt. Maybe even a heavy fur. That's what Myles Magnus Donal had done to her! And wait up for him? She'd been mad.

Kendran settled the tin onto the wicks, dimming the candles one by one, until only the fire coals were left for light. That was all right with her. She knew every speck of her room and loved every bit of it. It was an easy matter to leap from fur rug to wool, back to fur, and from thence to wool again, in order to keep from any contact with the chill of the floor until she reached her own bed. That structure was made of white ash and carved with great skill by an ancestor until it looked like a fairy forest of trees and vines and leaves. The carver had then entwined them all about the headboard and each foot post, meeting them all together at each post top to form the canopy above. Kendran hid the smile, the same as she always did when climbing between the ice-cold sheets. It just gave her so much satisfaction to own this particular bed.

Merriam had so wanted this bed for her own. Unfortunately, it had been assembled in the tower room more than a century before and no one wanted to risk destroying it by dismantling it. And Merriam wouldn't give up her own suite of rooms far below in order to possess it. That one had too much pride.

There was a sound at her door. Kendran looked up from pulling the folded quilt from the footboard and then she gaped. The door wasn't being knocked on. It wasn't even attempted. It was flying wide open, bouncing against the rock wall on its side and returning to slam back on the man who had swung through it and was standing brushing the snow from himself. He actually had the audacity to look well satisfied with the act.

At least that's what his wide grin must mean.

"Hush!" Her cry was loud in the abrupt stillness that followed his entrance. Then, there was a distinct groan just before the door finished a final sway, shook, and fell with another resounding boom right next to him.

"Blast and damn this entire heap of rock! I'll see it ground to dust! I vow it! Why—"

"Nae! Hush!" Kendran was at his side, her hand already on his mouth to halt any further angered male words that sounded very definitely male, and very definitely angry. Neither of which—angered males or angry words—were supposed to be in her chamber in the dead of night.

And then he kissed the palm against his lips. Kendran's gasp didn't make much sound, since he followed the instant jerk she'd made to remove her palm by gripping her to him, taking her completely off the floor and making certain she knew exactly who it was and exactly what he wanted as he took her mouth with his, imprinted his ownership, and turned everything into trembling female. He had an immense amount of material wrapped about himself, making it difficult to feel any part of him, no matter how she snaked her arms about him. She was forced to give it up and used them instead to pinion him in place, so she could return the kiss. She was drowning and he was air. She was sinking and he gave her wings. She was dry, parched, thirsty . . . and he was water. Kendran locked her arms about his neck, breathed exactly with him, and returned the kiss with as much fervor as he was giving it. Kendran knew the moan came from her own throat. There wasn't anything coming from him except grunting sounds—satisfied grunting sounds.

And then there came the sound of heavy pounding against her bolted entry door.

"My lady?"

Kendran didn't really hear the title. The door was too thick, the rock walls too stout, and the amount of air she was still sucking in was obliterating it, but she knew what it was. She also knew they hadn't much time before someone would investigate.

Myles groaned the moment she pulled away, and she hushed him with her lips against his cheek. "I must answer that," she whispered.

"I . . . ken."

He might say it, but he wasn't acting it. Kendran realized it as nothing about the hard arms holding her aloft changed, and nothing about the lips sucking along her jaw before reaching an ear stopped. He was creating shivers of heat that directly clashed with the tremors from the frigid temperature he'd allowed in, and the combination of them was seeking out every part of her that didn't match against him. It was intoxicating . . . heat and ice . . . fire—

There was another loud boom at her door, followed by three or four knocks.

"Lady Kendran?"

It wasn't one of the serfs. It was a guardsman, perhaps more than one. Kendran yanked her head back and glared at Myles. "I have to speak with them!"

"I ken that as well." He was returning her whisper, and then he started the litany of curse words in exactly the same sequence that he always seemed to use. She was back on her feet and freed, though.

The floor had never felt as insubstantial, nor as cold. She caught her breath with the shock of it. If there were such a thing as a frost-covered cloud, she was standing on it. Then, she was walking across it.

"My lady?" They were louder.

"Aye?" She hadn't much voice, but she put all of it into the word.

"We heard a noise."

Kendran was at the door, then she was looking over her shoulder at the wreckage of wood scattered near her oriel, and then she was openmouthed at the man who was tossing clothing aside and dropping it on the broken door as if the temperature wasn't freezing, and there wasn't a contingency of men at her door, probably getting ready to break through it.

"I . . . fell," she told the door. She had to say it loudly enough to be a yell, and behind her she heard the snort of reaction from Myles.

"Fell? Shall we fetch Lady Sybil?"

"Nay! 'Twas a bad dream. 'Twas naught."

"A bad dream?"

A hard, bare arm reached about her from behind, lifting her effortlessly from the floor and holding her against him. Kendran couldn't answer for a moment. She could barely function. The man was mad. He'd ruined her oriel entrance, stolen all the heat from the chamber, caused such a ruckus they were in danger of being discovered, and then he was starting such a throb of ache and want within her she couldn't think. He wasn't even supposed to be here! She wasn't allowing it! She had yet to berate him over it, and he was stealing her wits and her tongue as well.

"I do . . . have them! Now go. Leave me!" She said it in her haughtiest voice, rivaling Merriam's for stridency, and felt the reaction in the man holding her as their combined weights moved. He'd better not be laughing. If he was laughing at her, she was giving him an earful; the moment the guards left and he put her back down, but not one bit later than that.

And then the tip of his tongue touched her ear before going down her neck, while he was lifting the hair out of his way in order to reach farther.

Kendran barely kept from squealing aloud as the firelike trail he was leaving turned to such ice there wasn't any way to prevent the instantaneous shaking, thrilling, and race of reaction right to her nipples, which hadn't any way of staying hidden, since he'd pulled the material taut about her. One of his hands was unerringly there, kneading, rubbing, stealing her sanity, her will, and every bit of her anger.

"Nae!" She tried to hiss it, but it sounded more like a moan.

His answer was a chuckle, sending more warm air onto the surface he'd just licked, and that just caused more riotous shivers, and more response, and more angry sensation to the tip of her breast in his hand.

"Oh, Kendran . . . sweet. I dinna' come here to make love to you. I dinna'. I canna' . . ."

His words were accompanied by more movement as he spread his hand wide across the surface of her lower belly and used that grip to lift her against him, holding her buttocks to his heat, strength, and bulk.

"Myles. Nay."

"I ken that as well . . . sweet. I do."

He might be agreeing with her, but nothing on his body was obeying.

"You canna' be here," Kendran whispered.

"Nae?"

"I canna' allow it. . . ."

This time his reply came with a grunt of amusement attached to it.

"You shouldn't have climbed, either. It was too . . . dangerous." She wasn't doing a very good job berating him. Her voice had too much depth, whisper, and moan accompanying it. It was his fault, too! He was moving them in a slow, swaying fashion, toward her bed. There was one thing the winter air he'd allowed entrance in had done. It had stirred the coals in her fireplace, making it easier to see. The white ash bed loomed large, the sheets already tantalizingly turned down . . . warm . . . clean . . . readied.

That should have made it easier to stop him. Or, at least, made it easier to say the words.

"I dinna' climb here."

He said words. It took a moment for the comprehension of them. "But—" she began. He interrupted her.

"'Twas too slick. Just . . . as you say." His voice had the same catch in it, the same low roar she'd always heard, and it hit such a chord deep within her that Kendran arched back against him, making it easier to move.

"Then . . . how . . . ?" she murmured it and felt his shudder of reaction.

"Rope."

"Rope?" she echoed.

"Aye . . . attached to the battlements. 'Twas simple, except it was worse slick. I had na' counted on that."

"Slick?" That was the exact description of how it felt to slide forward from him when they reached the mattress, arching her back so she stayed in contact with him where it was so hot it was defying the elements.

"I dinna' break down . . . doors as . . . a normal occurrence. I fell."

Myles was having a hard time speaking. She knew the reason. He wasn't the one holding her buttocks in place; she was, although she had to go to the tips of her toes in order to do it. The arch she was in was even more agitating to him, if his words were any indication.

"I dinna' come . . . here for this . . . sweet. Ah! Sweet!"

And then he was assisting her, holding her down against shockingly cold linens, with a hand that wasn't so much pressuring as it was massaging, caressing, covering—and making everything warmer than it could possibly be.

"I came . . . to tell you. To beg of you—"

"Tell me?"

Kendran leveraged herself by planting her forehead on the mattress, in order to reach both hands behind them, to his kilt-covered hips, in order to hold him exactly where she needed, so she could gyrate back and forth. Back. Forth.

"Jesu' . . . Kendran! Cease! I canna' think! I canna' . . . ."

His voice dribbled off, leaving her wondering what the rest of it would have been. He was shuddering, too, making it difficult to keep any kind of contact where she most wanted it. And then he was shoving himself away, by placing both hands on her waist and heaving himself backward.

Instant cold blasted her thighs, backside, and lower back, making shivers that were harsh enough her back clenched with the power of each twinge. She swiveled, sliding up and onto the bed, pulling the coverlet over herself. And then she was blowing a fog-filled breath into existence through lips that chattered.

Myles was standing, silhouetted in the firelight, with both hands to the sides of his head, holding back his hair, while he scrunched his face into a grimace. And he was shaking. So much so it was difficult to tell which was a firelight flicker and which was emotion.

"We have to cease! I canna' abide the torment much longer! You dinna' understand!"

"I do," she mumbled.

That had him cracking his eyes open. "Oh, love. I dinna' come here to ravish you. I canna'. I will na'! Nae matter how much I long to! I canna'!"

"Why did you come, then?"

He heaved a sigh, moved both hands to his hips, and cocked his head. With that move came a waterfall of loose black hair, falling about his face, shielding whatever expression he had. He tossed it back, glared at her, and filled his chest with air. "To explain. To beg forgiveness. To worship."

"Wor . . . ship?"

He cleared his throat. Took another deep breath. And spoke, although he stuttered the first word. "I-I-I love you, lass. Only you. Kendran. Forever."

Kendran gasped, put both her hands to her breast to hold the emotion in, and then just let it fill her. "You . . . love me?"

He grinned. It was cold enough there was white vapor coming off every bit of him, and he was creating more of it with every breath he exhaled. It didn't seem to affect him. He was still grinning.

"Aye. With a rightness to it that defies this future I have encased myself with. It makes one weak when one needs to be most strong. I will na' take you now, my love. Na' that I dinna' wish to. My entire form is angered at me over the denial. I will na' take you because

I canna'. You are na' mine. I should na' have touched you at all. It's just——. It's hard. Almost too hard to fight."

"I dinna' understand."

"And I explain poorly. I love you. I took you because of that. I took your innocence because I thought you were she."

"She?"

"My betrothed. I dinna' lie to you then. I wanted you. I still want you! But I want to be wed with you. Na' her! You!"

"But it's Merriam you've trothed."

"And it was a shock, I tell you."

"What was?"

"That it was na' you."

"You thought I was . . . Merriam?"

He nodded. "I dinna' wish to wed with you. I mean, her. I dinna'. Why do you ken I left her sitting on a shelf for so many years? I fought it. With everything I had. You saw the results. You tended to some of them."

"Your bruising?"

He nodded again. "And it was all for naught. I lost. I never lose! But over this, I lost. And then I met you. I was in heaven. You dinna' understand. I thought you were her. I mean, she was you. You ken? I would never have taken you if I hadn't thought you were her. My betrothed. The harridan."

"You thought I was a harridan?" Her voice was rising.

Myles's head lifted and he blew out another huff of white-shaded air. "Being in love and stating such must give one a thick tongue. I would never have called you a harridan."

"You just did."

"I said I thought you were my betrothed, the harridan. I thought it was all just tales spread about the glens about you. I dinna' know you had a sister. An older sister. Why dinna' you tell me?"

"Why would I? I dinna' ken you were The Donal. Why dinna' you say something?"

"What? And ruin the surprise?" His grin faded. "It was a surprise, all right. All of this is. What am I to do, Kendran?" And then he moved, sitting right on the bed next to her, sinking the spot with his weight, while he lifted one of her hands with both of his. He was matching his palm against hers, like the dance had been, only better, and then he was lacing his fingers through hers in a handhold she helped him achieve. He sighed heavily when he was finished and looked at their joined hands.

"I've made a pit for myself that I canna' see out of. She truly is a harridan. Truly. What am I to do?"

"What you pledged to do, of course." She didn't know how she got the words to come out of her own mouth.

"Why should I? I dinna' wish marriage to her! And she does na' wish marriage to me! She hates me!"

"How do you ken that?"

"She's already told me of it. At least six, nay, seven times. She is worse than a harridan! She's a banshee."

"She's unhappy."

"Well, she's na' the lone one. What am I to do?"

"Myles?" Kendran waited until he moved his glance from the hand he was now gripping into a bloodless state and looked across at her. She reached over and smoothed a lock of black hair from his forehead and grazed his cheek with her fingers as she moved away. "It is na' what are *you* to do. It's what are *we* to do. You ken?"

He lowered his jaw just slightly, giving the firelight

a bit of moisture to glint from off the surface of his lash-shaded eyes.

"You are na' in this alone," she whispered.

"I'm na'?"

She shook her head.

"Why na'?"

"Because love just works that way."

"Love?"

"Aye. Love. Mine. For you."

Kendran leaned over and touched her lips to one of his fingers twined with hers. If she lived to be a hundred, she doubted she'd ever see such a beauteous expression as the one he was giving her.

CHAPTER 17

The weather took a turn for the better, letting the sun warm through for a span of nearly a sennight and turning the grounds into a soup of mud-encased slog. It also made it possible for the menfolk to issue warlike challenges to each other as they took to a higher section of the stable yard, since the land beyond the walls known as the list was still iced over and maintaining footing out there was treacherous. This way they could daily pummel each other into mud-covered masses of bruises. The laird wasn't allowing swordplay. But all got their choice of mallets and poles and shields. The laird even required everyone to attend the impromptu festivities, which were showcasing Merriam's betrothed, Myles, and his superior abilities at warfare. Kendran made up excuse after excuse until even Mother looked askance at her to avoid it. Then, she had to attend, too.

She had to admit, after the third Eschoncan knight Myles took on in what ended with hand-to-hand combat, that he was impressive. Even streaked with mud, filth, blood, and grinning through all of the muck once he was declared the victor—again—he was still impressive. Most. She couldn't understand how this was the same man.

This Myles could move about like a dancer, swinging his pole, hitting with his hand-ax mallet, and swiveling with such grace and power she wasn't the only lady panting and openmouthed just from watching him. And yet, he was the same man who couldn't seem to come through a door to see her without breaking it from its moorings? The same who fell through shuttered windows? The same who couldn't hit a pan with pitched broad beans? It didn't seem possible.

He'd been avoiding her. Daily. Minutely. Every pounding of her heart kept telling her of it and seemed to make all of it worse. That was stupid. She didn't *want* him noticing her! She didn't! She wanted him out of her mind and out of her life—but most of all she wanted him out of her heart.

Myles finished with another challenger, making that his fourth. He was bowing to all the cheering and clapping, and then he was planting his long stick into the ground like it wasn't frozen underneath or any kind of an obstacle. Kendran watched the sway of the wooden stick. She watched the way The Donal pitched his shield to one side. She ordered her eyes to move, her hands to unhinge themselves from each other, told her entire frame to cease aching, and she failed at all of it.

"Merriam has done well. Wouldn't you agree?"

Kendran caught her instant reaction to Lady Sybil's slight breath of words, since she was speaking in a whisper just for Kendran's ear. She failed at that, too, as her heart lurched fully and painfully within her breast.

"In . . . what way?" she answered finally.

"She has the tongue of a viper, detests the very ground any man stands on, and has all the warmth of a dull winter day. Yet still she managed to gain herself that one, the Donal heir for a husband? Quite impressive, nae?"

Kendran swallowed around the lump that was probably withheld tears. She dabbed at her nose with a corner of her embroidered handkerchief, since a head sickness had been her latest excuse not to attend, and she waited for her heart to cease pumping the hurt through her at Sybil's words. It was probably her own fault, too. She'd not taken the place to Merriam's left, where a long bench had been put for the laird's immediate family to use. That bench was being kept warm by fire-heated rocks that servants kept placing in a long pan beneath it. The bench was covered with velvet, horsehair-stuffed cushions, too. It was also beneath a jut of roofline that protected it from the elements. All of which Kendran was foregoing in order to sit as far from Merriam as possible.

It was the lone way she could survive watching him. And knowing he was never going to be hers. Ever. It wasn't her fate . . . and she knew what was.

Her hands clenched on the handkerchief, hard. It wasn't as noticeable as it could have been, since her fingers were already white from the cold. That was a payment of sitting so far from the family dais. And from any proximity to Father, who hadn't ceased mouthing his enjoyment and appreciation of his soon-to-be-acquired son-by-law; or Merriam, who seemed to do naught save frown and complain; or Mother, who, from time to time, gave acidic comments about the idiocy of menfolk and their games. All of which would have been intolerable and given her an ache in her head to rival the one burning deep in her breast.

It hadn't been difficult to gain absence from their

dais. All she'd had to do was mention her illness and she'd been banished far enough down the benches none should have noticed her. Except Sybil.

Kendran sighed and tipped her head slightly toward her half sister. They were on the end of a long, unpadded and unwarmed bench, protected only by the setts wrapped about their bodies, and the volume of fabric women were required to wear to such fests. It was the place where outcasts were sent. There was a distinct gap between where Lady Sybil sat and the next attendee.

"Haven't you a mix brewing that you'd best watch over?" she asked.

Sybil snorted her amusement. "I've three of them. One for your mother's worn and stiff hands and wrists, one to relieve our father's gout—although if he'd stay from the table it would be of more benefit—and one for Merriam."

"What would you brew for her? She will na' touch it. You know what she thinks of you."

"Savory," Sybil answered and then she winked.

Kendran caught the sob before it sounded, but it hurt. All the way back to the depths of her belly and then farther than that. Damn her own tongue for asking it!

"You worry needlessly," Sybil added.

Hope flared all the way to her cheeks, making them rosy enough the cold wasn't even an issue. Kendran fought that reaction, too. She failed yet again.

"I dinna' worry," she replied finally.

Lady Sybil answered with another snort of amusement. It was probably better than a giggle, but not by much, Kendran decided. Myles was moving away, going toward the loch. He was taking his skinny squire with him. He was also being trailed by most of Eschoncan's men. Kendran didn't know why he kept the squire at his side, since the lad never seemed burdened with anything. Myles was always toting his own saddles, or weaponry. The lad seemed only to point. That was odd.

"They go to swim the loch," Sybil said at her side.

"'Tis frozen over."

"Not all the way. And that man busts through ice to reach water. Ice water. I've never seen such strength. 'Tis why they all follow. They canna' believe it, as well."

"He swims the loch?"

"Nae man can swim the loch, even in summer. You know that. He takes a dip. All of him. And then he races back to his clothing."

"He . . . takes a dip . . . without his clothing?" She was choking the words. It was obvious.

"Of course na'. He strips himself of it whilst in the water. How else do you think he gets clean so quickly?"

"I've na' paid enough attention to the man to ken such a thing. Nor would I care." Kendran pantomimed a yawn and used the handkerchief to cover it over. She didn't think it worked. A moment later, she knew it hadn't.

"The man holds your heart and you say such a thing? I may have to change my viewpoint of this emotion so touted."

"What emotion?"

"Love."

"I dinna' love him! I dinna'!" Kendran's voice gave the lie away.

"You gave yourself to him, and you dinna' even love him? That is na' good, Kendran. You make me regret speaking."

"Does that mean you'll cease it and leave me be?"

This time it was definitely a giggle. "Of course na'. I already told you. The castle is boring this time of year. And lonely. I am finding it vastly entertaining this year. I'd na' change a moment of it."

"I'm your entertainment?"

There was a pause. Then a sigh of sound. "Not just you. All of you. 'Tis most entertaining. Most."

"Canna' you just brew a potion to save yourself boredom? Must you play with lives as well?"

If Kendran wasn't careful, Lady Sybil was going to make a spectacle of herself with the laughter. That would be so rare they'd probably receive all the notice she was trying to avoid and more besides. She waited while the other choked back what was probably an out-burst of laughter . . . at Kendran's expense.

Then Lady Sybil was dabbing at her own eyes with her embroidered handkerchief. The moisture wasn't sadness induced. "I dinna' play with lives, dearest sister. Nae one can do such a thing. I simply watch what is . . . and then I guess at what is to be. I dinna' even try to manipulate. Unlike you."

"I dinna' manipulate!'

"Nae?"

Kendran's own handkerchief was in a ball in her hands, her entire frame was trembling, and yet nothing about the day felt cold. She was tired of being baited by her own sister; tired of being ignored by Myles; tired of going sleepless with the tears; tired of the jealousy—she was tired.

"He'll get here in time, Kendran. As I already said, you worry needlessly."

"Who?" she asked, automatically.

"Kenneth."

Everything stopped. Even her own heart. Then it decided it really would continue pumping life through her, but with such a huge painful thump it restarted her inhaled gasp of breath and sent ice-cold reaction everywhere. She was frozen with it and more ice cold than Myles and the Eschoncan guard could possibly be, even if they were bathing in the loch.

"I . . . dinna' ken a bit of your words," she replied finally, and every word felt like an ice shard cutting her lips.

"Kenneth Kilchurn is na' here to accept a challenge. He is missing. In the midst of the winter . . . he is missing. Odd. 'Tis a four-day journey on foot over the drum to his land. Four days. And then four back."

"So?"

"That makes eight days. It's been seven since he left. The weather has broken, making it possible to get over the hillock in order to reach Drumrig Tower."

"You think he went to Drumrig Tower?"

"Nae." Lady Sybil replied.

"Then why do you speak of it?"

"He is the Kilchurning heir. And he is na' here. He'll be here tomorrow. Just as I already said."

"You already said you dinna' think he went to Drumrig."

"True. I dinna' think it. I dinna' have to. I already know he went."

"You dinna' ken anything. You guess."

Sybil shrugged. "Look about. He is na' here, is he?"

"I hadn't noticed."

Lady Sybil continued as if Kendran hadn't spoken. "And if he is na' here, he must be somewhere. Somewhere that would have a man missing for more than seven days. Seven. He must have gone for a decent reason. Nae man risks foot travel over the hill known as a drum without a reason. A decent reason."

"He's likely ill."

"You say such and dinna' even check?"

"Why would I do such a thing?" Kendran replied.

"The man is heir to your betrothed and you dinna' worry over his absence? In the heart of winter? With a Christmas wedding coming up? And all else about us planning, and worrying, and war playing, and feasting? That has interest."

"How do you ken he's missing?"

"The Donal is an impressive male. Thus far. Perhaps the reason he's so impressive is because he has na' lost in this warfare game they play. If one thinks further along this line, it may bring notice that perhaps he is na' losing . . . because he's yet to face a challenger of worth. Kenneth Kilchurn would present one. I dinna' think that battle would go easy—for either man. I believe the reason Kilchurn has na' entered into the fray is because he is na' here to enter into it. And then I had to reason out the whereabouts of such a man. Which led me to the reason he'd go to his home. And then return. It will take longer to return. I may yet be wrong. I only hope he reaches Eschoncan afore the next storm."

Kendran sighed. "You wish me to ask why it will take longer?"

"Are you?"

"Am I what?" Kendran bit out.

"Asking why it will take longer."

"I think he's ill. This is what I think."

Sybil snorted again. Kendran decided it was better than laughter.

"A man like Sir Kenneth . . . too ill to make a showing? At this fighting? 'Tis a poor husband to be he'll make."

"Sir Kenneth is na' my husband to be! His uncle, the earl, is!" Despite every control she was exerting, her voice rose. Kendran couldn't prevent it. She knew the other heard it, as a smile curved her lips.

"I dinna' say he was *your* groom to be. Now . . . did I?"

"The exhibition is over. We can go inside now, afore we freeze in one spot. Aside from which, I have tired of your words and the puzzles with which you always speak them."

"Methinks you have tired more of the waiting."

"Waiting?" Kendran lifted her cloak covering over her head, wrapping it just below her nose, and stood. She hadn't been fabricating the temperature, nor the emptiness of the stable yard in front of them. While Sybil tormented her with words that may have a thread of intent and meaning, but took forever for the saying, the crowd had gone back into the warmth of the great room, where the Eschons would have casks of mead opened and the three boar carcasses roasted and spread for the feast.

Beside her, she felt the little figure of her sister shrouding herself as well. It didn't stay any of her words.

"They'll arrive in time. They will."

"I dinna' ken your words, nor why you feel free to speak them to me. Nor the reason why you would want to. Can you na' leave me be?"

Sybil tilted her head, then waved with an arm for Kendran to precede her onto the wooden planks that had been put there to walk on, and to keep elegant slippers from reaching stable yard mud, or dark-crusted drifts of resilient snow in the shadowy recesses, or even touching the slick sheet of ice over puddles.

The boards were still uneven and coated with the wet of other shoes stepping up from the elements. Kendran had her eyes on that when the next bit of her sister's words reached her.

"He'll arrive in time. He'll have the ancient earl with

him. That is what will make the return longer. The elderly dinna' travel well. When they travel. If they travel."

"What are you speaking of now?"

"The earl. Of Kilchurning. Your betrothed. And the reason for Kenneth's absence. Which you already knew. Because you are the one who sent him. There is nae one else with reason enough."

"I have no power to send anyone anywhere."

"A bit of a pout. Perhaps . . . a kiss."

"I have na' kissed Kenneth!"

"Good thing. I would na' wish to see The Donal's anger if he found out such a thing had happened."

Kendran sighed. "I thought your talents lay more in brewing poisons than storytelling, Sybil."

The woman giggled. "I'll na' assist anyone with a poison. Na' when they destroy themselves so willingly and easily without any assist at all."

"And this makes you giddy?"

They'd reached the security of rock steps. Kendran leaped to them before turning back. They had listeners about now, for there were two men standing on either side of the door. And beyond that, she could see how crowded the great room was.

"You set things in motion. Regardless of the cost. You dinna' have a care to what you do. Again. Always."

"What are you talking of now?"

"Adding the earl to this keep. Here. Now. With the turmoil within it. His heart canna' take the work you would force on it."

"The earl has a heart? Strange. He has na' had one afore."

Sybil's lips shifted to show she appreciated the humor. Then she sobered. "True. Remember this, as well. Whatever you think of, others will also think of. It will be set up. They may even come to it first."

"What makes you say such a thing?"

"I've reasoned out your intent, haven't I?"

Her back was clenching on itself, and it wasn't from the cold. It was from Sybil's words. And then, the woman made it worse.

"It was all for naught, as well . . . for the earl will na' wed with you."

Kendran swung on her, but the woman was already moving away, moving the cloak from her head, so torchlight could gleam off her dark hair, as she disdained the festivities and passed beneath the arch to her tower.

Sybil was wrong! She had to be. The laird of Kilchurning would wed with Kendran! He had to. That was the intent behind summoning him, and sending Kenneth with the mission. And blast her own sister for seeing through all of it! She was not manipulating anything. She was saving herself. And she was saving the child—if there was one. She had to. Her time was late; that much was true. But Sybil wasn't a witch. She wasn't a sorceress. And she wasn't a soothsayer. She was a strange girl who had nothing more to do than meddle. That's all she was.

And the Earl of Kilchurning would wed with her! She'd demand it. On the heels of Merriam's own vows and not one moment later. She was afraid of the alternative.

The fear was still there that evening. Along with the worry, the loneliness, and the ache of loss. It was getting worse, too. Especially late into the night, with none to listen or know. Kendran lay in her huge four-poster bed and watched the leaves and vines carved in her canopy as they melded into a wash of brown. Such stupidity. It was useless to cry. All that happened was her nose turned red, her eyes pounded along with the pain in her head, and her chest got thick with a tightness that no amount of coughing dissipated or relieved. None of which made any difference. None of it brought any succor.

The room was still heavy with the steam her bath had put into existence. The window was still coated with the frost; the fire was still burning merrily; and the door that Myles had propped back into position, and that he had shoved bolts back into bolt holes to disguise the damage, was still standing across from her, mocking her. Everything did so anymore.

Lady Sybil had been right about almost everything but she wasn't going to be right about the earl. Kendran wasn't allowing it. He would wed with her! He had to. It shouldn't be difficult. He'd made no secret of his desire for it, ever since she'd been visited by him more than a decade earlier, when he'd watched her with beady bluish eyes set in a wrinkled face. The lone thing that had kept her safe was her father's desire for a better match. Kendran secretly thought her father was holding out hope that the earl would pass on, leaving Kenneth to fulfill the betrothal that had taken place almost the moment Kendran had been placed in a cradle. Kenneth would be a worthy son-by-law. Father had known it. He'd almost set it up.

It was a fair match. The Kilchurnings hadn't enough gold to rub together, but they had land, although their keep known as Drumrig was little more than a pile of rubble, and they had masses of clan to their name. It was a fair match. Especially when you factored in Sir

Kenneth Kilchurn. Sent to her father on his fifteenth year to train as an Eschoncan knight, he'd more than excelled.

Father would do well with him for a son-by-law. Which meant it was going to cause an uproar when Kenneth returned bringing the earl with him. Kendran shuddered, fought the gag her body gave her, and crossed her arms about herself. Father wasn't the only one who'd be in an uproar. Kendran almost couldn't stomach the thought of making the ancient earl her groom. But she had no choice.

She had the bairn to consider. Kendran rubbed her hands all over herself, following the path of shivers that came from the realization. She was going to have a babe, and it was that man Myles who'd given it to her! And she couldn't possibly stay and watch him give the same to Merriam. She couldn't! She'd rather die!

She turned to face the wall, reached out and etched her finger along a score in one of the rocks she'd long ago memorized, and breathed through another sob. It didn't help. The wall mocked her, too.

And then the door to her oriel creaked once before it fell.

CHAPTER 18

"Blast and damn! Jesu'."

The male voice started going through the litany of curse words in exactly the same listing as always. Then there was another creak. Kendran caught the mirth that sounded suspiciously like a sob with the palm of her hand. It would never do if Myles saw this! He'd think things of her that no one knew. She had her face wiped clear with the coverlet before she rolled over.

He wasn't paying her much attention. He was trying to get the door back into its slot, but every time he let it go, it wavered and then tilted outward from the top. She wondered how long it would take before he moved the bottom out a fraction to make the weight keep it in place.

"I swear on all I hold holy that this door is—"

He had it in place, turned about, and then took the brunt of it on his head. Kendran couldn't keep the laughter back, then. This was the same man who gave no mercy out on the field? The one born to the art of warfare? The same one who couldn't get through a door unscathed?

He had his jaw locked, his chin down, and his eyes narrowed as he looked at her. Kendran couldn't hold to her mirth. Even if he was holding the door at an angle with his head, there wasn't any desire to laugh. Not with a look like that.

This time, he wasn't gentle. He wasn't quiet, either. There was more knocking and pounding, and it was a very good thing they were probably still celebrating far below, but he had the door jammed into place, and it didn't look capable of moving anywhere this time. Nothing on her body felt capable, either. Nothing. She couldn't even take a breath. It felt like the entire world had stopped to wait. Kendran heard a hiss from her fireplace, and not much else. She blinked. He turned, put his hands on his hips, defining them through all the layers of woolens he wore, his head lowered, and a knot was bulging out one side of it. He was incredible.

"Well?" he asked.

"You . . . should na' be here," she whispered.

"Nae secret, that."

"You'll . . . be discovered."

"If none heard my entrance, I dinna' ken how I can make more noise. Although I can try."

Then he was smirking, tossing the cowl of his sett to his shoulders, and next he was working at the brooch fastening at his shoulder. Kendran couldn't get her mind to work. She couldn't get her mouth to form words. She couldn't get her eyes to move. She watched as he unwound the covering of plaide he wore and let it unravel to lie on the floor at his feet. Then she was watching as he stepped out of it, and that brought him nearer to the bed, and to her.

"You . . . still should na' be here," she stammered.

"True enough."

His hands had moved to his doublet, and her mouth went completely dry as she watched him unfasten the ties one by one. He wasn't watching his fingers, either. He was watching her. And he was taking another step toward the bed and then another.

"Tell me what I should be doing. Kendran?"

"What?"

He had to say it twice before she heard it. There was the strangest sound akin to a fresh running burn in her ears. Loud. Roaring loud. She blinked again.

He had his black doublet unfastened, and then he put his arms back and let it fall off as well. She was not letting him do this! She was not allowing Merriam's intended husband to disrobe in her bed chamber this late at night! She wasn't allowing it at any time of the day or night! She only wished her mouth would say the words and not stay slack jawed as he started on the ribbon fastening his shirt placket.

"Verra well. I'll say it," he said, just before he had the tie pulled out of its bow shape.

"What?" she echoed again.

"I should be below. Celebrating. Drinking to my great, good fortune. And trying to ignore the knot of ache. Trust me, love, there's na' enough ale. And your family brews it too poorly, even if there were. I canna' ignore it. Every moment of every day. I canna' forget. I'm near to losing my mind with it."

"With . . . what?" Kendran asked.

"Longing. Wanting. Desiring. Aching. Dinna' you feel it, as well?"

If the sheen of moisture on his eyes was what she thought it was, Kendran was going to howl the pain aloud. She had no choice. If she said the right words, he'd leave. He'd go to the life fate had decreed for him, and she'd be left to follow her own path. She swallowed, moving the thick knot in her throat, opened her mouth to reply, and had to settle for a nod. She couldn't lie. She couldn't even get her throat to work.

One side of his mouth lifted. "That is what I was afeared of. You'll need forgive me, then, love."

If he called her that one more time, the tears were going to spill. Kendran wondered how to alert him to it.

"I work and I battle, and I waste time, and I ache. All over. All the time. I could na' stay away another moment. Forgive me."

Forgive him? she wondered. She'd been torturing herself with thoughts of why he'd been ignoring her. Now she knew. He was trying to do what was right. What was honorable. What was his duty.

And he was failing.

"Aside from which, I had to wait for the snow to melt a bit."

"What?"

"I lower myself from a rope. 'Tis wrapped about a merlon of the battlement. Same as last time. It will na' have the same result tonight, however."

"I dinna' understand."

"Snow leaves marks. Easy to read. The rope cleaved a line right through the drift, showing all exactly what transpired. I had to sweep it away last time. I dinna' ken how alert the guards are, but I'd na' like it discovered that I'm visiting the Lady Kendran in her chamber at night. Alone. You ken?"

She nodded.

"And I vowed then that I'd na' put you at risk again, as well."

"Then why are you here now?"

He shrugged, put both hands on the sides of his

shirt, and started tugging it from the belt, and then he was lifting it over his head and dropping it to the floor as well. He had welts across him again. Kendran couldn't move her eyes.

"I already said it. I canna' stay away. The ache is too great. Forgive me, lass. Either that, or tell me to go. Say it with anger. Or hate. Or any of the emotions your sister uses. Make me believe it. Then, turn about. If you do all of that, I may be able to leave." He gulped. Everything on his body showed it. "And I might na'. The pull of it is too great. I canna' fight it. Not anymore. Well?"

She didn't know what he was asking. And she couldn't see through the veil of tears to guess at it. He wasn't taking any more of his clothing off, however.

"Will you tell me to go? Tell me you have nae desire for this? Tell me you dinna' ache? And will you make me believe it?"

She shook her head, shut her eyes, and let the tears fall. He'd reached the bed and was settling onto it right beside her. Then he was pulling her toward him, wrapping her in his arms and placing his chin atop her nose. She knew that was his position by the touch of his breath on her closed eyelids, cooling the moisture she wasn't capable of staunching.

"I dinna' ken love felt like this," he whispered.

"Like . . . what?"

"All vast. Large. Like I can do anything. As long as I know where you are, and sense you, and can see you. Anything. 'Tis as child's play."

"Does . . . it feel like that?"

"That and more. 'Tis also enough to make a man weak. Make my arms quiver and my belly clench. If I dinna' know that somewhere in the world I have this. Do you ken what I say?"

She nodded.

"Good. I would na' fare well if I was alone in this."

Kendran sniffed; rubbed her nose against his chin, where the slight scratch of freshly scraped skin greeted her; and knew exactly what he meant.

"What am I saying? I am na' faring well already."

"How so?"

"I eat. I drink. I talk. I fight. I exist. I am na' living. I'm a shell. And your sister hates me. I dinna' ken what I've done to her, but she hates me. I dinna' ken how a man can live through the waspish words she uses without backhanding her. And I never hit a woman. Ever. I'm frightened."

"You?"

"Aye. Me. The Donal heir. The man who never loses. I'm a coward. There. I admit it. You dinna' think less of me?"

"You're nae coward, Myles. You . . . win every man you face."

"That's a simple matter. I win because I'm not afeared of the loss. I welcome it. If he'd allow swords, I'd welcome it more."

"You wish . . . swords? But that's— It's too dangerous. Someone would get gravely hurt. Someone might die."

"I know," he replied. "Why do you ken I'd welcome it?"

"You want . . . to kill?"

He shook his head and trembled. Kendran felt it.

"I am na' afraid of dying, lass. 'Tis the living that frightens me. I would welcome death. It has honor."

"Myles. No. Please?"

"I am verra afeared of what I must do, Kendran. Verra."

"You? Nae."

"I. Me. You think less of me?"

"That depends on what it is," she whispered back.

"Bedding your sister."

Kendran's eyes went huge. She couldn't hold back the shock.

"You think it an easy thing to bed a wench?" he asked.

"I never truly thought of it."

"Well it is na'. Well, mayhap it was. I mean, it used to be. But, now that I have you . . . now that I've had this"—he squeezed his arms, moving her slightly until she could hear the echo of his heartbeat through the chest she was pillowed against—"I dinna' ken if I'll be able to do it. And with your sister? If I canna' perform, she would na' let it pass. She would use it. She would."

She shook her head.

"Day in and day out, I'd hear of my failure. I thought mayhap if I imagine it's you in my bed, keep the fire dim . . . do you think that might work?"

"You want me to help you bed my sister when you have to?"

He shook his head again. "Nae. I only want to hold you. To feel you. To know you're in the world. To know for a brief moment, I touched heaven. Because of you. This is what I came here for. This is all I want. I'll na' wish for more. Tonight, anyway. Tomorrow is far off. I may need more then."

There wasn't any way to answer that. Kendran was aching too hard to make anything in her throat work for other than swallowing.

"Aside from which, I have to still survive the wedding night. I have to bed that harpy, and I have to watch and wait for her to birth my son and heir. And all the time this is happening, I have to know that it's na' you at my side with the right. It's her. And she hates me. I dinna' ken why. Most lasses find me fair enough. Not her. I'm afeared, Kendran, and with good cause. She unmans me with her expressions and her tongue. Now, do you find me a coward?"

"Nae." The word was whispered.

"I've spent some of this time thinking. I wondered at the fingers of fate, of the turn that took me to that croft. I could have fallen and perished. I could have made it to this keep. I could have passed by without even knowing you, or feeling this. And I wonder why God felt I needed it. Do you think this, too?"

"Aye."

"And do you ken why?"

"Nay."

"I wonder who does. Why would I get to know this feeling just to have it taken away? That is na' fair. So much about this is na' fair. Why is that?"

"I dinna' know," Kendran answered.

"I dinna' wish to bed with her. I dread it. I dinna' ken one man who would wish it. You ken that much, too?"

"I . . . never thought of it, Myles."

"Of course na'. 'Tis because I am supposed to be big and fearless and strong and manly. Now you ken the truth. I am neither. I am a coward. 'Tis the true reason I'm so victorious on the field. I am na' afraid of loss. I'd welcome it. Would your sire consider steel when next he calls me into the game?"

"This war play that you do . . . 'tis na' usual. I dinna' ken if he'd allow it or na'. I do ken one thing, however. I would na' allow it."

"Why not?"

"Because then I would have to live this life without you. That would be most unfair, Myles. Most."

He shuddered again. "I told you I was a coward, Kendran. And God curse my own mouth for making it take place on Christmas Eve! I have all the luck of a bit of sweetness surviving in your sister's mouth."

"It may na' be as bad as you fear."

She felt the finger beneath her chin, moving it, raising it. He waited until she opened her eyes and met his. Kendran's heart skipped at the expression he wore. "I was raised among men—by men. Only men. I dinna' have a woman's hand in my life. I dinna' ken this love feeling existed. None ever spoke of it, if it did. I ken it now. With every beat of my heart, and every breath that I take. I ken it. I live it. I own it. I cherish it."

Kendran nodded when he seemed to wait for it.

"And now you tell me I can forego it for another? I can put another right here in my arms . . . and it will na' be as bad as I fear? How bad is that to be?"

Her eyes filled again. She blinked the tears down her face, and more came. His expression got more tender. He smiled slightly.

"Could you do it?" he asked. "I dinna' ken why I even ask such a question. You'd have nae choice, just as I dinna' . . . and then I'd have to be forcefully restrained from ripping that man apart."

Dearest God! Her stomach rebelled at the thought. Her only choice was to keep it hidden from him. If he knew what she was to do—and the man she was inviting into her bed! She blinked the tears away again and watched as he stayed in focus for a moment before more moisture blurred and then obliterated him.

"We are in hell. I was right the first time. Hell."

"This is na' hell, Myles. 'Tis life. Others have gone afore us. They lived through it. We can, too. We will. We have nae other choice."

"You've seen the results, as well. Your own family. Your mother hates your father. He is na' verra fond of her, either. And in time, this will be me. And her. Ugh. She grows ugly with just the thought of such a thing. I canna' bed her, Kendran. I canna'. I'll be revealed as a coward, and unmanly. How am I to live through that?"

"I have another sister, Myles. She-she brews potions. She's been known to . . . cast spells. I will ask her—"

"I ken all about this sister of yours. I have even met the sorceress."

"You've met her? And you know about her?"

"That . . . and more. Endless amounts more. I hear of it from my squire. He's ceaseless with his words. Makes my ears ring worse than a sword blow to the side of my head. Ceaseless. Meaningless. He tells me of her. He's mightily afeared of her. With good cause as far as I can tell."

"Sybil is . . . strange. I grant you that."

"Can she make a potion that will have that harpy feeling like this in my arms?" He ran a hand along her arm and linked it with her hand. Then he was bringing their conjoined hands to his heart. "Will it make her smell as you do, feel as you do, sound as you do? If I close my eyes, I would na' be able to tell the difference. She can do this?"

"I dinna' ken. I can ask her."

"Trust me, love. There is nae spell capable of such a thing. All there is . . . is oblivion. And your clan does na' brew good enough mead to guarantee such a thing. I may resort to hitting something. I only hope it is na' her. God. I'll say it again. I am na' only a coward; I'm a base coward."

"You are neither, Myles. You are brave. And strong.

And honorable. And everything needed to be the man I love."

His shaking intensified. And then it calmed. Just like that. When Kendran looked at him again, he looked defeated and older somehow. "There is nae potion on earth that can replace how I feel for you, Kendran Eschon. None. I dinna' have to guess at this. I ken it."

"Sybil can make something to get you through the wedding night, Myles. I ken she can!"

"Can she brew a potion to get me through the rest of the nights? Can she make a brew that will render me heartless? That will turn back the days and make it so I never met you? Never felt you? Never kenned you? Because that is what this is going to take. And that's only the beginning of it."

He was speaking in a dead-sounding tone. That was worse somehow.

"It will come right, Myles."

"Aye, lass. That it will. There's nae other choice anyway, is there?"

"We can run, Myles."

"Run?" he echoed.

"Aye. Away. Take me away. We can do this. I am na' dowered with this keep. 'Twas always meant for Merriam."

He sighed again. She moved with it. "She'll na' have it, either."

"She will always have it. It's part of the dowry—"

"It's a heap. And when I own it, 'twill be naught save rubble. I'll make certain of it and greatly enjoy every butt of the ram I will use."

"But . . . why?"

"It's poorly constructed, worse maintained, and full of memories. I'll na' live here. Ever. I canna'."

"You'll run away?"

"I canna' do that, either, Kendran. I'm to be the Donal laird. 'Tis a great clan. Large. With clansmen and women scattered about eight glens, and encompassing three lochs. 'Tis a great responsibility. One I'll na' shirk. Ever."

"Na' even for me?" she asked in a small voice.

This time when she looked at him, he'd paled, and his trembling had increased. "If I had nae honor," he finally replied.

"And you call yourself a coward." Kendran shook her head slightly, and then she shifted up to touch her lips to his. She might as well have touched rock. Trembling rock.

"Lady Sybil gave me a warning for you," she murmured when she'd finished her kiss and pulled away. Not enough to bring him into focus, but enough to allow the movement of her lips as they brushed against his.

"What is it?"

She heard the words, felt the breath against her flesh, and that started her own trembling. It was too much to bear! Kendran moved farther away until she was in a slant from him and keeping herself that way with the stiffening of her arms and locking of her elbows.

"You must control this spin move you do. In battle. To your left. With your shield out. You must learn to control it better."

"What?" His eyes went wide and angered, and the form she was still touching did the same movement as everything on him tightened and clenched, making her rock slightly. "She dared slur my battle form? A wench?"

Kendran giggled, which had him glaring even more. From the shadow of his own forehead, it was impossible to see the amber gleam he had deep in his eyes, but she imagined it was there all the same.

"I am faultless in battle, flawless in attack. I never lose. Never. And now a wench calling herself fey tells me I lack control? I have never been so insulted."

Kendran reached her free hand upward, combed her fingers into the hair at the top of his forehead, and pulled it back, letting what firelight there was highlight and sculpt the masculine beauty of the warrior at her fingertips. She smiled again. "She dinna' say you lacked control, my love. She said you must learn to control it better. I dinna' ken why. I think you wondrous as well. And na' just in battle."

His lips twitched. Then, there was a gleam of teeth as he smiled. "You are na' helping, wicked wench," he whispered.

"With what?" she asked.

"Desire. Passion. Longing. The depth of it that I feel for you." He blew the sigh upward, feathering it across her wrist and palm. "And I'll na' take you again. I canna'."

"Why not?"

His eyes closed and a shudder ran him. She felt every bit of it. When he opened them again, there wasn't an emotion showing anywhere. "Because I must wed with your sister. And na' you. Never you. That is why."

CHAPTER 19

Myles watched Squire Beggin falter back three disjointed, shuddering steps before falling. It didn't bring any satisfaction. It didn't bring the amusement of the first time it had happened. It didn't bring anything other than frustration. He strode over to the lad, put out a hand, and yanked him back to his feet, where he wobbled.

"Concentrate! And learn!"

The leather helm atop Myles's head and splicing his face in two by the trail of it down his nose was drenched in sweat and sending each drop onto his lips. It was far shy of the other's sweat. That lad looked like he was melting in place.

"You must learn to withstand a blow. And if you canna' withstand it, then dodge it! And always—always!—keep an eye out. All the time. From any angle. From any side. The attack can come from anywhere . . . and it will!" Then Myles spun to the left, his shield out first, the long stick they used in place of a sword directly behind it. Such a motion slammed first the left arm and then the wood into the lad. This time there were no footsteps marking his collapse. He sailed two full body lengths before landing on his back in the ice-mud mixture of the stable.

"Ah!" Myles yelled it heavenward, before shoving his stick into the mud. The shield wasn't far behind it, as he planted the tipped bottom end into the muck as well. The lad wasn't assuaging any of Myles's pent-in emotion, he wasn't deflecting any of the self-hate, and he wasn't even a decent sparring partner. He was also slow on his feet. Unfortunately, he was also the only one willing to meet in mock battle with Myles since the laird wasn't commanding it. Myles was about ready to decree them all a bunch of craven cowards.

He strode over to Squire Beggin again. About the only thing he was good for was information. The lad was still twitching. He was also groaning.

"Now, do you see why you must never let down your guard?"

"You . . . dinna' even let me . . . rest," the lad panted.

"In a battle there is nae rest, lad. All there is time for is life. Or death. Your choice. And it all hinges on your expertise and training and skill. All."

"I dinna' . . . have your . . . upbringing," the lad continued with his complaints.

It figured that even if he was physically defeated his mouth never ceased. Myles had a smirk on his face over that thought as he reached down, put both hands into the sides of the lad's linked mail, and hauled him back onto his feet.

"That much needs nae explanation, lad. 'Tis obvious you're fit more for wielding a quill and parchment than a sword and shield."

The lad straightened and glared from his own leather helm. "I am a decent squire, Lord Myles. I'm no scribe."

Myles reached out to flick the leather flap on Squire

Beggin's nose. The lad flinched backward. It didn't give him any satisfaction. None. Not much did, anymore, Myles decided. "Get that taken off and washed. And see to my shield. I'll see to my own armor." He reached over and yanked out the stick.

He would have turned then, but there was a shout and then the gate was opening, sending a contingency of horses in to fill the courtyard. At their head was the missing Kenneth Kilchurn. And with him were seven of the eight Donal Honor Guard. Myles narrowed his eyes. Even astride a horse and surrounded by Donal men, the Kilchurn man had bulk, size, and muscle. He looked to be a worthy adversary. Myles felt his arms clench at the pleasantness of the thought.

"Oh, good. Your competition has finally arrived. Thank the lord."

"Him?" Myles motioned with his head.

"Aye. The Kilchurning heir. He's the castle champion. He'll see you taken down a peg. Or three. I'm hopeful it will be three."

Myles tipped his head and gave the lad a narrowed-eye look. "You think him good enough, lad?"

Squire Beggin thought for a moment about it and then started twitching his shoulders and arms again. "'Twill be a great contest should the laird see it set up. A great one."

"That's nae answer. You'll resemble the witch Sybil at this rate."

Squire Beggin grinned. "Verra well. I'll answer. In any battle atween you two, I'd na' bet any gold on him," he replied.

Myles returned the grin.

"He's got his uncle with him, as well. The laird will na' be pleased."

"He also has my Honor Guard. You see?"

Squire Beggin whistled. The Donal men did look impressive. Especially as they were all dismounted and walking toward him. He noted there wasn't much bruising or limping among them. Even the blackening about the youngest's, Egan's, eye had all but disappeared. Rolf was nowhere in sight.

"I suppose you'll na' have need of my services . . . now." The lad, Beggin, sounded woebegone, and for once there wasn't another word coming out of him.

Myles slapped him across the back, sending him forward two steps in a clumsy motion, but at least he didn't fall. "You're wrong, lad. I'll na' allow one of them near me. Not ever again. I'd na' even think of replacing you with one of their sorry arses."

"Truly?"

The lad looked shocked. He also looked so happy every bit of weakness seemed to disappear. He also stood straighter.

"I'm na' in the habit of speaking lies. Of course 'tis truth. They've na' proved themselves deserving of a place at a future laird's side. Especially mine."

"They haven't?" The lad was backing as he said it, until he was standing beside Myles. Both of them got the full impact of seven men clad in Donal colors, and fully armed, as they stopped and fanned out to form a semicircle.

"You left us for dead, Donal," Arthur, the largest, said finally.

"I left you—true. You'd only be dead if you continued eating that man's fare. I can see the lie of that myself," Myles answered easily.

"We sent Rolf to Donal Keep with word of your death."

"That was . . . bold of you," Myles replied. "And untrue. I hope they can survive the shock of your next message telling them of my continued great health." He couldn't help it. He knew he had a grin on his face. He watched as Egan shifted from one foot to the other.

"We had nae other choice!" the lad spat out.

"Loyalty is always a choice, Egan. That's why I selected you. Each of you. Now I ken where your allegiance lies, I'll be selecting others. You may leave my presence. You have done what my father ordered."

He turned his back on them. Beside him, he knew Squire Beggin had done the same. He glanced sidelong at him and winked. He was hoping it would bolster the boy. He looked like he was going to faint.

"Once the ceremony is complete, we leave."

That was definitely Arthur speaking. Myles tipped his head. "'Tis a foul stench that has arrived, Squire Beggin. I feel the need of a swim."

"Right . . . now?" the lad stumbled through the question.

Myles turned sideways to the lad, keeping the Donal men in his peripheral vision. "Once the stench clears away will be soon enough. And that will na' happen until these men leave. They dinna' realize they're dismissed. They will soon. Perhaps they'd be better served speaking with the laird of Eschon. They'll need quarters assigned to them. With any luck, they may na' even freeze within them."

Beggin was wide-eyed at his words. They both heard the huff of annoyance. It was probably still coming from Arthur. Myles didn't care. They'd proved their loyalty to a Donal laird—that was true. Unfortunately, they'd chosen the elder, seated one. They weren't going to enjoy it once his father passed on. He turned fully back to them then, bent his chin down, and looked at them through hooded eyes. Not one was meeting his gaze.

"Come men. There's more welcome in that keep than with him."

There was more mumbling amongst them. Then they turned. Myles hadn't realized how tautly he'd been holding himself. He let his back slowly unclench, and the wooden stick in his hand felt compacted there.

"What did they do?" Beggin asked at his side.

"'Tis a long story."

"We've time."

Myles took a big sigh. This was going to complicate things even further. He couldn't possibly escape a guard long enough to sneak in to see Kendran. His jaw set. He'd find a way, if he had to beat them into unconsciousness. He only had a fortnight of days before *Cristes maesse*. He wasn't wasting one of them.

"Well?" Squire Beggin had a second wind, if his head bobbing was any indication. Myles nearly groaned.

"'Tis a Donal clan issue. Na' Eschon. You dinna' need to know."

"I'd keep silent."

Myles looked heavenward. The lad couldn't keep a secret long enough for the words to dissipate. If he knew something, everyone else would. A rift between the Donal heir and his Honor Guard wasn't going to be one of them.

"I keep you about for information, Beggin. Which is a powerful good thing given the work still needed on your abilities on the field."

The lad gave him a solemn look. "What do you wish to know?"

"The auld man with Kilchurn. Start with him." It was the best Myles could think of. Once his Honor Guard had left, there wasn't much of interest in the stable yard, save the activity accompanying the old man who was with Kenneth. They both watched as a litter was brought from the house, and then Kilchurn was helping the decrepit man to the ground, where the skeletal figure went into a hunched-over position, nearly disappearing beside the form of his escort. He didn't look capable of walking the distance to his litter and proved it as Kenneth had to assist with that, as well.

"Oh, him. He's the earl of Kilchurning. Our neighbor."

"This crag sports neighboring clans? Impossible." Myles was still watching and evaluating. There was going to be a challenge made and before long. Every portion of his body was experiencing the thrill of it, sending strength and will to the tips of his fingers and everywhere in between as well.

"Kilchurning is the lone one. That much is true."

"And Laird Eschon dislikes the man? This is odd. A neighboring clan?"

"He does na' dislike the man, as much as what he represents."

"And what would that be?"

"Loss of more ground. And more gold. And more wealth."

"Truly? Why?" Myles pulled his own shield from the ground. If he waited for Beggin to do it, the leather would be caked with more stable mud and would therefore need more oil applied. The lad made a pathetic squire.

"Dowry."

Myles wiped at a clump of mud, grass, and snow-melt that was clinging to the steel framework of his shield. Then he bent to swipe it onto the bottom of one upheld boot. He was actually grateful he was bent forward and in such a position. It had his face averted.

"The man is his daughter Kendran's betrothed. That's why. The earl may be forcing the marriage. Finally."

Myles went to a knee and fought the rush of sickness that flew his entire frame. Then it was gone, obliterated by the pure, unadulterated rage. His jaw locked as he fought it. None must know. None must ever guess. Kendran's name would never be linked to his. Ever. It wasn't getting linked to Kenneth's either. Myles was going to see to it. He was accepting the challenge, and he wasn't losing. His Kendran wasn't matching her frame against the sandy-haired knight's form. She wasn't! Myles wasn't allowing it! The handle of his shield was made of steel and formed into a hand-fitting shape. It was also taking up all the rage and anger he felt as his fist tightened about it, revealing the noteworthy craftsmanship with which it had been made.

"The laird will be land poor by the New Year. He'll na' be pleasant. 'Twas most unfortunate the earl thought to visit now. And most unfortunate his nephew went and fetched him."

"Wouldn't he need to be present for the wedding?" Myles asked. He was gaining control over his own body again. His hand no longer locked on the handle, nor was there a tremble to any part of him. He stood, stretched his arms upward and then backward to loosen the knot that had formed between his shoulders, and then he rotated them.

The squire tipped his head back and showed more energy than he'd exhibited all morn with his laughter. "Of course. It couldn't take place without him. That's why the Eschoncan laird will be so unhappy. Why now? Why? He's held off the union for seasons now. Nearly a half score's worth. Why now? When he's already losing Eschoncan Fells and his own keep to you . . . he has to lose Kendran's dowry, too? 'Tis most amusing. Most. I may stay from the mead tonight in order to watch."

"That isn't mead, lad. 'Tis worse than brine water." Myles shook his head. So. His Kendran was to wed Kenneth. It was fitting. The laird of Eschoncan had done well by his daughters and for his progeny. It was apt. Too bad it was never happening.

"This Kenneth may na' make the ceremony," Myles said, through clenched teeth that probably showed the emotion he was attempting to hide.

The squire shrugged. "Why?" he asked.

"He has to survive my challenge."

"The laird is na' allowing true swordplay. Kenneth may lose to you, but he'll make the ceremony. He just may na' be standing."

"Perhaps I'll change the rules," Myles offered.

"Why would you do that? The earl needs Kenneth. He has nae other heir. Unless he begets one with Kendran."

Myles felt his belly roil, his eyes widened, and he had to swallow the taste of bile that churned up his throat. "Ken . . . dran?" he asked.

"If he's na' too auld and useless. 'Tis what a marriage is for. Begetting heirs. You should ken this. You've got your own to beget with the harridan."

"The auld earl is . . . her betrothed?"

Squire Beggin grinned again and bobbed his head. "Exactly. And despite the prayers of all involved, he dinna' do what he was supposed to."

"And what . . . would . . . that be?" Myles was choking. He was amazed the squire didn't notice it.

"Die off. Then Kenneth could have taken his place at the altar. 'Twas what they hoped for, why the laird delayed the wedding."

"You ken this?"

"Everyone kens it! Except perhaps . . . the earl. He may na' ken it. He's probably the lone one wishing the wedding take place. I dinna' understand it. Why now? Why?"

Myles turned his back on the squire. He had to reach his chamber. He had to get to his knees in prayer before the sickness filling him took him there. The squire was at his heels.

"You dinna' want to know the rest?" the squire asked.

Myles shook his head. "I've more to do than listen to gossip."

"Oh. Right. You've a wedding to prepare for, a night of drinking and feasting to accomplish, and a challenge to place. You've far too much to do to listen to castle tales."

"I also dinna' care," Myles returned.

"You may na' have a care, but I'm curious."

"Can you na' obey the simplest thing, squire?" Myles asked harshly over his shoulder. He was striding for the castle, leaving a trail of muck.

"Like what?" the lad asked.

"Seeing to my shield." Myles spun and shoved it into the squire's midsection. That didn't even stop his words.

"You've a harsh way of dealing with those who serve you. I pray it changes as you age."

"Can you na' see my shield cleaned and oiled? I'll

need it on the morrow. First light. Or I can find a Donal guardsman to assist me."

"You'd have a fight on your hands, then."

"I have a fight on them now."

"With whom?" Beggin asked.

Myles had his teeth clenched too tightly to answer at first. He forced his own face to relax. Now that he'd dismissed his own men, all he had was Beggin. He was beginning to think he might not have enough patience. "I need my shield cleaned—for the challenge. I need a bath—for my presence at the banquet this eve. Again, for the challenge. Can you see any of that done?"

"You'll challenge him that soon?"

"If they have enough torchlight, I may need it this eve."

"You have a death wish. That is what you have. You should be exhausted."

"From what?"

"Sparring with me. I've nae strength left."

"You had little to begin with," Myles replied.

"My thanks."

"Here." Myles pulled the padded leather he'd been wearing as armor from his torso and tossed it at the squire, also. This left his linen shirt, plastered to his frame with the adhesive of drying perspiration, and his kilt. It was enough. If he didn't stand in the draft of the hall while it dried.

"Can you na' see to my belongings now?"

"What of your bath? Who's to see to you then?"

"A mute. Send a mute."

"What would you want that for?"

"Self-preservation." Myles muttered it beneath his breath as he pulled his chamber door open. There was no way to bolt it from within. He checked the outside of the door. Both sides had bolt holders. The locking mechanism was worked from the hall. Only dungeons needed such. Stupid design, he decided. Good thing he was razing the entire keep. A shadow fell across his threshold.

"Well?" He swiveled to ask it. Beggin wasn't at his heels. The little waifish sister was. Despite everything, Myles pulled back swiftly and markedly. He couldn't help it . . . in the event she had a handful of her dust again.

"You're issuing the challenge this eve?" she asked.

Myles's eyebrows lifted. He leaned against his door frame, folded his arms and regarded her. From across the length of the hall. She couldn't reach him with any potion from where she was standing. It gave him a sense of security.

"And if I am?" he asked, finally.

"I watched you today. Verra cunning. Verra sly."

"When?" he asked.

"In the yard. You practiced restraint. Good. You'll need it."

"I had to. My squire canna' take a full hit."

"Neither can the Kilchurn heir."

Myles smiled. "Surely . . . you jest," he answered.

"Mark my words. Use them. Think about them. Your happiness depends on it. Everything you want and desire hinges on it. Dinna' make another mistake."

"Another?" he asked.

She nodded. At least her cowled head dipped. He assumed it was a nod.

"What was the first one?" he asked.

She giggled. The cloaked form moved with it. It was a light, gay sound and made him narrow his eyes at her. He'd slighted her earlier. She was actually quite lovely, but it was a muted form, far removed from the beauty of her sibling Kendran. And then she ruined his reverie by speaking the reason for her mirth.

"Dear knight, there are too many to recount. I dinna' ken where to start."

He grunted the reply and shifted his back against the wood frame.

"I mustn't be seen here," she told him.

"So, leave. Dinna' be seen. Go."

"Not until you give me your promise."

Myles wrinkled his brow. "To what?" he asked. "Restrain a hit on the Kilchurn heir? And allow him a win? You're too late, my lady. Such a thing has already occurred to me. And already discarded. I never lose."

She took a step toward him. Myles backed one, taking him through the door and into his room. She giggled again.

"You needn't fear me," she said once she had her breath back.

"I dinna' fear you. I practice caution. I canna' issue any challenge if I'm asleep again."

"Promise me, then."

"Promise what?"

"That you'll na' issue one."

He lowered his head, glared down at the sprite-sized figure, then shook his head. "I will na' promise such."

"You must!"

She took another step toward him. Myles backed a corresponding one.

"I need you aware. And awake. And conscious. I dinna' use the dust for a reason! Men! They canna' see beyond their noses at times!"

Myles took another step back from her. "You can just stay right there." He pointed across at her.

"Promise me you'll stay your tongue tonight. Dinna' issue the challenge. Fight your own men, with any weapon you choose, but na' the Kilchurning heir. Your men will accept. They wish to prove themselves to you again."

Myles frowned. She couldn't have learned of the Donal rift from Beggin. There hadn't been time. "I will fight him. I have to. You dinna' understand."

"I never said you would na' fight with him."

"Beggin was right. You speak naught save riddles. I long to fight with him. And I canna' challenge him? What sense does this make?"

"Every sense! Listen to me!"

She was in the chamber now and pulling the door closed behind her. Myles was surprising every bit of his upbringing by moving as far to the other side of his room as he could from her. Beggin wouldn't have believed it.

"You must wait. You must let him do it!"

"Let him do what?"

"Let him make the challenge! If he says it, there will still be a fight! You'll still get the chance to show your supremacy."

"He'll challenge me?"

"Aye."

He considered that. "You may be right. He has much to gain from issuing a challenge. You're verra bright. And verra fey. No wonder they all fear you."

She giggled again. "Do I have your promise?"

"Aye."

"Good. Now I need another one."

"What?"

She was walking toward him, and he took a leap up onto his hearth stone. There wasn't anywhere else he could go. Such a position put her face level with his waist. She was grinning as she shoved the cowl back. It wasn't returned. He wondered what anyone would say if he saw him perched on the hearth stone with his arms wide to the stone walls at his side. It was obvious he'd been chased there. It was also obvious that it was a wench doing so; and a wench of such small proportion she'd fit in a bag. Easily.

He didn't really want to know what anyone would say.

"I said I need another promise from you."

"And I already asked what it was," he replied.

"Has it na' been questioned what brought Kendran's betrothed to our step, yet?"

"What?" he asked.

"Dinna' your squire speak of it? Beggin? The lad has little use, unless one wants gossip. That he has. He had to have spoken of it."

"What of it?" Myles asked.

"The earl was fetched. Kenneth was sent to fetch him."

"So?" he asked.

"He has to live long enough to make a wedding night with her."

Myles clenched his hands on the stones at both sides. It didn't do much except make his form arch out slightly at the increase of muscle size. "He'll na' live long enough to have her. I vow it."

"Listen! Now!" she hissed.

"Have I a choice?"

She tipped her head and considered that. "Nae," she replied finally.

He sighed. "Then say something to make sense. Make me understand."

"Kendran had him fetched. Kendran. Your love. Her."

Myles gaped. Everything on him went to the same reaction, making it difficult to even remain standing. *Kendran had seen the ancient earl fetched? Why?* he wondered. "She couldn't. She didn't. She wouldn't," he said.

"She could. She did. She would," she replied. "You lose."

"I already lost. I continue to lose. I can see naught save loss in my entire life. Say something to change that."

"This loss will be a win. You just have to see it and make it happen."

"Make sense, blast you!" He was shouting it at her, and that had her stepping back a bit. That wasn't normal for her. He wondered what would be considered normal for someone like her.

"You have to accept his challenge. When he speaks it, you must accept."

"Easily done. I promise," Myles replied.

"And then you must lose. Completely. Fully."

"What?" If his mouth hadn't dropped open yet, it did then, completely and mortifyingly. He couldn't prevent it.

"Promise me."

Myles pulled his own mouth shut, lowered his jaw, and glared down at her. "I already told you—I never lose."

"In this you must. You must! There is nae other option. None. Practice at it."

"Practice at what?" he asked.

"Losing."

She didn't even wait for his reaction. She simply put her cowl back over her face, picking up her skirts with the same fluid motion, and then she was at his door before her last words sank in.

He was still perched on his own hearth staring at the door when Squire Beggin returned, leading two serfs carrying a tub, and behind them was a file of more men bearing buckets of warmed water. And behind them were at least three men of the Donal Honor Guard, no doubt wondering what would have been frightening enough to scare the Donal heir up onto his own hearth.

CHAPTER 20

Kendran clutched her arms about her middle and kept the sickness at bay through sheer will. This wasn't the illness she suffered every morn. It was worse. It was because of *him*. The earl. Kendran wasn't used to being ill. She'd rarely suffered even a slight bout of chill. Yet it felt like she spent every morn hunched over at the privy chamber, and then emptying her own chamber pot once she'd finished. She'd then be ravenous at the noon meal because of it, making it easy to nap away the afternoon in the lady's solar, where she should be knitting, rather than oblivious to her sister's sobbing at the other side of the room, or her mother who was knitting at such a cadence the clicking of her needles could be danced to, and pointedly ignoring both of them the entire time.

And then came the evening meal. Then she'd have to sit beside *him*. The earl. Her intended groom. The man she was going to give her body to, so her son would be safe. And she'd have to do it with Myles glaring at her nearly every moment, since he was too occupied with training his squire how to be a knight, practicing the spin move Sybil had told her of, and turning every day into a battle with two more of his Donal men to visit nocturnally with her.

So every evening, she sat beside the earl, and everything on her rebelled. Absolutely everything. He didn't eat. He didn't converse. Most of the time it looked like he wasn't even breathing. And there was no one she could share the anguish with. Nobody. Sybil was the lone one who guessed at the state of affairs, and Myles hadn't visited in over six days! It was tortuous, even though she knew it was just and right. In three days' time he was wedding Merriam. He was staying from Kendran for a reason. An honorable one. It still hurt. Kendran was determined that her own vows were going to take place before the New Year. She'd demanded it, and Father hadn't even argued. He hadn't even attended the eve's fest, either. Mother said he was ill. She was accomodating to all, watching over the festivities from a place beside her daughter, Merriam, and directing everyone with an authority none would have guessed at if the laird of Eschon were attending.

Kendran wasn't staying a moment longer than she had to. She was wedding with the Kilchurning, and they were leaving for his castle the moment it was done. It wouldn't be so hard. She wasn't going to allow anyone to count the days until her first son was born, she wasn't going to watch as Merriam blossomed with carrying her own child, and Kendran didn't think she'd be able to stand the sight of Myles or Merriam on Christmas Day, following their wedding night. Aside from which, she had her own to face.

If she was really lucky, just the sight of her nakedness would be enough to give the old earl apoplexy and save her. Kendran giggled, clapped a hand to her mouth as the bile warned her from the base of her throat, and she swallowed it away again. Her own body wouldn't allow a giggle now? This was not good.

"Kendran?"

The name came in a breath of air over her shoulder, since she was facing the wall. That was better than facing the room, the dimness beyond her fire's light, and a night portending all sorts of other things. Sensual, warmth-imbued, sweat-inducing kinds of things. The things that were making her nights a mess of sleeplessness, and her body a solid mass of want.

She knew what it was. She just didn't know what to do about it. She'd never felt as wanton, as brazen, or as frustrated. She blamed the bairn. That, and the man who had given him to her.

"Are you awake, sweet?"

Kendran gasped and swiveled to her other side. Her woven flax nightgown didn't make the move, and it wound into a curve-enhancing twist of material about her. She probably should have been beneath the covers, and well into what sleep she could gain. That way she wouldn't be catching her breath as the man standing at the side of her bed roamed his dark eyes over her, and then groaned. He wasn't wearing a cloak—which was highly stupid of him, considering the weather—and his black hair was made even darker by the way it was plastered to his skull with a moisture sheen that glinted in the firelight.

"You're wet," Kendran pointed out. The words had a touch of giggle attached to them, making them sound as stupid as they were. She couldn't help it. Pleasure was filling her entire body. That, and anticipation.

He grinned. That made every bit of air she'd managed to gain fly right out again.

"'Tis snowing," he answered.

"It is?"

"Aye. And briskly. Move over."

He didn't ask; he simply gave her a moment to decide whether to do as he ordered or take the brunt of his weight as he sat beside her, and then turned. His hair wasn't the lone thing on him that was wet. Kendran lifted a hand, placed her fingers atop frozen-feeling, iced-over flesh on his hand . . . his lower arm . . . all the way to the end of his tunic sleeve just above his elbow. He was wet the entire way, making a drip that meandered down her own hand and onto her wrist.

"Why?" she asked.

"I had to exhaust them first. It took days."

"What?" she asked.

"And then, I had to beg a moment's relief of their presence long enough to run the steps by myself. They think me a madman. I'm tempted to agree."

"What?" Kendran repeated.

"There were only two to keep up with me, and I lost them near the kitchens. At least I think them lost. It's na' hard. Your buttery is a disaster. The entire keep is that, though."

"I dinna' understand a word you say, Donal."

He grinned again. The motion made snowmelt drip off his nose, where it glimmered on his full lower lip. "And I've been in hell. I can feel you. I can see you. I can smell you. I canna' touch you. Do you ken how hard that is?"

She nodded.

"Why, Kendran? Why?"

"Because I love you," she answered.

He grunted and lifted a leg, making every bit of flesh

that she could see bulge with the motion. She didn't say a word as he unlaced his boot, pulled it off, and then started on the other, although the activity of his arms as he made the movements was tying her tongue and making her fingers tingle. She didn't move the ones that were still resting on his arm. She liked feeling the ripple of movement his sinews were making beneath the skin.

"You canna' be here," she said, finally, once he had the boots off, and then peeled wet socks followed.

"You always say that. You already ken the answer."

He was standing, and her hand felt the loss immediately as it fell to the covers he'd dampened with just that short bit of contact. He'd moved so he could pull the soaked shirt from beneath his kilt, and start unfastening the ties holding the placket together. It didn't look to be easy. Kendran watched as each tie held to its hole with all the tenacity of wet rawhide. Myles wasn't being patient; he was making a big enough gap to get it from his head and he didn't look interested in much else.

The shirt opening went to midbelly. He didn't get it separated that far. He had it yanked apart, making creases in the material where he'd wadded and forced it, and then he was peeling it from him, turning it completely inside out, since the wet material wasn't giving up any grip on the flesh it was covering.

Kendran was jealous of it. Myles had a body meant for running her eyes and hands over. She had to settle for just her eyes. He was wet beneath the shirt, too, proving how soaked the material was. She watched as he took it over to the fireplace and hung it using a dirk from his belt in the wood of her mantle to hold the material.

"Well?" he asked the fireplace.

"Well . . . what?" she whispered. She had to gulp midway. Her mouth was too full of spittle to make sense.

"You ken what I'm here for, yet?"

"Nae," she answered.

"Torment," he replied, and then he was unfastening his belt, letting it drop to the floor, although he plucked another dirk from it before it fell. That way he had one ready, once he unwound his kilt, and could pin it to the mantle beside the shirt. His clothing was making a screen of the light, and now it wasn't bright enough. It was only showing shadows and indentations and valleys of flesh. She wanted to see more . . . more . . . so much more. Kendran watched him until the vision felt imprinted on her eyes, burning them; then he turned toward her; and she had to close her eyes. She couldn't stand it much longer. She was trembling with holding off the sensation. Myles was perfect. He knew it. He had to know of it. He had to know every part of him was formed in order to draw the feminine eye. He was doing it on purpose! He had to be.

"You feel the torment yet?" he asked. It wasn't said lovingly, either.

She nodded. Her hands went into fists, holding to the flax nightgown.

"I'm a fine male," he continued.

She nodded again. And tightened her fingers.

"Perhaps . . . the finest?" It was a question. He was getting closer, too, if the sound was any indication.

"Why . . . are you doing this?" It wasn't sobbed, but it might as well have been.

"You wish to touch me? Again? With abandon? Nae rules?"

Kendran nodded. She still wasn't opening her eyes. She couldn't! She was already panting, wondering where he was, and frightening herself with the torment of putting such a rein on her own body.

"Well. I may allow it this time. I may na'. I may never allow it again."

"Dinna' do this," Kendran whispered it. Her entire frame pulsed. She would have given anything to prevent it, and she knew he'd seen it, as his voice hoarsened.

"I was blessed with beauty, Kendran. Male beauty. I dinna' ken why, until now. Open your eyes. Look."

She shook her head.

"Why na'?" He snarled it.

"Please?"

"Please what, lass? What is it you wish?"

The mattress swayed, dented with the volume of his weight as he joined her on it. Kendran gasped. She didn't open her eyes.

"Dinna' do this," she finished.

"I haven't even begun yet, love," he replied.

The answer was choked. She couldn't help it. The spittle in her mouth caused it.

"Reach out. Touch. Now."

He was speaking so softly it was almost whispered. It ruffled the hair on her forehead, giving her a clue of his whereabouts. She didn't move.

"Obey me, Kendran. Now. This night."

"Why?"

"Because it's all I'll have in the bleakness of my future, and it's going to be what you dream of when you're pressing your frame to that creature you've brought here! That's why!" He punctuated his speech by grabbing up her hand, pulling the nightgown even further awry until she released it. Then, he was putting her fist fully in the center of his chest. Kendran's hand opened from the knot of tight fingers it had been and spread wide, filling her palm with the deep beat of his heart. Her eyes filled with tears. She felt them slip beneath her lashes.

"I hate you, Kendran Eschon," he said.

Her heart leapt right into her throat, torturing her with the pressure as it beat from there.

"I hate this emotion you've given me. I hate the endlessness of my days. I hate the fates that would make all this possible. I hate myself. I am so full of hate."

Kendran shuddered through a sob and licked at the tears that had reached her mouth.

"I hate the thought of that creature. Pressing himself to you. Making love to you. I hate you, Kendran." The last was said against her lips, since he'd put a hand behind her head and pulled her into his embrace.

Then he was sucking at her lips and stealing her breath and pulling her against him with a moan that had to have come from her throat, since it dislodged the lump there with the force of it.

"And I hate your sister." He whispered the words against her jaw, moving his kiss from there to the flesh below her ear, teasing the flesh with the promise of a kiss, and then denying it as well.

"All . . . hate her," Kendran mumbled.

"Na' that one. The other. The witch."

"Sybil?"

"Aye, the one called Sybil. The fey one. She frightens me. Me, the Donal heir. Unmans me. Me, the scourge of the Highlands. Tells me things I'd rather na' ken. Me, the man who never loses. Me. I hate her, as well. And her words. And the havoc she creates with each and every one of them."

Kendran's heart had stopped the moment he mentioned her sister. If Sybil had told him of the bairn, she was strangling her! The baby was her secret, and her bane, and her future torment every time she looked into devil-dark eyes that were going to be the image of his sire's. It was her secret; it was her future; it was her pain. It wasn't going to be his. If he knew . . .

There was no telling what he'd do.

"What did . . . she say?" The words were panted. That was the lone way she could make them. He'd moved a hand to the curve of her buttocks and was bunching and grabbing material, pulling it up until he reached flesh. Kendran couldn't avoid it. The moment his palm touched the soft back of one thigh, she was sliding, moving, trying to match herself to the frame he was denying her. She knew he was, too, since he was using her thigh as a handhold to keep her from reaching him. He'd also moved his tongue to the juncture of her shoulder and was running it along the neckline of the modest nightgown that now felt like the most erotic garment made. Then he was moving, sliding all along her, imprinting heat through the twisted wreck of her clothing.

"You sent for him. You."

There was the sound of cloth ripping. She knew it was the meticulous stitching at her neckline. She knew it since his breath touched flesh that was immediately pulsing and aching and ready. And getting denied.

"Whom?" she asked.

"The earl." He was biting each word out and sending rivulets of shivers all over the bared skin he was just hovering over—not touching.

"I did?"

"She told me of it. She wanted to torment me further. She dinna' ken what she does. Or if she does, she's truly vicious. Hateful. Wicked. I do hate her. I do."

"Sybil?" she asked.

"Aye. Sybil," he answered, and then God help her, he licked at a nipple.

Kendran squealed and pulsed so viciously everything on her body felt like it left the mattress for a moment before being pushed right back down. Her entire world melted into the sensation of his lips as he suckled, bringing her to the brink of ecstasy, letting her dangle, and then lifting from her to blow slightly at engorged flesh. And then he was tormenting the other one. Kendran was trembling. She was crying. She was begging. And he wasn't listening.

She tried sinking her fingers into the wealth of black hair and pulling it into locks separated by the presence of her fingers. She tried gripping him and forcing him up to her, so she could return the kiss. She tried everything. He denied it.

And then he was away; lifting from her, sitting beside her, and waiting. She didn't even know what for.

"Open your eyes, love," he whispered. "Look. Memorize."

Kendran opened her eyes. There was a slight trail of moisture in the middle of his chest. It glinted and glimmered with every heave of breath he was taking. He was tremendously aroused, too. And he had his chin lowered, his jaw set, and his eyes half hooded. Kendran had never seen anything like it. She didn't know if she ever would again.

"Memorize?" she repeated, since there wasn't anything on her that felt capable of thinking.

"I'll na' take you, Kendran. I canna'."

"But why?"

"Because it was na' meant to be."

"You'll bring me to this . . . and then leave me?" Her voice was cracking. He heard every bit of it and smiled. The motion wasn't gay. It was the saddest smile she'd ever seen.

"You dinna' belong to me, Kendran. You never will. That is what you made me face."

"I dinna'!" She cried it. He wasn't listening. He was lifting himself from the bed, stretching a bounty of male beauty that made her catch her breath, and then starting an echo of pain that she knew was just going to get worse in her future. She *knew* it!

"I'll na' visit again. Never again. You hear me?"

"Myles."

"Dinna' say my name. It makes it worse!"

"But . . . why?"

"Because you had him fetched! You made me face the reality that is this life. You did. You."

He strode to the fireplace to pull a steamed, damp shirt from where the dirk had it pinned, ripping material in the process.

"Nae, Myles."

"There is naught left to say, Kendran."

He shoved the shirt over his head and pulled it down, where the chill of it had an effect on what he'd been denying her. Kendran watched it happen.

"I have deceit and betrayal all about me. I must learn to protect myself from it."

"Deceit?" Kendran repeated.

"My own Honor Guard. They were the ones who beat me into submission. You wondered about my state when we first met. That was it. My own men. My father turned them on me, and they obeyed. Him. Not me."

"Myles," Kendran couldn't help the way his name caught. She watched as he flinched. Then, a vein bulged out the side of his jaw before he turned from her and plucked the dirk out of his plaide.

"And then you. I canna' even challenge the man you'd give yourself to. He's already half into his grave. I have nothing. Nothing. And your sister! She promises me the Kilchurn will challenge me. Give me a way to solve this and keep my honor, and what happens? The man ignores every insult, every chance."

"You want to challenge Kenneth?"

"I did. Now, I dinna' care."

"Why?"

"Because I was na' letting any man near you. Ever. And then what happens? You bring the one man I canna' challenge right into my life. And flaunt it!"

"Myles . . . no," Kendran said. "It was na' like that."

"It was very like that."

She still wasn't telling him of the child. She wasn't!

"You had . . . days to tell me this. Why now? Why, like this?"

"I have been shadowed every moment by my Honor Guard. Have you na' noticed? I move, and at least two of them have already decided my intent and are there afore me. They seek forgiveness from me. They're na' receiving it."

"You canna' hate all of us."

"I can do whatever I wish. Put your clothing back together."

He said it as he looked her over dispassionately from beside the bed. Kendran didn't move. She watched him roam those dark eyes over her, felt the shivers it induced, and hoped she could survive looking into her own son's when he was birthed without her eyes filling with tears as they were now.

Myles bent to the floor, retrieved his socks from

where he'd placed them, and then he was sitting on his haunches and pulling his boots on. He was being rough intentionally; he had to be, for there was an intensity to his movements that threatened more than once to pull a lace completely from its hole. And then he finished and sprang to his feet.

"Myles?"

He stopped, and then he turned. There wasn't a movement made anywhere on him. He might as well be a statue. A gorgeous, large, manly statue. He was right. She was memorizing it.

"I love you."

He didn't so much as blink. Then, he turned and left her, pulling the balcony door closed with a softness belying the size and precarious berth of it. He was right about something else as well. It was snowing. Thickly.

Myles reached out and plucked the rope from where he'd dropped it. And then he swung free, sliding a good body length down the wet, iced hemp before any of it grabbed. He almost wished he didn't have such a sense of survival. Plummeting to his death might be easier than living with the heartache that was filling every pore of his entire body, and then turning inward on his soul.

It was apt punishment, he decided. He'd been trying to punish her. It felt more like he'd taken a whip. Over every inch. And nothing could reach the solid fire spreading through his chest.

He didn't think he'd been in her chamber very long, but the air had turned to a frost-filled burden to breathe, and the rope was the consistency of an icicle. He was forced to wind it about his hand for each pull upward, making the pulls take longer, and be more precarious once they were achieved. And then he heard the cry that stopped everything, even coming through the muffling quality of the snowfall.

"Intruder! There's a man on the wall! Get a light! Call an archer!"

Myles slid another good body length. If he hadn't experienced it, he'd never have believed it as absolute fear went right through him, weakening every muscle until he almost did plummet from the wall. It wasn't fear for himself. It was fear for Kendran. His slide stopped, and then his hand started throbbing at the burn of hemp wound about it. And then the rope started moving.

Myles was hanging by one hand and being pulled upward in long, jerked motions when there was a commotion below—far below. It was far enough it was impossible to guess at the amount of men gathering there to shoot arrows into him, even if they weren't muffled by the amount of snow between them. He was nearing the top, hanging between two crenellations, and then four hands were reaching down, yanking on his shoulders, and hauling him over the wall.

"Christ! You could have lost some weight in the interim, Donal. You're still as heavy as a fresh-killed hog." It was the Honor Guard Arthur, and at his side was Egan, and if Myles wasn't mistaken, there was Wills hovering in a crouch behind both of them.

Myles shook his head to clear it. His arm felt like it had been pulled from the socket, and his hand was a mangled mass of throb from where the rope had been wound about it. And he felt frozen in place, as well.

Egan was the man moving closer in order to unwind him from it.

"Lack of sense must be a Donal trait," Arthur continued.

"What are you doing here?" Myles asked finally.

"Saving you. That's our right, and duty. Remember? Wait! Go at a crouch. They canna' get the light this high, but there's nae sense taking chances, is there?"

Myles dropped to his knees beside them.

"There he is!"

They heard the cry and all four of them went flat to their bellies in the fresh snow. That had an invigorating effect, Myles decided.

"This is na' going to look good on our record," Egan mumbled.

"Hush!" Arthur whispered it. It still sounded loud.

"'Tis the Kilchurn! Fetch him. And fetch the laird!"

Myles lifted his head and met the others' eyes. Kenneth Kilchurn was on the tower as well? That made no sense. None of it did.

"The lasses both receive visitors," Arthur whispered. "We've known of him for some time. We dinna' ken of you. That was a surprise."

"Sir Kenneth?" Myles asked.

"Aye. He has his eye on the heiress. Begging your pardon, my laird. I mean your betrothed. He has his eye on her. He visits with her."

"Merriam?" Myles couldn't prevent the note in his voice. He knew what it was: hope. For the first time he felt it.

"Aye. The elder lass. We dinna' know of your leanings toward the other one, though. As I just said, that was a surprise."

"You knew of his actions toward my betrothed?"

"We did."

"And you dinna' tell me of it?" Myles's voice was rising, which was stupid. He didn't even know why it did.

"'Tis your pride talking now, my laird. Did you wish the lass?"

"You already ken the answer is nae. You had a hand in making certain I was forced to claim her, remember?"

"And you would na' speak with us due to it. How were we to tell you of our knowledge? And why would we?"

"It's a verra good thing you just rescued me, Arthur."

The other grinned. "True. Otherwise, that could be you out there. Being escorted from the tower and marched in front of the laird. That would have been verra entertaining. This could prove to be, as well. It might also give you someone else to pummel besides us."

"You deserved it."

"Aye. We probably did." Arthur had his hand stretched out across the snow. Myles took it. He knew now what the little witch had meant. All he had to do was wait for the challenge. He knew it would come now. Kenneth had no choice. All Myles had to do was lose.

"Come lads," Myles said. "We've melted enough snow and for nae good reason that I can see. I've a fire roaring in my rooms. We can continue this there."

"That would be a different state of affairs, that it would. We've been bedding down in the stables. A stall. He gave us a stall."

"He did so poorly by my men?" Myles's voice was rising again.

"And you cared enough to check, as well," was the reply.

"Oh." Myles cleared his throat. It was true. "How are his lordship's stables, then? Will I need to raze them as well, once I own this heap?"

"Na' much for hospitality, but they're warm and dry. The stables have a roof that does na' leak. I would leave them be, were I you. If the betrothal still stands. And if you still wish to own any of it on the morrow."

"I dinna' wish anything more of Eschoncan Keep than the lass Kendran. That, and a swift good-bye as I leave it."

"And I would begin to wonder what the younger sister's dowry consists of, were I you," Egan added.

"Nothing worth consideration, given the state of these holdings." Myles went to his feet, although he still stayed at a crouch. He watched as the others did the same. He couldn't help the grin. "The best way to see Eschoncan Keep is from the backside of your horse as you're leaving it. Trust me, lads. Now follow. And keep low. Nae sense adding to his lordship's anger and letting him out of this easily."

CHAPTER 21

Myles looked for the challenge all day. He put himself into every room, wandered every place this Kenneth might be, and couldn't find the man. He found everyone else, however. Even the laird, although he was looking pale and sweaty and had to be assisted from his chamber to the great room and back.

Still, there wasn't a challenge spoken. There wasn't a word spoken. It was as if the previous night had never been. And before the evening meal had finished, Myles was getting more and more frustrated and more and more angry. They thought to hide it? His betrothed committed such perfidy, and they hid it from him? What were they planning at the consummation? A fraud? If he really was wedding with Merriam, and he really was planning on staying and creating heirs with her, what would happen if the firstborn was blue eyed, rather than dark, like any offspring of a Donal was bound to be? He couldn't believe it. If he wasn't intent on making it a certainty that Sir Kenneth Kilchurn challenged him, and if he wasn't going over each and every battle move until he felt certain he could accomplish a loss, then he would have been insulted to the point the old laird of Eschon would be accepting a challenge. And dying over it.

He'd sent the Honor Guard into each room trying to locate Sir Kilchurn. He'd sent Beggin about looking for any tales of where the "great" castle champion had gone to. Nothing. They'd found out nothing. He was still missing at the supper banquet, and Myles had dressed with great care for it. He'd gone so far as to scrape the two-day growth of beard from his face and he'd pulled his hair into a queue. He'd entered the great hall with the newly restored Honor Guard flanking him, and he knew it was impressive. He knew why he'd done it. He knew who he was trying to impress.

And he knew she'd be avoiding him.

Myles sat beside his betrothed and noted how quiet she was, for once. She was also very pale and more than once had tears fill her eyes. He'd thought her heartless. He'd been wrong. She was heartsore. Just as he was. That was one of his mistakes. The little lass had been right. He was making a lot of them.

The Lady of Eschoncan had left her ailing husband's side to preside over the meal. That held his interest, but not for long. Kendran was seated next to the frail figure of her intended, the earl of Kilchurning. She wasn't paying him much attention. It didn't look to affect the old man.

She wasn't paying much attention to anyone. Not even Myles, and he tried to catch her eye more than once. The entire meal, he tried. He knew why. He'd been brutal. He was making her pay for making him face the reality that was her future, and that he wouldn't be in it. He'd tried to turn her from him. He knew it was best. It still hurt. And it was pumping through him with every beat of his heart. First the hope . . . and then the hurt. He licked his lips, then glanced at Kendran again. She quickly averted her face.

It was still there when he prepared to bed down for the night, when he was feeling the silence that came of having Beggin busily engaged with his new education, which had started as Arthur's apprentice. From there, he'd gone to being Wills's apprentice, and by eve, he was making Egan wish for deafness with the lad's continual chatter. Myles would have smiled to himself as he unwound his kilt, except everything was pumping the problem through his veins.

He had to receive a challenge from Sir Kilchurn. And once he got it, he had to lose. He was ready. Now all he had to do was find the man. And he only had one more day. The wedding was set for sunset on the twenty-fourth. Christmas Eve. It was what he'd requested and what he'd paid for. He had tomorrow. He had the morning of the next day. That's all he had.

Myles went to his knees and started praying.

Kendran stumbled to her knees and almost didn't make her goal—the chamber pot. Behind her she heard the door opening and was too ill to care.

"You're ill?"

It was Sybil. That was only a bit better than if it had been Merriam. No one else ever came to the top of the north tower. There weren't enough serfs to attend every Eschon daughter, and even if there were, they were needed at the laird's bedside. And with her mother. The woman who was turning into a saint who had nothing but goodly things to say about her husband, much to everyone's disgust.

Kendran choked, gripped her arms about herself, and moaned.

"I had heard this about carrying bairns. I hadn't thought it true."

Kendran groaned again. Her sister was deaf to suffering. She seemed to enjoy it. She seemed to enjoy it more if she caused it.

"Are you ill every morn? And is it the same?"

"What?"

"Carrying a child makes a woman ill. Some of them. Especially in the morn. I just wondered if the strength of your sickness is the same, or if it varies?"

"Why? So you can torment another with your knowledge? And why canna' you knock for entrance?"

"Nae need. The door was na' barred. Had you na' wished granting me entrance, you'd have barred it."

Sybil had a strange sense of logic. It was probably true, too. The one in charge of barring the door was Kendran. It hadn't seemed necessary. Myles was never visiting again. Despite her efforts, a shiver ran her frame. She pulled tighter on her torso with her arms. It didn't help. The lonely feeling was still there. As was the emptiness. And the ache. It was never-ending and permanent. It made her answer harsher toned than she meant it to be. Sybil could usually be dealt with as long as she didn't guess at how accurate she was.

"As to your question . . . as I'm na' carrying a bairn, how could I comment on whether any sickness has a sameness to it or na'?"

Sybil chuckled. "Oh, you carry a bairn, although I may have to change my determination as to the gender. I think now it shall be a daughter."

"Hush!" Kendran said.

"She will still favor him. The sire. You will na' be able to hide it."

"Can you na' hush when requested to?"

"Definitely a daughter," Sybil said instead.

"I am na' carrying a bairn, and you are na' claiming otherwise. Aside from which, how would you ken whether 'tis a girl or boy bairn? You dinna' ken. You are na' fey. You are a useless, stupid sister, with little to do save cause trouble."

Sybil sighed loudly, and then she bounced up onto Kendran's mattress, making the straw stuffing rustle. "I dinna' ken either way. I simply guess and have a fair chance of being right. Actually I have every chance of being right this time, since I've claimed it was both."

"I'm na' carrying a bairn!" Kendran cried.

"You missed your time, dinna' you?" Sybil asked, instead.

Kendran rose, picked up her pot, and took it to the balcony to empty it. Her sister was still sitting there watching her when she returned.

"It goes away quickly, then?"

"What do you want, Sybil?" she asked instead.

Sybil turned aside and ran her hands along the unmade bed, lifting the covers a bit before pulling them back into position. "He is a verra handsome specimen. I dinna' ken men like him existed. I thought them all big, and brawny and rude, and arrogant, and mean."

"He is mean," Kendran replied.

"He is na' mean. He is suffering. Everything that comes from his mouth speaks of it."

"You lie." Kendran went to the great carved wardrobe that matched her bed; opened it; pulled out a pair of long, woolen stockings; and lifted the front of her nightgown and pulled them on, one at a time, while keeping her mind on mundane things.

"And you dinna' listen. None of you. That's why you miss hearing what is really worth the listening."

"Are you going to tell me Waif is speaking to you again?" Kendran teased, as she tied a garter in place above each knee to keep the stockings in place. Then she was rooting about in the drawer for the long shift that was to be donned next.

"Did you tell him of the babe?"

Kendran's fingers stopped on the ribbon tie of her nightgown, and she had to consciously make them keep moving, pulling them apart, so she could get the neckline over her head. It didn't matter that the material had recently been mended. Sybil wouldn't have known of that. Kendran's hands hid the stitching she'd put in, anyway.

"If there is no bairn, why would I say there was?" she answered carefully, and then she pulled her nightgown off.

Sybil's gasp alerted her to the idiocy of that. Kendran had forgotten how much her body had changed in little more than a month. She'd increased so in breast size she was having difficulty squeezing into her chemise, and the problem grew daily.

"That is most impressive," Sybil said, in awed tones.

"What?" Kendran had the chemise in place, and then was forced to find room for her enlarged breasts, one at a time.

"What does he think of that?"

Kendran glared across at her. "He hates it. There! I said it. He hates me. He hates himself. He hates everything."

"What makes you say that?"

"Because he told me so."

Sybil was speechless. That was so different Kendran couldn't help but smile. She didn't even bother hiding it.

"Not a night hence. In this very room. He told me of it. In nae uncertain terms. I'll never see him again. He'll never see me again. He'll na' care whatever happens with me. Ever. He said that as well."

"That's odd, then."

Sybil was at the wardrobe now, fingering through the two frocks that were there. It wasn't a hard selection. Kendran's other two needed laundering.

"What are you doing?" Kendran asked.

"I'd select the blue. It goes well with your coloring. Especially the greenish shade near the neckline. That should work. I'd wish to draw the gaze there, if I were you."

"What are you speaking of now? I've naught to do but oversee the breakfast clearing, and make certain the noon meal is started. Then, I'm to see to the listing of the root cellar. You know my duties."

"The blue will also match your silver cloak. That one with the fur trim. That will go well and be warm."

"I'm na' going to need a cloak. I'm na' going outside. What has gotten into you this morn, Sybil?"

"There's been a challenge issued."

Kendran's heart stopped. She actually felt it. She reached for one of her woven ecru underdresses, one made from the finest, thinnest strands of wool, for warmth and fluidity of motion. It draped well, too. They were both styled with an open bosom, however, and once she had pulled it over her head, she watched with annoyance as Sybil's attention wouldn't leave her chest.

"So? There's been a challenge issued daily. Hourly. That is nae great event worth wearing my best dress,"

Kendran remarked. She barely kept from putting her own hands over herself.

"This one is different," Sybil said.

"And what makes this one so different?" She took great satisfaction in reaching for her dark maroon overdress rather than the blue. She watched as Sybil shook her head.

"'Tis the Kilchurn heir making the challenge," she answered.

Kendran's hand wavered above the blue dress where it hung from its peg. "And whom is it Kenneth has challenged? One of the Donal Honor Guard?"

"Nae. He has challenged The Donal, himself."

"Myles?"

"The blue also has a wimple of silver. 'Tis see-through. Most enticing. Eye-catching. The red does na' have one. You really should choose the blue. It will look nicer, it will be warmer, and it's clean. All told, it's the best choice."

"I'm na' needing warmth."

"It snowed last night again. Makes the ground slick, and the air frost filled. Here. Let me assist." Sybil reached for the blue.

"It snowed? Again? They canna' take a challenge on the field, then. It will be too treacherous."

"The Kilchurn does na' care. I dinna' believe The Donal does, either."

"This is so stupid. Canna' they wait until after the wedding to kill each other?"

"I suppose they could, but then there would be nae need of a challenge."

"Why na'?"

"Because men fight over the strangest things."

Sybil was cinching the back of the gown as she

answered. She was probably right about the blue. It was perfect with Kendran's complexion, it had all the accompanying garments that it needed, and it was doing a very good job of drawing the eye to cleavage she hadn't possessed a fortnight earlier. Kendran looked down at herself and frowned.

"They'll na' notice my face with this attire," she commented wryly.

Lady Sybil ignored her to pick up the large brush that lay on the table beside the bed. "Men. Who can decide the why of where they look, or what they do? Take this challenge of theirs. What do you think they fight for?"

"You bait me without reason, Sybil, for I dinna' care," Kendran said.

Sybil sighed, pulled the brush through Kendran's hair, and then spoke. "They fight for supremacy. They fight over conquest. They fight . . . over rights to wed, or na' wed."

Kendran's heart felt like it sank that time, right down into the pit of her belly, where it started pounding.

"Wed?" she asked.

"The Kilchurn has challenged The Donal for the right to Merriam's hand. Your sister, Merriam. Sir Kilchurn believes himself a better groom for her, and more deserving of the dowry she possesses. He's fighting for that."

Kendran couldn't contain the joy. She felt both sides of her mouth splitting with the size of her smile. She didn't even care that Sybil saw it. "Well, why dinna' you say so in the first place! Come! We must hurry. When does this challenge begin?"

Sybil forced her to pivot back around. She lifted her

arm high in the air and pulled the brush through Kendran's locks again.

"You have time. You dinna' understand. You must find calm, Kendran. Calm. Aside from which, we're near finished."

"How much time do I have, Sybil?"

The other shrugged. "Moments. Hours. Days. Years."

"Could you say something without making it a riddle? For once? Just once? This once?" Kendran's frustration was coloring every word. She couldn't help it. She was itching with the sensation and every slow stroke of Sybil's brushing made it worse.

The other sighed, drew the brush through Kendran's hair again, and then started another trail through another long lock. "The battle will last some time," she said finally.

"And?"

"The Donal has been practicing."

"What does he practice for? He's deadly. He always wins."

"That's why he's been practicing. He has to lose. He has to lose and he has to make it look like he dinna' lose. That will prove difficult for him. He needs all his concentration."

"So?"

"I've been watching him. He almost has control of his spin move. He might be able to lose. He dinna' wish to, though."

Kendran gasped, and that was the only sound that made it past a lump forming in her throat. *He dinna' wish to?* she wondered. She managed to swallow around it. "He does na'?" she asked.

"No man would." There was another stroke of the

brush. Another. Then, another. Kendran's hands went into fists, making her nails dig into her palms.

"Myles does na' wish to lose? He wishes to wed with Merriam now?"

Sybil giggled. The sound grated all along Kendran's spine. She decided she really did hate her youngest sibling. She hated the way she spoke, the length of time she took, the puzzles she created, the havoc she put into play, and the way she toyed with others' lives. Kendran spun away.

"We've finished," she announced. She put her own wimple on, wrapping the gossamer fabric about her head to shroud it, although Sybil had been correct about the silvery material. It was opaque enough to hint at the wealth of hair it covered.

"This challenge . . . is to the death, Kendran. What man would wish to lose that? Only a man with nae future. That's who."

"Oh, dear God!" Kendran had the cloak in her hand and donned it while running the steps. She didn't bother with Sybil. She didn't care. She had to stop this. Myles alive and wed to Merriam was better than no Myles at all.

Myles spun to his left, slamming his shield first into Kilchurn's advance, and barely missing a blow to the other's chin with the hilt of his sword at the same time. He was pleased with it. Until he slipped, went to a knee, and then rolled back into a crouch. Blood was pumping through him, filling his ears and drowning out the sounds of all the crowd lining the yard. Sweat stung his eyes, and he swiped at it with a leather-wrapped wrist, and then he was on his feet before the arc of the other's sword had a chance to lop off his head.

This Kenneth was a worthy opponent. He was good. He was very good. He was also fit. He was very fit. He was well trained. He was almost Myles's match in bulk and strength. Kenneth was still losing, and for two other reasons entirely. First off, he lacked Myles's finesse. He hadn't the ability to dance around sword blows and dodge slicing blades, hammering fists, and arcing projectiles. The lone reason the fight was still making the crowd gasp and cheer was the length of it. That was Myles's fault. He could have finished it off within the first few blows. He didn't. He was determined to lose this battle. He was also going to keep his head. And that was taking all his expertise to keep the image of a great fight while still losing. It was going to take time enough to wear out his opponent. And that was going to take great skill and greater endurance.

The second reason for Kenneth's inability to win was his inattention. The reason was sitting up on the dais, a handkerchief wound in her hands and such a look of anguish upon her features she didn't resemble the same woman to whom Myles was betrothed. She looked like a lass in love, and watching her man with every bit of worry at her disposal.

Myles knew Kenneth was aware of her, too. That was hampering his blows and making him look more than once in her direction. Myles was grateful Kendran hadn't joined the onlookers. He might have had the same trouble.

Another sword blow came flying through the fog his own breath put into existence, glancing off his shield and putting the Kilchurn heir into a spin that hadn't anything accompanying it save awkwardness and ineptitude. He watched as the man went to his haunches. Myles was stalking him the moment he landed.

Myles then made a large movement with his own blade, making certain the other saw it, and wasn't surprised to find his blow deflected and landing in the crust of ice-mud the ground had been reduced to. He used the sword for leverage, leaning fully on the implanted length of it to turn about. It was a good thing he had, or Kenneth's incoming blow would have halved his skull. Myles realized it as his shield took the brunt of it, and then his shoulder.

The man was deadly earnest. He didn't know Myles would give him the battle. Myles pivoted on the implanted sword, using it for ballast as he swung outward, and caught the Kilchurn in the midsection with both feet. The force of the blow separated the man from his shield as well as sent him backward, causing him to glance against a railing with enough force the top pole cracked, and then split, and then fell.

Which only gave his opponent another weapon. Myles's eyes widened as the Kilchurn took up the split pole in his left hand, his sword in his right and began another advance. That took all his skill, all his ingenuity, and all the patience at his command not to bring the battle to the only conclusion every inch of him was demanding.

Bloodlust filled Myles's eyes, and he tempered it. Anger boiled to the surface and he sent it back. Rage made him tremble, and he ignored it. Intensity was like a drug filling him with strength and power and making every move calculated and death dealing, and he reined that in, as well. He wasn't going to win, but he wasn't going to die, either.

Kenneth was tiring. Myles realized it as each blow

came with less and less frequency, and when the blows did come, they hadn't the stinging power they'd once had. It was almost time to fall. He practiced it in his mind. Went over the sequence of events that would have him nearly unconscious, and with it, gain the Kilchurn a win. As long as there wasn't any energy left to put a death blow into place.

Sweat was pouring over him, coating him with a chill that was invigorating rather than hampering, and the fog of each breath coming out was joining the steam-filled aura that surrounded him already.

And then he heard her: his Kendran. She was calling his name with such anguish it ripped through his gut and made everything on him clench. He made a mistake. He lost his concentration and glanced over at her.

The blow sent him to his knees, and he retched the blood splatter into the snow as he crawled away. He didn't know if it was a sword that had given him the blow across his back, or the pole. Whatever it was, it had a crushing force he hadn't known Kilchurn still possessed. Myles was stunned. He shook it off. He was blinded. He wiped a hand across his eyes, got to his feet, took a heave of breath, and then he spun. His left arm with the shield hit first, and then his fist, since he'd lost his sword.

He watched with horrified fascination as Kenneth Kilchurn took the blow, swayed on shaky knees, and toppled. Myles couldn't even blink as the figure at his feet pulsated once, and then was still as only the unconscious can be. And then Myles did something that had them all gasping. He went to his knees, put both fists to his face, and shook with emotion no warrior would ever put on display.

CHAPTER 22

Heartache was the worst. It was. It had to be. And it was endless. There wasn't a poultice, there wasn't a cure, and there hadn't been a warning. Kendran kept her nose in the wadded coverlet she held with both fists, tried to find solace in tears, and failed at that, too. They wouldn't come. That made her head and throat pound. Almost enough to ignore how her breast hurt. The ache wasn't just staying there, either, although that's where it had begun. It was radiating down both arms, pulling them into the fray. Kendran was very afraid it was going to reach her legs as well. There hadn't ever been any warning. That was what made it even worse.

Her door opened, and Sybil's slight form entered, her ever-present cloak swaying with the breeze she created. Then she was shutting the door and barring it. Kendran turned her face back away. She wasn't interested in company, and she really wasn't interested in Sybil's puzzles.

"You cry?" Sybil asked.

Kendran shook her head.

"He'll na' be able to stand your tears, you ken? He's still trying to absorb how it feels to shed his own. He's na' doing well with it, either."

"Who?" Kendran asked the thick weave of her cover.

"Who? Your love! That's who! Lord! I'll wash my hands of all you lovelorn fools afore we're finished. I vow it!"

The voice was moving and Kendran heard the sound of slippers scraping across her floor. *Lady Sybil is pacing?* she wondered. She rolled her head and looked over at her sister. She almost smiled. She'd never known Sybil to even raise her voice, let alone pace.

"I'm na' crying," she remarked, finally.

Sybil stopped, pierced her in place, said "thank the lord," and then resumed pacing.

Kendran raised her head. She forced her entire aching form to move into a sitting position. This was odd. This was more than odd.

"He's on my heels, and he canna' see you crying! He canna'!"

"I just told you I am na' crying," Kendran replied. "And then I proved it."

"I have enough on my hands just keeping Merriam from disgrace."

"What?" Kendran asked.

"Merriam! Your sister. She has more troubles than you. And all of you bring it upon yourselves! Constantly! In a never-ending supply! Why does nae one listen?"

"If you see the future so well, why dinna' you tell me?" Kendran asked.

Sybil stopped. She shoved the cowl from her face and put her hands on her hips. She still looked small, and insignificant, and frail. She was standing between the two fading beams of sunset that came through Kendran's high windows, making a shadow land in which, for some reason, Sybil looked perfectly at home. Kendran frowned.

"I dinna' see anything! I dinna' ken anything. Nothing! I never have!"

"You knew about me . . . and Myles." Kendran's voice caught. She couldn't help it. "And the babe. You knew."

"I guessed about you and Myles. Guessed. You answered it for me."

"I dinna'!"

"How else would you have been nigh a sennight alone in a blizzom, and yet actually gain weight to your frame? And what would cause such a glow on just about every bit of you? I guessed. This horrid thing that they call love. And then there was him. Showing up as he did. Right afore you did, and looking about the same as you did."

"Him?"

"Your sister's betrothed shows up, having survived in the open—in a death-dealing blizzom . . . and without one bit of damage? I thought not. And so I asked. He was found atween you and the keep, mired to his knees in deep snowfall. I guessed he'd been with you. I guessed what would happen if two beautiful people are forced together for that long. I guessed at it. And you both answered it for me. This is how I come by my knowledge. Everyone speaks when I'm there. They dinna' even notice me! They say things. Lots and lots of things. I guess at the holes in the speech. It's na' so hard. Now, get up! Receive your love. He's coming. He needs comfort and solace, and you're the lone one who can give it to him! Up!"

"You're wrong. He hates me."

Sybil stared. "You truly believe that?" she asked, finally.

"I heard him. From his own lips. He hates me."

"I would na' believe him if I were you," Sybil replied.

"You think he lies?"

Sybil giggled. "Na' with intent. I'd heard of the thin line that exists atween these emotions labeled as hate and love. One shadows the other and either can be tipped. Hate turns to love, and love to hate. I dinna' ken the truth of it until now. With all of you. All."

"He does na' hate me?"

"He surely wishes he did. A man capable of weeping on a field of battle has too much heart to hate. Unless he has reason. Did you give him any?"

"How could I have done that?"

"How should I ken that? I'm na' at your side every moment! I have my hands full with your sister and mother."

"Mother?"

"A plague. That's what this love emotion is. A plague. It makes one blind. To all. I must go now."

"You're the oddest creature, Sybil."

"You are na' the first to say such. I trust you'll na' be the last, either." She was at the door. "And na' one word to your love. He needs you as never afore. And whatever he pleads and begs for, say nae."

"What will he plead and beg for?"

"The same thing you would in his shoes! By the saints! Is everyone dense? He wants you. He had what he wanted in his grasp, and he failed. Now, he's got two choices: live with his failure, or run. If I were in his boots, I'd be for running. And far."

"He's going to leave me?"

Sybil rolled her head backward, then returned a solid glare at her sister. Kendran felt the shivers just from receiving it. "He's going to want you to go with him! Can you na' see anything in front of your nose?"

"You're wrong. I already offered. He refused."

"He was na' this close to wedding with Merriam afore. Trust me. He'll ask. Now, it's your turn to be honorable. Do the right thing. Now. This once. Dinna' make another mistake."

"What mistake have I made?"

"There are too many. They intermingle. I have to go. He canna' see me. He's frightened of me. He runs when I'm near. Your big, strong, handsome Myles . . . frightened of a little slip of a lass like me. Fancy that."

"Everyone is frightened of you, Sybil. 'Tis a smart man who knows it."

"Really? If he has much in smarts, he's keeping it hidden."

"You've never been in love! You dinna' ken what it feels like."

"I dinna' ever wish to be! It turns the smartest into a fool, and the bravest into a coward. Na' to mention what it does to honor. Recollect my words. All night, if need be. All night. You ken?"

"If I run away . . . we'll be together."

Sybil had the bolt lifted and was about to pull the door open. She stopped and turned. "Would you want a man with so little honor?" she asked. "And would he be the same man? Ask yourself this. A man living with a dishonorable act is a tormented man. I dinna' ken enough of this love emotion to know if it's strong enough to combat that. I dinna' know. I would na' wish to find out. Promise me, Kendran. Promise. Now. You'll na' run."

"I'll na' run with him. I promise."

Sybil slid through the door before Kendran's words finished. And four heartbeats later, the door she was watching tipped open again. Unless Lady Sybil practiced the art of disappearing, she had to have been in the hall when he passed by her. Kendran wondered if it was true. Sybil was so silent and shrouded and insignificant looking that none noticed her, even when she was there.

It was Myles, but it wasn't the Myles she knew. It was an older, grayer-looking version. Kendran's eyes widened as he approached. He wasn't dressed for leaving anywhere, she noted, as she ran her eyes over the massive, strong, supremely masculine shape. He was dressed for evening, with a black doublet atop his kilt; a white linen shirt with large, embroidered sleeves; and a plaide crossing his chest where the medallion of the Donal clan was pinned. He was impressive. He went to a knee onto the floor beside her, reached to pluck up her hand, and held it to his cheek. He was shuddering, too.

"I have tried everything I can think on, Kendran," he whispered.

"For what?" she asked.

"Everything. And I have na' been able to kill it. Still."

"Kill it?" she asked.

"This feeling. The immensity of it. It grows. I tried to hate you. I tried to turn your feelings for me to the same. I tried to lose today, and barring that, to die with honor. Nothing works. I canna' do it. I canna' kill any of it off. I have nae experience with this love emotion.

I dinna' ken its existence. I wouldn't even wish this upon my worst enemy. That is how shattering it is. I'd rather die a horrid death than live with such ache."

"Oh . . . Myles."

Sybil should have given her a potion if she wanted tears held at bay. Kendran shook with suppressing them and failed miserably. She watched the teardrops plop onto the coverlet beside their entwined hands and knew he saw them, as well. His breathing grew deeper, more tormented. She blinked enough to bring his black doublet into focus.

"All I had to do was lose. I could na' even do that."

"You canna' lose a battle to the death, Myles. 'Twas unfair to believe it possible. Death is the penalty for losing. I could na' have borne a life without knowing you were in it. You dinna' understand!"

"Aye, lass." He reached over with his free hand, cupped her cheek, and ran a thumb along a tear trail. "I ken it well. Too well." He took another deep breath. "The good Lord has seen fit to see me blessed with an emotion most men can only dream of. And, then, He takes it away! I dinna' ken what I have done to deserve this. I have na' been a saint, true. But—"

Kendran lifted her free hand and ran it through the locks at his forehead, pulling them back, and halting the bitterness of his words. He was so beautiful . . . so heart-stoppingly handsome. Especially with the depth reflecting from the dark, almost red tone that was deep in his eyes.

And he was Merriam's. Not hers. Ever.

"One more day. We have one more day," she whispered. "Then . . . it will be over. I'll be the wife of Kilchurning . . . and you-you—" She couldn't even say it.

He was shaking his head. His mouth went into a thin

line, destroying the full, feminine look of his lips, and his eyes narrowed to the point all they looked was black. Deep, bottomless black.

"You'll na' be wed off. Na' to that auld man. I forbid it."

Kendran smiled slightly. "You canna' prevent it, my love."

"He'll na' touch you! I'd na' be able to live with myself if I allowed it."

"Myles—" she began, only to be interrupted herself.

"I canna' have you, lass. I accept that. I will live with it. Somehow. But I can only do it if I ken that you're in sight. Somewhere I can watch. And envision. And create something in my mind that I canna' have in reality. I will na' allow that man to touch you. I canna'! It would kill me."

"I'll wed with him tomorrow. It's been decided. The betrothal canna' be broken." Her heart could be. Every dream could be. But her wedding to Kilchurning? Never. That was ironclad. Kendran blinked again, bringing the man at her fingertips into focus before he started blurring again.

"It can and has been," he replied. "You'll na' have any other man touching you. Ever."

Kendran's heart stopped. She actually felt it happening. It only started back up into a ragged rhythm when she gulped. And that made her ears pop, too. "What . . . have you done?" she whispered.

"I won," he replied.

"Won . . . what?"

"The battle. And I dinna' kill the Kilchurn heir. The earl is verra grateful to me for that. Verra."

"What did you do, Myles?"

"Demanded a different penalty."

Kendran was afraid to even breathe. "What . . . was

it?" she asked, through lips so strangely cold and numb feeling she didn't think they'd work.

"Freed you. You're na' wedding with that man. You're na' forced to wed with any man! Ever."

"Oh, dear God. Myles, you dinna' ken what you've done!" Every desire to cry was immediately changing. She was wide-eyed with the shock and horror. She knew what it was as cold invaded every bit of her. She pulled her hand first from his hairline, leaving several strands to trail his cheeks, and then she used the one he was gripping hers with as a counterweight in order to sit up.

"I got you a release. That's what I've done."

"No, Myles. God, no."

"You wanted him in your bed?"

His hand was finally opening a fraction, due more to his surprise than anything else. Kendran pulled her hand free and put both of them to her cheeks. All she felt was cold. Cold cheek flesh, cold palms. Cold. "I dinna' wish any man in my bed!"

"Well, you need never have one, either. Unless it's me. Perhaps in time, the Lord will be gracious and allow such a thing. That's one thing. Time. We have that."

"I dinna' have time, Myles. You dinna' understand."

"You're right. I dinna'. I expected gratitude, and what do I get? Anger. I dinna' understand this, Kendran."

"Does this mean you'll na' be asking me to run away with you?"

"What fool said I'd run?"

"This fool! And you'd best start afore I manage to launch something at that hard head of yours!"

Myles was pulling back and then he was standing.

He had his hands on his hips and was glaring at her. That was better than his sorrow, she decided.

"You have no reason for such anger at me," he announced.

"No reason? You have ruined all and say I have no reason!" Kendran reached for the first thing she could—her pillow—and threw it at him. He dodged it.

"You wanted that man?"

"I dinna' *want* any man. I had to *have* one. That one! There's a vast difference!"

She had the chamber pot now. He dodged that as well. It made a great, clanging noise when it glanced off the doorjamb behind him, however. Kendran ignored it. She was looking for another missile.

"You need a man that much?"

"I dinna' need any man . . . you-you great, bloated ass!"

She had a brush. She didn't bother aiming but rocketed it at him. It didn't help that he was as physically agile at dodging women's items as he was at parrying death-dealing sword thrusts. But she detested that about him, too.

"Great, bloated ass?" he repeated, shaking his head.

"I had to have him in my bed. Just once. That's all. Just once. Condoned by God. Just once!"

"You need a man, you come to me. You hear?"

"I already got everything I need from you. Thank you verra much!"

She launched the silvered reflective tray at him. He caught that one, and then he used it as a shield when she threw a slipper at him. That made even more noise than the chamber pot had, since the tray echoed.

"I dinna' understand this anger, Kendran."

"Why dinna' you come to me? Why dinna' you ask!"

"I dinna' need to ask! You were being forced to wed him, just as I'm forced to wed her! What need is there to ask?"

"Every need!" The tears were starting again. And they were coming with a vengeance that was going to be difficult to stave off. Kendran had spent her entire life, it seemed, running from emotion and now she was paying for it. That's what it was. She could hardly see through them to pull her other slipper off.

"He would na' have been able to satisfy you."

"Satisfy me? Satisfy?" She was sputtering, struggling with tears, and still sounding like there was laughter welling from deep in her chest. She was amazed the words made sense, since they were burning the throat flesh needed to make them.

"Aye. Satisfy you. That's what a man is for. Remember?"

"I dinna' wish him for that." She was going to gag now. Kendran caught the reflex and swallowed it away as well. She wiped at all the moisture on her face and spoke the rest of her words to the slipper in her hand. "I only needed him for one night. One. That's all."

"You only need a man for one night? What sense does that make?"

She glanced over at him and wished she hadn't as the lunge within her entire body was nearly impossible to fight. She knew he saw it. "It would na' have needed to be a whole night. I only needed him for a portion of it. A wedding night. That's all . . . I needed. All." Her voice was dying. There wasn't anything left of it at the end of her sentence. He still knew what the words were.

"He wouldn't have made it an entire night. He's too auld to even have memory of what his manhood is for!

You make no sense and then attack me! He'd have been nae good to you. He'd have probably fallen asleep."

"I dinna' care if he'd slept. That would have been better. God! Are all men so insufferably dense?"

Myles pitched the tray to one side, took one step toward her, and then another. Kendran backed up. She had to. The bed at the back of her knees was what stopped her.

"You have need of a man for one night, you come to me. Always. No other. You ken?"

"I could have evaded him. I would have done it. That's all I needed, Myles. A few moments. Alone. With him."

"Never."

He was right in front of her, chest heaving and his jaw jutting out in anger. Kendran reached out, touched velvet, and then she was against him, wrapping her arms about his neck and being enfolded in a hug she'd only dared dream of. Then, his lips slammed onto hers.

Every impulse ceased, muted, changed, and then became hunger. Kendran didn't even know how it happened. She filled her hands with his hair, pulling it back and gripping onto it as his lips plied hers to soreness. Then he was moving to her neck, trailing wetness along her jawline before he reached his goal, and started sucking marks into being on her throat.

"Tell me he'd make you feel that," he murmured as he went, sending the breath from the words along flesh that was already wet. Kendran was trembling. She didn't need to answer.

"Tell me you want him. You'd put him in my place. In your dreams. In your moments. Tell me."

"Myles. Myles. Myles." What began as a gasp of sound turned into a prayer-like chant. That had him chuckling, and that had his suction easing.

Kendran was off the floor. She hadn't even felt it. Myles had one hand beneath her cupping her buttocks, while the other made certain she couldn't move far. He moved his head, lifting it so he could look at her from less than a hand span's distance. And he had the most tender expression on his face she'd ever seen.

"Tell me you can live without that," he commanded, with every bit of arrogance and self-confidence he possessed. And with very good reason.

Kendran took a trembling breath, which forced more of her bosom into contact with more of the rock-hard mounds that were his chest. He raised an eyebrow as he too felt it, and then he smiled slightly. "Well?" he asked.

"I . . ."

"Dinna' force me to show you more," he continued, and then he blew her a kiss. Her eyes filled with tears again. She blinked them away. They came back, turning his face into a wash of flesh that had devil-dark eyes at the core. Kendran had never been so emotional or felt so foolish. And it was all his fault. Every bit of it. His. For being as gorgeous and manly and beloved and persistent.

"Now what?" he asked.

"You have made our firstborn a bastard," she whispered.

He sucked for breath. Then he swayed, giving her a moment of warning. And then he dropped to his knees, with her in his arms.

CHAPTER 23

It was better to stay numb. Much better.

Myles wore out every one of his Honor Guard, beating on them until they were all a mass of bruising and he was starting to think he'd have to chase after Squire Beggin if Arthur hadn't been able to take him down into the snow and hold him there until he almost lost consciousness. Even that hadn't inflicted much more than a temporary discomfort. Everything else was numb.

He wasn't going to have a wedding night with Merriam. He wasn't going to allow his firstborn to be a bastard. If she wouldn't run with him, he'd rather not live. That was the pact he'd made with Kendran. Better not to live at all. Better not to be born at all. Anything was better. Anything.

He gave each handshake like it was his last. Every blow like it was the same, and there wasn't anything getting through the haze of numbness he had cloaking him. Nothing.

Arthur let him up for breath, shook his head, and walked away. That was all right. They could soon go back to being his father's men, since they'd already proven that's what they were. Unless and until he was their laird. That was never happening now. Myles had told her he preferred death. Kendran had agreed.

He hated lying to her, but it was all he had. There wasn't going to be any death tonight. There was only going to be life and it was going to be with her. The Stewart boy-king needed a strong sword arm at his beck and call, and with Myles, he was gaining one. All Myles had to do was wait. And lie. And look like a man capable of collapsing at an altar before he said any vow.

He'd told Kendran about the dried tansy leaves in a pouch sewn into his trews. They all had it. Useful in battle conditions. Took care of the most gravely injured, allowing a swift, relatively painless death. He'd promised Kendran she wouldn't suffer before she died. He'd lied about that, too. She wasn't going to suffer at all. She was going to be packaged up and slung across Rafe's backside, and she was going to be kidnapped. That's what was going to happen to her.

She was going to be angry, though. Myles rotated his head on his shoulders at the thought of the upcoming battle. She'd probably screech herself into a mute state again. That might actually be a good thing. They'd get nearer to Drumrig if she wasn't making noise and he rather liked her when she was silent. All he had to do was get through the day. And it was better to be numb.

His guard all looked at him strangely. He didn't care. He didn't even care about the fist he'd taken just above his eye that had opened a cut, which was now making everything on that side of his face blur nicely as it swelled. Not to mention starting a dull throb that would have been much worse if he wasn't controlling every heartbeat with a vengeance born of desperation and finality.

Come the morrow, they would be disowning him. He'd be without a clan, without a friend, and without honor.

They laid out the Donal chieftain *feile breacan* and then they helped him don it. Myles took his time. That's all he had left to him, anyway: time. Beggin was holding out the last piece of his wedding attire. A black strip of ribbon that he was to tie about his queue, pulling his hair back so the male beauty that the Donal heir was noted for could be easily seen. He knew Kendran loved it that way. He set his jaw even more firmly, making a vein pulse out the side, and accepted the ribbon from Beggin. He didn't say a word. He hadn't one to say.

They nodded at him. He nodded back. And turned away.

Then, the knock came.

Myles had never been in the laird's private rooms. He truly didn't wish to be there now. If the summons hadn't come with such a feel of urgency he'd have ignored it. Seeing the man at the ceremony was going to be soon enough.

The laird's chambers in this keep were a far cry from the ill-kept tower they'd put Myles in. He was escorted into a richly appointed antechamber by a servant and stood surveying the tapestries that seemed to fall from the very tops of the rafters all the way to the floors, not a speck of dust muting the rich blues and golds of the threads. The pattern was repeated in the four stuffed chairs flanking the fireplace. Blue with gold. It was stifling with all the richness apparent there. It made his split lip curl. If he'd still had responsibility for the keep, he'd make certain the entire room was gutted by fire even before the battering ram reached it.

"Thank you for being so . . . prompt . . . when summoned, my laird."

It wasn't the chieftain. It was his wife and consort. And she was also Kendran's mother. There was little resemblance, he decided. She wasn't looking as stooped and cowed and beaten as usual. In fact, she looked peaceful. Myles shook off the impression. He didn't truly care.

He nodded. He wasn't speaking. Not yet. There was only one person worth speaking with, and only one evening left to do the speaking. He wasn't wasting it, either. He blinked and waited.

"If you'll follow me? Just you. I beg you."

Myles had taken a step, and the seven guard at his heel had done the same. At her words, he hesitated. *Just me?* he wondered. That was odd. Then, he shrugged, turned to his men, and nodded again. They stepped back.

The lady opened the door and waved him into the inner sanctum of the laird of Eschon's bedchamber, where the smell of illness immediately stopped him. The laird was still a huge, bulbous man, even reclining as he was in his bed. There was a man hovering at his side and dabbing occasionally at the drool that was coming from slackened lips on one side of the laird's face. Myles stood in the center of the room and forced his mind to overcome the physical numbness he'd willed upon it so he could think.

"My husband . . . has had an attack," Lady Eschon said softly.

Myles nodded in reply.

"It is na' the first, although it's never been quite this . . . this . . . severe?"

The physician man nodded, as if validating her remark. Myles waited. He was deciding the vagaries of fate. The laird was suffering? Well and good. He wouldn't be raising his fist against his womenfolk again. That saved Myles the effort of breaking his arm later, after the ceremony.

"I—I dinna' ken how to go about this."

Myles waited. He didn't give her any assistance with what they wanted of him, one way or another. The day would lengthen to eve, the ceremony would take place, and then the fate he'd put into place would happen. And little else was of any matter.

"My daughter caused this! Just look!"

Myles felt his back clench before he could tell it not to. Her daughter? She'd better not be referring to Kendran.

"You dinna' speak, and I'm left to wonder at why!" She put her face into her hands and hunched forward over the figure of her husband. Myles's lips twisted. He took a deep breath.

"Get . . . on with it, my . . . dear." The figure on the bed managed to slur through the words. Myles watched impassively.

"Verra well." She said it and then gently touched her lips to his forehead, showing a depth of love that shouldn't be possible given what Myles knew of his treatment of her. Myles took another deep breath. What did he care? There was no deciphering women. He wasn't about to start now.

She stood, faced him, although the sallow light only made her look more pale, and held her husband's hand in hers as if for bravery.

"The dowry. It included this keep," she said.

Myles nodded. The dowry had definitely included the castle. They weren't going to enjoy what he thought of it.

"'Twas always Merriam's. Always. No matter what happened. It was given to her by my father. He was the first Eschoncan."

Myles nodded again. She was waiting for it.

"She does na' gain Eschon Fells, nor the seacoast, however. That was for my husband to decide."

They are taking her dowry away now? Despite every effort, he could feel his shoulders twitching and barely kept from making fists at the insult. Their daughter had his hand due to her holdings. He'd fought having to take her hand because it came with the dowry and now they were changing it? They were not going to enjoy the war his father would start. Myles nearly smirked.

He settled for a shrug. She seemed to be waiting for it.

"I can nae longer give you the castle."

"What?" His voice croaked. It was from nonuse. She flinched at the harshness of it.

"Merriam has run. She left last eve. With the Kilchurn heir and the earl. I dinna' expect it or I would have had her tied into her chamber. I assure you—"

"What . . . did you just say?" Hope flared so swiftly and with such power he surged forward two steps before catching the motion and stopping it.

"The shock has nearly killed my husband! We canna' afford a war with the Donals! I beg it of you!"

Myles had stopped his own steps forward. Needle-like

sensation was pricking at every bit of him, making every bruise he'd suffered start pounding, and his head was rapidly becoming a mass of pain where the cut above his eye was.

"I have another daughter I can offer. I ken that she's na' as lovely as Merriam. Nor has she had the upbringing of her sister. She is still of Eschon blood! She will still be dowered with the land. I just canna' give you the keep. I canna'!"

"You think to put another lass in my betrothed's place?" Myles said it so loudly even the dust motes seemed to halt their floating progress from the rafters at the sound of it.

"I . . . " she began. Then, her voice must have failed. She nodded.

"And you think there will be nae consequence?"

"Kendran is a lady. She's been trained in all lady pursuits. She has na' been trained to the running of a keep, nor is she well versed in court protocol, but she's lovely. Mayhap not in comparison with my eldest, but Kendran—"

He had to stop her before she said another denigrating word. "You think to hand over this Kendran? And the Donal clan would accept? You think my feelings would na' be engaged?"

There was a garbled sound coming from the figure on the bed. Myles watched as she bent down and spoke with him. Then, she straightened and faced him again.

"We . . . will return the gold you have given us," she said.

Myles stood to his tallest and pierced both of them with the narrowest lidded stare he could. It was all he could think of to halt the supreme joy flooding all through him. It also made his head feel like it was about to pound right off his shoulders.

"And this Kendran? She agrees?" He asked finally.

He watched her sigh, her shoulders went back straight again, and she smiled.

"I believe Kendran will be amenable. She is ever a passive, obedient daughter."

Oh, she is, is she? Myles thought.

"She'll agree. I promise you."

"And she'll wed tonight? You can force this? I'll na' have to send for more of my clan?"

The relief in the reclining figure was almost palpable. Myles watched him dispassionately as he wilted even further into the mattress. He only hoped the man didn't expire before they could make it official.

"She'll wed with you this eve. You have our word on it."

Myles turned before they could see the grin spreading so far across his face he felt his lip split. Again.

Kendran dawdled about her bath. She dawdled about everything. The entire day had a slowness to it that existed only in her nightmares. That was fitting. Her entire existence resembled one. She smiled wryly to herself at the thought.

"You really shouldn't waste much more time. You'll be late." Sybil said it from her position beside the fire. The weather had turned, which should have been making it viciously cold and miserably damp in her bedroom had it not been for the immense fire she'd built. None of which affected Kendran in the least.

"So?" she replied.

"They'll hold the ceremony. Everyone will be waiting."

"Why would they do that?"

"You're sister to the bride. They'll na' start without you. 'Tis enough of a whisper attached to the litter on which our sire is reclining."

"Father?" Kendran asked.

"He's had another attack. A bad one. He may na' last a fortnight. That will make your Myles our laird. He'll control everything."

"Nae," Kendran replied, soothing the rag across her belly. Strange. It was still flat and had no sign of the life residing within. Her breasts were another matter. They'd easily doubled in size now, and that was considerable. She'd have suspicioned her condition, even without Sybil's words, her sickness, and the lateness of her woman time. "He will na'. Merriam will."

"Merriam will control the keep? Your Myles must be a rabbit to allow something like that. And I dinna' think him a rabbit. You're wrong. If you wish to guess at the future, you need to work at it. People give great insights to how they'll react. You have to get better at reading them. Your Myles is na' one to take orders from anyone, least of all a woman he's forced to wed. She'd be lucky if she is na' locked into a tower whilst he tears the castle apart around her."

"He was going to tear the castle apart?"

Sybil giggled. "Well, na' by himself. He'll need to await time to get a battering ram built. For that he'll need to await spring. We've time."

"Hmm." Kendran stood and accepted the warmed towel. It felt nice. Eschoncan Keep was safe. Myles wasn't going to be battering down anything come spring. The certainty settled like a stone into the pit of her belly, starting a dull thud from there. She only hoped it didn't make her ill.

"Why did you get my wedding attire readied? The earl has fled. I'm na' being wed."

"You had it prepared. I dinna' ready anything. 'Tis well and good, however. It looks verra nice. It will do."

It looked better than that, Kendran decided. If she could keep the front ties together enough for coverage. Her sheer chemise was made of softest, tightly woven flax and flowed like it had been poured over her. She'd made it knee length. It was better to have coverage since she'd known whom she was wedding.

The bodice of her overdress was fitted to her with a large shiny ribbon tie laced through little loops on either side. In order to get it closed now, Kendran had to stand tall, then watch as her bosom was pressed upward, creating a valley of shadow no man could resist looking at. She thanked God silently that the old earl wasn't to be gazing at her, ever again. Only Myles.

That sent a slight smile to her face. He'd appreciate the view. And from his height, it would be an easy thing to see, too.

"You've gained such size to you. I'd heard of that," Sybil commented as she finished the lacing and wrapped it around to the back in order to tie it.

"You hear of a lot," Kendran commented. "I sometimes wonder from whom."

"Yours is na' the lone child to be brought into this world. There've been others. And I've been in the room when whispers were spoken. I'm always about. Nobody ever notices. Strange."

"Have you seen him?" Kendran asked.

"Whom?"

"The groom."

"Oh. The Donal. Aye. I've seen him. He's fair of

face, brawny and sturdy of frame, and will make any woman proud to be his wife."

Kendran sighed loudly. "I mean today. Have you seen him today?"

"Aye," Sybil answered. She was speaking more to the large weight of skirts that had beads attached all along the front seams, and onto the bottom of all three sets, each one of a differing length. They made a clinking of noise whenever Kendran walked and had the skirts looking as though ice crystals were clinging to the material and scattering about the hem to the floor.

The same crystal beads were scattered throughout the large weave of her veil, making it look as if frost coated the material. It was fitting. She'd wear it if she were the woman getting wed. She already felt like she was made of ice. She might as well look it.

She sat on a cushion in front of the fire and waited as Sybil unwound the braids her hair had been in since last night. Then, she narrowed her eyes on the fire as her sister slid the brush through each lock of hair . . . over and over, clear to the ends that brushed against the floor. That way there was a ripple to the entire length.

There was a message in the fire and it seemed to be just for her. Kendran watched the flames dance about on the four logs she'd allowed herself this evening. She'd never been that wasteful. She didn't care. She wanted to be warm when she had her bath and dressed. She wanted this evening to be perfect. It had to be. It was the last one she'd have.

The wedding dress she'd made for herself so many years earlier was an excellent choice, as well. It had a sanctity about it that made her look like the virginal maid she no longer was. It was also beautiful. It made her feel beautiful just being in it. If she had a choice, she'd want to wear it when she was placed in the crypt as well.

She wondered if they'd allow her to rest beside Myles in the family crypt, felt the stab of tears at the impossibility of even asking it, and let it go. It took a bit of effort, however. She trembled slightly, held her breath to see if Sybil had detected any sign of it, and let the breath back out.

"You'll spoil it if you cry," Sybil remarked from behind her.

"I'm na' crying."

"Good thing. He's na' looking for tears from you. He needs strength. Your strength. Tonight. It's going to be a verra long night, too. For both of you."

"How would you ken that?" Kendran asked.

Sybil giggled again. "A fairy told me," she replied.

Kendran swiveled, the material enfolding her making it an easy movement on the cushion. She faced her sister squarely. "There's nae such thing as fairies," she replied.

Sybil smiled. "Perhaps," she replied.

"Why does it feel as if you ken something that I dinna'?" Kendran asked.

Sybil shrugged. "Perhaps I do."

"What?"

"I know Merriam is in love. And getting what she deserves. Finally."

That hurt. Kendran felt the stab of tears this time, all the way through her face, down her throat and into her breast, where it would hurt the worst. She swallowed all of it away. Very soon, Sybil's puzzling words wouldn't hurt her anymore. Nothing would.

"Is . . . she now?" Kendran asked.

"She was verra brave to do it, too."

"Do what?"

Sybil shrugged again, put her hand in the air, and made a motion for Kendran to turn back around. She did. The fire had more empathy to it, she decided.

"You know what I wish?" she asked the flames.

"For your love, Myles, to be your groom," Sybil replied.

That answer brought sheer agony. Kendran stanched it the only way she could think of. She sucked in a breath and held it until it burned worse than her heart was burning. Then she let it out. Slowly. With a shudder that was barely noticeable. She was very proud of it. "Aside from that," she replied once she had use of her voice again.

"You wish more than that?" Sybil's brushing stopped. "I hadn't considered that. What more could you want?"

"That you find this emotion called love. That a man so far from what you would consider worthy of love will steal your heart and leave you with burnings such as you torment others over. That's what I wish."

The brushing resumed. "I would na' hold my breath awaiting that," she said, timing each word with a stroke.

"Oh, I would na' be so sure. God does na' care for the whims and desires of humans. Nor does fate. You'll suffer it. I'll make it my last wish. I vow it."

"Last wish?" The brushing continued. Then the brush was set aside, and Sybil gathered locks of hair and started weaving a loose mesh waterfall of gold and red. She'd only done it once before. It had been beautiful. "That best na' mean what it sounds to mean," Sybil continued. "You have too much to live for."

"I have a bastard child to birth, and a world of pain

while I watch my sister receiving the man who should be mine. That does na' sound like much to live for, Sybil." Kendran wasn't successful at keeping the bitterness from her voice. She did keep any tears from evidence, however. That was a major victory.

"We've finished. I'll escort you."

"I'll be down directly."

Sybil had stood and was waiting for her. Her face was shrouded with her hood again. "I would na' wish you to get lost on the way," she said finally.

"I've lived in this keep longer than you have. I will na' lose my way to the chapel. I go there every Sabbath day."

"I'll escort you. 'Tis my duty. I was given it this day."

"By whom?"

"Your mother. She speaks for our sire. She wished me to make certain of your . . . presence."

Kendran went to her feet, leaving her to tower over the smaller sibling. She hadn't known Sybil's mother. The laird of Eschon had wed her off to another before Sybil was even birthed. She'd come to them as a small child. They'd made room for her. She hadn't been welcome. She hadn't been unwelcome. She just hadn't been anything. Except strange. She was that.

"Lead the way, then. I'll follow."

"We'll go side by side," Sybil replied.

"Why?"

"It's *Cristes maesse* eve. All kinds of things could happen."

"Like what?"

"Like wishes could come true."

"You're going to fall in love with an unsuitable man?" Kendran asked.

Sybil giggled. "Nae. Other things. Bigger things. Things that could never be. And yet, because it's Christmas . . . they are."

"You make nae sense, Sybil. Sometimes I wonder why I bother listening."

Their steps hadn't made much noise on the stone steps of the keep, due to their slippered soles and the fresh rushes that were scattered. Fresh rushes didn't have the rustling sound of dried, old ones. There were also scattered sprigs of mistletoe about, gracing sconces where torches were flaring. Such an expense would never be tolerated if it wasn't Christmas eve, and if Merriam wasn't wedding into a very rich clan, and if father hadn't suffered an attack, leaving him prostrate while Mother controlled everything.

The carved door to the hall loomed before them, thick and hard and echoing silently with the succor and peace that awaited inside, once one got to the sanctified chapel itself. Kendran shuddered through another sigh of breath. She was breathing shallowly, to keep the tears at bay, and to hide any hint of how much the upcoming ceremony was going to pain her.

"Afore we enter, I've a present for you." Sybil whispered it at her shoulder. "'Tis a gift . . . a bit afore the time, but I wanted you to have it early."

"I dinna' need a gift." Kendran moved her fingers from the long hammered-metal door handle.

"You need this one," was the reply.

Kendran turned, folded her arms, and straightened her back. She didn't know what Sybil intended, but it was better to be prepared. She swallowed on a dry throat that made it a scratching sensation. "What is it?" she asked when she had her voice again.

"I have delayed telling you something," Sybil

whispered. "Something large and wondrous. Almost too wondrous to keep secret for as long as I have."

"You always keep secrets. What difference is one more?"

"This one is . . . special. Verra special."

Kendran's shoulders tightened a fraction in the wedding finery she wore, making the chilled material touch her neck. That started shivers that went clear to the top of her head. She hoped it wasn't as noticeable as it felt like it was. "What is it?" she asked again.

"I wanted to make certain you had time. Actually I wanted to make certain you took the time. To be as beautiful as you are. Right here. Right now."

Kendran blinked, looked down at Sybil, and blinked again.

"'Tis what he deserves."

"What?" Kendran thought she asked it. The buzzing noise in her ears was making it impossible to hear if that's what she voiced or not.

"Your man. This Myles."

Unbidden tears smarted behind her eyes again. Kendran blinked again and sent them to purgatory, where they belonged. She turned back to the door.

"You see, while everyone slept, or fretted, or begged God for release . . . or planned something that had nothing of heaven to it, things changed."

The ringing was louder. Sybil was acting like she already knew what Myles and she planned! That was impossible. Kendran's room hadn't any listeners.

"What things?"

There was activity happening from somewhere beyond the door. They were probably coming to see what was holding up the sister to the bride. Kendran smiled sourly at wood that hadn't any emotion to it.

"Our sister, Merriam. She's in love with Kenneth of Kilchurning. She has been for years. 'Twas the reason behind her acidic tongue and her behavior."

"What of it?" Kendran was grateful she was facing the door. That way all she had to control was her voice.

"And he's in love with her. 'Tis a strong thing, this love."

"How do you ken this?" For some strange reason, hearing that the man Kendran had planned for her own spouse loved another had a strange effect throughout her entire frame. It dried any desire to cry and made a spark of anger start deep in her core. She wondered if this was how Myles had felt when he'd learned any of it.

"Well? What of that? Women wed with men they dislike, while the ones they love wed other women. We are na' the first to suffer it. We'll na' be the last. I've tired of your gift, Sybil." Kendran reached to pull open the door. They still had the length of the vaulted hall to walk before they'd reach the chapel steps. No doubt it was aflame with every torch and candle they could find and put fire to. It was probably much warmer, too.

"The Kilchurn heir and Merriam took fate into their own hands last night. That is your present."

"What?" Kendran's hand tightened on the metal handle.

"They have run. Away. Together. Last night."

"Who?" The ringing was louder, stronger, and making everything spin as well. Kendran opened her eyes fully on the door and watched the carvings rotate.

"And that meant this Myles had a choice put to him."

Kendran barely heard the words. She was swallowing around clumps of tears that kept rising without end.

"He was given it this eve."

"He . . . was?" There wasn't any hiding it. Emotion was flooding her. She gulped around it, fought it, breathed through it. Nothing worked. Her nose was starting to run as well.

"Aye. War atween the clans . . . or another bride. An Eschon bride. With a dowry. He did well with his choice. He even hid how much it meant."

"He . . . did?"

"They dinna' suspect. They think he actually resists. That is your gift, Kendran. Open your eyes. Accept your future. He's na' waiting at the altar for Merriam. He's waiting for you. Only you."

"Me?"

"The Eschon's offer of another bride was na' for my hand. Dinna' fret. I will be far too busy. I have to avoid this curse you have placed upon my head."

"What curse?"

"That little wish of yours. That I shall find a totally unacceptable love. For someone of my ilk, any love is unacceptable. 'Twas a stupid waste of a wish."

"Myles . . . has accepted this?"

"The offer of your hand? Easily. Although he made them give back the gold as well. You must ask him of that. Make him give it back. We have more need of it. Here. You're going to need the veil if you canna' control tears any better than this." Sybil was clicking her tongue as she pulled the veil from somewhere in her always present cloak and shook it out. Kendran couldn't see any of it.

CHAPTER 24

The only thing she'd envisioned correctly was the candles. They were everywhere. At the end of every pew, all along the altar; even high in the rafters, flickering from more candelabra than Kendran had known the family claimed. It was putting a glow to the chapel that dispersed some of the angry voices that reached out for them the moment the doors were opened.

". . . offer! And then you fail?" Myles's voice was the loudest, although there was a cacophony of sound that reached out and swelled with the force of a blow.

Then there was silence. Everyone turned. Kendran's eyes went wide. She hadn't known there were this many people at Eschon Keep. They were all standing, staring, totally unmoving, as though holding in the same indrawn gasp she was suffering.

Then Myles was moving, shoving through all the men about him, and striding down the aisle with purposeful steps. Kendran stood on the threshold holding on to Sybil's arm, as though permanently locked in place. Myles was wearing his chieftain raiment in

Donal colors. Every man following him was in the same colors.

It was effective. It was raw. It was domineering.

Then her own Eschon guard were coming from behind her, leaving their posts at the door to surround where she and Sybil were, and making the aisle of the chapel very small and tight and filled with men and weaponry that wasn't allowed in a drawn state in the Lord's place.

"Are you the maid Kendran? Kendran Eschon?" Myles stopped in place, put his head back, and yelled it above everyone.

She'd known he had a large, loud voice. Now everyone knew it as well.

"Aye," she answered in the stillness that followed his action.

"You have heard of this change your family would have?"

"Aye," she answered again, louder this time.

"And you agree?"

He lowered his head and pinned her in place with devil-dark eyes that already stopped her heart. Kendran flung the veil open and smiled back at him.

He looked almost as bad as when she'd first seen him, although there wasn't any pallor to his skin this time. There was a vicious-looking gash above one eye, and his lower lip had a split in it, made all the more noticeable since he was grinning so widely. He wasn't the only one suffering battle wounds. All his men looked like they'd been in a brawl since breakfasting.

"On one condition," she yelled back, using just as loud of a voice.

Myles straightened even further, making him loom even larger than before.

"Name it!"

He shoved through more bodies until he was right before her, his chest heaving and his grin spreading even wider.

"You give the bride price back to my family. Now. I have as much value as my sister to the Donals. Perhaps . . . more."

He pursed his lips, tipped his head, and winked at her with his unhurt eye. "Arthur?" He had to clear his throat to say the name. It didn't truly matter. No one was saying a word. He might as well have been yelling.

"My laird?" The largest of his guard stepped closer.

"Pay the bride price. Double it. Nae. Triple."

"Triple?" Arthur asked.

"Do you question your laird?" Myles asked softly.

"Never again, my laird. Never. It shall be done as you command."

Myles took the last step toward her, taking up all the space in front of her. Kendran's guards allowed it. She didn't know where Sybil had gone to. Her feet didn't feel like they were even touching wood any longer.

"Now, will you wed with me?" he asked.

"You need ask?" she replied.

EPILOGUE

It took the first seven months of his wedded life to locate the cousin they called "The Viking": Vincent Erick Danzel of the Donal clan. Then it took another fortnight to spirit him away from the Sassenach dungeon into which he'd thieved himself. It was a chore and it was dangerous, but it was done. It was a matter of payment. For Vincent was the gift Myles had slated for his beloved bride . . . the Christmas present he'd promised her the morning after their wedding. It was equally a gift to himself.

The Lady Sybil deserved it. That woman needed her own medicine.

Vincent Danzel was the man to give it to her. Long known for brawn, charm, the Donal long-lashed devil-dark eyes, and a wealth of honey blond hair that had gotten him in woman troubles more than once, Vincent had a standing bet with anyone. There wasn't a woman birthed whom he couldn't charm. No woman he couldn't make his own, and then leave. His betting price was steep.

Myles was willing to pay it.

In that nearly eight months' time, Kendran blossomed into the most beautiful lass the Donal clan had ever seen. Doted on by all, and attended by any male she even looked like she was going to turn toward, the woman could get quite spoiled at Castle Donal. This was as it should be. Myles had it decided. She had a sweetness to her disposition that only an Eschon female could have. And when the time came to birth the Donal heir, everyone anxiously awaited the outcome. None so much as Myles.

He'd rather take a beating by his own Honor Guard than spend another full day and night pacing the entire length of the castle grounds with his father and brothers at his side. And when he was finally called, it turned out Lady Sybil was full right after all.

They named their son Brently, and his twin sister, Dacia.